Fanny's mouth went dr
in the sugar-pink turba
taller than she had tho
thought as she had whe
like a god. He stood for
of roses, looking at her
Fanny swept him a low curtsey. Considering her own rank
and who he was, it was greatly overdone. She couldn't
remember curtseying as low as that to anyone but Queen
Victoria. Here, in Delhi, she had contented herself with a
small bob of recognition, even to the Governor and his
lady, and yet here she was curtseying to this barbarian as if
he ruled the whole world!

ELIZABETH DE GUISE

Dance of the Peacocks

GRAFTON BOOKS
A Division of the Collins Publishing Group

LONDON GLASGOW
TORONTO SYDNEY AUCKLAND

Grafton Books
A Division of the Collins Publishing Group
8 Grafton Street, London W1X 3LA

A Grafton Paperback Original 1988

ISBN 0-586-20036-3

Printed and bound in Great Britain by
Collins, Glasgow

Set in Garamond

For the Begum Roshan Horabin,

Mrs Ingeborg Deal,
My youngest nephew Damien,

And for Jack and Jeannemarie Holterman
who kept sending the books.

Prologue

The year was 1850. The Raja of Kattyapur looked at the scarlet-shrouded figure of his bride and, for the first time since he had come to the *gadi*, the cushion or throne of royalty, he thought he might have found someone to share the burdens of ruling his small State. The moment had come for the *Saptapadi*, the irrevocable 'Seven Steps' which would make them man and wife, and he took them gladly.

Leading the way round the sacred fire he repeated, 'Take thou one step for the acquirement of force; take thou two steps for strength; take thou three steps for the increase of wealth; take thou four steps for well-being; take thou five steps for offspring; take thou six steps for the season; take thou seven steps as a friend; be faithfully devoted to me; may we obtain many sons; may they attain to a good old age.'

Maneka, his new Junior Rani, followed him with a firm step. He had only spoken with her once, but he knew her to be as true as Agni, the god of the fire, who witnessed all such ceremonies and was the most straight-dealing of all the Hindu gods.

He had felt himself completely alone ever since he had lit the funeral pyre of his dead father, and helped his mother take her place amongst the flames, cradling her dead husband's head on her lap. His father had been a distant, awesome stranger who had meant little to him: his mother, on the other hand, had been his best friend all through his childhood years and her determination to fulfil her destiny by becoming *sati* had torn the heart out of him.

All that had been left to him had been her handprint on the Gate of Ganesha, made as she had passed through it for the last time, and a feeling of despair that had never left him until this moment.

Certainly his Senior Rani had been no comfort to him. They had been married as mere children for political reasons and it had soon been discovered that his wife was an idiot, with the mental age of a three-year-old. The marriage had never been consummated.

In Maneka, he felt he had found the Rani he needed to protect his back from the endless plots and ambitions of the women in his *zenana*. She had borne the ceremonies of the last few days with a dignity that had appealed to him. Would she also be his friend?

It had been his mother who had taught him that a ruler owed his position and privileges to his *praja*, in a two-way contract between Raja and people. It was his business to guide and protect them; theirs to reward him with their obedience and a proportion of their possessions. That was the way it had always been and that was the way he meant it to continue for as long as he lived.

He glanced round the marble hall, picking out his own courtiers one by one, knowing in his heart of hearts they were living in times past and would be useless to him when the British came closer and made yet more demands from them all. He knew little enough about them, but he had heard much. They were eating away at the sub-continent bit by bit, in the name of trade and their own concepts of law and civilization. He feared that one day he, too, would be forced to given his allegiance to these red-faced strangers rather than to his own people. Yet none of his courtiers were able to perceive this danger. Rather, they regarded the British as a temporary annoyance that would be swept away the moment they willed it that way.

The dancing came to an end in a flurry of scarlet skirts. He was pleased with his new Rani, but he didn't expect to find in her the confidante he dreamed of having one day, someone who knew the modern world, with all its excitements and dangers, and yet who would respect the old traditions. His new bride, no matter how willing, would be like all the other women he had ever known: pretty, pious, and bred to be a suitable receptacle for her master's seed. Perhaps there was no other kind of woman, only a dream that would never become a reality for him. He turned and smiled at his Junior Rani, making a conscious effort to put her at her ease. Poor girl! He hoped she would never know she was a disappointment to him before he had even taken her to his bed. The memory of his mother would demand he always gave her the gentleness and respect to which she was entitled, and for that reason, if for no other, he would keep his secret dreams to himself.

BOOK ONE
Lady Frances

Chapter One

Lady Frances Grogan stared down with distaste at the clothes the maid had laid out for her to wear.

'Fanny!'

Lady Frances turned, without any change of expression, to see her stout governess in the doorway, red-faced from the exertion of toiling up the stairs.

'Fanny,' that lady entreated her, taking in the look on her face, 'you have to do it. Your father knows best! What would your sainted Mama think of you, arguing every step of the way to the altar, just as though the decision of who you are to marry was yours to make!'

Lady Frances picked up the crinoline and dropped it on the floor. 'As I don't remember her, I haven't the least idea what she would think, and neither have you!' she pointed out. She sat down on the bed where the crinoline had been placed for her convenience. 'I am not getting dressed. I am not marrying that dreadful man. And I am not going to India!'

The governess clung to the last point with something like relief. 'Of course you shan't go to India. It's all arranged, your dear Papa tells me, that you shall live in England, managing your own house, and with everything you can possibly need to make you happy, while your husband returns to India and continues to make his fortune there. Everyone agrees that the Indian climate is not good for family life – '

Lady Frances laughed. 'The Indians seem to manage, if all one hears is to be believed!'

The governess's mouth opened and shut again, her face going an unnatural shade of puce. 'My love, I beg you won't make that kind of remark in front of anyone else. They'd think the worse of you. I may know you haven't the least idea of what you're talking about, others may not be so willing to give you the benefit of the doubt.'

Lady Frances gave the small, agitated woman her whole attention. She was fond of her on the whole, for she had known her ever since she could remember, drab and disapproving, but always loyal. Poor Agnes Fetton! She had come from a respectable family who had fallen on hard times and in these days, when all the men were abroad, either fighting to retain, or building up the Empire, before either the French or the Germans got there first, there was not the least chance that she would ever marry. She had fallen back on that hardy standby of the impoverished Victorian lady and had become a governess. She herself was the first to admit she had been fortunate to gain a position with the Earl of Cashel, for his lordship was an easy-going master and his Countess had died giving birth to Fanny and therefore hadn't been able to interfere with Agnes's ideas of the best way to raise the three motherless daughters she had left behind.

The one drawback to the position was that Miss Fetton was obliged to live in Ireland for, while she recognized that the Irish gentry were acceptable anywhere in the British Isles, she could not accustom herself to the Papist practices of the greater part of the population. She had been born and bred into suspicion of the awful things Catholics did in the privacy of their own homes and, although she no longer quite believed the worst of the stories she had heard, she still felt a *frisson* of horror when she saw one of those pious Religious Sisters going amongst the poor while Agnes herself knew that a nun like that was also the whore of any priest who chose to lift her skirts.

Agnes had never been able to share this secret knowledge with anybody else in Ireland. Most of the other upper servants were Catholics themselves, and even had her charges believed her, it had been her duty to protect them from all such terrible goings-on. Agnes regarded innocence as the most precious possession of any young girl and as, like most people of her time, she confused innocence with ignorance, she had striven valiantly to guard Fanny, in particular, from all worldliness, as she referred to such things in her own mind. It was all the more galling, therefore, that it had been Fanny, rather than either of her sisters, who had somehow managed to acquire a most unseemly knowledge of what it was that made the world go round. Unable to blame herself for this state of affairs, Miss Fetton had placed the responsibility on her employer's indifferent shoulders for allowing her young charge to ride all over the countryside at will, with only a groom for company.

Why, just the other day, Fanny had actually told her that she thought Catholics to be quite as Christian as any Protestants she had ever met! It had been that which had convinced the governess that it was just as well Fanny was to be married to a man who was well known for having no truck with any such nonsensical views. Agnes, on the one occasion she had met him, had heartily approved of his opinions of the greater part of the Irish population, to say nothing of those dreadful heathens, the Hindus of India. Imagine going about the land, strangling strangers to please some terrible-looking idol that was supposed to be a living goddess! Not that Catholics could claim to be any better, worshipping their statues of the Virgin Mary and their

15

Saints, bowing and scraping before bits of plaster and wood!

'Agnes, you always told me that if I disliked a man out of all reason, Papa would never make me marry him.'

'That was before, dear. Things are different now your father has been offered this important position at Court – '

'Important enough to sell me into misery and despair?'

'No, no, dear. Your father wants only what is best for you. It hasn't been easy for him to find suitable husbands for you girls, for he is far from being the rich man your grandfather was in his day. Lord Bantry is something of a catch under the circumstances. True, he's only a Baron, whereas your father is an Earl, but since when did you care about such things? Lord Bantry's title is an old and respected one. You could have done very much worse. You might have had to make do with a mere younger son, as your sisters had to, without any money to smooth your way!'

'Love in a cottage?' Fanny scoffed. Poverty was no stranger to any of her family. Her expression changed. 'I'd rather anything than Lord Bantry, even if he's the richest man in the world!' She poked angrily at the heap of silks and satins that lay in profusion at her feet. 'I'm afraid of him.'

Agnes pretended not to hear that last comment. There was something about Lord Bantry she couldn't like either. He had a cruel, mean mouth and, when he rode to hounds, he whipped his poor horse into a lather, turning the beast mad as often as not. She could well understand Fanny's reservations about becoming his wife. Oh well, it was not as if he would be home often. He would be in India, adding to his already vast fortune, while Fanny would be safely in London, with Agnes to chaperon her and keep her on the paths of propriety. Really, they could not have hoped for a better arrangement for either of them. Dublin society was all very well, but London was the centre of the whole world these days and Agnes longed to see it all for herself. Imagine, but she might catch a glimpse of the Queen herself! Perhaps she might even speak to her one day, especially as Fanny had no one else to take about with her into society. Agnes had a great love for Queen Victoria. She was convinced that, in some magical way, the Queen had been invested with the power to change the life of every one of her subjects for the better; therefore, it seemed reasonable to hope, or so Agnes fondly imagined, that the Queen would somehow manage to change the circumstances of Agnes's own life, maybe even finding her a husband amongst the brave fighting men who had just successfully added the Punjab to the other Indian possessions. It was just possible that it wouldn't be too late for her to have children of her own.

Accordingly, she hardened her heart to the misery that was clearly written on Fanny's expressive face. The navy-blue eyes were shadowed with despair and her usually beautiful complexion had broken out into the most unpleasant bumps. Maybe for once the child was going to have to paint her face, for she could hardly go to her wedding looking as if she were about to come down with the pox.

Agnes produced the one card that she knew would galvanize her young charge into action. 'Come now, Fanny, it isn't like you to play the coward. Anyone would think you were the first woman in the world ever to have been married off to a man she had not yet learned to care for. Your sisters made no complaint and look how happy they both are!'

Fanny smiled wryly. 'Happy? Oh, Agnes, how can you say so? They may have schooled themselves to be content

17

with their lot, but good, dutiful wives seldom know what real happiness is, or so it would seem to me! Perhaps they're not meant to, but I did hope to have some kindness from my husband – '

'My dear child, whatever makes you think Lord Bantry won't be kind to you?'

'Look around!' Fanny advised her. 'Most of the men of our acquaintance treat their horses better than they do their wives, and Bantry treats his horses worse than anyone I know.'

Agnes was shocked to the marrow. 'Decent people don't remark such things! As you'll find when you get to London, Lord Bantry is a much-respected man and it will be you who will come to grief if you criticize him to all and sundry. When you go out and about in English society, you must keep a proper guard on your tongue!'

Fanny looked more dejected than ever. 'I can't like him, Agnes!' she exclaimed. The mere thought of him nauseated her. When she shut her eyes, she had one single picture of him: Lord Bantry, with every appearance of enjoyment, applying the whip to the sides of his unfortunate, foaming horse.

'Fanny, you really must get dressed!'

Lady Frances heard the exasperated note in her governess's voice and responded to it out of habit. 'I sent Bridget away,' she said.

'Very proper under the circumstances. What would the girl think if she were to hear you carrying on like this?' She didn't like to add that she thought Fanny a great deal better off without the superstitious nonsense the maid would have poured into her receptive ears. Bridget had never been her choice of a suitable maid for a young girl. She would merely have put Fanny into still more of a fright, reeling off a whole pantheon of saints as the only

18

sure remedy for what every young wife has to come to terms with by herself in the end. 'I'll help you myself.'

It seemed unreal to Fanny to think she was dressing for her wedding. She thought back to the weddings of her two elder sisters and how different things had been for them. Lady Pamela, the eldest of the three girls, had married a younger son and clergyman; Lady Evelyn an obscure English baronet who loved her to distraction, while having little of this world's goods to offer her. Unfortunately, it was the latter quality that would have appealed to her sister more, for Evelyn was as acquisitive as Lady Pamela was self-effacing. As far as Fanny knew, they were both reasonably happy, largely because they had had the good fortune to marry before their father had gambled away his entire fortune in one reckless night. Neither of them had been asked to repair the damage by making Dublin's marriage of the year to the dissolute, abominably rich Lord Bantry, whom Fanny despised with all her heart and soul.

The Earl of Cashel had been more than frank when he had told his youngest daughter of the future he had arranged for her. 'Made his fortune in India, m'dear, not that he needed one to add to all his father left him. He's somewhat strange, I know, but I doubt there's any real harm in him. Comes from an old family and fancies having the daughter of an Earl as the mother of his son and heir. The Lady Frances Grogan doesn't have to look up to anyone socially and that appeals to him!'

'I hate him,' Fanny had responded with a quiet passion that was all the more persuasive because it was so unlike her usual manner.

'You won't need to see anything of him,' her father had reassured her. 'Won't expect you to go to India with him, made sure of that. There isn't any other way out, Fanny. The Queen has done me the honour of asking me to be one of her equerries and I no longer have the money to live at Court without Bantry sporting the blunt. Damned expensive business, you know, but I've had enough of Dublin and being away from the centre of things. You'll see how it is when you've set up an establishment of your own in London and have had a taste of London society. Why, I might even repair my own fortune eventually by making a suitable marriage of my own – '

'You'd replace Mama after all this time?'

The Earl had looked decidedly uncomfortable. 'Why not?' he had demanded sharply.

'We've always been happy in Ireland,' Fanny had begun.

'Glad to hear it!' her father had boomed at her. 'But you can't stay a child for ever. No, no, it's more than time you were married like your sisters. It's time, too, that I put my own life in order. Bantry has been pretty generous on that score. You'll see, it'll all work out for the best in the end.'

Fanny had known better than to argue with him any further. Charming and feckless, her father was incapable of seeing anybody else's point of view but his own. It was quite clear to Fanny that Lord Bantry had bought her for reasons of his own, and her father had been more than willing to sell his youngest daughter to anyone who would help him achieve his own ambitions to become respectable again and return to fashionable society. In that moment Lady Frances had known herself to be completely alone in the world and she hadn't liked that sensation at all.

She had been feeling much the same ever since. Agnes had suggested to her that she might like to be married in a youthful cream, or even white, but Fanny had shuddered at the thought. She had chosen a pale lavender, reminding everyone she was in half-mourning for an aunt she had never even met. This had unexpectedly received approval from the other matrons of the family, who decided she was at last beginning to show the proper sentiments of her age, giving up the unbecoming, hoydenish behaviour they had always deplored in her.

Fanny's shoulders sagged a little as she allowed Agnes to help her on with her wedding finery. She felt defeated and there didn't seem to be anything she could do about it. The dress she had chosen still had the lower waisted bodice that had been so popular in the forties. Fanny, who had a lively interest in fashion, eyed the dress with dislike. It had proved to be useless to point out to the Dublin dressmaker that such a cut would now be considered absurdly old-fashioned in London, not that anyone would care about that but Fanny herself. At least she had insisted on sleeves shorter than the wrist-length ones the woman had wanted, with puffed and frilled undersleeves that matched the dozen petticoats she wore under the flounced skirt.

It was not a style designed to suit Fanny. Flounces, no matter how well placed, looked as if they had got there by accident, and the bow she wore at her neck wouldn't sit straight, but twisted and was as uncomfortable as it looked.

'Well,' said Fanny with a rush of spirit as she looked at herself in the glass, 'I have seldom looked plainer. I hope he thinks he's getting his money's worth.'

'My dear, every girl looks well at her own wedding,' Agnes told her. What was more, she believed it implicitly. True, Fanny was a trifle pale, despite the little rouge she had applied. The excitement was bound to add to the girl's colour as soon as she went downstairs. It was only natural that Fanny should be a little nervous as she prepared for the ceremony that was about to change her whole life. Despite her present doubts, Fanny would be happy. Fanny always was.

Seated beside her father in a black coach emblazoned with his coat of arms on the door, Fanny came face to face with the fact that she couldn't be more miserable and also that, for the first time in her life, there was nothing she herself was able to do to change matters. In that moment, she almost hated her father for not realizing exactly what he was asking of her, for it would not be he who would have to suffer the consequences of this day's work. So angry did this conclusion make her that she arrived at St Patrick's Pro-Cathedral with more colour in her cheeks than even Agnes could have hoped for. Fanny was in a mood to tell everyone concerned what they could do with their wedding and everything that went with it. She even opened her mouth to say as much to her father as he helped her down from the coach, but one look at his apologetic, grieving expression changed her mind. It seemed there was nothing to be done but to make the best of things. However, if Lord Bantry thought he was acquiring a biddable young girl for a wife, she would quickly teach him otherwise! She had a will of her own and he would soon be learning all about it.

Fanny was unused to long sermons that said nothing to the purpose: their own parson knew better than to try his patron's patience with any sermon longer than a few minutes of racy comment. When the Bishop had spoken for twenty minutes by the clock, Fanny turned and stared pointedly at her father. The Earl nodded in sympathy, wishing Fanny would behave herself. It was bound to be noticed that she was unbecomingly full of her own opinions and that was unlikely to appeal to young Bantry. He had heard enough from that young man to know his opinion of women was low and unpleasant. He hoped Fanny would have the sense to keep a still tongue in her head when she was in his company. After all, other women had had to put up with far worse from their husbands.

But Fanny seemed unable to behave with the propriety

22

that quite ordinary society demanded. Her shuddering dislike for the man she was marrying was all too plain as she accepted his ring and promised to obey and serve him during their life together. That she shrank even from the brief contact of their hands was as obvious to all present as if she had shouted it from the rafters.

'Poor girl!' the Dowager Baroness Bantry breathed under her breath. 'I don't envy her tonight if that's how she feels about my son.'

'Nonsense!' the Earl retorted. 'Fanny will come about. Thing is, she doesn't like the way he treats his horses.'

'Astute of her!' the bridegroom's mother said with feeling. 'I felt exactly the same about his father. I saw as little of him as I could when he was alive, and even less of our son! Good God, Cashel, how could you do it?'

The Earl wished the ceremony over. He didn't like being made to feel guilty, a feeling that had been compounded by the set of Fanny's shoulders, advertising the belief that he had condemned her to a life of martyrdom. Nobody seemed to understand that he had had Fanny's interests at heart as well as his own when he had arranged this marriage. She, at least, would never have any money worries, and her husband would be absent far more often than he would be at home bothering her. She didn't know when she was well off! She was a very fortunate young woman. In the years to come she would have a great deal to thank him for – not that he looked to be thanked for his efforts – but he'd feel better if she could be brought to see some of the advantages in this match now.

The choir sang an anthem while the newly married couple went into the vestibule to sign the necessary papers. Somehow or other, Fanny had always thought she would be the custodian of the marriage lines, but Lord Bantry snatched the document from her before even the ink was dry and, folding it clumsily, placed it in his pocket.

'Well, m'dear, there's no going back now!' he leered at her.

Fanny couldn't remember that he had ever addressed her directly before and it was cold comfort to her now.

'I believe so,' she answered him clearly. Not for the world would she let him know about the hollow feeling in her middle that alternated with a sickly churning of her stomach. 'At least our wedding breakfast will be in familiar surroundings,' she added, more to herself than to him.

'We've no time for that!'

She couldn't believe her ears. 'No time?' she repeated stupidly.

'There's no one who matters to me over here. I mean to get back to London and civilization as fast as I can. As my wife, you go where I go – '

'Not to India!' she stammered.

His smile revealed bad teeth and the stench of bad breath. 'That depends how well you please me, madam wife. If rumour is to be believed, we'll deal very well together.'

That she couldn't believe. She murmured some nonsense that could have meant anything at all and glanced about her, seeking the support of someone, anyone she knew.

Both her father and her governess were as shocked as she could have wished for at this turn of events.

'Now, look here, my boy,' her father began, his face mottled as he took in the insult that was being offered to him. 'Will you treat my daughter like a tramp, sir?'

'I paid you well for the tramp, didn't I?'

An appalled silence greeted the remark. Lord Cashel pulled himself together with difficulty. 'If that is how you think of her, I wonder you should have wanted her as the mother of your children.'

'Why not?' his son-in-law returned. 'She was by far the best-bred tramp on the market and doubtless worth every penny I spent for her. I have no time for mewling and puking virgins in my bed.'

Fanny confronted her husband with clenched fists. 'I am afraid you're destined to be disappointed, my lord,' she announced in a voice meant to be heard the length and breadth of the church. 'Not only am I a virgin, I intend to stay one. I may have been foolish enough to have gone through a wedding ceremony with you, but nothing would induce me to share your bed!'

'You'll do as you're told!'

Fanny lifted her chin. 'I believe no man enjoys forcing himself on his wife!'

Lord Bantry laughed. 'You're mistaken, my dear. It's exactly what I enjoy! If no stable boy has already initiated you, I shall be happy to take on the task myself!'

Fanny swallowed a lump in her throat that was threatening to strangle her. She was deadly afraid and there were tears gathering in her eyes which, given the slightest excuse, she was sure would overwhelm her. She concentrated hard on the fact that she never cried. Her sisters cried easily and often, but Fanny had always been made of sterner stuff.

'I'm not going anywhere with you!' she declared.

Lord Cashel looked anywhere and everywhere but at his daughter. If she baulked now there would be such a scandal that, sooner or later, it would be bound to reach the ears of the Queen. Why did this have to happen to him? There were plenty of other fathers who were more deserving of being pilloried by polite society, so why not one of them? Why had the fates picked on him just as he had achieved the means of bringing himself back into fashion?

'You have no choice!' he barked harshly at his miserable daughter. 'You'll go with your husband and like it! I will not have a scandal on my hands – not now!'

Fanny looked at him with contempt. Was it really so important to return to Court as a man of means? She wondered if the Queen would be impressed by the manner in which he had acquired his wealth – or if she would ever know. It was said the Queen positively doted on her own husband, so perhaps she was without sympathy for those who did not. It would seem that Fanny was on her own, with no allies anywhere. She took a step towards her father as he turned away from her.

'I'll never forgive you!' she hissed at him. 'I'll never forgive any of you! Don't look to me for any favours in the future, Papa, because I'll have none to give you!'

The only way she could get out of the church was to concentrate very hard on the importance of keeping her head up and her back straight. She put her hand on her husband's arm and looked neither to the left nor to the right all the way down the aisle. The only time she nearly broke down was when Lord Bantry led her to a shabby-looking carriage that had been hired for the occasion, without any thought for her comfort, and she saw her luggage had already been strapped to the roof.

'Bridget,' she whispered. 'Where's Bridget? I can't go without her!'

'Your maid?'

She nodded, her eyes very bright. 'I've known her all my life!'

'All the more reason to leave her behind,' her husband snapped. 'You'll have me to act as your maid tonight, my dear, as is my right. Once we get to London, my own servants will attend you. You'll need a dresser more up to snuff than a country girl straight out of an Irish bog.'

26

'She's my friend as well as my maid,' Fanny said flatly.

Lord Bantry handed her up into the coach. 'Another reason to leave her behind. Lady Frances Bantry must learn a different way of life to the one you've been leading over here. India is the key to our future – '

'I won't go to India!'

Surprisingly, Lord Bantry didn't press the point. 'One thing at a time, m'dear,' he advised. 'Everything's strange to you now. You'll soon learn how to go on.'

She hadn't expected kindness from him and she didn't know what to do with it when she had it. She was better off hating him, she told herself, because the kindness wouldn't last – any more than it did with his horses!

She took her last look at Dublin, caught up in her love for the city where she had spent so much of her childhood. She had always thought it beautiful. A few people sneered at the classical lines of the buildings and Regency terraces, wanting a more Gothic appearance to their buildings, but she liked the clean lines and the wide streets. Of course the poverty, once one left the main streets, was terrible; the tenement buildings full of damp and infested with rats and other forms of animal life. It was a wonder that anyone survived in such places, but they did, many of them begging for a meagre living, the rest working every waking hour God sent them.

People had told her that London presented an even more ragged appearance. She hadn't believed them. She knew that London had to be something wonderful, full of characters and delightful people. She remembered her brother telling her of the boy he had befriended who swept the street outside his house whenever he wanted to cross the road. Geoffrey took after their mother and would notice things like that. Fanny twisted her fingers together. The next Earl of Cashel was a very different man to his father. She considered asking him to come to her rescue. Could anyone get her out of this terrible marriage? She knew in her heart they could not. There wasn't any power in the land that could come between a man and his wife. A wife was her husband's property, his possession, his chattel, a very part of him in that she had no legal entity of her own. Geoffrey would be sorry if she was miserable, but he wouldn't see it as his business to do anything about it. All females should find their contentment in doing their duty by their husbands and bringing up their families. And, indeed, most of the women of her acquaintance at least appeared to be content with their lot in life. Why did it have to be she who was different? For a moment she considered praying to God to deliver her, but she already knew whose side he was on. God himself had been born a man.

There was an argument over the fare when they reached the docks at Dun Laoghaire. Fanny stood by in an embarrassed silence as her new husband argued the toss with the unsavoury individual who had brought them from Dublin. Even in his most pecunious days, the Earl of Cashel had never lowered himself to argue with such persons, not even if they had demanded twice what he knew to be the going rate. Perhaps, Fanny thought with a spurt of returning humour, that was why her father was poor, whereas her husband was reputed to be at least a millionaire. Look after the pennies and the pounds will look after themselves! If that was his motto, what would he make of her cackhanded efforts at keeping house? She hoped it wouldn't be yet another thing for them to quarrel about.

The fare was finally settled. Lord Bantry summoned a couple of porters and gave them the task of getting the luggage on board the waiting packet.

'Come, Fanny,' he addressed his wife. 'I've reserved a

cabin and we'll repair there immediately away from this hoi polloi. You'll only make yourself miserable if you stay up on deck and look back to Ireland. Learn from me, and forget you were ever there. You'll find all the people you want to know in London – from Ireland and from all over the Empire. Only the slowest and dullest Britons stay at home these days. The fly ones go to where the rewards are there for the taking.'

'To India?' she asked almost humbly.

'Maybe. India fascinates. We talk of bringing civilization to the many different peoples there, but it's the trade that matters. All the time we hold India, there's no one in the world who can oppose our power in the world. Sometimes I think our government is too stupid to realize what a jewel they have in their grasp, but the time will come when they'll be forced to take over India themselves and not leave it to a single Company to run the whole continent and gather most of the profits. High-minded men interfering with the local customs are the very devil, and the Company listens to far too many of them. I've no time for such nonsense. They may think they're doing God's work by stopping widows throwing themselves on their husbands' funeral pyres, or dacoits murdering innocent travellers on the road, but they'd do better to leave them alone. It isn't they who pay the price when the natives rebel and turn in on themselves. Live as they do is what I say, and fleece them for every penny you can. That is what they understand. Anything else is asking for trouble!'

Fanny, knowing nothing of India, thought it sounded the most unpleasant place in the world, and dangerous besides. She had no wish to have any part of it. She licked her lips to give herself courage and sought for a new topic of conversation to distract her husband.

29

'Could someone bring us something to eat in our cabin?' she asked him with a calm she was far from feeling.

'Certainly not! The expense would be out of all proportion. You'll have to make do with a sandwich, my dear, if you want something to eat.' His twisted smile was as cruel as she ever remembered it. 'You won't have to wait alone down there for long, I promise you. Think about that and I doubt you'll have much appetite for anything else!'

Fanny hoped she had misunderstood him. She followed one of the sailors down the companionway with a sinking heart. She wasn't quite sure what was about to happen to her, but her instincts told her that her enjoyment would be in an inverse proportion to his.

Down below deck, the stale air came up to meet them, turning Fanny's stomach. Surely, the best cabins couldn't be so poorly furnished and without air? Fanny stumbled and almost fell. It was all of a piece, she thought. Her husband was turning out to be a miser as well as a blackguard. And, on top of everything else, she was turning out to be a thoroughly bad sailor. She only hoped she could hang on long enough to be alone in the cabin before she disgraced herself entirely!

Chapter Two

The cabin was small and cramped. Fanny looked at the two berths, one above the other, and felt as if the walls were caving in all around her. Holding a handkerchief in front of her mouth, she went back into the corridor, seeking a friendly face, and came upon a frightened-looking Irish girl who was as pleased to see another female as Fanny was.

'Oh, miss, such a small boat doesn't look as though it's going anywhere, does it?'

'It's making me feel remarkably unwell,' Fanny answered her.

'Oh, miss!'

The girl was resourceful, Fanny granted her that. Besides, she reminded her of the missing Bridget, having the same soft accents and the same bouncy, healthy look about her. Fanny relaxed into her care as if she had come home.

'What's your name?' she whispered when she could sufficiently control the spasms of sickness that wrenched at her whole being.

'Eileen.' The girl turned and surveyed Fanny's luggage. 'Saints alive!' she exclaimed, taking in the significance of the Cashel crest that decorated the leather trunks. 'My lady! I'm ever so sorry, my lady, but what are you doing in one of these cabins? The gentry don't have inside cabins!'

Fanny could believe it. 'My husband booked the cabin.'

Eileen swelled with indignation. 'I don't know how this

31

can be so, my lady, indeed I don't! Whatever are things coming to? If I may make so bold, though, I shouldn't be moving just this minute. Perhaps a little food – '

'A bowl!' Fanny commanded firmly.

'Yes, my lady. At once, my lady!'

The girl was kind. She bathed Fanny's brow and kept up a non-stop flow of chatter, laced with episodes in the lives of saints Fanny had barely heard of before and which speedily became confused in her mind with the various members of Eileen's family, amongst whom there was never enough food to go round. What did emerge was that her ex-maid's patron, St Bridget, she of the sunbeam fame, who in a fit of absent-mindedness had hung her cloak on a shaft of sunlight where, apparently, it had magically remained until she had needed it again, would undoubtedly come to her aid.

'She has the ear of Our Blessed Lord's Holy Mother,' Eileen assured her. 'If I hadn't put myself under her protection I wouldn't dare set foot in a pagan city such as I've heard London to be.' Her eyes grew as round as saucers. 'They're all pagans, so they are, in London, not knowing right from wrong. Father McGilligan warned me to keep myself to myself and to insist on my right to hear Mass on Holidays and Sundays. He said there isn't anyone in the world who can stop me from doing that, because it's legal now, even in London.' She shivered. 'The English aren't about to murder us Irish Catholics in our beds nowadays, are they, my lady?'

Fanny didn't know, but she thought it unlikely. It was not her experience that the English cared enough about anything to go to such lengths.

'I don't think anyone will want to murder you, in your bed or out of it,' she reassured the girl. 'They're far more

32

likely to work you to death and pay you far too little if they think you anything different from themselves.'

'Poor souls!' Eileen sighed. 'They'd not know any better, not having Father McGilligan to keep them on the straight and narrow.' She broke off, aware that Lady Frances's attention had left her. 'Shall I be after going myself, my lady?'

'Yes, girl, go about your business,' Lord Bantry ordered from the doorway. He presented her with a penny-piece and pushed her bodily out of the door, slamming it shut after her, and locking it. 'I'd have thought you'd be undressed by now,' he said silkily to his wife.

Fanny thought she was going to die. 'I've been otherwise engaged, sir.'

'So I see. Feel unwell, do you? Well, we'll soon give you something else to think about. Sea-sickness is all in the mind, my love. You have other duties to attend to right now.'

Fanny sat up. Her head swam and she grasped the bowl more firmly, fearing the worst. 'You'd be better advised to leave,' she warned him. 'I'm about to be extremely unwell again.'

'Nonsense!'

Lord Bantry snatched the bowl away from her and reached down for her hand, hauling her out of the berth where she had taken refuge. Her head came into sharp contact with the upper berth and she cried out in pain.

'That's only a beginning,' he snarled. 'You're mine now, Lady Frances, to do with as I will. Ain't that so?'

Fanny thought it better to agree with him. Indeed, her mind was almost totally taken up with the fear of being sick all over him. He would not have taken kindly to that, she was certain, and he would undoubtedly hold her to blame.

'My lord – '

'My name is Edwin. Didn't anyone tell you?'

'No, no, I don't believe they did.'

'And you weren't sufficiently interested to find out?'

She shook her head. All she had been interested in was the depth of her dislike for him. She noticed the cruel twist to his mouth and saw, too late, that she had angered him. She made a swift attempt to repair the damage.

'I must have heard it in church today – '

'Ay, you would have done, if you could have spared the time from regretting all your lost lovers. Lady Frances Bantry will have only one master, her husband. Is that clear to you?'

She nodded, tongue-tied. He'd been right about one thing; she didn't feel sick any more.

'The daughter of an Earl is the same as any other woman without her clothes,' he went on. 'It's only when she goes out in society that she has the cachet of being a Lady in her own right. I wanted that in a wife, I'll not deny it, which is why I bought you body and soul from your father. Between the two of us, we don't need such courtesies. I have the right to do as I will to your body, and don't think the men of your precious family will be interested to hear any complaints from you. They were as hungry for my money as the thief is for his swag!'

Fanny couldn't deny it. She shivered as he reached out for her, afraid of what was about to happen. And yet she was curious too. The stories she had heard of what took place between a man and his wife were too ridiculous to be believed, but what did they do? It seemed she was about to find out.

'Don't expect the same respect from me your father's stable lads offered you!' Lord Bantry grunted, lifting her skirts waist high and wrenching them further upwards.

'They have to be untied,' Fanny told him. 'If you'll wait a moment –'

There was a hideous tearing sound and one skirt followed another on to the floor of the cabin. Buttons, hooks and eyes flew in all directions. Fanny put her arms up to defend her naked breasts from his hot gaze, but he would have none of it. He tore the remainder of her clothing off her back, laughing full-throatedly at her obvious fright.

'Afraid of me now, are you?' he mocked.

'A little,' Fanny admitted.

'One could almost believe you are the virgin you claim to be! Is it possible that all the stories I heard about you are untrue?'

'Wh-what stories?'

'Didn't you ride out alone with the stable hands?'

'With a groom sometimes.' Her brow furrowed in bewilderment. 'What has that to do with anything?'

He raised a hand and brought it crashing down on her backside. 'You'll soon know, madam wife. Come over here and do me the favour of undressing me as I undressed you.'

Fanny shut her eyes, biting back a sob that threatened to break from her throat, the leader of many. In all her life, no one had ever seen her totally naked before, not since the day she had been born and that she couldn't remember. Nor was she accustomed to seeing her own body in such a shameless way. It was as much as she could do to remain upright and not collapse in a weeping huddle on the floor amongst her discarded clothing.

A rough hand caught her by the upper arm, dragging her round to stand in front of him. 'Kneel down!' he commanded her. 'A Lady should always kneel to her Lord.'

On her knees, Fanny could no longer restrain her grief. She knelt in silence, the tears streaming down her face, as her husband divested himself of his outer garments, handing each article to her to be folded and placed neatly to one side.

'Poor Fanny,' he commiserated at last. 'You're woefully ignorant of your new duties, aren't you? The more you cry, the more I long to school you in what's expected of you. It pleases me to see you alone and afraid. Are you going to plead with me to let you go?'

'No,' Fanny informed him through her tears.

'A pity, my dear. However, you won't have your pride for long, you may be sure of that. By the time I've finished with you, you'll be and have nothing! D'you hear that, my lady? Nothing!'

Fanny clenched her teeth. She couldn't bring herself to look at him, afraid of what she might see, so she was completely unprepared when he pulled her close up against him and she became aware of his thrusting manhood for the first time and of his hands groping between her legs.

'Don't!' she exclaimed, deeply shocked.

'Would you deny me?'

She looked at him in earnest, her eyes widening. Was this what marriage meant? If it was, she supposed she would have to suffer it, but she was sure it would do her a devastating injury, if it didn't kill her. She looked away again, trying to stop herself from shaking.

He tipped her over backwards, grasping her breasts in his two hands, laughing loudly all the while. He was mad, Fanny decided. She tried to release herself from his cruel fingers, but she soon saw that a battle was what he wanted from her. He meant to degrade her utterly, to hurt her in a way she had never suspected she could be hurt, through her womanhood where she was at her most vulnerable. She lay still, praying for deliverance. None came. His knees parted her legs and he entered her, pressing home without a thought for the pain he was causing her. She cried out, unable to help herself, knowing the sound would be music to his ears.

When she tried to ease her bruised body into a more comfortable position, he belaboured her with his clenched fist. Black spots appeared before her eyes and she was very much afraid she was going to faint. Perhaps it would be better for her if she did, for she could feel her spirit shattering inside her and she knew she would never be the same person again. She could taste her hatred for him and she clenched her jaws tight shut, denying his mouth and tongue entry to hers. His breath disgusted her and she was beginning to feel sick again. She blanked out her mind, telling herself that her revenge would be all the sweeter when it came. Never, never would she suffer this again at his hands. She didn't know how she would prevent it, but she didn't doubt herself for a moment. She might have married him; she might be forced to bear his name; but know herself to be his possession, his private whore, never! Not while there was breath in her body and enough spirit left within her to recognize herself as a person in her own right.

His climax came and he slumped against her. 'So you were a virgin after all!' he grunted.

'Yes, I was,' she hissed, and then she was greatly and gloriously sick all over his inert body.

Fanny dragged her bruised body on to the lower berth and wished she were dead. The cabin smelt foul and so did she. The remnants of her clothes were everywhere, unwearable and as broken as she. Oh, but he had hurt her! She had thought after a while that nothing worse could happen to her, but it had been then that he had beaten her so severely that even he had begun to wonder if she would be able to walk off the ferry by herself. If was no part of his scheme to have his wife carried off on a stretcher, yet he could still blame her for being unable to absorb any more punishment.

'Any harlot would have served me better!' he had roared at her, his face convulsed with fury.

'Go and find one!' Fanny had retorted.

He had lifted his hand, making to hit her again, changed his mind, and let it fall to his side. He was a ridiculous sight, his whole body covered with dark, matted hair. He looked more like a monkey than a man. She would have done better to have kept the thought to herself, but she hadn't been able to resist the jibe, even while she had been sickened by the uncontrollable rage that had met her mockery.

'What would you know about me?' he had jeered.

'A man wouldn't have hurt me so,' she had answered with dignity.

He had gone away after that, leaving her where she lay on the floor in a mess of vomit and ruined clothes.

'You have an hour to make yourself presentable,' he had shot at her from the doorway, pulling his own clothes on as he went. 'You won't want anyone else knowing what took place between us, will you?'

Fanny was past caring. Her ribs were bruised and she ached all over. When she pulled herself to her feet, she thought her bowels were about to fall out on to the floor and, clutching her stomach, she threw herself back on to the lower berth and cried her eyes out.

She didn't know when Eileen had come into the cabin. She heard her flustered, 'Jesus, Mary, Joseph!' and then a silence. A minute later a wet flannel was thrust into her hand.

'The saints preserve us!' the girl wept. 'Whatever happened, my lady?'

'My husband happened,' Fanny told her roughly.

The girl crossed herself. 'He must be the devil himself!'

Fanny struggled up on to one elbow. 'Yes, I think he may be every bit as bad as that,' she agreed.

Eileen set about righting the cabin without another word, her pinched features revealing the strength of her shock and disapproval.

'I can't pay you,' Fanny felt obliged to say.

Eileen turned on her. 'I wouldn't take it if you could! I wouldn't leave my worst enemy in a state like this! I'd be as bad as he is if I passed by one the other side! I'd not have believed such things of a well-to-do gentleman – and him with a title and all! But that's the English all over! Pagans every one!'

'Lord Bantry is an Irishman,' Fanny told her.

'Then he ought to know better!' Eileen snorted. 'If I were his mother, I'd box his ears for him!'

Fanny found herself laughing and thought she might live after all. 'He's stronger than I am. I don't think I could do it,' she said.

'No,' Eileen agreed grimly, 'we need Father McGilligan for that! He'd make short work of his pretensions to nobility!'

'Lord Bantry wouldn't listen to any priest.'

Eileen opened the nearest valise, seeking something for Lady Frances to wear. 'Father McGilligan is more than a match for any man!' she declared. 'Why, my own father, the best fighter you've ever clapped eyes on, knows better than to take on the good Father. One word from him and they all turn from their sinful ways. There's not a man in our parish who doesn't know he'd have Father McGilligan to answer to if he treated his wife as you've been treated!

They may not all know the fear of God, but Father McGilligan – that's another story!'

Fanny wondered what her governess would have had to say to that, but Eileen was rattling on.

'When it was decided I should go to London to make my fortune, for there's little enough for a girl to do back home, and we're all of us hungry most of the time, it was Father McGilligan I turned to for advice. He went to London once – for isn't his brother a missionary priest who was ordained over there? – and he told me what it would be to live amongst so many pagans. They can't help themselves being drunkards and worse because they know no better, Father McGilligan says, but that doesn't mean that a good, Catholic girl should go amongst them unprepared to take care of herself, so he gave me a knife to hide in my stocking – and showed me how to use it too! If I'd known what that husband of yours had in mind for you, my lady, I'd have given you the loan of it! There's not many men, heathen or not, who want a blade in their gizzard!'

Fanny's interest was caught. 'A knife?'

Eileen nodded soberly. She reached under her skirt and produced a well-polished handle that she only had to press at one end for a wicked-looking blade to appear. 'I plan to convert more than one gentleman to my way of thinking with the help of Father McGilligan's knife,' she said with satisfaction.

Fanny looked at her with a new respect. 'Are such knives easy to come by?' she asked.

Eileen smiled, a knowing look in her eyes. 'Is it wanting it yourself you are?'

Lady Frances shivered. 'Yes,' she said. 'It's exactly what I want!'

* * *

London was crowded out despite it being the new year after the Great Exhibition in which the Prince Consort had taken such a personal interest. Lady Frances put her head out of the hansom in which they were travelling and looked about her in wonder. She had never seen so many people, horses and coaches crowded into so small a space. There was a large congestion in the Strand, involving a great altercation amongst the drivers who were all in a hurry to get nowhere as fast as they could, their horses' hooves and the wheels of their carriages slipping on the wet surfaces.

Fanny had slept for the greater part of the journey, uncomfortably curled up in her seat, and that had added to her stiffness if not to her bruises, which now showed black and blue all over her body. Even her face bore the imprint of her husband's hand, which had done no more than serve to annoy him.

'Why aren't you wearing a veil?' he had demanded when he had first seen it.

Fanny had retreated a little further into her poke-bonnet. 'I don't have a veil,' she had said.

'Then you'd better acquire one!'

He hadn't waited for her answer, which was as well, for she had had none ready for him. There were going to be no more bruises, however, no matter what he thought. He would have to find another female to torture for his pleasure, and she hoped it would cost him a fortune as she had done, because she would sooner kill herself than submit to him again. Her hatred of him roared through her body every time she set eyes on him.

She could see at once that the house he had taken for the season was not in the best part of London. When he was gone to India, Fanny decided, she would ask her brother Geoffrey's advice as to where she should live, for she meant to make herself as comfortable as any lady on her own could be without her husband by her side. She wasn't afraid that she wouldn't soon come to terms with London society. With her father at Court, and a great many other acquaintances from Dublin in positions of importance, she had no fear that she wouldn't soon have a wide circle of friends of her own. She might even become one of the noted hostesses of the day. It would require money, of course, but she doubted even Lord Bantry would leave her completely penniless in his absence.

The servants were waiting for her, lined up in the hall in their best bibs and tuckers. Fanny gravely shook each one by the hand, from the greatest to the least, doing her best to ignore the wave of speculation that passed through them at the sight of her bruised face.

'We presumed my lady would be bringing her own personal maid with her?' Dancer, the butler, boomed lugubriously. 'But if – '

'My maid is with the luggage.'

Her husband's mouth compressed itself into a tight line. 'I told you to get rid of that girl!' he jerked out.

'You told me to be rid of Bridie, Bridget, who has been with me since I was a child,' Fanny reminded him sweetly. 'Eileen is my new girl. She helped me dress and was with me when I came ashore. I couldn't have managed without her.'

Lord Bantry didn't like the sound of that, but there was little to be gained by crossing his wife in front of the servants over a stupid girl who could be disposed of later. He didn't want any tittle-tattle getting out about the way he treated his bride. Nothing would be said, certainly not to him, but he knew it would count against him in the circles that mattered to him. The gossip might even follow him to India and that would never do. On the other hand,

Lady Frances needn't think she was going to defy him in anything and get away with it. There would be time enough, however, to remove any props she tried to surround herself with. She was going to learn she was his, his property, and no silly girl was going to come between him and the lessons he meant to teach her about being his wife. The more alone she was, the easier it would be to break her to his will. A few bruises were nothing to what was to come!

Fanny mounted the stairs, her head held high. Her skirts swept the banisters on one side and the wall on the other. She had never been inside such a small, poky house before and she could only hope the upper chambers were better than anything she had yet seen.

They were not. The sitting-room wouldn't have held above a dozen people in comfort, and was so crowded with ornaments and aspidistras that she despaired of ever making herself comfortable in it. The bedrooms were worse. There was only one of any decent size, with the smaller room next door to it turned into one of those new-fangled bathrooms. That would be her husband's room. She walked briskly into one of the two remaining bedrooms and smiled in a friendly way at the two maids who had followed her up the stairs.

'This will be my bedroom. Perhaps one of you would be so good as to run down and tell Eileen where I am?'

'Yes, my lady.' Both maids bobbed a curtsey, one of them disappearing down the gloomy staircase. The other bobbed a second curtsey, taking a step forward into the room. 'My lady, you must be quite exhausted,' she said with quiet sympathy. 'Eileen, too, will be tired after the long journey, and so, maybe, you'll allow me to help you just for tonight. I'll warm your bed and help you undress and have Cook send you up a tray of supper.' She hesitated, remembering that while her new mistress was not yet twenty years old, she was also a lady and used to having her own way. Then there was the bruise on her face –

'What a lovely idea!' Fanny said gratefully. 'I'm so tired, I could sleep for a week!'

Eileen appeared with the luggage. She allowed the other maid to apply the warming-pan to the sheets, but she was determined to supervise her mistress's undressing herself.

'I think it better, my lady,' she insisted when Fanny would have protested. 'There'll be enough talk without anyone else seeing what that brute did to you!'

Fanny could have wept at her kindness while she was helped out of her clothes as if she had been a small child, Eileen anointing the worst of her bruises with a salve she said her mother swore by, it having proved itself a regular life-saver whenever Eileen's father had come to her, battered and bruised from a bout in the ring.

'You have the knife, my lady?' she asked, her duties done.

'I have.' Fanny placed it carefully under her pillow. 'Go and get some sleep yourself now, Eileen. I'll see you in the morning.'

'That you will, my lady!'

Eileen shrank into the shadows as she passed Lord Bantry on the stairs. He behaved just as if she didn't exist, and Eileen thought she knew why. She crossed herself and spat on the stairs behind him. He was the devil incarnate and he was not coming anywhere near her! She wished, not for the first time, that Father McGilligan were on hand to send him back where he belonged, stoking up the fires of hell down below, and not bothering good, honest folk who were doing their best to earn a crust in a perilous world, and save their souls besides.

She said a quick prayer to Our Lady to keep Lady

Frances safe, wishing she had thought to remind her she would be even better protected if she had her rosary as well as her knife under her pillow. Ah well, if it came to a battle between Lady Frances and that devil, Eileen would have put her money on the lady, now she knew what to expect. Eileen smiled happily to herself. Father McGilligan would have approved of Lady Frances, and that was good enough for her! All in all, she could have done a lot worse than find such an employer on her very first day amongst the pagans.

Fanny was waiting for her husband when he came to her room. She seized the knife from under her pillow and hid it carefully beneath the bedclothes.

'I didn't hear your knock,' she said.

'On your door? Don't be impertinent, my dear. Where you're concerned, I'll come and go as I please.'

Fanny stared at him, her navy-blue eyes shadowed by her long, black lashes. 'Never again. You'll never come near me again, Edwin. If you do, I'll kill you and take the consequences. I shan't in the least mind hanging for you.'

Lord Bantry was thrown off balance. 'I didn't marry you never to come near you, my sweet. I married you to get an heir – '

'Then you'd best hope you already have, because you're not going to get another opportunity!'

'My dear, you're talking rubbish. I may have frightened you a little, but all women find it an ordeal to make the change from maid to wife. I have to have a son! It's well known virgins don't conceive at the first time of asking, so you'll have to put up with – '

Fanny clenched her teeth. 'Never again, Bantry! Never with me!'

Lord Bantry was sure she was bluffing. What could she

do, after all? He had proved himself her master and if she needed another lesson he was more than ready to oblige her. It had been a mistake to mark her face – he'd take more care next time – but what else was a woman for? He walked over to the bed, pulling the bedclothes away from her. Her nightdress fell open to the waist and it gave him a jolt of pleasure to see the dark bruises against the white ivory of her breasts.

'I'll show you who has the ordering of things in this household!' he said between his teeth. His hands trembled as he reached out for her, but she was there before him.

Fanny stood beside the bed, the knife firmly held in her hand. She pressed the button and the blade flew out, looking doubly dangerous in the flickering candlelight.

'If you touch me – if you *ever* touch me again – I'll stick this blade between your ribs!'

He couldn't believe she meant it. 'So that's what the stable lads taught you!' he sneered at her, reaching out for the knife.

She moved so fast he didn't see it coming. A welt of blood appeared on the palm of his hand, followed by a stinging pain in his arm. She did mean it and it was his turn to be afraid.

'Don't think you'll get away with this, my lady!' he sobbed, terrified by the sight of his own blood. 'You won't always have that knife with you!'

'Always,' Fanny assured him grimly. 'If you can be sure of nothing else, you can be sure of that! Wherever I go, the knife goes with me, waiting for you, just as it did tonight, and I'll use it on you with as much pleasure as it gave you to inflict pain on me. Goodnight, Edwin, and don't ever try to come to my bed again!'

And for the next seven years he never did.

Chapter Three

1858

The Viscount Oughterard watched his sister come into the room and thought how well she had fulfilled their father's highest hopes for her. The Lady Frances Bantry was a recognized hostess in London, popular with the Queen and her daughters, and without a breath of scandal attached to her name despite the rather unpleasant gossip there had been when she had first arrived in the company of her husband. Lord Bantry had left for India almost immediately, however, and the family had been able to ignore the tittle-tattle of what had gone on between the two of them, especially as his brother-in-law had made his sister a decent enough allowance in his absence, if only to put an end to the unpleasant gossip. Geoffrey didn't hide to himself the fact that he had always preferred not to know what had gone on between them.

'How's tricks, my lady?' he greeted her, warmed by the affection she always showed him.

'As well as your political ambitions will allow,' she responded. 'Whatever made you think you'd like to become a Member of Parliament, Geoffrey?'

Her brother's eyes twinkled. 'Nothing else to do,' he complained. 'Our respected parent looks like living into his dotage and, until the House of Lords will receive me, I have to get by on my own efforts in the Lower House.'

'That for a hum! Everyone knows the House of Commons is the place for an ambitious young man to be these days! When you do go to the Lords, you'll complain as to how the move has blighted your career midstream!'

'Very likely, sister dear, if the tendency of moving the power to the Lower House continues. They hold the purse strings nowadays.'

Fanny pursed her lips, her navy eyes as shrewd as ever. 'Is it true that the Crown is planning to take over in India? Will the Company be brought to accept the inevitable?'

'Quite true. The East India aren't being given any choice in the matter.'

'Because of that terrible Mutiny last year?'

'Maybe.'

'Oh, don't be so aggravating, Oughterard. You know I'm interested in all that happens in India.'

'Afraid your husband may come home?'

Fanny took a deep breath, expelling it very slowly. There was no point in pretending otherwise. She was afraid he might choose to return to England. 'Yes,' she said.

'About time he saw something of his daughter, isn't it?' Geoffrey mused. A doting parent himself, he couldn't understand his sister's ambivalent attitude towards his niece. Any mention of her was enough to bring a guilty frown to Fanny's face. Sometimes, he noticed, she seemed more upset by his mentioning the child's name than ever she was by any of the snippets of news he brought her about the goings-on in India. 'Where is Mary?' he probed delicately.

'Upstairs with Agnes, I should imagine.'

'Does she like Agnes any better than you did at that age?'

'I suppose so.'

'Suppose? Fanny, don't you know? Worse, don't you care? Sometimes you give the impression you don't even like the poor child!'

Fanny frowned resentfully at her brother, knowing she could never begin to explain her fears to him that Mary might have inherited any or all of her father's worst characteristics. 'I told you,' she excused herself. 'Bantry was disappointed she is a girl. He wants an heir.'

'That's not Mary's fault –'

'Nobody said it was!' Fanny cut in, stung.

'Besides,' her brother pointed out, 'that may explain Bantry's attitude, but it doesn't say much about yours?'

Fanny's lips trembled. The iron control she usually placed over herself slipped alarmingly. Couldn't he see she was afraid of liking Mary too well and thus making herself even more vulnerable to her husband?

'Mary is a Bantry,' she said. 'Not that that will satisfy her father. She isn't the heir he wants.'

'And you don't?'

Fanny shuddered. 'He will have to make do with Mary!' she concluded with a snap. 'He had his chance. He won't get another one!'

Oughterard wished he could remember more clearly exactly what the gossip had been when his sister had first come to London. Perhaps he'd been wrong to close the matter out of his mind, telling himself it was none of his business. Of course he had seen for himself the bruise on her face, but he had chosen to believe her story of falling on the packet coming over, barely credible though that yarn had been when anyone could see it had been made by the open palm of a man's hand.

'You have a duty as his wife,' he muttered uncomfortably. 'It's said the Queen doesn't like childbirth above half, and she does her duty.'

Fanny opened her eyes wide. 'What d'you know about it?'

Geoffrey backed down hastily. 'She has enough children,' he muttered. 'What is it? Eight or nine at the last count?'

'The Queen,' Fanny said, slowly and clearly, 'adores her husband and the proof lies in the number of children. Though how she can like it is beyond my imagination!'

Geoffrey cursed his brother-in-law as a clumsy fool. Secretly, he thought Bantry had missed a fine opportunity with Fanny, who had never been at all missish or lacking in affection for her family. Far too many well-brought-up females these days thought of any contact with their husbands as being sinful. He sighed heavily.

'Has Edwin written recently?' he tried to change the subject.

'Lord Bantry communicates with me through his solicitors,' Fanny told him distantly. 'We really have nothing to say to one another.'

This was much worse than Geoffrey had thought. 'Not even to discuss Mary's future?'

'Least of all about Mary's future. Lord Bantry – '

'He is the child's father!'

'He sees fit to doubt that!'

'That's doing it too brown!' Oughterard exclaimed. 'I must say, between the two of you, one can't help but feel sorry for the little girl!'

Fanny's notion of justice was exact, even when it was inconvenient to herself. It was one of her most endearing traits, winning her many trusting friends and the enduring devotion of her servants.

'Yes, poor child,' she said at once. 'She's in an impossible situation and none of it of her own making. I wish I could get on better terms with her, but I can't bring myself to. I can't get it out of my head that she may have inherited some of her father's cruelty!'

'Shouldn't have thought there was much danger of that,'

Geoffrey offered hopefully. 'In looks she favours you. She has those large, Irish eyes all you girls have,' he added, referring to his three sisters.

'So Agnes is forever telling me. But she must have inherited something from her father, don't you think? Anyway, I'm not prepared to take the risk. I won't allow myself to love her and I expect nothing back from her in return. It's better that way. What a child's never known, she won't miss.'

Geoffrey was appalled. 'You hate Bantry so much?'

'More,' his sister informed him. 'Let's talk about something else. I have a horrid feeling Bantry means to return to England for a while. When the Crown takes over in India, there'll be more of a social life out there, and he may make me go back with him. I won't have any choice, will I, if he sells this house over my head?'

'None,' Geoffrey agreed uneasily. He knew as well as she did that women had no rights over their own property or person. Everything belonged to the husband. He thought this quite right and proper, but with it went a certain responsibility to ascertain the happiness of one's dependants. It was one of the marks of a gentleman. 'Why don't you let Mary come to me for a bit? It would be good for her to be in the company of her cousins for a while.'

Fanny spread her hands against her skirts. 'Why don't you ask her yourself?'

Oughterard swallowed down his belief that no child of seven should have to decide for himself what he should do next. It was his opinion that both women and children should be governed firmly but fairly by their husbands and fathers. He doubted the wisdom of expressing such a view to his sister at that moment, however, and by the time Mary came reluctantly into the room, he felt as helpless as she did. The child, the image of her mother, with the same navy eyes and thick black hair, had a depressed look about her. She hung back when Fanny bade her enter, her eyes enormous with unshed tears. With relief, she saw her uncle holding out a hand to her and scurried across the room to him, hiding her face in his coat-tails.

Fanny made an impatient sound, but she said nothing. In her opinion, Mary was always crying, just as her sisters had done. It did nothing to put her in better charity with her offspring. Fanny liked laughter and the wit of clever men: Edwin Bantry had offered her only cruelty; Mary offered her nothing at all. Fanny felt nothing but contempt for her daughter's damp mutiny whenever she came into her presence.

'Do you want to go and stay with your cousins?' she asked the bent head.

'I don't know,' Mary whispered.

Fanny shrugged, abandoning the task of getting an answer from her. 'I'll leave the two of you together,' she said with a pinched look. 'You may be able to come to a sensible arrangement between you if I'm not here to distress you further.'

Oughterard sat on the edge of the sofa and took the little girl on his knee. It hurt him deeply that neither mother nor daughter was prepared to do anything to build a bridge across that yawning void that Edwin Bantry had created between them.

'We are planning all sorts of treats this summer,' he encouraged her. 'It would be fun if you were to come with us, don't you think?'

Navy eyes scanned his face with infinite care. 'Will Agnes come with me?'

'If you want her to.'

'And not Mama?'

Her uncle sighed. 'No, not Mama,' he agreed.

'Then I'll come.'

By the time Fanny came back to see what had been decided, Geoffrey had heard his niece laugh for the very first time. She was an engaging little piece, he thought, with far too much dignity for a child of her age. She reminded him very much of Fanny at the same age, only Fanny had always been full of laughter and mischief. This poor child was afraid of her own shadow and was plainly terrified of angry voices.

'What angry voices?' Fanny demanded impatiently, when informed of this by Geoffrey. 'When is anyone ever angry with you, Mary?'

'You are,' her daughter squared up to her. 'You're angry now, even though I've done nothing.'

Fanny had the grace to look ashamed. 'It's nothing that you do,' she said at last. 'It's something I can't help.'

Mary snuggled her hand into her uncle's. 'It doesn't matter, I'm going to stay with Uncle Geoffrey, and I may take Agnes with me.' She hesitated for a long moment. 'You won't be lonely all by yourself, will you, Mama?'

Fanny looked at her long and hard. 'Why should I be?' she asked wryly. 'We don't see much of each other when you are here, so why should I miss you?'

Surprisingly, though, she did miss Mary. Fanny lay awake for a long time that night considering her relationship with her daughter. In some ways, she admitted, she was an attractive little thing, but she still felt she could do no other than keep her at arm's length. She had only to know she was in the same room to remember the manner of her conception, the terrible pregnancy she had suffered, and the culminating birth that had gone on for days and days, until she had been sure that neither she nor the baby would survive. Mary had finally made her appearance on the day

53

of the Duke of Wellington's funeral, so Fanny had missed the fine sight of his cortège being hauled through the streets of London, his coffin borne on a specially built carriage that was still on show to the curious.

Fanny had tried not to blame Mary for any of it. There had been a brief moment as she had first taken the baby into her arms when she had thought she might come to love her, but a small birthmark on the infant's hip had been enough to remind her of Lord Bantry's face when he had seen the bruises he had inflicted on Fanny's body. Immediately, revulsion for both father and child had set in and she had longed never to have to see either of them again.

Of all Fanny's acquaintance, the only person who had shown her any understanding had been Queen Victoria. Head over heels in love with her own husband, the Queen yet knew what it was to take one of her children into dislike and to regret it. The tiny, diminutive creature had embraced Fanny warmly when she had been told of the difficult birth.

'What we women have to suffer!' she had exclaimed. 'Nothing would persuade me to go through it again if it were not for dear Albert! And you didn't even have the comfort of having your husband on hand!'

'That was no loss to me,' Fanny had told her.

The Queen had looked distressed. 'My dear child, I had no idea! How very terrible for you! Don't you love him at all?'

'No, ma'am, there is absolutely no love lost between us.'

'Then it might be best to keep Lord Bantry away in India for as long as possible,' the Queen had murmured. She hated changes herself, had fought the inevitable marriage of her eldest daughter, feeling she was being taken away from her, and she felt much the same about Fanny, one of her clear favourites. 'Of course, not even the

54

sovereign may come between a man and his wife, no matter how bad things are between them, and I'm sure that this is right in the general way. We women weren't born to rule ourselves, or God would have made it plain to us long before this. I'm so glad you had a girl, Fanny! Sons often seem more important at the time, but one's daughters are such a comfort to one!'

Fanny had smiled her agreement, not agreeing at all. Being taken up by the Queen had been the best thing that could have happened to her. The Queen was at her best, surrounded by her family, into which she had included Fanny, ostensibly as a suitable model of what a lady should be for the Princess Alice and the Princess Helena, but actually as a confidante for herself. Fanny had soon discovered that being the daughter of an Irish Earl and the wife of an Irish Baron cut little ice in English society compared with being acknowledged as the personal friend of the Queen herself. And Fanny had enjoyed her success, as she was always the first to admit. For the first time she had understood why her father had been so anxious to return to London and the social life there, and it had been on his advice that she had found a wet-nurse for her daughter, sending for Agnes soon after to look after her development.

She sighed heavily. Her brother hadn't approved of her handling of her daughter and she didn't blame him. She was a bad mother. It would do Mary good to go away and live the life of a normal little girl for a few weeks. Meanwhile, she had her own nightmares to keep at bay. Fanny reached under the pillow for the comforting feel of the knife she still kept there, knowing it wouldn't be long now before she might find herself needing its protection once again.

* * *

Exactly one week later, Fanny's worst fears were realized. She heard Dancer himself go to the door, despite it being the middle of the night. There was no one better able to deal with a drunken intruder than the butler, and the man who was demanding entrance was plainly drunk.

'You're in no condition to see her ladyship at this hour,' she heard Dancer say sternly. 'I'll help you to bed in your own room, my lord.'

Her husband!

'Gone over to her side, have you, Dancer? Not to worry, I spent a splendid evening with some real women! Wouldn't do to treat my wife as a real woman, would it? Because she isn't. Doesn't like that kind of thing at all. Did you know that? They always say one's servants know everything. By God, she'd still be a virgin, if she'd had her way, instead of a wife and mother.' He cracked a laugh. 'Going to be a mother again now, whether she likes it or not, because I can't allow the title to die out and have all my money go to that brat she's foisted on me, now can I?'

Dancer's answer was unintelligible. Then her husband's voice came again: 'Not as easily deceived as she'd like. Never heard of a brat taking root at the first attempt, did you? If you ask me, I gave the bitch a taste for it, no matter how hotly she denies it. Somebody else's daughter that she's passing off as mine! And don't tell me she ain't capable of it, because she is!'

Fanny was beyond feeling humiliated by anything her husband might say; he had said it all before, to anyone who would listen, prior to returning to India and leaving her to make out as best she could. Besides, Fanny was far too busy rallying her defences against him, should he try to come anywhere near her before she was ready for him. The Queen could talk of a married woman's duty to her husband as much as she liked, Fanny would never again submit to any man's brutal demands on her body. She would die first.

Her husband didn't present himself to her until morning, however, by which time Fanny had worn herself to a frazzle waiting for him to make his appearance. He bent over the bed and studied her for a long time in silence. She had forgotten how badly his breath smelt and how hairy he was. He was quite as thickly covered with fur all down his chest as was any monkey she had ever seen. His dressing-gown gaped open as he bent over her and she turned away in distaste.

'I need to talk to you, madam wife!'

Fanny flinched. 'I can't prevent you,' she muttered sullenly.

'I'm taking you back to India with me in six weeks' time. See that you and the brat are ready to go.'

'And if I don't choose to go with you?'

'You have no choice in the matter, my dear. And don't go running with your complaints to Her Majesty again. She's been mighty busy, putting in a word here and there to keep me in India out of your way, but she won't help you more now. Not even she can deny me my right to have you by my side. I'm an important man in the India of today – saw the way the wind was blowing long ago and took steps accordingly! The new government won't be able to manage without the advice and knowledge of old hands like myself. There will be perks in plenty until they're sure they're not going to have another mutiny on their hands!'

'Pity those murdering dacoits didn't put an end to you while they had the chance!' Fanny spat at him.

'A pity for you maybe,' he acknowledged. 'India is much harder on your sex than on mine! Nobody will be at all surprised if you and that brat of yours succumb to the climate before the year's out. If you won't give me an heir,

57

it begins to look as though I must look round for a way of replacing you, as I'm sure you'll be the first to understand. Your future is in your hands, my Lady Frances!'

Fanny's hatred was something tangible and the only thing she wanted at that moment was to be free of him.

She said, 'Very well, I'll go with you to India. Mary would be better left in England though. She's a delicate child at best. My brother would be willing to have her live with his family, I'm sure. She's staying with him now.'

'Your brother would like that, I suppose?' Edwin looked amused. 'And he'd bring her up in the same mould as you were, to think herself more important than her master. I think not, my dear. Your undoubted affection for her will suit my ends very well. Daughters are as expendable as wives in India. If you won't bend your will to mine for your own sake, perhaps you will for hers? Children's graves are common all over India wherever the British have set up homes for themselves. One more won't surprise anyone.' His smile was a tortured representation of the real thing. 'This time I mean to have my way with you, my lady, and there's nothing you can do to prevent me, or you and that brat of yours will find your way into an early grave!'

Fanny believed him. She set about packing up her household in such a black mood of despair that none of the servants dared do more than creep about, hoping to avoid their usually easy-going mistress's attention. Only Agnes dared to remonstrate with her.

'How can you think of taking poor little Mary to that heathen land? No good will come of it!'

'Because poor little Mary's father says she must come with us. Would you have me disobey my husband, Agnes? That isn't what you've been telling me these last years.'

Agnes was caught in a cleft stick. 'Then I'm sorry, my

lady, but I won't be going with you.' Agnes only ever called Fanny my lady when she was really put out. 'I know it to be my duty to see that child is given a good, Christian upbringing such as you had yourself, but I won't set foot in that nasty heathen land! It was bad enough being asked to live amongst all those Papists, never knowing what they'd take it into their heads to do next, but at least they know the name of their rightful God! I'll not go amongst people who worship graven images and go round murdering each other for no reason!' She had another worry, but she was reluctant to have Lady Frances know it. Fanny listened far too much to Eileen these days, choosing to ignore the strictures of her old governess.

'Don't you think it might be interesting to find out if Hindus are worse than Catholics?' Fanny suggested.

An ashen face answered her. 'We'll all be murdered in our beds! I've read all about the Mutiny, if you haven't!' She became more agitated by the moment. 'If one were to die out there, one might be lost for ever. Have you thought, Fanny, that Jesus wouldn't know where to find one's soul so far away from home? I'd be afraid to turn round out there!'

Fanny knew in that moment she was alone again. If Agnes wouldn't go with her, who else would? She sat long after her old governess had left her, contemplating the future and wondering if she could bear it, all her courage having temporarily deserted her.

But there was one person who decided that India would be the greatest adventure imaginable. 'I wrote at once to Father McGilligan,' Eileen announced, 'and he tells me St Thomas, one of the Apostles, chosen by Our Lord himself, was the first to take the Good News to India. I'm coming with you, my lady, if only to see what kind of a job he made of it!'

'Aren't you afraid of being lost for ever in a foreign land?' Fanny had asked Eileen wryly.

'Mother of God, is that what's bothering you?' the maid had replied, pert as ever. 'If Miss Fetton has been putting these ideas into your head, she ought to be ashamed of herself! Neither of us is in any danger, not with Father McGilligan praying for the two of us every day of his life. Since when have the Irish been afraid of a heathen or two? Wasn't it ourselves who kept the faith alive all alone in the Dark Ages? I daresay Indians aren't so different from the rest of us, if the truth were known.'

'They look very different,' Fanny had warned her.

Eileen's face had shone with excitement. 'I'm sure they look magnificent, dressed in silks and satins of every colour under the sun, just like the gentry going to one of their balls. It'll be lovely to see it all, sure it will!'

Fanny had felt a first stirring of interest in the country herself. If she had been going on her own, and not accompanying Edwin, she might have looked forward to seeing such a distant land. She began to ask questions of anyone she thought might know about India and was much surprised to discover that one of the best-informed people on the subject was the Queen, who was never happier than when discussing the manners and customs of her latest subjects.

'Wait until you taste some of their food!' Princess Alice had joined in teasing Fanny. 'One of these days Mama will probably import an Indian cook for herself.'

The Queen bridled. 'Certainly I shall! It will be only right to do all we can to make them feel at home when they come over here, and more and more of them are bound to make the journey to gain a good education and to be taught to be better rulers. There are more Princely States in India than I can count, forever making war on one another. All my subjects are entitled to the same benefits of the British way of life. We must teach them more peaceful ways and a respect for the law, but they are already, I'm sure, a spendid people.'

Fanny had always thought of India as being one massive country. 'The East India Company –'

The Queen snorted. 'Will have to learn that they, too, are subject to our laws!' And then, because she shared Prince Albert's enthusiasm for all the modern inventions, she added, 'They won't be able to get away with one half as much now our communications have speeded up so much, for I mean to see to it personally that my government introduces a proper code of law for India, and a proper seat of government in Calcutta. Is that where you're going, Fanny?'

'No, ma'am, to Delhi.'

The Queen furrowed her brow. 'Delhi? You won't see anything of Lord Canning then. Never mind, my dear, now that the last of the Moghul kings has been sent into exile, you'll find that the British will be in control there too.' She cast a worried look at her young friend. 'Leave us, Alice,' she commanded her daughter, 'I have something private I wish to say to Fanny.'

Princess Alice left, with a conspiratorial smile of sympathy for Fanny.

Fanny didn't notice. She was wondering if she didn't regret ever seeing the effete Moghul Court of Delhi. She had read that the Red Fort had been a veritable paradise on earth before the terrible Nadir Shah, the Emperor of Persia, had sacked the city and had carried off the famous Peacock Throne as well as everything else of value. Only the rump of the Moghul dynasty had remained to be sent into exile in Rangoon by the new rulers of India, a sad shadow of his magnificent forebears.

61

The Queen's face held a bleak, sad expression. 'You will be all right in India, Fanny, with none of your family and friends to support you?'

'I shall try to be, ma'am.'

The Queen put a hand on her arm. 'If there were anything more I could do, I'd do it gladly. My dear Albert, so tired as he is these days – he does far too much for us all, never sparing himself! – has explained to me what a terrible fate it can be for a woman to be married to a monster, as I'm convinced Lord Bantry is! I'll miss you – '

'With all the people you have about you?' Fanny's eyebrows rose. It was well known how reluctant the Queen was to part with anyone of whom she became in the least fond. 'Oh, ma'am, I don't deserve your many kindnesses to me.'

The Queen looked away, to hide the tears in her somewhat prominent eyes. 'I count you as one of my very dearest friends, Fanny. Still, you may be sure we'll do all we can to have you brought home to us as speedily as possible. Meanwhile, you will write often?'

'As long as I survive . . .'

The Queen was shocked. 'Good God, do you expect to die out there?'

'I think I do, ma'am. My husband tells me that women's lives are held very cheap out there and that my chances of surviving more than a few weeks are not great. The climate, you know, and my husband's determination to have an heir.'

The Queen interpreted this last exactly as Fanny had intended. The diminutive monarch had not survived her childhood and her first years on the throne without learning a great deal about human nature under the most trying conditions.

'Oh, Fanny!'

Fanny smiled a wintry smile. 'You'd be the first to advise me that it's my duty to submit to him, as you very well know, ma'am. I can only tell you that to me that would be a fate worse than death. I don't expect ever to return to England. My daughter, though – your goddaughter, ma'am – deserves a better fate and, I believe, is equally threatened by her father.'

'Your little Mary? I've never heard anything like it!'

Fanny pressed home her advantage. 'I gave Mary life once, very reluctantly, and she's had little enough from me ever since. I don't seem to be possessed by the maternal feelings I so admire in you! Will you do me this one favour, ma'am, that if anything should happen to me, Mary's future will be assured by your personal interest in her well-being? You see, I cannot bear that she should suffer further because she chose such a bad mother. My own death I can contemplate with equanimity. I shan't welcome it, I shall do everything in my power to prevent it, I assure you; but Mary is another matter. Will you do this for me?'

'You have my word on it! It would be a brave man who would seek to hurt any goddaughter of mine, let me tell you! And, Fanny, don't judge yourself too harshly. I used to think my own mother a very bad mother indeed, but I learned better after my own marriage. When I think how my father drove her halfway across Europe in a dreadful old coach, and without even a driver besides himself, and all so that I should be born in England, I'm surprised she survived the ordeal. My uncles did little to make her feel welcome and all she had were her ambitions for me. For her sake, as well as for yours, Mary will always be assured of my interest. I hardly think Bantry will care to take on his Queen and win?'

Fanny averted her face. 'My husband is not brave enough

for that,' she agreed. 'But, I should warn you, I have frequently found him to act from stupidity rather than reason.'

The Queen pursed up her lips and shook her head at Fanny, but they both knew the younger woman had made her point. Altogether, Fanny was content she had done all she could to protect the child she was afraid to love. The Queen might be convinced men were born to rule and women to obey, but she was very conscious of her own dignity as monarch. Gifted in many ways, she might hold all the conventional views of her circle, reinforced by the sober, Low Church views of her spouse, but she would yet work tirelessly to get her own way when she was interested in any particular cause. Fanny had formed a deep respect for her on first acquaintance, and nothing she had learned of her since had caused her to change her mind. If Mary were known to be under Queen Victoria's personal protection, she was as safe as any person in the realm could be. One way and another, it had been a good day's work.

Mary was crying again. She had hated leaving Agnes behind, the one constant being in her increasingly confused world. She was afraid of the man who she was told was her father, who had entered her life so abruptly, and who had even less time for her than had her admired, but distant, Mama. Fanny longed to be able to offer the little figure some comfort, but she had no idea how to go about it.

'If your Papa sees you crying, he'll send you to bed without any supper,' she tried to stiffen her daughter's backbone. 'If you let him see you're unhappy, he'll soon find a way to make you more so.'

This Mary had already discovered for herself. She looked up at her mother with shrewd, almost adult eyes. 'Are you afraid of Papa too?'

Fanny set her chin at a jaunty angle. 'I'm not afraid of anyone! If I think I'm going to be, I remind myself that I'm the daughter of an Earl, and that they're far more likely to be afraid of me!'

'Am I the daughter of an Earl?' Mary asked.

Fanny shook her head. 'You're the daughter of a Baron, not nearly such an important person!'

Mary was glad of that. She had learned long before she could walk the advantages of not calling attention to herself if she could help it. She was only standing beside her mother now because she didn't know of any place where she could hide.

'When will we see England again?' she sniffed.

Fanny gave her an impatient look. 'Missing your cousins already?'

'Yes,' said Mary. 'What are you missing?'

Fanny put a gloved hand up to her face and was dismayed to discover the tears pouring down her cheeks.

'Nothing! It's a mistake to get fond enough of anyone to miss them,' she instructed her daughter carefully. 'One is always alone in the world, and it's best to remember that. Nobody else will ever really care what happens to you. If you think they will, you'll only be disappointed. It's better to know you're alone and act accordingly.'

Mary looked worried. 'But you aren't alone, Mama. I'm here.'

Fanny brushed her daughter's face with a gentle hand. It was the nearest approach to an affectionate gesture she had ever made her. 'Could you protect me from Papa?'

'N-no.'

'Then don't talk nonsense. You'll have enough to do learning how to look after yourself without worrying about me.'

'Yes, Mama.'

Fanny did her best to ignore her daughter's pathetic bewilderment. 'Don't ever love anyone, child!' she advised her in a rush. 'They'll only make use of you if you do!'

It was a relief to both of them when Eileen came and took Mary away, promising her some innocent delight in another part of the ship. 'She's not been after bothering you, has she, my lady? I came as soon as I could, but there was all the luggage to be seen to, and nobody to do it all but me. His lordship has an Indian man to attend him – far too grand he is to help a mere female like myself! And he hardly speaks a word of English!'

'Good,' said Fanny. 'When he has nothing better to do, we'll employ him to teach us the rudiments of his own language. It will be an advantage to us to be able to make ourselves understood when we arrive in India.'

Eileen didn't share her enthusiasm. 'If you say so, my lady.'

She caught Mary by the hand and went off down below with her young charge. Learn a foreign language she would not! If her ladyship chose to amuse herself during the long voyage learning a whole lot of meaningless syllables Eileen was quite sure no civilized person would ever understand, she would have to do it all on her own.

Chapter Four

1859

The kites circled overhead, their black shapes graceful against the interminably blue sky. Fanny swung herself back and forth on the cushioned swing she had found in her husband's garden. So far, she had won the silent battle between them, but she didn't fool herself that that state of affairs would go on for ever. She was far more vulnerable in India than she had ever been in England.

Despite the danger she was in, Fanny loved India from the moment of her arrival there. She loved the colour; the shape of the buildings; the silent curiosity of the people; the stoical good nature of the babies and the children, who never seemed to cry; and the grace of both the men and women as they went about their daily tasks. Compared to the suffocating formality of the British abroad, the soft, indifferent good manners of the Indian Princes intrigued, even while she knew a *frisson* of fear when she met them because she couldn't begin to guess what thoughts lay behind their bland good looks.

Less attractive, to her way of thinking, were the endless rules of precedence the British insisted upon. It was soon obvious that the agents of the Crown were suspicious of everyone connected with the East India Company and had no intention of allowing the Nabobs, as those who traded in India had been known for more than a generation, to forget it had been their Company's rule against which the Mutiny had been organized. In vain had the Company tried to dismiss it as a local affair of very little significance outside a small area of their territory. The ferocity of the rebellion and the bloodcurdling tales of the survivors had left an indelible mark on British opinion, both in India and at home. The Nabobs were under suspicion and were having to prove their worth all over again.

Edwin Bantry was constantly angered by the treatment he received, the more so as Fanny was found completely acceptable no matter where she went. Being a female, she took her rank from her husband, her own title being no more than a courtesy, but few would forget that her father was the Earl of Cashel, an equerry to the Queen, and that Fanny herself had been well known as a hostess in London and a personal friend of the royal family. There were very few of her quality who had so far graced the sub-continent with their presence and she was immediately popular with one and all for her gracious good manners and her interest in everyone and everything that went on about her. Besides which, as they all admitted, she was a most welcome diversion from the endless talk of death, and the fear of death that stalked the corridors of government, no matter how dedicated the new rulers were in their service to the Queen's new domain.

Mary had developed prickly heat on landing and, despite Eileen's best efforts to soothe her, she seemed to her mother to have been either whimpering or crying ever since. Fanny herself spent most of her time in the garden, refusing to cower behind lowered *chik* curtains, under a *punka*, a length of material that was pulled back and forth on cords to stir the humid air, usually by some child sitting outside the room. In vain did the women warn her what the sun would do to her complexion; in vain did they discuss the ill humours that were rife in the Indian air: Fanny rejoiced in the climate, was fascinated by the exotic flowers and colourful birds, and was endlessly curious about the lives and customs of the native women, with their dark, unrevealing eyes and gentle gestures. Nothing delighted her more than to try out a few words of the local language, enquiring into the day-to-day details of the running of her household in a way that frankly appalled her compatriots.

'But, Lady Frances, you can't *approve* of the way these people live?' the other ladies would reprove her, a little shocked by this interest of hers.

'I don't know enough about them to approve or disapprove,' Fanny would answer. 'The only thing I'm convinced about is that they are more appropriately dressed for the climate than we are. I'm sorely tempted to ask our bearer's wife how to manage one of those long, graceful lengths of material they wind about themselves. Wouldn't you like to try it for yourself?'

Fortunately, her audience always thought she was funning. Lady Frances became known as a wit, and eccentric with it. If she cared to try her hand at learning the local language, her social standing was more than sufficient to allow her to get away with it, and nobody credited her with either the ability or the stamina actually to master the vocabulary and grammar of a language that was not European.

In fact, Fanny was reasonably competent in Hindi, though not, to her disgust, the pure Hindustani that was spoken on official business. Hindi was the dialect of the Rajputs, a land of Princes with whom the British had formed many alliances but had no interest in ruling directly, for Rajputana seemed very far away from Delhi, and further still from Calcutta, the Bengali capital and the chosen seat of government of the British.

Fanny looked up from the book she was reading and

saw with surprise that Edwin was joining her in the garden. He looked hot and angry. She wondered why it was that, in all his years in India, he had never learned to let the climate flow over him, attempting only one thing at a time, instead of the half-dozen that might have been possible to him in a more temperate zone. She eyed him with distaste, disliking the odour of perspiration that accompanied him wherever he went almost as much as she disliked his bad breath.

'Ah, you're at home!' he greeted her.

'I frequently am when I know you to be out,' she answered, turning the page of her book.

'Be careful you don't forget that knife of yours one of these days. I suppose you have it with you now?'

'I have indeed,' she assured him.

He was irritated beyond measure that she thought so little of him that she didn't even bother to look at him when she was speaking to him.

'I should have thought you'd be preparing for this evening,' he went on. 'Didn't you get my message? We're obliged to attend a function in honour of a Maharaja fellow. He's just got married again, I hear, and is making sure he has British approval for the alliance. Sensible of him! These Princes are forever marrying this one and that one. It's all supposed to bind them into various family alliances that will prevent them from going to war with one another. The sensible realize that British rule is more likely to do that, however.'

Fanny favoured him with a mocking glance. 'Let's hope they enjoy their marriage more than we do ours!'

'Not the same thing at all! You don't have a whole lot of other wives to contend with.'

'Any other wives you had would have all my sympathy,' Fanny goaded him.

Edwin frowned. 'A little competition might put you in your place, my dear. You don't seem to allow that even the Governor's wife should take precedence before you! As everyone fawns on you every time we go out, a little healthy neglect might prove salutary at home!'

'Your neglect at home and abroad is all I ask for,' Fanny smiled. 'Nor would I be averse to being neglected by what passes for British Society out here. It's like an elaborate and rather silly dance, with everyone curtseying to every-one else. The Governor's wife even curtseys to her husband as if he were some kind of monarch – '

'He does represent Queen Victoria to the people out here. Surely you approve of that?'

Fanny chuckled. 'She'd certainly enjoy the spectacle we make of ourselves, like a lot of peacocks strutting up and down, all trying to outshine the others.'

'The trappings of power are important in bringing home to the natives who rules the roost. They expect a display from the people they're supposed to look up to. It's something they understand and respect.'

'It's strange to me,' Fanny commented, 'that people's happiness has so little to do with it all. Is anyone the happier for our coming here, I wonder?'

Edwin shrugged. 'Most people get their happiness from doing their duty – something you have yet to learn. Perhaps you will tonight – '

'Are you going to dare my knife, Edwin?' she asked him with contempt.

'You won't have your knife!'

Fanny's heart missed a beat. 'I never go anywhere without it. Be warned!'

And, to her relief, her husband said nothing further.

Lady Frances dressed with the greatest care for the evening. Her London reputation for being in the very forefront of fashion had followed her to India and, even while it amused her that anything so essentially trivial should be of the first importance to the rather dowdy set of women of the Delhi government circles, she was quite prepared and very able to play the game with the best of them. Her gown was so low at the neckline as to be almost indecent, with small, puffy sleeves. The skirt was enormous, worn over a cage-like crinoline foundation that was tied securely round the waist with tapes. It was ridiculous to wear such a garment in the crushing heat of the hall, but Fanny carried it off with an air that made it impossible not to notice her. It took Fanny only a few moments, however, to decide that any party she gave in India would be held outside and not in the still, lifeless atmosphere of any room, no matter how large.

She was shown to her place amongst the other women on one side of the formal reception room. The men took their places according to rank on a stage that had been set up behind two padded thrones, on one of which, his feet drawn up under him, sat a small, much-bejewelled boy with an unhealthy, pudgy look and a bored expression. Next to him sat the Governor in full dress uniform, his face scarlet from the oppressive heat, his neck falling in sweaty rolls over his collar. The Indian guests sat on either side of a wide aisle up which the various princelings who now lived under nominal British rule took turns to advance, make their gifts of a symbolic coin, and retreat again. It was, Fanny realized, another dance of power, making it clear to one and all who had the ordering of things now.

No Indian women, she noticed, graced the occasion. She wished the British had been as sensible, for the English ladies had no purpose there that she could discover other than to produce a foil to the extravagant silks and satins the Indian notables had chosen to wear. By comparison the British civilian men looked like a wall of crows and were about as argumentative, each one on the alert for any slight to his rank, his wealth, or anything else that could offend his complacent view of his own importance.

Fanny accepted one of the Indian sweetmeats that were passed round on gold and silver trays at regular intervals and became conscious that she was being scrutinized, in her turn, from afar. Shaken for the moment out of her role as observer, she sought the ranks of guests to know who it was who was making her so self-conscious. She found him almost at once, a shock of recognition passing through her although she knew clearly she had never seen him before. He wore a sugar-pink turban that emphasized the darkness of his skin and the peculiar liquid quality of his eyes, which seemed to be as amused by the futility of the proceedings as she was herself. He was not of very great importance, she reasoned, for his seat was far from being one of the best. His jewels, however, were spectacular, and his embroidered coat and slippers were of a much finer quality than any others she could see. He spread his hands on either knee and she saw they were as hairless as any woman's.

He turned and looked at her, putting her in a fine rage at having been caught out staring at him like any adolescent girl overcome by some man's beauty. She fanned herself crossly, refusing to look away, and he actually had the temerity to smile at her. Worse still, she was tempted to smile back. He was exotic and exciting in a way no man had ever been to her, certainly not the other Rajas and Maharajas, nor the pompous, flushed faces of the British grandees.

He moved his head in an incomprehensible Indian gesture and lifted his eyebrows, making her blush. She

73

closed her fan with a snap, pursing up her lips in disapproval, vowing not to look his way again. A moment or two later, however, their eyes met again and this time she smiled before she had thought and was rewarded by such a broad grin of appreciation that she wanted to laugh out loud.

Opening her fan again, Fanny turned to her neighbour, an awkward, large-boned woman she probably would have dismissed as being beneath her notice at home. She had a kind expression, however, and her boiled-sweet eyes were decidedly sympathetic as they rested on Fanny's face.

'Have we met before?' Fanny asked her.

The lady laughed. 'That we haven't, my lady. Took some doing, I don't mind telling you, to get myself placed next to you now. Wouldn't have bothered for myself, but I felt I owed it to my husband, Sir Arthur Cunningham, poor lamb. Some of them won't give him his due when they see what a poor dab he married. So I thought to myself, Lady Frances looks all right to me and I daresay she wouldn't mind lending me a little of her consequence.'

Amused by her directness, Fanny began to feel the evening might not be too bad after all. 'I'd be delighted – if you think anything I can do will help.'

'It will. I'd like to see them snub the friend of Lady Frances Bantry as easily as they do the ex-Miss Jukes! Sir Arthur may have married beneath him, but he don't want his nose rubbed in it by a lot of jumped-up Jacks and Jills who are no better than he is! They can put me down all they like, but I do resent it when they try to do the same thing to him!'

Fanny understood that only too well. She gave her new acquaintance an encouraging, guilty smile. If she had never lived outside London, she knew she would have snubbed the unfortunate Lady Cunningham herself. In Ireland, though, society had never been as stiff or as rigid in its notions and, if it had been, Fanny's natural friendliness would have welcomed Lady Cunningham's good-natured realism even had she liked her less than she did. As it was, she thought the artless woman to be quite the most interesting female she had yet met in India.

While she was considering what to say next, Fanny was approached by a servant in a green coat that reached to his knees, with a scarlet belt and turban. She didn't recognize the uniform, but that didn't surprise her, for she had yet to meet any of the local rulers. He presented her with a note on a silver tray, his face impassive as she silently took it from him, trying to ignore the pervasive curiosity of the women about her.

'Open it, do!' Lady Cunningham advised her. 'You'll never know what it has to say – nor who it's from! – if you don't!'

Fanny did so, attempting to look as though she received such intriguing missives every day of her life. She did not, immediately, connect the scented message with the Indian Prince she had smiled at earlier. Nor would she have thought that such a person would be able to read and write in English as well as she could herself.

Her fingers trembled slightly as she read the line of the script once, and then again: *I shall be in the rose garden immediately after this affair has ended. Where will you be?* She fanned herself vigorously, certain that the heat was about to overcome her for the first time in her life. Surely, she was not about to do anything as foolish as visiting the rose garden herself? The last thing she wanted was to be the centre of spiteful gossip and she was far too experienced not to know what a flutter such an action on her part would cause in the narrow community in which she found herself. Edwin would be more than justified in

75

calling her to account, using her ill-judged assignation as an excuse to make sure that, for once, society would be on his side if he should choose to punish her for her behaviour. A knife could prove to be a paltry weapon against a determined man, as she very well knew. Edwin was both a bully and a coward and, so far, she had successfully used both these characteristics to her own advantage. She would be foolish beyond belief to throw away that advantage and give him the very excuse he sought to force her back into his bed.

Fanny crumpled the note, wondering what to do with it, a little relieved when Lady Cunningham took it from her, dropping it unread into her reticule.

'Best not to let others see his impertinence,' she murmured to Fanny. 'Handsome devil, ain't he?'

Fanny swallowed. 'Some of them do have a look about them,' she conceded.

Lady Cunningham chuckled comfortably. 'I've often thought the same myself, but it doesn't do to say so, not happily married as I am to my Sir Arthur!'

Fanny turned her attention back to the ceremony before them, but the picture she retained in her mind was the face below the sugar-pink turban, with the laughing eyes. He was as different from Bantry as it was possible for a man to be. Her husband always looked to her what she knew him to be, a cruel pervert whose hatred for her was only outdone by hers for him.

Edwin Bantry, she noticed, was seated closer to the Governor's throne than he had any right to be, probably as a compliment to his wife's rank, Fanny thought cynically. It hadn't taken her long to discover that her husband was not popular amongst the small British community. Nothing had been said to her directly, but somehow she had been made aware of many things she was sure he never suspected were common knowledge amongst his so-called friends. Servants everywhere would gossip about their employers; Indian servants had ways of their own of spreading the secrets that these red strangers amongst them thought were securely locked away in their own hearts. It hadn't taken Fanny long to know all about Bantry's taste for young girls. Before her arrival, he had bought them from their parents in the streets, throwing them out to starve when he had done with them. The British had been prepared to overlook such excesses at first, justifying themselves with the stories they had heard of child prostitution in temples, and convinced as they were that all Indians were without morals or any sense of decency, it had been easier to look the other way. When Edwin had turned his attention to a young European girl, however, their reaction had been very different. It hadn't only been his need for an heir that had led Edwin into forcing Fanny to accompany him back to India: he was as much in need of her respectability and her consequence as he had been on the day he had married her.

Fanny's heart had gone out to the little girls he had abused, but she had schooled herself to a complacency she was far from feeling, determined to protect Mary and herself from his uncertain temper for as long as she could. She had even employed her considerable talents as a hostess on his behalf, smoothing over his social lapse and concentrating everyone's attention on her own dazzling display as the most sought-after lady in Indian society. Although she secretly despised the small British community for their narrow-mindedness and the speed with which they rushed to stand on their dignity at any imagined affront, she remained affable to one and all, answering their many impertinent questions about her previous life in England, never once showing what she really thought of their ill-mannered curiosity. She, who had never suffered fools gladly, had allowed her clothes to be picked to pieces, her friendship with the Queen to be commented on by one and all, and had assured the more insecure of those she met that the Queen was indeed still wearing plaids and checks, her enthusiasm for all things Scottish undimmed. Not by so much as a word or gesture had she shown that she minded when her clothes were copied by the inelegant and her name bandied about by virtual strangers claiming friendship with her.

Today, she had her revenge by choosing to wear a Court dress of such daring that she knew none would dare imitate. The Indian Prince hadn't been the only man who had spent much of the evening staring at her half-revealed, half-concealed charms. It had been unkind in her, she knew, but it had been too good an opportunity to miss of showing her husband exactly what attention the Lady Frances Bantry could command without the least effort on her part.

Her thoughts were interrupted by her Prince, as she was beginning to think of him, rising to his feet and bowing in a half-hearted way towards the Governor and the juvenile bridegroom. Apparently the durbar was coming to an end. Fanny wondered what the Indians thought of it all because of one thing she was quite convinced, there wasn't a British official there who could have told her what was going on behind those brown, enigmatic faces.

'Wondering who he is?' Lady Cunningham's voice came to her.

'Not really,' Fanny denied.

'I would be,' her new friend assured her cheerfully. 'You mustn't mind my saying so, Lady Frances, but I have met your husband and you must be bored stiff with all of us out here. I am myself, and I'm happily married! That's my Arthur sitting next to the Governor, Poor love, he hates everything to do with this sort of thing, but he'd better get used to it because he's been appointed the next Resident at Jammu and Kashmir.' She became even more confidential in her manner. 'If you want to take a turn in the rose garden, I wouldn't mind taking a breath of fresh air myself!'

'I think I'd do better to find my husband,' Fanny began, much tempted.

'Please yourself, dear. Sir Arthur don't receive Lord Bantry, but he'd be very pleased to make *your* acquaintance. In fact, if ever you feel the need, you'd always find a welcome in our home. Shouldn't say so, I know! You know your own business best, but your husband does seem to have a rather uncertain temper, if you know what I mean. All of us ladies have been worried about you ever since you came out here, though none of the others would have dared say anything to you. You mustn't mind me! Never did know my place, as Sir Arthur would say!'

Fanny's humiliation knew no bounds. Did everyone know the full details of her married life? Probably they did, as she knew theirs.

'Shouldn't have said anything, should I?' Lady Cunningham concluded gloomily. 'Arthur would be furious if he knew I'd presumed so on your good nature, what with him only being knighted this year, and you the daughter of an Earl and a personal friend of the Queen's besides – '

'I have never claimed as much!'

'You didn't have to, your husband saw to that!' Lady Cunningham told her dryly. 'You'd be a fool if you didn't see that your high position makes you even more alone out here. There's few who'd dare approach you to offer you any assistance, no matter how bad it gets.' She put a comforting hand on Fanny's arm. 'I've been alone and afraid in my time too. It'll do us both a bit of good if we become friends. I wouldn't want you to think I mean to take advantage of you, though. I've said my say and I shan't refer to it again. Now, shall I find out for you who that handsome young man is?'

'You're being very kind,' Fanny said stiffly.

Lady Cunningham laughed. 'I'm not easily frightened by rank or position, though I expect you wish I were. Not that I wouldn't have held my hand if I hadn't taken a rare fancy to you as a person.'

She pressed firmly through the crowds, undismayed by her husband's lack of welcome as he struggled to keep his place in the procession of personages who had been invited to pay their formal respects to the Governor. A few words were exchanged between them and then she sailed back again to Fanny. Fanny watched her approach with rueful appreciation. If they ever saw London again, she thought she might enjoy sponsoring her unexpected friend into the first circles of society. The Queen, she was certain, would welcome such a doughty matron to her Court, for the Queen, too, was possessed of a warm heart and a fierce loyalty to those whom she chose to honour with her friendship.

'Sir Arthur says he's a guest here tonight, quite independent of British rule – though how long that state of affairs will last is anyone's guess. He's the Raja of Kattyapur, a small city State out in the desert of Thar. An impossible place to get to. He makes a very good living though, taxing the caravans that come through his lands from Persia and places like that. It's rumoured he feels too small to be safe from our interest and is trying to expand his territories, the very thing, Sir Arthur says, which may be his undoing, though he thinks it'll be years before we bother with any but the greatest of the Princes of Rajputana.'

'Only a Raja,' Fanny pretended to dismiss him. 'I thought everyone here was a Maharaja at least?'

'Probably seeing how the land lies. Shouldn't think he willingly bows the knee to anyone!'

Fanny had come to that conclusion herself. She watched the Raja take his turn at greeting the Governor and paying his respects to the boy bridegroom, and wondered at the excitement he engendered within her. She must be missing her friends in London more than she knew if she could find the barbaric splendour of some foreign despot so compelling. It was more than time that she pulled herself together.

Lady Cunningham dug her in the ribs. 'Are you thinking of seeing him, Lady Frances?'

Fanny gasped. 'Oh, I don't think – '

'With me there to chaperon you, who could possibly object?'

Fanny's eyes changed to an even darker shade of blue. 'Lady Cunningham, you're a wicked woman, and the best thing to happen to me since coming to India! He does look more interesting than the others, doesn't he?'

'A most handsome fellow!' Lady Cunningham agreed comfortably. 'The Rajputs are a very handsome race. They're all descended from the sun, the moon, or from fire, or so I heard tell. Your young man has the sun in his emblem, though what it means exactly I can't tell you. The ones who are descended from the moon have the Lord Krishna as an ancestor.'

'Isn't Krishna one of their gods?'

'An incarnation of a god. He was a very naughty boy and is much loved by all his adherents.' Lady Cunningham didn't sound in the least bit shocked. Fanny warmed to her, delighted to find someone who had taken the trouble to find out something about the country she was living in.

'If he has descendants, he must have had a wife,' she supposed.

'My dear, he was disgracefully prolific. It's said that when he met his wife, she was with a group of cow-girls, milkmaids, who had come to town to sell their milk and butter. The other girls were dreadfully jealous when he picked out the one of his choice and he was obliged to reproduce his body a thousand times over to accommodate them all in what turned into a positive orgy. Radha – she was the one who became his consort – well, no one thought to record what her feelings about it all were, but Indian women don't seem to have a jealous bone in their bodies. I suppose they're brought up to know they won't be the only woman in their husbands' lives.'

Fanny uttered a yelp of laughter. No one had spoken so frankly before her since she had left Dublin and her girlhood behind her.

'Are we any better off in England?' she heard herself ask dryly, and wished she hadn't when she met the quick look of sympathy in the other's eyes.

'My poor Arthur doesn't get the chance to take an interest in other women while I'm about. I meant to have him from the moment I first set eyes on him, despite my being so far beneath him socially. Happily for me, he was of the same mind and we were married before anyone could change it for him. That's why we came out here. I thought people would accept me more easily. I should have known better. If anything, they're worse than they are at home!'

Fanny recognized her cue. She tore her eyes away from the Raja's form. 'Lady Cunningham, I'd be very honoured to have you as a friend.'

'That's what I hoped you'd say,' Lady Cunningham acknowledged. 'That'll be one in the eye for the lot of them! Sir Arthur will be ever so grateful to you, Lady Frances. It hurts him more than it does me when they don't treat me as they should. If only I could mind my tongue better – '

'I hope you never will with me!' Fanny said, laughing.

The two women nodded happily at each other in complete understanding, both equally pleased to have made a friend whom they could genuinely like, as well as being prepared to be made use of by one another to gain their own ends.

The rose garden was very pretty in a formal kind of way. Fanny was in love with English gardens, having long ago discovered that the Irish, by comparison, didn't have gardens at all. At her father's house in the country there had been a walled garden, but only vegetables had ever been grown there. Round the house had been only shaggy, ill-kempt grass, kept down by a few sheep, and the old mounting-block which she and her sisters had used as soon as they had grown too old to ride bareback and had had to put up with the constrictions of a riding-habit and side-saddle.

Here, a profusion of roses grew, smelling heavenly in the starlit darkness. Servants had brought lamps to edge the paths and Fanny thought she had never seen anything prettier than the rows of tiny flames, gusting in the light breeze.

'You know,' she said to Lady Cunningham, 'I could grow very fond of India. I visited the Red Fort earlier in the week. It's truly magnificent.'

'The Moghuls were very clever with water and fountains. I'm told the word paradise comes from their name for a water-garden. As for India, I'm too English to appreciate the perpetual chaos and, while the people are beautiful, whether they be Pathans or Bengalis, I never know what they're thinking. I can't feel quite the same about them since the Mutiny – not even my own servants! I'd always thought we were good friends before.'

'That's exactly what the English say about the Irish!' Fanny told her. 'Oh, not about us, the nobility and the landowners, but about the general run of people whom they don't know at all. They're always trying to be friends, but ordinary people don't have the time or the inclination to cultivate friendships when they're starving to death. What they want is food and justice, not kindness and sentimentality. Their priests don't help, insisting they pay their rents to absentee landlords before they feed their own children! The Queen started a charity at once when I told her about them, but she couldn't persuade her ministers to do anything for them. Apparently they think that if they send emergency food to Ireland, the whole population will give up working for ever and live on English charity for the rest of time.'

Lady Cunningham sighed. 'I suppose it *is* much the same here. They don't rebel often because they hope for better things in the next life, as do the Irish, I suppose. Only here they believe they keep coming back, you see. You fashion your next existence by your deeds and choices in this one and your past lives. The Bishop may hope to make good Christians of them, but I don't believe we ever shall! They have no idea of right and wrong, only of good and evil forces loose in the world. The cow is the Holy Mother and an object of worship. That's how the Mutiny began, they say. The rumour was spread among the *sepoys*, the native soldiers, that their ammunition had been smeared with beef-fat, and they had to tear the cartridges open with their teeth when they were loading up. Nobody can possibly tell now whether it was true or not, but I can't believe even the Company would have been so insensitive.'

'More likely they hadn't bothered to find out what it would mean to them,' Fanny said disparagingly. 'I wonder if the Crown government will turn out to be any better?'

'We'll have to wait and see. It may stop all the fighting that goes on between the petty States, those that weren't already subservient to the Company for one reason or another. However, a united India seems to me to be as far away as a united Europe. A pipe-dream! The peoples are too different, speaking hundreds of different languages, and what Mohammedan is going to have anything to do with a Hindu?' She rescued Fanny's skirts from the flame of one of the little lamps. 'Here comes our hero now. D'you still want to make his acquaintance?'

Fanny's mouth went dry. She couldn't answer a word. In silence, she watched the man in the sugar-pink turban progress towards them. He was taller than she had thought, well over six feet, and, she thought as she had when she had first seen him, he moved like a god. He stood for a moment on the far side of a bed of roses, looking at her. Put out of countenance for once, Fanny swept him a low curtsey. Considering her own rank and who he was, it was greatly overdone. She couldn't remember curtseying as low as that to anyone but Queen Victoria. Here in Delhi, she had contented herself with a small bob of recognition, even to the Governor and his lady, and yet here she was curtseying to this barbarian as if he ruled the whole world!

Nor did he bow in reply as any decent man would have done. He leaped over the roses, extending a hand to her, drawing her upright once again. Lady Cunningham took a step forward.

'Lady Frances, may I present – ' she began.

'Lady Frances,' the Raja repeated. He made it sound like a caress. 'You are welcome here in India.'

'Very pretty,' Lady Cunningham approved. 'That is, if you owned India, Your Highness.'

'It's more mine than yours,' he retorted, with such a charming smile that both ladies immediately forgave him his presumption. 'Are you always called Lady Frances?' he went on to Fanny, refusing to give up her hand.

She lifted her chin. 'My friends call me Fanny.'

'Then that is what I shall call you.'

Fanny stiffened, amused despite herself. 'While I go on calling you Your Highness?'

If she had hoped he would notice the set-down, she was doomed to disappointment. It was like water off a duck's back.

'What's wrong in that?' he shrugged. 'My name is Sajjan Ramakrishna Singh, if you're curious, but nobody now calls me that.'

'I shall call you Sajjan,' Fanny decided, in exactly the same tone of voice he had used to her.

'I mean to have you call me Lord.'

Her head jerked backwards, unable to believe she had heard him aright. She was more startled than shocked, however, and excited, too, by the promise that lay behind the words.

'I'm afraid that's impossible,' she said tartly. 'I'm a wife and mother.' She suspected he wasn't even listening to her.

'I know all about you, Fanny. I've always known you.' He smiled gently at her. 'You're far too beautiful to be left to wilt here, in Delhi, without love and without anyone who understands you.'

Fanny licked her lips. 'You must be married yourself,' she said on a note of desperation.

'Of course. I have two Ranis and several wives of affection – '

'Then you have no need of me!'

It wasn't at all what she had meant to say. She had meant to insist that he should respect her married state, that he treat her as she was accustomed to being treated, not descending to his own level as if – as if she didn't strongly object to being classed in the same bracket as these other women of his!

His smile was as soft and sensuous as the silks he was wearing. 'We have no choice, either of us, Fanny,' he whispered to her. 'We each have to fulfil the destiny life has marked out for us. Sooner or later, you will be mine!'

Chapter Five

'Well I never!' Lady Cunningham exploded. 'I never thought to hear anything like that! Lady Frances, I hope you'll believe me that I had no idea – What arrogance! What presumption!'

'Yes, wasn't it?' Fanny agreed. 'Magnificent presumption!' She felt a strong desire to laugh when they regained the lighted area and she caught sight of her companion's shocked face. It was so long since she had really laughed at anything that she was grateful to the Raja for that, if nothing more. 'Don't concern yourself, Lady Cunningham,' she went on lightly. 'The chances are that neither of us will ever see him again.'

'I hope not!'

Fanny inclined her head, though she was far from being in agreement with her friend's sentiment. She thought the incident had done her good. Since she had first determined to set up as one of the leading hostesses in London, she had been in danger of being as stuffy as were the rest of them. She had always known the British were a stuffy people though, as an Irishwoman, she had naturally blamed the English as the chief instigators of the prudery and self-importance that refused to acknowledge anything calculated to upset their complacent view of themselves. That had been before she had met Prince Albert who, despite his many worthy qualities, had done nothing so well as to quench his wife's high spirits and affectionate nature, making the whole of life a duty rather than a pleasure.

Now, Fanny thought it might have had more to do with the times they were living in. She had done her best to subdue the wild side of her own nature, giving way to no one in her determination to outshine all others when it came to respectability and acceptability amongst the great and good of the land.

It had done her good to find someone who had been unimpressed by all that she had achieved. He had known at a glance that all her lofty pretensions were no more than a part she was playing. Not even Geoffrey, who had known her as a child, had guessed what went on inside her as she had held court amongst the most powerful men of the day, flattering them, occasionally pushing a policy of her own without in the least appearing to do so and, as often as not, gaining her own way for no other reason than because it amused her to do so.

Not once had any of these astute, ambitious men challenged her vision of the world, or of her own place in it. Emotionally unruffled, her inner core untouched, she had gone her way with intelligence, humour, often with a touch of brilliance, and had grown a little lonelier inside with every day that passed. She couldn't remember the last time anyone had stirred her up so thoroughly, openly mocking her rank, making a nonsense of her defences against the attractions of the opposite sex and, worst of all, inviting her to share his amusement that anyone should have been taken in by her charade.

What, she wondered, would happen if she decided to bring her barbarian to heel? It never occurred to her that she might not be able to do it. Lady Frances Bantry had put down the pretensions of too many hopefuls not to have developed her technique to a fine art. It would be amusing to try – if she dared? For a delightful moment, she allowed herself to contemplate the treatment she would hand out to the gentleman in the sugar-pink turban before she grew tired of the game. Then she remembered her husband and what had brought her to India in the first place. She had more than enough on her plate to be going on with, without chancing her arm and her reputation on someone polite society was undoubtedly right in condemning as a heathen savage.

Lord Bantry watched his wife as she came in out of the darkness, with that terrible woman, whom he thought she would have despised as much as he did, in attendance. She had changed since that day she had walked down the aisle towards him in Dublin on the day of their marriage. She was more mature, of course, less a frightened little dab of a creature, but he had never seen her in such good spirits. The sight of her fed the brooding anger that lived inside him these days. More than ever did he need to reduce her to the helpless being he fantasized all women to be. Her confident manner was an affront to him. How dare she set herself up as his equal in a place he had spent years making his own! Did she imagine he would admire her for cultivating the right people, encouraging them to gloss over his supposed sins and accept him back into the fold? Did she hope he would be grateful for her efforts on his behalf? It was time she learned better. All he needed from her was a body he could humiliate and torture in his bed; *her* body because there was more pleasure in defiling the gently reared daughter of a British aristocrat, rather than the brown body of a child from the streets, let alone the pallid daughters of the British soldiers who had sometimes come his way.

Watching Fanny's progress across the hall afforded him no pleasure at all. He had thought she would be alone and vulnerable out here, but he had soon discovered she was nothing of the kind. Before her arrival, he had carefully allowed it to be known that the Lady Frances had much for which to be grateful to him. He had chosen the Governor's wife as the audience for his final barb, ensuring that she understood his drift even while he had actually said very little. It had been an act of charity for him to marry Lady Frances, he had implied. True, they had consummated the marriage, but they had had only one night together before duty had called him back to India. He was sure Lady Allen knew, as well as he did, the chances against a virgin conceiving on the night of her initiation? Lady Allen had been as shocked as he could have desired, but all this had counted as naught as soon as the ladies had made the acquaintance of his wife. They had been enchanted by her. He had tried to blame her acquaintance with the Queen for the respect in which they held her, but he had soon been obliged to acknowledge to himself that she had done it through sheer charm and strength of personality. It had been one more thing to fuel his hatred for her.

In his mind, he had always thought of Mary as Fanny's bastard. It was the kind of revenge he would have thought up himself, foisting another man's child on to him. It was a good thing the child had turned out to be a girl and not the son and heir he would have found impossible to acknowledge. As it was, he was prepared to tolerate Mary as the key to the revenge he planned on the woman he'd married. If she wouldn't submit to him for her own sake, she could be made to do so for the sake of her daughter. He remembered with pleasure the fear in her eyes when he had told her as much in London, fear she had successfully hidden from him at all other times. It excited him beyond belief to think of Fanny at his mercy, Fanny pleading with him not to hurt either herself or Mary, Fanny reduced to tears. The contrast between the elegant, charming lady he was watching, and the terrified, bruised and hurting creature of his imagination, made him shake with excitement. His eyes glittered dangerously as he turned away, making his way to the bar. It wouldn't be long now before he would have Fanny on her knees before him. Meanwhile he needed another drink.

Lord Bantry's gait was unsteady and his eyes glazed as he escorted his wife out to their carriage. He was in no condition to notice that his usual footman was missing, replaced by a tall, copper-coloured individual with the accents of a Rajput when he opened his mouth to wish Fanny a pleasant evening. Lord Bantry wouldn't have noticed him anyway: he had long ago come to the conclusion that all Indians looked exactly the same. As long as they bowed and scraped and served him as they ought, he preferred not to know too much about them. Their women were a different matter. They had as many tricks up their skirts as had surprised even him when he had made his first visit to one of the local bawdy houses. No, Indians were all very well when they kept their place, making better servants than his own compatriots ever would. For one thing, he could be reasonably certain than none of them would dare to interfere when he finally taught Fanny the lesson she so richly deserved, whereas in London he had never been sure that Dancer, or some other flunky, wouldn't have come running to her aid.

'Don't know what the world is coming to when our government feels it has to put on a show like that to entertain a lot of popinjays! They'll get above themselves if we go on like this.'

'I thought the idea was to show them the advantages of being dutiful subjects of the British Queen,' Fanny answered.

Unlike her husband, she had noticed the stranger who had helped her into the coach and who had wished her a good evening. She had particularly noticed the way he had smiled at her with open approval, without any of the servility of the other servants. The only Rajput they had on their staff was Gupta, the bearer who had accompanied Edwin to England and who had taught her the rudiments of his language, so who was this fellow and where had he sprung from?

'A firm hand is the only thing they respect!' Lord Bantry insisted.

'Some of them helped put down the Sepoy Mutiny, didn't they? The Maharaja of Jaipur – '

'A peacock if ever there was one!'

Fanny put her head on one side. 'The British did look rather dull by comparison,' she ventured, 'even those in military uniforms. Wouldn't you have liked to be seen in a more colourful costume?'

'Heaven forbid! Providing the crowds with bread and circuses is a sign of weakness. The Romans learned that to their cost. No, what is needed is a build-up of political and military power where it matters most and force our will on them. They can put on their own spectaculars, when we tell them they may, of course, as long as the real power lies with us.'

Fanny was hardly listening. She had summoned up a picture of Edwin in a sugar-pink turban and was wondering why she was so convinced he would merely look ridiculous. Her barbarian hadn't looked ridiculous at all! But she would not think of him again tonight, she vowed, not if she could help it, a small voice amended the promise inside her, and she almost laughed out loud.

Delhi was as crowded by night as it was by day. Peering out through the netted windows of the brougham, Fanny wondered where they all came from. As many people

93

seemed to live in the streets as in the houses, cooking their food, relieving themselves, even sleeping in the road, reluctantly moving out of the way of the passing carriages and pedestrians of a higher caste than themselves. If she had been forced to live that way, Fanny knew she would never have survived, yet these people managed their pitiful existence with both dignity and calm. They moved about in silence, even the children, forming and re-forming knots of colour against the dun walls of the buildings. As they left the walled city, the blackness of the night closed in about them. Fanny felt the loss of the cooking fires and the security lights that burned on every corner. The contrasts of India awed her as much as they attracted her. The other wives she had spoken to were made uncomfortable by them, a little afraid perhaps; only she seemed to find it all so familiar it was as if she had lived here once before and was only now returning home. Lady Cunningham had told her the Hindus believed they lived many lives on this earth. It was a strange idea, but no stranger than Agnes Fetton's conviction that Jesus wouldn't know where to find her soul if she died amongst the heathen in a foreign land.

Fanny was almost asleep when the carriage turned into her husband's drive. Startled into wakefulness by the jolting of the horses as they were brought up short in mid-stride, she felt from habit for her knife. Reassured, she waited for the carriage door to be opened, a little put out at the noise their arrival had occasioned. Gupta's voice, harsh and angry, rang out from the open doorway; another voice answered him. Fanny hadn't expected to understand either of them, but she did, and the shock of knowing what they were saying took her breath away. They were Rajputs, both of them, and subjects, it seemed, of the Raja of Kattyapur, who had sent his own servant to guard a pearl of great price, someone whose destiny was inextricably bound up with that of his small desert kingdom.

Herself? Even allowing for the flowery images of their language, she couldn't believe anyone had the arrogance to assume that she, the Lady Frances Bantry, would be party to a shabby affair of the kind the Raja seemed to have in mind. How dared he! What insult would he offer her next? For two pins, she'd send this man of his back to him with a message that would make his ears burn! Did he think she had found him so desirable that she would commit social suicide, and worse, for his sake?

She didn't look at either servant as she allowed herself to be handed out of the carriage and swept inside the house. She was far too angry to trust herself even to wish them her usual goodnight. When she had calmed down, she would consider what was the best thing to do, because she had little doubt that something needed to be done, and quickly!

From her own room she could hear Mary crying. The sound increased her irritability until she began to wonder if the famed climate wasn't affecting her after all. But she knew it wasn't really that. It was that that savage had dared to send his personal servant to keep an eye on her! Was he so sure of himself that her rank and marital status counted as naught to him? It was a thought that intrigued her and was therefore one to be dismissed from her mind as quickly as possible. Good heavens, he couldn't seriously suppose she would jeopardize everything she had built up for herself at a word from him, could he? She, who had shuddered away from any number of highly advantageous liaisons, had something better to do than to make herself an object of derision and speculation from India to London, even to Dublin and beyond. To be a social pariah, an outcast from her own people, had never been an ambition of hers! She knew the ways of the world too well to be cozened by a passing attraction into losing everything that was dear and familiar to her.

She had only just begun to undress when Edwin appeared at her doorway. She hadn't realized before how drunk he was. His shirt was hanging open and his trousers half-unbuttoned. Fanny eyed him with distaste.

'What do you want?' she mocked him.

'No more than my rights, my lady wife.' His speech was blurred and indistinct.

Fanny shrugged and turned away. 'I still have my knife, Edwin.'

'I'll have it taken away from you! We have enough servants to do the trick. The lazy bastards may prefer their mistress to their master, but they won't help you to defy me, not while I pay their wages!'

Fanny's confidence faltered for a single, fatal moment as her husband sauntered across the room towards her.

'Wait a minute! I can't tonight. I'm not well.'

She could feel his anger rising and winced away from him, hoping he would never find out she was lying to him. Where was her courage when she most needed it? If he were to discover how afraid she was, she would never be able to refuse him again, that she knew. It was only because she had been so sure of herself, so sure of her power over him, that she had escaped his attentions so far. Surely, her courage wasn't going to fail her now.

'I must go to Mary – she's crying!'

She stood up, pushing her husband to one side as she rushed out through the door. She heard him fall, crashing to the floor, but didn't stay to see if he were hurt. Eileen met her in the corridor, her eyes wide with shock.

'Are you all right, my lady?'

'How's Mary?' Fanny asked her breathlessly.

'How should she be, afraid of her own shadow? Send

her home to England, my lady. There's nothing for her out here, ignored by both her parents, and more afraid of her father than any child should be!'

'Afraid of Edwin? What's he been doing to her?'

'Nothing – yet. He never lays eyes on her, but he's threatening her with a good whipping. He says she has no call to think he's her father because he has reason to know she's your bastard, foisted on him to give you credit before the world. Mary doesn't understand what he's telling her, but she's none the less afraid of him for that! She'd be better off living with your brother in London, or even at your father's home in Dublin. Miss Fetton would welcome her back; she wouldn't be alone as she mostly is out here, poor mite!'

Fanny went into her daughter's room, her own troubles forgotten, and picked up the child, cuddling her close against her.

'He threatens to take my knife away from me,' she told her maid over Mary's head. Mary listened carefully.

Eileen busied herself with putting away Mary's clothes. 'And how does he intend to do that?'

'He'll get the servants to help him.'

Mary snuggled closer, hiding her face against her mother's breast. Fanny felt almost embarrassed by the contact. She started to push her daughter away, changed her mind, and brushed her cheek with a gentle hand instead.

'You ought to be in bed and asleep, my child,' she told her.

'I can't! *He* says he'll come and wake me up – and then he'll whip me until you come to stop him. You – you will come quickly, won't you, Mama?'

Fanny hushed her as best she could. 'Better still, would you like to have Eileen sleep in your room?'

The small girl nodded. 'Could I sleep in your room with you?'

'No, darling, you can't do that. He wouldn't allow it, even if I wanted you with me, which I don't.'

'Why not?' The small, fractious voice grated on Fanny's nerves.

'I've always slept alone! You should learn to do likewise!'

'I have bad dreams.'

'Only babies have bad dreams. Big girls like you should have grown out of them long ago. You must learn to face up to things with more courage, Mary. If you're brave enough, no one can hurt you! Tell your father you're not afraid of anything he may do to you, and see what happens then!'

'He'll whip me,' Mary insisted.

'He may, but he probably won't do it twice if he sees you don't care how much he hurts you. Some men are like that. They enjoy seeing other people in pain. They're more to be pitied than feared.'

Great tears welled up into Mary's eyes. It was Eileen, though, who rounded on her mistress. 'How can you burden a child with things like that, my lady?' she demanded. 'More to be pitied indeed! Will you still be thinking that when he's murdered the pair of you?'

Fanny sighed. She wished there was some way she could send Mary back to England. It came to her with a sense of wonder how much she would miss her, and that led her on to thinking how stupid she had been to bring the child with her in the first place. If she'd made enough trouble for him about her, Bantry wouldn't have gone against her decision. His only use for his daughter was as a way of bringing pressure on Fanny to give way to him. He wouldn't be interested in torturing Mary if he didn't hope to reap the benefit from Fanny. No, if Mary were to be kept safe, one or other of them would have to leave Bantry's roof and as not even Fanny could see her husband consenting to her departure, it would have to be Mary.

'Very well,' she said aloud. 'Eileen, you must take Mary home to England as soon as I can arrange a passage for you both. Will you – will you come back to India, and me, once you've got her settled?'

Eileen picked Mary off Fanny's knee. 'I will, my lady. Between the two of us, I'd as soon be in heathen India as in pagan England. Mind you, I'll not deny it'll be good to see Father McGilligan face to face once again. He'd have something to say about all this! Grown men frightening little children indeed! But then the English never did have the sense they were born with, locking their little ones away in dark cupboards and sending them away to school, saying they should be seen and not heard, just as if they weren't people at all! I thank the Good Lord I was born into an Irish family where nobody minded what we looked like and listened to us all the time! What I'd give to have the good Father here now and listen to what he'd have to say about this carry-on!'

Fanny actually laughed. Father McGilligan had become an old, familiar friend to her. She would miss his second-hand strictures while Eileen was gone – and she would miss Eileen. How very much she would miss Eileen!

'There!' said that individual. 'That's one of you settled for the night! And now, my lady, will you be after going back to your own bed and let me get to mine?'

Lord Bantry was still on the floor where she had left him. Fanny poked him with a foot, unwilling to awaken him but more unwilling to leave him where he lay. He groaned, swearing under his breath. She had never heard half the words before, but the general drift was clear to her. She felt sickened by the sight of him, reluctantly acknowledging to herself that she was afraid of him, as Mary was afraid. If she were to move him, however, she was going to need some help.

She thought the servants would have been in bed long since but, in case there was still someone lingering in the kitchens, she wrapped herself in a cloak she kept on a hook behind the door, and went to find them. Immediately, Gupta and the strange Rajput footman materialized out of the shadows.

'Is there any way we may help you, *memsahib*?'

It was the footman who spoke and she deliberately answered him in his own language. 'Please put my husband to bed!'

There was a whispered consultation between the two men. It was quite obvious to Fanny who was giving the orders, and it certainly was not Gupta. A slight frown appeared between her eyes.

'Gupta, who is this man?' she asked.

Under other circumstances the bearer's consternation would have amused her. Tonight, her nerves were too raw for her to be other than infuriated.

'Well?' she demanded, a slight tapping of her toe betraying her ill temper.

'He serves the Raja of Kattyapur.'

'I guessed as much. What is he doing here?'

'Guarding you, my lady.'

'Indeed?'

'He will be here a few days – '

'He will go tomorrow!'

Gupta writhed with embarrassment. 'He cannot go, not until His Highness the Raja tells him he may.'

'Then he'd better hide himself away in your quarters,' Fanny ordered firmly. 'My husband has drunk too much to notice him tonight, but he's neither blind nor a simpleton. He won't be impressed to hear he's here at the whim of the Raja of Kattyapur! The Raja's writ doesn't run in Delhi!'

Gupta's face was totally without expression. 'There have been many cities called Delhi, since long before either the Moghuls or the British came here. Which Delhi are you referring to?'

Fanny's annoyance gave way to a new emotion, one she had never experienced before. 'The British mean to unite the whole sub-continent in the end!'

Gupta spread his hands. 'If that's their destiny, there's nothing any of us can do to stop them. We none of us can escape our *karma*, my lady, not even you.'

'Christians don't believe such nonsense!' she snapped at him.

Gupta dared a broad grin. 'My lady goes to church every Sunday, it's true, but does she believe everything the other British ladies believe?'

'If I don't, it's because I was brought up in Ireland!' Fanny retorted. 'They'll believe any superstitious nonsense in Ireland!'

It wasn't what she had meant to say at all. If anyone knew the art of disguising her true thoughts from the vulgar gaze of others, surely it was the Lady Frances Bantry? She certainly knew better than to discuss either religion or politics with anyone, let alone with her own servants! The fact that she had listened to them often enough may have given her a small insight into some of their beliefs, but that in no way excused her parading her own reservations in front of them.

She tried to regain some of the ground she had lost. 'Of course I'm as much a Christian as any of the other ladies!'

'Yet you sometimes bow to our gods too,' Gupta murmured slyly.

Startled, Fanny tapped her foot again. 'I do?'

'Perhaps you remember the Lord Ganesha from a long, long time ago, he of the elephant head, who guards the crossroads of our lives.'

'I hadn't realized he's a god,' Fanny defended herself. It was true, she had become attached to the tubby, elephant-headed, jolly-looking statues she had seen about the city. The other god to appeal to her was the Lord Síva, who, surrounded by flames, seemed always to be dancing on the head of some dwarf. She had no idea why he should do so, but she had been captivated by the beauty of his statues.

'India has many gods,' Gupta instructed her. 'They all speak to us of the one reality until we are wise enough to be able to do without them. In the end all things are the same. Even India will be the same, long after you and I, and the British, have come and gone. The god will blink his eyes and a whole new cycle of time will begin.'

Fanny could only wonder at herself that she should be standing here in a corridor of her own home, in the middle of the night, discussing such things with her butler. Dancer would have been deeply shocked if she had tried to involve him in such a conversation. Neither would Agnes or Eileen have welcomed a discussion about what they regarded as heathen gods. Each was convinced that she, and she only, belonged to the one, true faith. Fanny wished she knew why it was that she was unable to be certain of anything to do with her Maker. Her only hope was that God would understand that the muddle was not entirely of her own making – if there were a God at all! Of one single thing was she certain: that no human being, not even the holiest of all, could ever hope to understand more than a small facet of the Being they called God.

Gupta signalled to the other man to remove Lord Bantry from Fanny's bedroom. The man slung his unconscious form over one shoulder. It was easy to see he was as reluctant to touch the unconscious lord as Fanny herself was. She felt doubly humiliated that he should have vomited all over the floor where he had lain.

'I'm sorry to give you the trouble,' she said in his own tongue.

'It is nothing. You have nothing to fear from him now, *memsahib*.'

Fanny knew better. She had much to fear from him. When she had first seen him lying on the floor, she had hoped he was dead, and that had been enough to frighten anyone. She might not be an ardent believer, but she had been raised to follow the tenets of the Bible, and so she knew that wishing a thing to be true was quite as bad as making it come true – well, almost as bad! – because of the damage such wishes did to oneself.

She forced herself to look again at her husband's lolling head and saw his eyes had opened.

'I'll get you yet!' he groaned. 'You won't escape me for ever!'

Fanny watched his departure with relief. Eileen was right, Mary would be both safe and happy in England. But how to arrange matters? Would Lady Cunningham help her? Someone would have to, because she didn't think Edwin would do even that much to please her.

Chapter Six

Fanny was watching a bee-eater out of the window and, entranced by the pretty bird, hoped it would nest in the garden where she could watch the young hatch out and grow. She couldn't remember ever having seen such a colourful bird before, but then look at the people it had to compete with! The Raja in the sugar-pink turban for one!

The moment was spoilt for her by the appearance of her husband, a silver-knobbed cane in his hand, who frightened away the little bird by a single poke of the stick. Her hands clenched and unclenched again. How long was she going to have to put up with –

'Oh, there you are!' Edwin came in through the French windows, completely unembarrassed by the way she had last seen him. Perhaps he didn't remember? 'I have to go away for a couple of days on business,' he announced.

Fanny took a deep breath. 'Edwin, I'm thinking of sending Mary home to England.'

'If your brother wants her, my dear, he can pay her fare. I see no reason why I should pay out any more for the benefit of your bastard.'

'She is your daughter every bit as much as she is mine. You'll never prove otherwise. Is it because you imagine her to have been foisted on you in some way that you threaten to whip her whenever you see her?'

'Did she tell you that?'

'You're giving her nightmares!'

'She hasn't your spirit, nor your courage. The only interesting thing about her is that you, contrary to every expectation, seem to have some maternal affection for her. It interests me that you'll do so much to try to protect her from me. It makes you seem more of a woman somehow. She's staying here, Frances, until you do your duty and return to my bed. After that, if you still want to send her home, I'll be glad to be rid of her.'

Fanny forced herself to be completely still. 'Have you no feeling for her at all?' she asked at last.

'None. I'd never speak of her if she weren't your daughter. Of what use is any girl, except to breed up sons for their husbands? Something else you have yet to learn, Fanny!'

'I will never learn it!'

'I think you will, my dear – over Mary's dead body if necessary.'

Fanny winced. 'You overrate my affection for our daughter if you think I wouldn't gladly see her dead before I'd submit to you again!'

His eyes narrowed. 'Every woman loves her own child! No matter how much you deny it, you love Mary and you'll sacrifice yourself to protect her.'

'You know so much about women, of course,' Fanny mocked. 'When did you find time to learn it? I thought you preferred to rape and beat us, not listen to what we hold in our hearts!'

Another point made, she thought, but had it been worth it? It hadn't taken Bantry long to discover her secret, a secret which she had successfully hidden from herself for years: that Mary was, indeed, very dear to her and that she would do everything in her power to protect her. She would never be the type to brood over her offspring's picture, or tear herself to pieces over a mere sniffle in the nose, as many mothers did. She was quite unsentimental about her, but she loved her better than she had thought possible. She had always tried to persuade herself she had done enough for Mary in giving birth to her, and in trying to instil into her some of her own fearless independence. Of what use was it to rely on anyone, even one's mother, if they failed one when one needed them most – as they surely would if it suited them to do so. She wished someone had taken the trouble to teach her that truth when she had been Mary's age.

Bantry stared at his wife, an indefinable expression in his eyes. He couldn't see that she had anything to complain about. 'If you won't fulfil your marital duties willingly, what do you expect me to do?' he asked her.

'You could treat me with the respect any human being owes to another.'

'If you expect that, you shouldn't have been born a female,' he said dryly. 'When you became my wife, you became my property, not another human being I need to appease and make much of before you'll extend me the privilege of using your body. No woman is ever a person in her own right, Fanny. It would be unnatural! What woman could ever manage her own life and money? Think of the muddle that would ensue if women were given charge of anything more important than the children they bring into the world!'

Briefly, Fanny wondered how Edwin had been brought up to have such a low opinion of the women in his life, then she dismissed the matter from her mind. He was as he was, that was all that concerned her now.

'How long will you be away?'

'A couple of days. It'll give you a chance to think things over. When I get back, I mean to get myself an heir. If you're wise, you'll put your knife away and co-operate. This time I mean to get my way, no matter who suffers for it. Do you understand me?'

Fanny didn't bother to answer. The mists of despair threatened to engulf her. What was she to do now? Two days were hardly going to be enough to lay any plans and do all the other things she would have to if she were to get Mary away safely. She could run away, taking Mary and Eileen with her, but who would help her against her own husband? There wasn't a soul who would do so, no matter how disgusted they might be by what Bantry was likely to do to her. There was nothing for it, she told herself dolefully, but bear him another child. She felt sick to her stomach at the very thought.

Granted the temporary respite of her husband's absence, Fanny returned to her contemplation of the bee-eater. If Mary were to cultivate an interest in the birds and flowers of India, it might help to reconcile her to her new life, she thought. At any rate, it wouldn't do any harm to find her and point out to her the brightly coloured bird, or the little green parrots that flocked from tree to tree. Their song was far from being as pretty as that of the blackbirds back home, but then how many blackbirds had Mary ever heard, living in the middle of London?

She was just about to go and fetch her daughter, when the Rajput servant came silently into the room behind her.

'*Memsahib*, His Highness the Raja is here.'

Fanny whirled round to face him. 'Here?'

The servant waggled his head, looking up to the ceiling and back again. 'He wishes to see you.'

'Then you'd better show him in.'

He had gone before she had thought to ask him why he should have been the one to tell her of the Raja's arrival. He was making himself very much at home in her household despite his lack of English. Fanny dreaded to think what might happen if Edwin were to notice his presence.

There was no doubt about it, the Raja needed taking down a peg or two, and she was in just the mood to do it! She moved into the centre of the room to greet him, relishing the task ahead of her.

She was every inch the lady when he was shown into her presence. She held out a cool hand to him.

'My husband is away on business, Your Highness, so I must ask you to be brief in stating why you are here.'

'No curtsey, Fanny?'

He was no longer wearing the sugar-pink turban of the evening before. Today, he was a vision of scarlet and white. She felt dazzled, nor was the excitement he engendered within her any less in the clearer light of the day.

Obligingly, she bobbed a distant curtsey. 'I notice you do not bow,' she remarked.

He put a hand up to hide his mouth. 'Your instincts served you better the last time we met.'

Instinctively, she lifted her chin. 'In what way?'

He made that funny movement with his head that Indians do, his eyes coming to rest on her face. 'Curtsey again,' he commanded her, 'or would you have me teach you a more fitting greeting?'

Fanny trembled inwardly. 'I have already learned to say *Namaste*.' Her frosty tones would have been more than enough to stop the gentlemen of London society from trying their luck with her any further.

'To a Raja?'

She was about to tell him there was no difference in her book between a Raja and anyone else, she didn't bow her head to anyone! Then her eyes met his and she was overwhelmed by the strength of his attraction for her. It was only fun and she most likely would never see him again, so why not, she thought. Even then, she wasn't sure how much she liked it when she found both her hands taken firmly into his possession and pushed, palms together, in front of her face. 'Now bow low,' he instructed, 'before touching the ground at my feet.' He watched her efforts critically, trying not to laugh. 'Perhaps we should each keep to our own customs while you are dressed like that!'

'What's wrong with my dress?' she demanded angrily.

'It rises at the back.'

Fanny choked back a laugh. 'I'll have you know that in London I am well known as a leader of fashion! What would you have me wear?'

He looked her up and down thoughtfully, his eyes pausing on the swell of her breasts and with disapproval at her concealing crinoline. Finally, his glance met hers. His was as enigmatic as ever.

'If I sent you a Rajputana costume, would you wear it for me the next time I come?'

Her stomach muscles tightened in an unfamiliar way. 'I don't think my husband would approve,' she said, lowering her eyes.

'Your husband is of no account to either of us.' He dismissed the absent Bantry with a graceful movement of one hand.

'He has to be – to me. Society doesn't look kindly on one who goes behind her husband's back.'

The black eyes searched her face intently. How much had he been told about the humiliating scene of the night before? She wished she could rid herself of the notion that he knew far more about her than was comfortable.

The Raja seated himself on the edge of the chair her husband usually used, leaving Fanny to stand before him, unperturbed by her indignant expression. 'You may sit if you wish,' he invited her at last.

'Thank you!'

Her sarcasm was lost on him. 'Sit here,' he bade her, pointing to the floor at his feet.

'I shall do nothing of the kind!'

He finally realized he had committed some kind of *faux pas*, but was nevertheless amused by her indignation. 'No?' He removed himself to an overstuffed sofa Fanny had disliked from the first moment she had seen it. 'Then sit beside me here!'

It annoyed her very much that she should want to obey him. She sat as far away from him as she could, trying not to notice the scent of sandalwood and other spices that seemed to be a part of him. She opened her mouth, determined to give him the set-down he richly deserved before her usual good sense deserted her entirely.

'I don't think you can understand our British ways very well,' she began in firm but kindly tones.

'No, nor do you understand mine.' He seemed to find her strictures as amusing as he did everything else about her. 'I have overlooked much from you, beautiful Fanny, because you haven't had time to come to terms with your destiny yet, as we all must in the end. It would please me, however, if you were to learn quickly what will be expected of you. Life in the *zenana* is very formal and there is little I shall be able to do to protect you from the spite of the other women if you should offend them with your arrogance.'

Fanny gasped. The whole conversation had suddenly got out of hand and, for all her social expertise, she could think of no way she could bring it back under her control. 'Me, arrogant?' she repeated. She dared a glance at him from beneath her lashes. 'Isn't that the pot calling the kettle black?'

He frowned over the allusion, making no sense of it.

'Will you wear the Rajputana dress for me?' He moved his ground.

'No. I told you, my husband wouldn't like it. You forget I'm a married woman.'

'I forget nothing. Your husband will be safe as long as he never dares touch you again. That is his only interest for me.'

Was that what his servant was doing in her household? Fanny stood. Her knees were as weak as water. She wished she had kept her seat.

'Your Highness, there has been some misunderstanding. It would be better if you left now and didn't come back, unless my husband is also at home to entertain you. My butler will show you out.'

He stood also. 'Your butler is from Kattyapur, Fanny. He'll take his orders from me. When the time comes for you to leave Delhi, there will be no difficulty on that score. It might be wise for you to tell Lord Bantry as much, in case he should get any inconvenient ideas of his own. I wouldn't like to see him come to any harm. It would be inconvenient for me to be seen in an unfavourable light by the British at the moment. I prefer to keep my independence, and the independence of Kattyapur!'

Fanny sat down again. 'That's it! If you remove me from Delhi, do you think the British will wash their hands of the affair? You'll be putting your head into a noose from which there'd be no escape! I'm not some nobody whose absence will go unremarked!' She swallowed. 'What makes you think I want to go with you?'

He seemed incredibly tall as he stood before her, rocking gently back and forth on the balls of his feet. She turned her gaze away from the gold embroidery on his coat, completely undermined by the knowledge that the temptation he presented to her was written clearly on her face.

'Afraid, Fanny?' His voice was as gentle as if he were coaxing a recalcitrant child to face up to the inevitable. 'I thought you claimed there was nothing in the whole world able to frighten you?' His voice became gentler still, making Fanny want to cry. 'No woman has ever complained of my treatment of her in *my* bed!'

Fanny closed her eyes to shut out the sight of him. 'Would they dare?'

His laughter made her realize the impropriety of that remark. She flushed, wondering what had become of the dignity and self-control that usually informed her behaviour.

'I think you would dare!' the Raja said on a note of admiration. 'In that, Fanny, I find you worthy of your destiny.' He ran his forefinger idly down the side of her nose. 'I shall have your nostril pierced on this side, I think.' He screwed up his eyes thoughtfully. 'Yes, it will look well on you, just as I thought.'

Fanny thought she was about to faint. 'Don't I have any say in all this?'

'It'll please me to see you looking more like one of our own women,' he went on, just as if she hadn't spoken. He tapped her cheek warningly. 'Open your eyes, Lady Frances, and see what I have for you. Won't that be worth a moment's pain?'

Realizing that she was not going to faint and miss a moment of this extraordinary man's conversation, Fanny did as she was bidden. Her eyes widened at the largest diamond she had ever seen lying in the palm of his hand. Did he hope to bribe her with that? Not that it wasn't a thing of beauty, but to wear it in her nose? The whole idea was ridiculous. She shook her head, suspecting that he was, indeed, mad.

'European women do not wear jewellery in their noses!'

she informed him loftily. 'Would you make me an outcast amongst my own kind?'

'Better an outcast than dead,' he answered.

She looked at him. 'Dead?'

'Isn't that what your husband intends for you if you continue to defy him?'

She felt a spurt of anger that he should know so much about her. 'I don't care to be spied on!'

'I'm only protecting what's mine. Would you prefer to give Lord Bantry the heir he needs?'

Humiliated, Fanny sought to dissemble. It was totally out of place to discuss such an intimate matter with any man, let alone one who was clearly bent on her seduction.

'I have to protect Mary – my daughter,' she found herself saying. 'I must know she's safe!'

'She'll be as safe as she'll ever be once you're gone.' It wasn't what she wanted to hear, particularly in those indifferent tones, and perhaps especially because she knew it to be true. 'You can't take her with you, Fanny,' he pointed out in the same, flat tones. 'What future would she have in Kattyapur? She has her whole life before her and she won't thank you for destroying her hopes of living that life amongst her own people. You won't be able to return – would you wish the same fate on her? The best you can do for her is to set her free to make her own way without you.'

Fanny threw back her head. 'My place is here! I don't know what you imagine you can do about it, Your Highness, but I assure you my life is already decided – '

'True. Your destiny is in Kattyapur, with me! Why won't you admit it, Fanny?'

She swallowed, seeking to still the pounding of her heart. She was being ridiculous even to consider going with this barbarian, and yet, and yet, she was far too fond of life to

113

want to die at Bantry's hand, and that, she knew, was the only realistic alternative before her.

'I must protect Mary!' She hesitated. 'She's afraid of him – '

'Then the sooner you leave the better!'

Fanny chewed on her lower lip. 'I still can't believe him to be such a monster! When we were first married, he raped me. Mary was the result. Poor child, it was a bad start in life. How can I abandon her to her father's whim?' She swallowed again. 'If you – if you think to take your pleasure with – with me, you'll be disappointed!'

The Raja smiled slowly, with a male arrogance that made the blood spin in her veins. 'When I take you to my bed, beautiful one, neither one of us is going to be disappointed.'

Fanny looked wildly round the room, seeking inspiration. It was wicked that anyone should be able to put her in such a taking with no more than a look, a gesture, or touch. She, who was known for her cool, detached view of life, had fallen headlong into a quagmire of emotion and need, such as she had never suspected was in her nature to feel for anyone. 'I must have time to think! I must be mad! Oh, I wish I knew what I should do!'

The Raja made that strange movement with his head again. He, at least, seemed to have no doubts on the subject. For an awful moment she wondered if that was the secret of his attraction for her, that he not only voiced what she wanted for herself, he seemed fully prepared to take the whole responsibility on to his own shoulders, leaving her the possibility of being guilt-free for perhaps the first time in her life. Oh, the guilt would return, she was sure of that! She had never felt in the least tempted to have an affair with anyone before, but she was tempted with this man! What bliss it would be to cast her cares on to someone else, if only for a few hours, and know he would never blame her for her weakness.

Then he was speaking again, reducing her efforts to stay cool and calm to chaos once more. 'You may stay with your daughter until Lord Bantry makes his first move against you, then you shall come to me.'

She didn't need to ask him how he meant to achieve this. He had already subverted her servants – and herself! She was quite sure he would have no difficulty in arranging the other details of her life to suit himself. The only thing left to her to marvel at was why she should fall in with these plans with no more than a murmur of protest. It seemed to her to be as inevitable as had been her first meeting with him. She felt a fleeting fear that he wouldn't carry out his promise when the time came for it. Perhaps this was his Indian way of carrying on a flirtation and he meant nothing more by it than that? No, that she wouldn't believe!

'What will you do if I don't come?' she dared to ask.

'You will come – *and* you'll have your nose pierced to please me!'

Fanny's finger strayed to her nostril, rubbing it thoughtfully. 'Behold me in terror!'

She smiled at him as she had not smiled at anyone for a long, long time. Of course, she kept telling herself, she would never really go anywhere with the Raja of Kattyapur, but it might be fun to pretend for a moment that she might. Her navy-blue eyes twinkled up at him.

'Will I see you again in Delhi?' she asked him.

He straightened his shoulders. 'Not tomorrow. Will you invite me to visit you the day after, in the afternoon when your husband will be about his business?'

She nodded, knowing she was playing with fire, but unable to resist the temptation. 'Shall we say four o'clock?'

He jerked his head in the Indian affirmative. 'Your

Rajput dress will be waiting for you an hour before my arrival.' He held out a hand to her. 'Make your curtsey, Fanny, for it's the last time you'll ever do so to me.'

Obligingly, Fanny curtseyed to the ground, spreading her skirts around her. Her brows rose significantly when he made no move to return the obeisance, merely watching critically as she rose again to her full height.

'I prefer our ways,' he said abruptly. 'If you want to please me, Fanny, learn them quickly and well.'

'That, of course, must always be an object with me, Your Highness,' she mocked, tongue-in-cheek.

He acknowledged the thrust with a narrowing of his eyes. 'It's your sole reason for living,' he answered.

He was gone before she could think of a suitable answer. It would be a hard task to keep that man in his proper place, but it might well be worth the effort. She was looking forward to their next meeting as avidly as if he were already her lover.

Mary's screams erupted through the house, nudging Fanny into wakefulness. Her first thought was that Bantry had come home, her second to feel for the knife under her pillow. She jumped out of bed, pulling on a lacy negligee, intent on putting a stop to the child's nightmares before she woke the entire household. If this were Edwin's doing, he would answer to her for it, though quite how she would achieve this she didn't know.

As she stormed down the corridor, Fanny almost tripped over the *punka-wallah*. The boy was fast asleep, as he almost always was at this hour. It was a shame to wake him for, young as he was, Fanny could only suppose it was the most boring job imaginable, but it was for her own child she was concerned now.

Mary's door was wide open. The first person Fanny saw

116

was Eileen, looking strange in her nightwear. She was completely shrouded in a nightgown of enormous proportions and had a mob-cap pulled down over her face so that only her nose was showing.

'What on earth is happening in here?' Fanny demanded.

'His lordship's the matter!' Eileen returned darkly. 'Next time he'll kill the child, and so I'm telling you, my lady!'

The scene that met Fanny's appalled gaze was horrendous indeed. Her husband stood over Mary's bed, a riding crop in his hand, while his daughter screamed out her terror in case he should touch her again. One arm lay twisted at an unnatural angle behind her back, but it was impossible to assess the extent of her injuries in the candlelight.

'Bantry, are you mad?'

'Your door was locked!'

So that was it! She didn't make the mistake of raising her voice. Rigid with shock and disgust, she stood her ground, speaking slowly and clearly and meaning every word.

'Edwin, you have finally taken leave of your senses. Don't you realize that Mary is the Queen's goddaughter? That surprises you? Well, it shouldn't. Before I left England, I particularly reminded the Queen that our daughter – '

'No daughter of mine! The Queen will love to hear how she was tricked into being the godmama of your bastard daughter! When I tell her – '

'I've already told her the circumstances of Mary's birth – and her conception! No one is in any doubt she is your child. Would to God she were not! It's because she's yours that I've always starved her of any affection, but that's on my conscience, not yours. If, however, you should ever lay so much as a finger on that child again, I shall see to it that you are hounded out of society wherever you go! And don't think I can't do it! I won't need to do anything! Servants talk, my dear Edwin, servants always have!'

She went further into the room, sitting down on the edge of her daughter's bed. Part of her longed to gather the small, broken frame into her arms, to whisper soothing nonsense into her ears; another, more sober part wouldn't allow any such weakness.

'What happened, Mary?' she asked on a note of asperity.

'He hurt me!' the child moaned. 'And you didn't come!'

Fanny's accusing eyes met her husband's across the bed. His gaze fell away before the contempt in hers.

'It wasn't my fault,' he excused himself. 'It wouldn't have happened if you hadn't driven me to it. How else could I get you to open your door? I warned you what would happen if you didn't do your duty by me as a wife should!'

'You'd use that as an excuse to torture a little girl?'

He recovered himself a little. 'As I will again, if you don't give me the heir I seek. I've always known you'll do for her what you won't do for your own sake, or mine!'

Fanny stared at him across the bed. 'You fool! The bazaars will be buzzing with the whole story long before breakfast. The news will have reached the Governor's wife's ears by lunchtime! What will everyone think of you after that? You should have settled for my death –'

Bantry let the whip fall to the floor. 'I can buy my way out of trouble!' he mumbled. 'I'll bring you to your knees, if it's the last thing I do!'

'Never! I shan't be here much longer! Rest assured, however, that wherever I am, wherever I go, if I ever hear you've touched Mary again, I'll destroy you – and if I don't, Queen Victoria will!'

Edwin hunched his shoulders and began to whine. 'It

wouldn't have happened if you'd done your duty. I'd have got you where I wanted you tonight, if you'd come more quickly to see what was happening to your precious daughter! I have every right to father an heir on my own wife!'

'But no right to treat your daughter this way!'

'Then you'd better learn your duty! You won't always have your knife with you!'

Fanny dismissed him with a contemptuous look. 'I'll kill you before I ever let you come near me again,' she told him almost casually. 'If necessary, I'll kill you with my bare hands. I'd be doing the world a favour – '

Bantry put his hands over his ears to shut out her voice. 'You weren't worth your price, Lady Frances. I paid your father a pretty penny to have you as the mother of my children, and it bought me nothing! But be on your guard, my lady wife, because you haven't won yet, not by a long chalk. In the end, every woman is at the mercy of her husband and no questions asked! When I've had my way with you, I'll dispose of you as I would any other wench from the streets I've bought and paid for! See if any of your high-born friends come to your aid when they know you to be a harlot in a brothel. They'll look the other way and pretend to themselves that you're dead, as you'll wish yourself to be!'

Fanny, in a state of shock, watched him leave the room. That he spoke no more than the truth, she had no doubt. She well knew the hypocrisy of the polite world as they combined to draw a veil over the darker facets of life. The gentlemen would excuse themselves, saying they could not sully their wives with the contaminating influence of one who had experienced such things. They wouldn't approve, but none of them would lift a finger to help her. She was Lord Bantry's business, not theirs!

She heard Eileen's gasp and turned her attention quickly back to Mary's ills.

'It's her arm, my lady! We'll have to send for a doctor to set it, or she may never be able to use it again.' The Irishwoman broke into noisy tears. 'What are we coming to when a man will do this to his own child?'

It was obvious to Fanny that Mary's arm was broken in several places. She struggled against the despair that seized her, while Eileen audibly wondered what Father McGilligan's advice would have been under the circumstances. The impossibility of sending for an English doctor in the middle of the night to treat the child made Fanny feel sick to her stomach. The gossip would be intolerable and it would be Mary herself who would suffer most.

'Send Gupta to me,' she commanded Eileen, 'and tell him to hurry.'

The butler arrived in full uniform, his turban set at a jaunty angle on the back of his head. He took one look at Mary's arm and the crimson welts that ran down her back and sides.

'You wish me to fetch a doctor, my lady?'

Fanny nodded, refusing to look at him. 'I thought His Highness's *hakim* might be persuaded to come. Do you think he would, Gupta?'

The dark eyes were unreadable. 'For you, he will come, my lady. He'll be here before dawn. His Highness will insist on knowing all that's happened here, however,' he added slyly.

'Tell him Miss Mary has been badly hurt. He needs to know no more than that!'

Gupta bowed. 'If you say so, my lady. Shall I tell him he'll hear the whole story from your own lips?'

Fanny stirred restlessly. 'What business is it of his?' she demanded impatiently. 'Or of anyone else's?'

Gupta bowed again. 'I'll give him your message. Good-night, my lady.'

Fanny didn't move a muscle. She was afraid to go to her room in case Bantry came looking for her, and afraid to stay where she was in case her presence disturbed her daughter more than it comforted her.

'Goodnight, Gupta,' she said.

Chapter Seven

It was, perhaps, unfortunate that Lady Cunningham should choose that morning to call on her new acquaintance in order to cement their promising friendship. She happily accepted the fiction that Fanny was 'not at home', and was standing in the handsome portico of the Bantrys' house, bending the corners of the visiting-cards over to show they had been delivered personally, two of her husband's and one of her own, when who should come into her view in the garden but Lady Frances herself, peering into a bush, for all the world as if she had lost something most precious amongst its shaved branches. For an instant she hesitated, sorely tempted to call out to her, no matter what the conventions might dictate. It seemed too ridiculous to pretend that Fanny was invisible to her, the more especially as her curiosity to know exactly what she could be doing was whetted.

'May I help you look?' she offered at last, taking a few steps down the drive.

Fanny turned a distracted face towards her. 'I'm sure there's a bird nesting here somewhere; the prettiest bird imaginable.' She described it, still searching the bushes as if it were the only thing at that moment which mattered to her.

'A bee-eater,' Lady Cunningham said, pleased to be of service. 'If you don't mind my saying so, Lady Frances, it won't come anywhere near you with you beating the bushes like that.'

Fanny brushed an errant ringlet out of her eyes. 'You're

absolutely right!' Her shoulders hunched miserably, before she straightened her spine and pinned a smile on to her lips. 'Won't you come inside?'

'That's mighty good of you,' Lady Cunningham acknowledged frankly, 'but I know you're "not at home" and so I won't keep you. You don't look as if you can be bothered with people who are "absolutely right" just now, if you don't mind my saying so. You look teased half to death!'

Fanny managed an apologetic smile. 'And without a manner to my name? I'm so sorry! There, you have my full attention now. How can I serve you?'

Lady Cunningham took the apology in the spirit in which it was meant, privately considering it to be a very handsome one. 'I was going to ask you to attend a little gathering I'm thinking of holding in honour of Sir Arthur's new appointment,' she began, 'but it wouldn't be very well-mannered in me to invite you and not Lord Bantry, would it? I won't hide from you that I'm in a proper taking about it and could do with your support. Lady Allen has said she'll come, and she's a real stickler when it comes to the seating arrangements and things like that. I do so want to do the right thing – for Arthur's sake!'

'Of course you do!' Fanny agreed warmly. 'Tell me whom you're inviting and we'll get it all planned out over a cup of tea.'

'Well,' Lady Cunningham said doubtfully, 'if you could, I'd be ever so grateful! Lady Allen won't be half so difficult if I start right!'

Fanny turned her amused gaze on the other woman, suddenly liking her very much and longing to tell her that nothing was 'ever so' anything. What fun it would be if she could be brought to snub Lady Allen as that encroaching female deserved, but it wouldn't do. Lady Cunningham would never get away with it, despite being worth ten of the Governor's lady.

'It isn't at all difficult once you've grasped the rules,' Fanny explained. 'It's rather like playing those silly games we did as children; once you've got the hang of the basics, all you need is a good reason for doing exactly as you please.'

'That's all very well for you!' Lady Cunningham observed dryly. 'You can afford to have eccentric ways and do as you like. I can't!'

That was only too true, Fanny decided with mixed feelings. The poor woman was far too terrified of doing the wrong thing to be able to summon up the nerve to flick her fingers in society's face and make these intolerably self-important females accept her on her own terms.

'Come inside and we'll work out the details of your table, then let anyone criticize you if they dare! As for your invitation, nothing would keep me away from your party were it not that I may be forced to leave Delhi. After today, it would be much better for you not to claim any friendship with me – I'm afraid it would strain your credit with the other ladies beyond remission. Much better turn your back and have nothing more to do with me!'

'Leaving Delhi? Where are you going?'

'It'll be better for you not to know anything about it.'

The older woman plumped up her sleeves indignantly. 'I'll not deny I set out to get to know you for my own reasons, but I like you. A bit of tittle-tattle isn't going to change my mind!'

Fanny smiled wearily, touched by such unexpected loyalty. 'Then I shan't scruple to tell you that you're the only person I've met here I would truly want as a friend. You're a thoroughly nice woman, Lady Cunningham, and, because you are, I hope you won't be able to refuse me when I ask you to keep an eye on my little daughter for me. It's an unforgivable liberty to make such a request, I know, but I really don't know what else to do for the best. I can't take her with me, not without bringing her to ruin, and she's afraid of her father.' Despite herself, a tremble of emotion entered Fanny's voice.

Lady Cunningham observed her shrewdly. 'Like that, is it? Poor child! She won't like seeing you go!'

'She won't mind too much. I've never been a doting Mama to her. I'd like her to go home, to my brother in England, but Lord Bantry won't hear of it. With me gone, let's hope he'll ignore her altogether. She'll need someone to show her how to go on, however. Will you do it?'

Poor Lady Cunningham's dismay was only too obvious. She couldn't believe that what had begun as a simple call on someone she had met precisely once before and had liked, should somehow be turning into an involvement she was very much afraid Sir Arthur would dislike in the extreme. She was far too kind-hearted, however, to be able to refuse what she knew had to be a desperate request.

'If that's what you want,' she said roughly, hoping Lady Frances was not going to break down and embarrass her still further. 'The first thing is for you to show *me* how to go on though, don't you think? Lord love us, I don't know what you think I'll ever be able to teach the poor little mite!'

'Something she never learned from either of her parents – that there is still kindness and goodness in this world of ours. If you can teach her that, or anything near to it, I'll be in your debt as long as I live!'

Shocked that Lady Frances should speak so lightly on such a serious matter, Lady Cunningham followed her into the house, feeling more bewildered by the moment. One thing she was quite sure of was that Lord Bantry somehow lay at the back of all this. Hadn't Sir Arthur said only last night that he wouldn't stand in Lady Frances's shoes, not for all the tea in China, and in India too! He had refused to explain, when she'd asked him what he'd meant by that, but Lady Cunningham had her own ideas as to what kind of man Lord Bantry was and she had been only too willing to agree that he shouldn't be allowed out in decent society. She had been quite relieved when, on telling him of Lady Frances's condescension in befriending herself, he had expressly forbidden her ever to invite Lord Bantry to his house.

'I'll not receive him!' he had said flatly. 'Do as you like about Lady Frances – daresay she's in need of a good friend – but have nothing to do with that blackguard she's married to! Such is his reputation, my dear, I'm not sure even your married state would keep you safe from him if he were ever to get you alone!'

'Me?' she had echoed in disbelief.

'Why not? You're still a mighty attractive woman!'

Lady Cunningham preened herself on the memory. How many women, married only half as long as she, would have received such a compliment from their husbands? As long as she lived, she'd never find a better man, nor one she could ever love half so well. How terrible it must be to be married to someone one couldn't love, couldn't even respect!

Barely had the two ladies seated themselves than the butler came in and whispered a few words to his mistress.

'Yes, bring him in at once!' Fanny bade him. She turned impulsively to Lady Cunningham. 'Will you forgive me if I attend to a small matter of business before tea is brought?'

The older woman was given no chance to reply before the butler was back, showing an Indian gentleman into the room. His head was bare and his black hair glinted in the diffused sunlight. He had a thin, ascetic face, with deep grooves running down from his nostrils to the corners of his mouth. It was the face of a clever man, but not one whom Lady Cunningham would have cared to invite into her own drawing-room.

'How is Mary?' Fanny asked him immediately. She spoke without thought in English and was not surprised when he answered her in the same language.

'She is badly hurt,' he told her, 'but not as badly as I first thought. Most of her injuries are superficial and will heal well, though I can't promise she won't be scarred. There is little I can do to regain the use of her arm, however. I have set it to make it appear as normal as possible, but she will never be able to use it with any confidence. It's possible she may drag one foot as well, though she is still young and I have left instructions with the woman who is with her as to the best exercises she can do to correct this tendency.'

Fanny winced as if the injuries were her own. 'Poor Mary!'

Lady Cunningham's reaction was more robust. 'My good man,' she addressed the *hakim*, 'are you sure you're the best person to treat Lady Frances's little girl?' As the words came out of her mouth, she realized exactly why Fanny had called him in and, once again, heartily wished herself elsewhere, dismayed as she was to hear about the little girl's injuries, caused, as she had no doubt, by that terrible father of hers. 'Oh well,' she added unhappily, 'I'm sure you're very clever at your trade despite being an Indian.'

'If I were not, I wouldn't be in the employ of His Highness the Raja of Kattyapur.' The *hakim*'s tones were smooth but inwardly he seethed with anger. The *sahib-log* were best left to get on with their own affairs. He himself had nothing but contempt for them. He ran an experienced eye over the younger lady, noting her white, strained face, and wondered what it was about her that had attracted the attention of his master. He preferred the child to the mother. 'I understand His Highness wishes me to attend personally on you also, my lady,' he added softly, hoping to put her in her place.

Fanny glanced at him, startled. 'Me?' Her hand went straight to the side of her nose. 'That was only a joke!'

'His Highness seldom makes jokes!'

Fanny, only too conscious of Lady Cunningham's interest in this exchange, rose to her feet, holding out her hand to the Indian doctor. 'Even if he were not joking, I don't need a doctor for that!' she exclaimed.

The *hakim* couldn't have agreed with her more. Such things were better left to the old women who specialized in such operations. If he had dared, he would have told the Raja as much! He drew back, distressed that Fanny should want to touch him, and palmed his hands together, bowing his head.

'Thank you for coming so promptly,' Fanny said proudly. 'Gupta will see to your fees.'

'His Highness has already done so. You may see your daughter now, if you wish.'

Lady Cunningham prided herself on being more broad-minded than most, but she really could not feel comfortable with this Indian fellow prowling about the house. She was beginning to think Lady Frances had been right when she had advised her to know as little as possible about what went on in the Bantry household. She would keep her promise to do her best for Mary, who had done no one any harm, and she had every intention of telling Sir Arthur as much, should he try to talk her out of it, but get further involved she would not! It was obvious that Lady Frances

128

had embarked on a course of action that was best described as disastrous, but Lady Cunningham had her own family to consider, and not even her dearest friend could expect her to commit social suicide just because she was determined to do so herself.

'Lady Frances, have you thought – ' she began helplessly.

'Until my head aches with thinking. The thing is that if I don't go, Lord Bantry may kill Mary next time. Would you have that on my conscience as well as everything else?' She put her head on one side, her navy-blue eyes snapping with amusement as Lady Cunningham strove to come to terms with one shock after another. 'Don't worry about me,' she said more gently. 'I can't explain it to you – I shan't even try! – suffice it to say that whatever becomes of me in the Raja's care, I couldn't be more unhappy than I have been with my husband!' She looked down at her hands and was astonished to observe they were shaking. 'I've never been in love before,' she added, 'but I think it may be possible I've fallen in love with him!'

The wretched Lady Cunningham sniffed. 'With the Raja?' That was something she would have preferred not to have heard. 'That I don't believe! You can put a brave face on it all you like, but I won't hide from you I think you're doing the wrong thing. I'd sooner be dead myself than contemplate such a thing! Still, I can see that's not your way and I won't blame you for that! I won't say I understand, because I don't, but I'm not so stupid that I don't know it's a very different thing to be married to my Sir Arthur than to your Lord Bantry! You needn't worry that anyone will hear your secret from me, either, and I'll do my duty by little Mary as you asked me – ' She sniffed again, her mind reeling as she thought of trying to explain this interview to her beloved Sir Arthur. Lady Frances and

129

a *native*! She wouldn't blame him if he didn't believe a single word of it!

Fanny leaned forward and kissed her on the cheek. 'When you go to London next, go straight to the Queen and tell her I sent you to her. Don't forget! Now, let's arrange your table for your party and then I must go and see how Mary is.'

Lady Cunningham thought it just like Lady Frances to insist on doing that much for her despite the tragedy that had befallen her own household. She was even more surprised to find herself soon feeling completely at home, her outraged feelings soothed, and in a much more optimistic frame of mind, a circumstance for which Lady Frances gained her wholehearted admiration. By the time she rose to go, having commanded Lady Frances's whole attention for a good hour, she was ready to lie down and die for her. Sir Arthur could say what he liked, she was determined that Mary would come to live with them until she was able to meet her father on more equal terms. To do any less, she assured herself, would be failing in her Christian duty and she went on her way smiling and well pleased with herself and Lady Frances.

As soon as her guest had departed, Fanny went slowly into her daughter's bedroom. She wasn't sure she understood what she was about to do, any more than Lady Cunningham had done. All she knew was that she had managed to survive so far and that, if she had any say in it, she would continue to live every day she had left to her to the full, into a grand old age if she could manage it, and for as long as possible if she could not. Death might be the gateway into a new and better life, as she was assured every Sunday in church, but she was a long way from being ready to relinquish the one she was already living.

Mary was sleepy and a great deal more comfortable than

she had been before the doctor's visit. She opened her eyes, frowning at the unusual sight of her mother's tears.

'Did he hurt you too?' she asked stoically.

'Only because he hurt you.'

Mary thought about that. 'I tried to do as you told me! I tried not to let him see he was hurting me.' She ground her teeth together. 'I hate him!'

'I know,' Fanny said. 'Mary, you're too young to understand now, but the reason he hurt you was because of me. I'm going away so it won't happen again. You can read and write now and you must start to write letters of your own to your godmother, Queen Victoria, and she will write back to you. It's important, Mary! If you can't manage on your own, Lady Cunningham will help you at first. No one, not even your Papa, will dare to hurt you again if they know the Queen herself stands behind you.'

The child gazed at her with an unblinking stare. 'Where are you going?'

'It's better that you don't know. You'll soon forget all about me!'

'You're my Mama! When I'm big enough I'll come and find you! I shan't mind where it is as long as Papa won't be there!'

'Maybe. You'll probably get married and have children of your own. All I want is for you to be happy.'

Mary looked gravely up at her. 'I always thought you didn't like me, but you do, don't you?'

'Very much!' her mother answered. 'Much good it will do you!' she added bracingly. 'Now don't forget, Mary, write to the Queen as soon as you're able. Lady Cunningham will post it for you, if you ask her nicely. Eileen will stay with you, of course, but there are some things she won't be able to help you with and then you are to go to Lady Cunningham. Do you understand?' She bent down

131

and kissed Mary's cheek as casually as if she were going no further than the next room. 'Go back to sleep now, and don't forget all I've said!'

Mary shut her eyes again. 'Do you hate Papa?'

'Yes, I do,' Fanny confessed, 'but I mean to learn not to do so. One becomes less of a person if one gives way to hatred. I long ago made up my mind your father wasn't going to do that to me!'

'Then I shan't hate him either – at least, not very much. I can't help hating him a little bit!'

'Very understandable!' Fanny said dryly. 'Just don't give him the satisfaction of poisoning your whole life. One day, you'll find there are other men who aren't in the least like your Papa, thank God!'

'Do you know a man like that?'

'I'm hoping so,' Fanny said.

'I hope so too,' said her daughter.

The waiting seemed endless until the Raja's carriage finally turned into the drive. Fanny stayed where she was, allowing Gupta and the Raja's own servant to do the honours of the house for her. She was exhausted in mind and body. Nevertheless, she decided she would be very dignified and sufficiently distant to force him to make all the running between them.

Then she heard his voice in the hall and, picking up her skirts, she ran to him, no longer caring what the consequences might be.

'Take me away, Sajjan,' she begged him. 'I can't bear any more!'

He held her tightly against him, saying nothing. He was stronger than he looked, and much bigger than she had realized. She became slowly aware that his jewels were sticking into her flesh and she smoothed the brocade of his coat beneath her fingers, surprised to find it damp from her tears.

'Oh dear,' she remarked, half-laughing, 'I forgot you don't allow anyone to call you that. You must blame my impertinence on my upbringing. It has often been remarked that the British nobility have no manners to speak of!'

'That is one of the things I wish to talk to you about,' he said with a frown. 'Shall we go somewhere where we can sit down?'

Fanny made to lead the way, colliding with the Raja in the doorway as she tried to enter her own drawing-room. She smothered an embarrassed laugh, standing aside for him to go in front of her.

'I keep forgetting you take precedence over the mere daughter of an Earl,' she muttered darkly.

His only response was to seat himself on the most comfortable chair in the room. 'It's something you can't afford to forget, Fanny. When we are alone, we can behave as any other two people together; but when I am not with you, there is little I can do to make your life easier for you. In the *zenana* you will be of very little account. You are a stranger, from across the forbidden Black Seas that no Hindu may cross without a loss of caste. My two Ranis are both high-caste ladies, coming from families as distinguished as my own. They, and even some of their women, will all take precedence before you, even if they don't resent the attentions I pay you. You can expect nothing else from them.'

'I hate it that you have two wives already!' Fanny responded.

'Two Queens, Fanny. I have had many other wives. It's a matter of politics. I was married to my Senior Rani when I was eleven years old and she but three. I have no children

133

by her, but through her Kattyapur has formed a useful alliance with her father and brother. The Junior Rani is from another State with whom I needed to conclude a peace treaty. She is a charming person. We have two sons and one other child. You must refer to them always as First Her Highness and Second Her Highness, and will have nothing to say in front of either of them. You are dust beneath their feet, as you are beneath mine. A concubine, a wife of affection, can't claim the same respect as a Queen.'

'No.'

He approved her meekness with a slight smile. 'You may expect to be called to my bed more frequently, however.'

Fanny's eyes darkened until they showed black in her pale face. That was something else to which she hadn't given sufficient consideration. She had faced up to the fact that he might hurt her physically, but she hadn't guessed that her own feelings might be seriously involved. She was aghast when she realized that, far from being indifferent, she was consumed with jealousy of these other women whose claims on him were so much stronger than her own. And besides them, how many other wives of affection did he have?

Looking at her expressive face, he challenged her, still smiling, 'Aren't you looking forward to lying in my arms?'

Fanny swallowed. She decided the truth would be the best antidote to what was ailing her. No Englishman, to the best of her knowledge, would ever have asked such a question. Such things were never mentioned in Victorian England though, and she hardly knew the words with which to explain herself.

'I know little about it,' she confessed. She reached under her skirts and brought out the knife she always kept in her stocking, or under her pillow. 'After that first time, I would never allow Lord Bantry to touch me again. I threatened to kill him! I wish I had! Mary might have been spared last night's incident if he'd been dead and buried!'

The Raja took the knife from her, weighing it thoughtfully on the palm of his hand. 'Would you use this on me?'

She shook her head, tongue-tied and awkward. It was strange that she had had to wait for this barbarian, this heathen from another race, to make her feel the slightest joy in her womanhood. The mere sight of him was enough to send ripples of excitement coursing through her body. She was quite sure that once he had made love to her, she would never be the same person again.

'That's as well – for both of us,' he commented wryly. 'Think no more of this husband of yours. He's merely the wind blowing through your hair for a while and then ceasing. What his future is you know not, his path is not yours. Your *karma* determines a different way for you. It's not only as a beautiful and desirable woman that I have need of you: you are to be my means of keeping my independence from the British.'

'Me? A woman?' Fanny expostulated. It hurt unbearably that it was not just for herself he wanted her.

'A woman who understands the politics of her country very well.' He jerked his head to one side, his glance shooting upwards. 'I've heard you played hostess to all the greatest men in London. You've heard their talk and their advice to the Queen. You know what they're really thinking better than anyone else in India. It's important to me, Fanny, not to suffer the fate of Oudh. You can help me by giving me the benefit of your advice. Will you help me keep my independence?'

'I don't even know what really happened at Oudh!' Fanny murmured restively.

He pursed up his lips, watching her closely through half-shut eyes. 'One of the best men of the *sahib-log* is Sir Arthur Cunningham. I saw how eagerly he encouraged his wife to make your acquaintance – '

'And how the poor woman is living to regret it! I've done nothing but make the most shameful use of her! Sir Arthur married beneath him and Lady Cunningham's position in society is made awkward because of it. Everyone knows she was little better than a servant in the Cunningham household before he married her. She thought to take the wind out of the sails of the other ladies by making up to me. It would have worked, too, for I was more than willing to take her up – she's worth ten of any of the other matrons I've met out here. Her only reward was that I succeeded in extracting a promise from her that she'd do her duty by Mary. There aren't many people I'd trust to stand up to Lord Bantry, but if anyone can, she will!'

'Exactly!' he encouraged her. 'You've chosen your ally with care and good sense to protect your daughter – '

'I could have sent her to Charlotte Canning!'

'You're acquainted with the Governor-General and his wife?'

She nodded. 'Of course I am! Lady Canning was Lady of the Bedchamber to Queen Victoria for thirteen years. Poor Queen Victoria! She hates it when her friends go abroad and leave her. Fortunately Lady Canning is an excellent correspondent and a very good watercolourist. I'm afraid I haven't been such good value where Her Majesty's concerned!' Fanny chewed her lip. 'Perhaps it's not too late to send Mary to Charlotte. What do you think?'

'She would have to make the journey to Calcutta alone. She is too sick to go such a long way,' the Raja decided for her. 'Don't tease yourself any more, Fanny. You've done all you can for her. Now, you must think of the future and leave your past behind you!'

'Mary is a part of me – '

'A part of your past. Your future is mine!' His dark eyes burned with a fervour that scared her. 'Until recently, I thought myself to be safe from the acquisitive meddling of the British, because I'm far away and not particularly rich by their standards. Lately, however, there has been talk that the Company wishes to take over my revenues and I find it unlikely that the Crown will put an end to their ambitions. Will they, do you think, send an army to defeat me if I resist them?'

Fanny tore her mind away from her own problems with difficulty. 'Why don't you initiate a treaty of your own with the Crown before the Company has time to call you to its notice?' she suggested. 'What *did* happen at Oudh?'

'Your Lord Wellesley brought the Nawab to the point of abdicating – '

'Why is he a Nawab and not a Raja?'

'He's a Moslem ruler. A Mohammedan,' he added, seeing she hadn't understood him. 'It's an easy way of telling the ruler's religion, just as Moslem cities frequently end in "bad" and Hindu cities in "pur". It's a difference of language as well, of course. Anyway, the Nawab refused to abdicate at the last moment and that cost him half his state as a penalty for his obduracy. The rest was taken from him on account of his alleged misrule. The East India Company forced its trade on our States all over India, at the point of a gun, and often with the backing of the British government in London. First, they signed a treaty with a State, imposing their troops on the capital at their victim's expense, ostensibly to protect their trade. Then, if anything should have displeased them, their forces were already in position to take their retribution.'

'I can see why you don't want anything like that to happen to Kattyapur!' Fanny said seriously.

'Kattyapur is small, hardly appearing at all on the British maps.'

'Which is why you're only a Raja?' she teased him.

He leaned forward eagerly. 'That may all change soon – if only the British will look the other way!'

'By going to war?' Fanny asked doubtfully.

'That wouldn't be very subtle in times like these. No, we have long had a custom among the Rajputs of consecrating a milk-white stallion to the sun and allowing it to wander where it will for a full year, followed by a band of warriors to keep an eye on it. When it strays into the territory of another ruler, he has two alternatives: either he can capture the horse, thus declaring war; or he must do homage to the sacrificer, who thereby gains title to his lands. I consecrated such a horse several months ago, before I came to Delhi and saw the British for myself. They don't understand our customs and they don't wish to. They think we don't understand law, or how to rule our own lands. They won't be content until we do everything their way!'

Fanny tried to concentrate on what he was telling her, but her heart wasn't in it. All she could think about was that he hadn't wanted her for herself at all! All he had wanted was an adviser who understood the ways of the British and, unaccountably, his eye had fallen on her. All his flattery had been incidental to his ambitions for his small State, not because he had wanted her as a woman. Of course, she had been foolish to expect anything else – a moment's thought would have told her otherwise! – but that hadn't stopped her falling headlong in love with him, though how she could have done anything so stupid, and practically on first sight, was beyond her understanding.

'The Crown seems to be much more interested in Maharajas than Rajas,' she observed.

'A Maharaja is a great king; a Raja a small king.'

Fanny had always thought half a loaf to be better than no bread at all. 'If I were you, I'd be content with what you have and keep it safe. Forget the horse. Ask for the protection of the Crown before any of your neighbours informs against you and then, with any luck, the British will feel obliged to protect their known ally against all the rest. It may cost you a bribe or two, as well as the lands you'd hoped to gain, but it'll be worth it in the long run.'

'That's your best advice?'

'Unless you really are too far away and too obscure to be of interest to the *sahib-log*. But I should warn you that India is regarded as a great source of British wealth back home. I can't count the fortunes that have been made out here. The British won't give up easily, the pressures from home are far too great!'

The Raja's eyes glittered dangerously. 'I'll have to hope I'm too far away. If I forget about the stallion, I should lose face before my own people. Also, I still have to get you away safely. Your servants will put it about that you were attacked and abducted by dacoits and they will pretend to search for you for a while. In time you will be presumed dead. Only then will you be safe from the revenge of that husband of yours.'

Fanny was on the point of reminding him that she was only one person, that his first responsibility was to his whole people, but she was reluctant to put at risk the one tie that lay between them. Finally, her sense of justice came to her aid. 'You'd do better to protect your Kattyapur by leaving me to my own devices!'

His eyes blazed with a desire she knew to be reflected in her own. 'No, Fanny, I've already made my decision. Your

139

wisdom is more necessary to me and to Kattyapur than half-a-dozen treaties with the *sahib-log* for them to break at their convenience. You were made to be possessed by me and I won't wait for you any longer. I want to feel your ivory-silken skin next to mine and have you give yourself to me as you haven't to any other man. Isn't that what you also long for in your heart of hearts?'

Fanny twisted her fingers together. 'There may be children,' she pointed out. 'What of them?'

'They will have a place, as do all my children, though they can never come to the throne. My people wouldn't allow that. I am directly descended from the sun, and the mother of the Yuveraj, my heir apparent, must be of the same caste as myself. You are without caste. There is nothing either of us can do to remedy that. You must know, though, that my people take their customs as seriously as you do yours.'

Fanny essayed a fleeting smile. 'I've known the bastards of great men do very well for themselves!'

The Raja returned her smile with one of his own that was so loving, so affectionate that she could feel herself melting inside with pleasure. 'Our children won't be illegitimate, Fanny. I can't make you a Rani, but I can make you the wife of my heart.'

'If you love me a little, I shall never ask you for anything more,' Fanny murmured, 'though I find it difficult to know you have other women.'

'None of them will ever be more loved than you, Fanny Devi.'

She laughed out loud at that. 'Me, a goddess? I shall never be that!' Then she remembered having been told that Devi was a frequent honorific attached to a well-born girl's name. It amounted to Princess, or the Lady with which she was more familiar, it having always been her own title as the daughter of an Earl. 'I'm glad you remember I was born to better things!' she added with a touch of mischief. It was a novel experience for her to laugh and joke with any man.

'You were born to be mine!' he declared. Then he was on his feet. 'We have no more time to waste now. Go and put on your new dress and then I'll tell you my plan for getting you away without your being seen. Hurry, Fanny, we have very little time!'

She looked up at him through her lashes. 'No time for that *hakim* of yours to do his worst?'

He fingered her nose with an intimacy she found peculiarly exciting. 'Not now, but don't think I've forgotten. If anything should happen to me, your jewels will be your insurance for your future. Guard them carefully, and don't give them away to anyone else.'

Fanny couldn't imagine ever wanting to dispose of anything he chose to give her. She, who had never been much interested in possessions, was sharply jealous of his interest in her and the symbols of it were correspondingly important to her. The only reason she was prepared to wear Rajputana dress was that she knew it would please him.

Eileen was waiting for her in her bedroom, marvelling over the costume. 'Did you ever see the like, my lady?' she exclaimed. 'You're never going to wear that? It's indecent, that's what it is!'

'His Highness expects it,' Fanny returned calmly.

'You're wearing it for that one, are you? Oh, I'll not say he hasn't good reason to be so mightily pleased with himself, for a more handsome man I never saw, but if it should ever get out, how are we going to explain it away? It won't stop here in India either! What with that doctor of his being seen by Lady Cunningham, and now you entertaining himself just as if he were any other Christian gentleman, and not some heathen, even if he is a king! His lordship won't take it lying down and, for once, he'll have right on his side!'

Fanny undressed to her skin, puzzling over the unaccustomed garments that had been laid out on her bed.

'Eileen, I'm going away with himself, as you call him. I'm going to live with him in his palace and be his wife. Nobody must know of it, you hear me? I won't have Mary further hurt!'

Eileen swallowed painfully. 'If that's the way of it, I'll pack my bags and go with you. You can't go to such a place all on your own!'

'No. You must stay with Mary and take her to Lady Cunningham as soon as she can be moved. Do whatever Lady Cunningham bids you, but try to take Mary back to my brother in London. And whatever you do, don't discuss with Mary or Lady Cunningham, or anyone else, that you know what has become of me!'

'But my lady, you can't go alone, without any maid of your own!'

Fanny, her dressing completed, surveyed herself in the glass, feeling half naked. She thought she looked as exotic and as provocative as any *nautch*-girl. She pulled the end of her veil over her face and was surprised by the anonymity it gave her. How strange she looked!

She turned and faced Eileen, her friend through so many adventures. 'I'm old enough to look after myself,' she said sadly. 'Mary is not. I couldn't leave her with anyone better to look after her. Remember, I must be dead to you all, but Mary must live! I'm looking to you to see she does.'

Eileen was completely overcome, as much by the shocking, shameless appearance of her mistress as by the thought of parting with her.

'Yes, my lady,' she said.

Not even the wisdom of Father McGilligan could help her now. If she were to write and tell him all that had happened in the last couple of days, he wouldn't believe her. And she'd be the last one to blame him for that! She didn't know herself whether she was standing on her head or her heels!

Chapter Eight

He laughed when he saw her. Infuriated, Fanny stamped her foot. 'I thought I looked very well!' she said stormily.

'So you do!' He laughed again. 'I'll send a maid to help you dress before you come to me this evening. And something for your feet. I hadn't realized you are so small – '

Her bare foot tapped irritably. 'Small?' she repeated.

'Ah, Fanny, Fanny, don't mind so much! It's just that I've never seen you shy and uncertain before. You look more beautiful than ever. It pleases me to see you dressed as one of my own women.'

'That, naturally, is of the first object with me,' she said dryly. 'However, if I must appear before you half naked, I prefer to do it in as dignified a way as possible. Suppose you stop laughing and tell me where I've gone wrong?'

He spread his hands in apology. 'No time!' But he did stop laughing, surveying her from head to foot with a thoroughness that disconcerted her. 'I forgot to include the jewellery I have for you. That's what's wrong! The maid will bring it all with her, for your feet and your arms, everywhere!'

'I look like a barbarian!'

'A beautiful barbarian!'

Fanny sighed. 'A stranger. Is that what I am to become?'

'Will you mind very much?'

'Perhaps not, when I get used to it. What do we do now?'

He ran an exploratory finger down her jaw-line. 'What

you must do is to change into your own clothes again and make a morning call on the Governor's lady, where you will gossip about the parties you expect to attend in the near future and all the other things you Englishwomen talk about when you are together. Then you will come home and will dress again as you are now. As soon as it's dark, Gupta will bring you to me.'

'And what will you be doing?' she asked.

'I shall leave Delhi with as much pomp and publicity as I can contrive. By lunchtime I shall be out of sight of even the most curious. We don't want your disappearance to be connected with my departure from the city. The longer distance we can put between the two events the better.'

Thus it was that Fanny found herself spending what was left of the morning making a belated call on Lady Allen. It was obvious from her first greeting that Lady Allen felt both threatened socially by her guest and highly put out that she should have left it to such a late hour to call. Fanny did what she could to mend matters, apologizing profusely for having got lost in the crowded, narrow streets around the Red Fort. Nothing she could say, however, could reconcile the older lady to having the shine taken out of her leadership of local society by having the daughter of an Earl, and a friend of Her Majesty's, foisted on her and assuming the position of arbiter of fashion, manners, and everything else in a manner that was quite obnoxious in such a young woman. Fanny was tempted to drop her a hint that she was soon to have a most satisfying revenge, but she nobly resisted making any but the most ordinary and unoriginal comments, going out of her way to congratulate Lady Allen on her choice of headdress, which she privately thought ill-chosen in such a warm climate.

By the time she returned home, Fanny was exhausted by her efforts to flatter someone she could only despise for her narrow views on India and the life she was forced to live there. Not even her efforts on behalf of Lady Cunningham had met with anything other than a complacent snub.

'I'm surprised you should have any patience with her pretensions to be one of us, Lady Frances,' Lady Allen had said with a thin smile.

'I admire her very much,' Fanny had retorted. 'She knows more about India than all the rest of us put together, which must be such a help to her husband. A fine pickle we should all be in if London wives were as ignorant of their husbands' interests as most ladies pride themselves on being out here. Even the birds have been given English names, often of those to which they bear not the slightest resemblance!'

Lady Allen's smile had grown more wintry still. 'It's easy to see you don't suffer from the homesickness that afflicts even the least sensitive of the rest of us.'

'No, why should I? At least the sun shines here!'

Lady Allen had actually shuddered. 'Making it impossible for any but the most robust to make the least exertion. I know I feel washed out for the greater part of the year. I long for the green fields of England and servants one can trust! Wait until your Mary succumbs to one or other of the terrible diseases that lie in wait for our children, and then tell me if you don't prefer a little English rain!'

'We wear the wrong clothes,' Fanny had decided. She had learned that earlier that morning! Now, she couldn't help noticing how restrictive and confining were the clothes she had worn willingly all her life. She was actually looking forward to being set free of them!

If Fanny had had one fear left, it was that she might be forced to see her husband once more. She couldn't be more thankful that he was away, about his own business, though she couldn't help feeling an instant of sympathy for whomsoever would be luckless enough to fall into his hands tonight. If she ever were to see him again, she thought she would kill him for what he had done to Mary and she would be doing the world a favour. The bitter part of what she was doing would be her coming parting with Mary. When she thought about it at all, she was afraid she would choke on the pieces of her broken heart. What was going to be Bantry's reaction to her departure? Would he blame Mary? It didn't bear thinking about, but it was impossible not to as the afternoon stretched before her. She might think she was helping Mary, but was she? Round and round she went, until tired and dispirited she lay down on her bed and fell asleep, worn out by her morning's activities and her fears for Mary. Half Delhi must have seen her that morning, all determined to have a word with her and to make sure they were seen doing so. If they'd been a little surprised at the ease with which they had accomplished this, none of them had the least suspicion that far from concentrating on the snippets of news they were relaying to her, she was busy pretending that she wasn't sick with fear as to what the future was going to bring both her and the child she was leaving behind.

Gupta stood over her bed, hissing between his teeth to awaken her. 'The maid is here, my lady,' he whispered to her.

Still half asleep, Fanny greeted the young maid, who looked no more than a child herself, but a cheerful child for all that, who made good use of the few English words she had at her disposal to keep Fanny amused. She was efficient, too. Almost before she was aware, Fanny found herself donning the Rajputana costume once again, a pair

147

of baggy trousers that fastened closely about the ankles, a skirt edged with embroidery and a pattern of tiny pieces of mirror that caught the light when she walked, a *choli*, a bodice that reached barely to her waist, and a veil that was held firmly in place by a magnificent, jewelled headpiece. The traditional ivory bracelets covered her arms, mixed with others of gold and silver. They were surprisingly heavy and got in her way when she moved, but she was beyond protesting about anything, meekly submitting to whatever the young maid cared to do to her.

What surprised her most was the difference the sandalwood decoration on her forehead made to her appearance. It was as if, at one stroke, she had left her previous identity behind her, along with her old clothes, and had been reborn as an exotic stranger. She squared her shoulders as she studied her reflection in the glass, telling herself that she had chosen all this of her own free will and, if she didn't like the look of herself, she had only herself to blame. Suddenly, she was impatient to be gone, and Gupta couldn't come too soon to tell her it was time for them to leave.

It was a strange way they took through the narrow streets of Delhi to the Kashmir Gate. Fanny had never been so close to the teeming inhabitants of the city before and she was quite overcome by the sights and sounds of the truly poor as they scratched a meagre living for themselves out of nothing at all. Gupta had hired a handcart for the occasion, covered by all-enveloping screens through which she could see out but nobody could see in. Her new maid sat beside her, enjoying a rare feeling of importance as she peered about her, exclaiming over the various buildings and the height of the red wall that practically enclosed the city.

Darkness was falling by the time they reached the Gate.

Fanny slipped from the cart to the waiting palanquin and drew the curtains tightly about her as she had been bidden. She barely had time to appreciate the quality of the bedding and the beauty of the carved framework before she was lifted up on to four men's shoulders, another man going before them with a lamp to pick out the way as soon as the last rays of the sun disappeared.

She was soon to discover that there were four more men on hand to take turns with the first bearers. For a while, she worried that she was too heavy for them, but they showed few signs of tiring and she quickly grew used to the swaying motion and even slept a little as the minutes grew into hours and they were safely away from the prying eyes of the sophisticates of Delhi.

She saw the lights of the Raja's encampment through the curtains and longed to draw them back a little to see where she had come to. She was too afraid of incurring her new lord's displeasure to do more than lift a corner, and dropped it hastily again when she realized that quite a crowd had gathered, silently watching her arrival. Indian crowds, it seemed to her, were always still and silent, not at all like those she had known in Europe.

The palanquin was taken right to the doorway of the main tent and women stood holding concealing curtains to allow her to pass unseen into the magnificent interior. The Raja was waiting for her, seated on a pile of cushions. He watched her critically as she took in her surroundings, noting the fine embroidery of the hangings and the luxury of the appointments of his travelling home.

'Well, Fanny?'

Belatedly, she remembered he would expect her to fold her hands together as he had taught her. She had thought she would resent making her obeisance to him, but when

149

it came to it, it seemed the most natural thing in the world to bow low before him and place her hand beneath his feet.

'You ran into no difficulties at the last moment?' he asked her, drawing her down beside him.

'No, none,' she assured him.

He sighed with relief. 'Gupta will see to everything and will give that knife of yours to Mary in case she should need it.' He pulled her closer to him, his hand finding her bare midriff. 'Lord Bantry will be free of you at last!'

'Thank God,' she murmured.

His hand brushed her side, cupping her buttock in an almost painful grasp. 'Go and eat, Fanny,' he commanded her. 'Afterwards, your maid will prepare you for the night.'

It was the first intimation Fanny had that they would never eat together, that her own plates and implements would always be kept apart in case he should lose caste by coming in contact with them. She thought of the many meals she had shared with her friends, enjoying the conversation as much as the food. She didn't like eating alone!

'Sajjan, will it always be like this?'

He nodded, dismissing her as if she held no more interest for him. 'You must always live behind the curtain now. It's for your own protection. Besides, I don't care to have other men gaping at what is mine.'

'But can we never eat together?'

He was astonished. 'Never. You must always eat alone because you're without caste. You'll grow used to it.' He was already tired of the topic, which seemed to be of little importance to him. 'Women must expect changes in their lives when they first enter the household of their lord, no matter who they are. It's better to bend than to break. I can't live by your customs, Fanny, so you must learn to live by mine! Go quickly now!'

That was easier said than done. She didn't know where

to go. She opened her mouth to ask him, but he cut her off with a light drawl. 'Obedience is the measure of a woman's honour!'

Stung, Fanny lifted her chin, her expression mutinous. 'Where am I to go?' she demanded.

He burst out laughing and, leaping to his feet, led her through to an inner room where her maid was already waiting for her. It might have been her imagination, or sheer wishful thinking on her part, but his fingers seemed reluctant to part with hers as he left her. It more than made up for everything that had gone before.

Although Fanny had eaten an anglicized version of Indian food, she had never before come face to face with the real thing. Even the bread was strange, being the unleavened *chupattis*, made from a flour as coarse as oatmeal. She found them good, especially as they were freshly made and piping hot. The main dish was made from chicken, but it was the side dishes that caught her attention. There were so many of them, each an event in itself. There was yoghourt, various salads made from beans or chopped vegetables, moistened with sesame oil. And there was a huge bowlful of rice, in which she found both raisins and nuts of some kind. Altogether it was a strange but very satisfying meal.

After the woman had cleared away the silver *thal* from which they had taught Fanny to serve herself with the help of a *chupatti* and her right hand, the left having a quite different function which precluded it from being used at table, her new maid came back to help her prepare for the night to come.

There followed one of the most embarrassing half-hours of Fanny's whole life. She was glad she could speak a few words of the girl's own language, if only to tell her to turn her back. Her upbringing had been as sheltered as that of most well-born girls of her time, perhaps a little more protected than most as she had been raised by the puritan Agnes, who would have died sooner than look at her own naked body and had done her best to teach Fanny to be equally modest. Now, she was expected to wash herself from head to foot in the scented water they had brought her in a brass basin, called a *chillumchee*. After that her skin was rubbed with perfumed oils and turmeric to make it soft and beautiful, her body hair totally removed, her anguished protests being met only by giggles that a European woman should be similarly endowed as they were. Lastly, her hair was loosened and brushed until it shone and flew in a great cloud about her shoulders.

It was then that she had most reason to be grateful to Eileen, who had somehow managed to smuggle her favourite nightgown into the small bag of possessions she had brought away with her. Never had Fanny been more glad to see any garment. She thrust her arms into the sleeves, delighting in its familiarity, and wrapped its modest length about her, refusing to have anything more to do with the women's well-meant attentions.

'Don't you want us to put henna on your hands and feet?' Ila, her maid, asked her, shaking her head disapprovingly at the sight Fanny presented.

'No!'

'*Aa-cha*, don't you want His Highness to find you pleasing?'

'Not particularly!'

Fanny regretted the words as soon as they were spoken. Her natural good manners made her reluctant to upset people who were doing their best to be kind to her. To her relief, Ila was only amused by a claim she discounted as ridiculous.

'It's only because everything is strange to you. A little henna won't hurt you. Look, let me do the palms of your hands at least. The patterns are traditional for a bride and will bring you good luck. Perhaps you'll be nursing a son before the year's out.'

Heaven forbid, Fanny thought. The recollection of Mary's difficult birth made her shudder. 'I'm not made for bearing children.'

Ila's soft eyes were sympathetic. 'It'll be easier for you next time. Your next child will want to come into the world, knowing his father to be a great man. The first birth is always the worst.'

Fanny had more pride than to seek further reassurance from the girl. It wasn't only the thought of bearing another child that scared her. It was the more immediate ordeal that seized her imagination, tying her in knots of panic lest the Raja should expect more of her than she was able to give him. By the time Ila left her, seated in the centre of a mountain of bedding that had been unrolled and placed in the middle of the curtained bedroom area, she was pale and shivering. She looked down at her hands, the sight of the intricate patterns of brown on her palms adding to her fright. What had she come to? How would she ever be able to achieve a modicum of happiness amongst these strange, beautiful people with their delicate movements, speaking in a strange tongue and eating strange meals? Could she bear it for the rest of her life?

A movement of the curtain caused the gold embroidery to catch fire in the lamplight, alerting her to the fact that she wouldn't be alone for long. The richness of her surroundings seemed suddenly overdone. She thought back to the threadbare rooms of her father's house in Dublin and the cold which had eaten into her very bones as a child. What wouldn't she give now to feel the soft Irish rain on her face and to know herself a girl once more? There would be no freedom for her ever again. Once she was 'behind the curtain', as His Highness put it, she would never again be able to come and go as she pleased. She had heard what it meant to live in purdah, in the *zenanas* of the Rajas and Maharajas. As a subject, it fascinated the ladies of the British Raj who couldn't leave it alone, endlessly congratulating themselves that they had been born to another way of life, a vastly superior one in every way. Fanny doubted that was so for, in her experience, the women of Europe depended on their husbands' whims for their happiness just as much as did any woman in the East. She had been afraid all the years she had spent as Bantry's wife.

'Sajjan?'

The Raja came through the curtain and paused at the edge of the bedding, looking down on her. He, too, had been washed and prepared for the night by his own servants. In the flickering light of the lamps his golden skin blurred before her eyes. There was no mistaking the solidity of the muscles that rippled at his every movement despite the fact that she couldn't see a single hair on his naked chest.

'Will I never teach you to treat me with respect?'

Fanny tried to stop her teeth chattering. She hid her hands under the embroidered coverlet and tried to still the waves of panic that assailed her.

'Sajjan, I'm afraid.'

It wasn't at all what he had expected. 'Afraid? Afraid of me?' He knelt beside her as she nodded her head. His expression set in a grim mould as he reached for her shaking body. 'What kind of man was this husband of yours? I never expected you to admit being afraid of anything.'

His touch soothed her, although she expected no more

than the same agony that Edwin had meted out to her. He was the only solid thing in a changing world and she clung to him as if her life depended on it, burying her face against his scented chest. No other man of her acquaintance could possibly wash as frequently as did this man, and yet not even the oils that had been used on him could mask his own special smell and she breathed it in, allowing it to calm her jangling nerves.

He took her hennaed palms, kissing first one and then the other. He was relieved she had stopped shaking, making no effort to caress her further until she had recovered her normal courage. His contempt for the man who had had this jewel at his disposal and who had so mistreated her filled his mind and his heart. This woman of the ivory skin should have been taught only the joys of the bedroom, as he meant to teach them to her. He was glad of the many women he had known since his first days of coming to puberty, glad of the pleasure they had given him and the pleasure he had given them, though none of them had ever affected him as this pale creature did, catching at his heart-strings and making him long to give her the happiness she had never known.

He stretched himself out beside her, resting his head on one arm, while he waited for her to accustom herself to his presence. He had always been possessed of endless patience when it had come to breaking in his horses, and women weren't so very different in the handling they needed. If he made no move towards her, she would soon grow curious about his unexpected lack of urgency. Even this one, once she had come to terms with her past experience, would soon prod him into a warmer courtship to satisfy the physical needs of which she seemed to be totally unaware. Oh yes, he could well afford to wait. He doubted she was going to keep him waiting very long.

Fanny lay in silence, very much aware of the half-naked man beside her and of the hurried beating of her own heart. If she turned her head a trifle, she could glimpse his long, relaxed length, contemplating at her leisure the pride and strength in his every line. He claimed to be descended from the sun and the gold of his skin lent some credibility to the claim. He behaved as if he knew himself to be the son of a god, too, with far more arrogance than she considered proper in any man, but he could be gentle sometimes and more considerate than she thought she deserved. Most of all, she liked to remember him as she had first seen him, not looking a bit ridiculous in his sugar-pink *pugri*, while his English counterparts had managed to look both ridiculous and uncomfortable in their dress uniforms, their swords clattering by their sides.

How odd, she thought, that she, who had known only contempt for her legal husband and who had denied him any recognition of his manhood, didn't really object to bending her knee to the Raja, either as a woman or as his latest subject. In fact, she thought, before they slept that night, she might well be tempted into telling him so. She leaned up on her elbow, annoyed to see he was showing every sign of going to sleep. With a quick movement, she put her hennaed palm beneath the arch of his foot, hoping he was as ticklish as she was.

'Is this the respect you say I owe you?' she taunted him, her eyes flashing with laughter.

He lay disappointingly still. 'It's a beginning,' he smiled.

'Sajjan, do you really expect me to – '

'I expect you to conform to custom. If anyone else were to hear you call me Sajjan, they would dismiss you as a presumptuous, scheming woman of the worst sort.'

'But you yourself told me your name is Sajjan.'

'I also told you to address me as Your Highness. I assure

you, when anyone else is present, you will have to learn to keep that tongue of yours under control – as much as any woman can!'

'Yes, Your Highness.'

He reached out an arm and caught her to him. 'Fanny, I am not like Edwin Bantry, in any way. If I ask you to obey me, it's for your own good. The Rajputs are a proud, religious-minded people, and you are a foreigner from across the Black Seas, and mean nothing to them. You must learn to behave as one of us, or you'll be blamed for every ill that ever comes to Kattyapur. If the gods are known to be displeased by your presence, there'll be unrest, riots even, and I shall have to send you away. Now do you understand?'

Chastened, she stared back at him. 'A little. I don't know anything about your gods, only the one called Kali who inspires all those thugs to go about murdering innocent travellers on the road.'

'Kali is only one face of the goddess Parvati. She has many others, just as life has many aspects.'

'Don't you believe in her?'

He shrugged. 'All gods lead to God. Who can understand, or conceive, what God means in this life? We worship him as creator, as destroyer, as the one who holds everything in being, and the glimpse of the sacred we sometimes perceive in ourselves. It's all one.'

Fanny was prepared to accept that. She had never understood much about Christianity either. Eileen and Agnes had each held the other's faith in abomination, and yet she had felt quite at home with both of them. It probably wouldn't be much different with Hindus, not if they were anything like Sajjan.

She put a tentative hand on his chest, delighting in the

157

smooth warmth of his skin. 'You're beautiful!' she said. 'Bantry's like a monkey, he has so much hair everywhere.'

'He hurt you?'

She didn't pretend to misunderstand him. 'I thought he'd killed me.'

'And you're afraid I'll do the same?'

Her lower lip was caught between her teeth. 'Will you?'

'I've never hurt a woman before.' He reached for the hem of her enveloping gown and pulled it up over her head. 'To the best of my knowledge, my women are always delighted to be summoned to my bed.' He almost laughed when he saw her incredulous expression, and he kissed her quickly to save himself from betraying his mirth to her. 'They get as much pleasure from it as I do,' he insisted.

She had never been naked with a man she loved before. A hot flush crept up her body as she tried to escape the warm appreciation in his black eyes. She had always been taught it was indecent to undress completely before one's husband, let alone any other man. Did she dare ask him to turn out the lamps? No, he would only laugh at her again. Besides, she found that she, too, wanted to watch the changes in his expression as he gazed on her, delighting in her youthful breasts, the firm line of her stomach and her long, well-shaped legs. She felt the first curling of desire in the pit of her stomach, even while she pushed his hand away before he could cup her breast.

Instead, he kissed her mouth, parting her lips with his thumb and thrusting his tongue between her teeth against hers. She gasped at the unexpected liberty, not sure she approved of the way he obviously thought he could do as he liked with her.

'You're beautiful, Fanny,' he whispered against her lips. 'You were made to be mine!'

Excitement ran up and down her spine. She put her

hands against his chest and tried to push him away, to give herself time to think. To her relief, he ignored the small rebellion, crushing her body beneath his in an easy conquest.

'Ah, Fanny, why do you try to deny me? You've already given yourself to me by consenting to come to me. Would you deny me the right to make use of what is my own?'

Fanny was startled into passivity, trying to ignore the weight of his leg across hers. She tested her feelings carefully, wondering what had happened to the fear she had expected to engulf her when he had first touched her. She felt only excitement and a burgeoning desire to have him touch her in all the places she had been taught never to think about.

This time she made no objection when he fondled her breast, rubbing his finger across the nipple until it stood forth, making it easy for him to catch it between his teeth in a gentle bite that deprived her of what little breath she had left. She dug her fingers into his shoulders, making a few discoveries of her own, which she immediately forgot as his fingers found the very centre of her being and she had no choice but to arch herself against him in open invitation of his ultimate entry into her.

'Not yet, my Fanny, not until you want me as much as I want you!'

Fanny couldn't believe she would ever want him more than she did now. She wanted to tell him so, but she had no words to do so. Her excitement seemed about to erupt inside her and she did what she could to hold it back, ashamed she had so little control over herself.

'Do you want me, Fanny?'

'Yes!'

She felt his laughter against her mouth. 'But not enough! Not until you admit I'm your lord, the lord of your heart, and you give yourself, body and soul, as the women of my race are proud to do!'

She thought her heart would burst within her. 'I can't!' she exclaimed. 'You have no right to ask it of me!'

He parted her thighs with his knee, his hand still working its mischief between her legs. 'I've taken the right, Fanny, as I'll shortly take you! Come on, admit it!'

Did all men see women as their possessions? Yet this one had been kind to her in his own way. Perhaps all he wanted was her commitment to him in return for the sanctuary he was giving her. She wound her arms tightly about his neck. 'I love you!' she almost shouted at him.

He was completely undone. He held her closely against him, nuzzling his face into her neck. 'Oh, Fanny, I never hoped for that! I was content you should submit because you had nowhere else to go.'

'I didn't have to run away with you,' she said with dignity. 'I came because I wanted to. If I hadn't, I should have found another way.'

'Because you love me?'

She could feel his need for her pressed against her and knew that that was what she wanted too. She wanted to be a part of him, to feel him move inside her.

'Because I want to be your woman, Your Highness,' she whispered in his ear.

She opened herself to him, guiding him inside her as though it were the most natural thing in the world. Later, she would be astonished to remember how free she had made with his body, as he had with hers. She would blush at the thought of what he must think of her, consoling herself with the fact that she was indeed a new person, no longer the Lady Frances Bantry but the wife of affection of the Raja of Kattyapur, and that the latter was by far the prouder title.

160

Sajjan held himself back until he was sure he was carrying her with him. He paced himself with the greatest care, a little amused that it should be so important to him to make this a night for Fanny to remember. In Kattyapur, there were always five or six women waiting for his call and he knew they found him a satisfying lover. He took their praises as no more than his due, choosing between them with little more interest in their feelings than when he chose his dress for the day. It had never occurred to him to subdue his own needs to theirs. They were there for his pleasure, and he was glad if they were pleased also, but it would have been all the same to him if they had found his attentions distasteful. His Senior Rani, a large, gaunt, witless woman, had never known his bed as she would never be more than a mindless child, but his Junior Rani was a woman of another calibre and they had spent many nights of pleasure together; they probably would again. Yet it had taken this pale scion of the British nobility to make him tremble with anxiety that he might not be able to give her the satisfaction he craved from her for himself.

It was, of course, ridiculous that any woman's pleasure should mean more to him than his own – but then he had never known another woman like Fanny! He felt her reaching her climax beneath him and took off into the higher reaches of passion himself, knowing a fierce satisfaction that she had never known the exultation of flying into the sun in the arms of a man, of having the whole world tilt under her and come right again, as she clung to him, steadying herself as she slowly drifted back into her own body.

Fanny took his hand to her lips and kissed it. If this was what it meant to be loved, she could no longer wonder at the Queen's dog-like devotion to her Prince Albert, or of

Charlotte Canning's for her errant husband. In a few moments Sajjan had wiped away all memory of Edwin's parody of the act and made her feel clean again.

'I love you,' she said again.

Sajjan smiled a self-satisfied smile, taking a male pride in his own performance. 'That was only the beginning,' he boasted. 'It's a long way to Kattyapur and we shall spend many nights together. Does that please you?'

'Very much!'

He ran a possessive hand over her hips and up to her breasts. 'Did you know you're the colour of ivory all over? Even your breasts are ivory, tipped with rubies.'

It wasn't at all the picture she had of herself. She much preferred the golden hues of his colouring, contrasting with the blackness of his hair. 'And you're the colour of the sun!'

His eyes danced in the flickering light of the lamps. 'What else have you noticed about me?'

'What should I have noticed?' she teased him.

'Don't you like the way I look?'

She laughed. 'Oh yes,' she assured him. 'When I first saw you I thought you moved like a god.'

'And tonight? Did I move inside you like a god?'

She could afford to be generous. 'There will never be anyone else but you for me. You might well be a god, a god who created me for himself. You made me feel like a goddess in your arms.'

He bent his head, fondling her nose between two fingers, and asked the question that was the most important to him of all.

'Have I made you forget what went before, Fanny? Are you truly mine?'

She saw the urgency in his face and wondered at it. Was

162

it possible she could matter to him more than she had thought? It made her feel humble that it should be so.

She kissed him hard on the mouth. 'It's you I love, Sajjan, and only you. I never loved before. I'm not afraid any more.'

He pulled her into the circle of his arm. 'Good. Women should never be afraid. They should be brave and beautiful and make fine sons for their lords.'

Fanny's mouth curved into a relaxed smile. She was about to ask him if he didn't want any daughters when she saw he was already asleep. She wondered how many other women had watched him sleep as she was doing now: the two Ranis, and who knew how many concubines? She remembered Lady Cunningham saying that Indian women didn't seem to have a jealous bone in their bodies, and she wished she could have said the same about herself. It was as if she had exchanged one knife for another; the first had protected her from Lord Bantry for many years, the second was pointed at her own heart. Now that she had discovered a love of her own, it was going to tear her in two to have to share him with any other woman. And yet what choice did she have? It was a long time before she slept, however, curling herself into the curve of his body. It was the first time in her life she could remember ever having been completely happy in the company of another person. She would do as he advised her and try to forget her previous life, concentrating on all he was offering her in the new life she was embarking on. Goodbye, Lady Frances, she whispered to herself, and wished that it hadn't meant saying goodbye to Mary as well.

BOOK TWO
Behind the Curtain

Chapter Nine

The *hakim* pierced Fanny's nose first thing in the morning. What was more, he did it so well that she hardly felt a thing. She had been nervous when he had first produced the needle he intended using, as it looked far too big and too blunt for its purpose. She couldn't remember having her ears done, she had been just a baby, and she felt a baby now as she grabbed Sajjan's hand to give herself courage, blinking at the needle as it came towards her. The doctor's face told her nothing of what he thought of this liberty but as the two men exchanged glances, and he realized the Raja was not going to rebuke her, he was already reassessing her in his mind, deciding she must be even more important to his master than he had thought.

Sajjan, knowing very well what was going on in the *hakim*'s head, paid no attention to Fanny's cries that she was bleeding like a pig all over her new clothes.

'Such a fuss! I'll hear no more about it! I thought Englishwomen were born of a people who intend to rule the rest of us lesser mortals – and you afraid of a mere prick!'

'I happen to be an Irishwoman,' she corrected him.

He frowned at her. He didn't like it when he couldn't understand what she was talking about. Women had no right to talk in riddles! 'What does that mean? You come from a ruling family in Britain, don't you?'

'Yes, I do. I'm British as you're an Indian. You wouldn't like to be called a Bengali, would you?'

His eyes lit with a strange fire. 'I am a Rajputana, a descendant of the gods!'

'And I'm Irish!' she insisted.

'You are of no significance!'

She turned a knowing smile on him, enjoying a newly discovered talent for flirting with him. 'None at all. I exist only to please you.'

He eyed her warily, knowing she was teasing him and unsure how to handle her. Fanny's smile grew broader. It didn't matter how much he played the ruler on his dignity, underneath he was the man she loved, a man of intelligence doing his best for his people. It wasn't surprising that he should be suspicious of ways he didn't know or understand.

He played safe. 'That was well said,' he congratulated her dryly. 'It's good you know your place in the scheme of things.'

Fanny chuckled. 'Your place being my lover?' she riposted, wondering how he would take such a piece of impertinence from her.

To her surprise, he grinned back at her. 'Only you and I know that. It's not something I want generally known, so see you guard our secret well!'

It was the beginning of the happiest days Fanny had ever known. Travelling by *ghari* by day and camping out under the stars by night, she wouldn't have minded if it had gone on for ever. The *gharis* were not the kind of conveyance she was accustomed to, but she thought none the worse of them for that. The luggage was piled on the top and they were very rough inside, without the slightest comfort. Nor were the horses more than half-broken, moving only when they pleased, which was sometimes not at all. *Syces*, as the grooms were called, pulled them and pushed them until they were exhausted, but still the evil-tempered creatures refused to move until they were good and ready to do so. Nor, once they were on their way, were things much better. The roads were unmade and deeply rutted in places, and there were no metal edges to the wheels, which hung on the vehicles precariously, wobbling violently in every direction.

Her own carriage was carefully curtained from prying eyes, which made it unbelievably hot. Nevertheless, Fanny wouldn't have missed a moment of their travels. She couldn't get over the countryside they passed through, as golden as the people and as beautiful as the peacocks that walked wild in the land. Dotted about were the villages, the backbone of the economy of all the Princely States, where most of the people lived, their colourful clothes almost hurting the eye against the drab of their houses and land. They favoured the pure colours that looked their best under such a hot sun: the scarlets, purples, yellows, oranges and the shocking pinks that came to be designated Indian in later times. Fanny relished them all, glad to have thrown off the sober plaids, greys, dark blues, and the endless black of mourning that were the rage in London. Life was much more comfortable without such things as stays and underskirts, and the colours reflected her glowing mood of contentment. Not for one moment did she regret her headlong chase through the countryside away from the old life and towards the new. She was happy through and through, and she couldn't remember ever having been truly happy before.

It was the nights she enjoyed best of all, however. The Raja's tent was sent on ahead of them and was usually already erected by the time they drove into the camp, dusty and exhausted. Fanny was always hurried inside through a corridor of grinning women holding up swathes of colourful material to veil her from the eyes of any man who happened to be looking in her direction. She would change her dress, often putting in the diamond Sajjan had given to her because she knew it pleased him to see her so decorated. Then, carefully veiled, he would allow her to meander through the encampment at his side, explaining to her how the cooking was done, how the camels were trained for their burdens, even how the cows had come to be venerated as the source of life, giving of their milk and much else, their dung being used both for building and as a fuel for the cooking fires.

This was the time when the women would gather around the nearest source of water, carrying it back to the camp in brass pots on their heads, their hips swaying gracefully as they moved. The men mounted their camels and held races until the sky changed from blue to orange, to purple, to the silver of moonlight, before they gathered round the fires, unpicking themselves from their groups of friends to retire for the night at a late hour, leaving only the guards to keep watch against the prowlers of the night.

One night, Fanny saw their camp had been set up below a walled city, as golden as the hills on which it had been set. In the other direction, unbelievably beautiful, were some cupolas etched against the sky. Sajjan told her they were cenotaphs, commemorating the dead of the royal family.

'May we ride out and see them?'

'Not tonight, my Fanny. I have a surprise for you tonight. We are below the city of my brother-in-law and he will give me news of the progress of my sacred horse. He will also entertain us with *nautch*-girls and others. Be very careful what you do tonight, for he's not to be trusted! Stay behind the curtain until I send word for you to sit with the other women.'

'Will I meet your brother-in-law?'

'Perhaps tomorrow.'

Fanny didn't ask who his brother-in-law was, and he didn't volunteer the information. Rather, she would have tackled him about the horse, but he looked so forbidding when she tried to bring the subject up, she thought it better left alone for the time being. It seemed to her the very worst thing he could have done, if he was sincere in saying he wanted to avoid calling himself to the notice of the British. She couldn't imagine them welcoming an expanding State anywhere near those in which they already had a major interest. She pondered the matter all the time she ate her meal, alone as always, never coming to any conclusion. The best that could happen to the animal was for some awful accident to befall it, she thought gloomily, knowing Sajjan would never hear of it. The white stallion was a sacred being, dedicated to the gods, and he was willing to antagonize them even less than he was the British.

She hoped Kattyapur was as far away as he thought, too obscure to attract the tentacles of British interest in Rajputana, whose larger States had been amongst the first to make treaties with the East India Company. The first, because they had also been the richest. Such names as Jaipur, Marwar, centred on Jodhpur, and Mewar on Udaipur, were as familiar to the English as were the names of Delhi and Calcutta. For how long would the British be content with their booty from such States, that was the question? Their new-found missionary zeal, that they had been chosen by God to civilize a barbaric and heathen world, had been dealt a decided setback by the Mutiny of the *sepoys*, but Fanny put no trust in that lasting for long. The English frequently congratulated themselves on having won first place in the lottery of life, but such good fortune carried with it the responsibility of turning the losers into as near an approximation of Englishmen as they were able

171

to manage. The White Man's Burden, she thought, might well turn out to be the curse of the rest of the world.

Sajjan's brother-in-law, Hanut, brought two of his own ladies with him. They were both pretty girls and the very best of friends. Fanny found their enthusiasms a little overwhelming, but there was no doubting their delight in meeting her, finding her story romantic as well as being a source of great amusement. They peered through the *chik* curtains that had been erected for their benefit, congratulating Fanny at intervals on the physique and general appearance of her Raja, sighing audibly as they confessed the contempt in which they held their own lord. Hanut was a bad man, they said dismissively; so much the better for her that good fortune had smiled on her and brought her to the attention of such a fine man! It was indeed strange that someone as pale and uninteresting as herself had managed to make any impression on him at all!

'Don't you miss your own people?' they asked her.

'Sometimes,' she admitted. She never spoke of Mary, but it was surprising how often her daughter came into her mind, especially at night.

The elder of the two girls shrugged. 'It's the same with us. It's the same for all women. We must always leave our own homes and go and live somewhere else when we marry. When I came here as a bride, I didn't speak a word of the local language. I was very lonely.'

'I spoke only Hindi, and not the local dialect,' the younger confirmed. 'My mother-in-law was horrible to me, always talking about me behind my back, knowing I couldn't understand anything she said. You are fortunate to speak so well!'

Fanny accepted the compliment with only half an ear. It hadn't occurred to her that as well as the two Ranis, she might have Sajjan's mother to contend with also.

'There's no one of that generation in Kattyapur,' the younger wife consoled her. 'She became *sati* when her husband died. She was a great lady. You British have forbidden our women such honour, but you can't be everywhere. When my turn comes, no one will be able to stop me. What else is a widow to do? I have no wish to become a mere thing in the *zenana* where once I held sway!'

Fanny was glad when the subject was changed. Their casual attitude to what had to be an excruciatingly painful death distressed her. No wonder Sajjan had accused her of being a coward when she had cavilled at having her nose pierced! No wonder, too, when she had asked him if it hadn't been a shock to find himself responsible for so many people on his father's death, he had looked sad and said it was his mother's advice he had missed. She hadn't known then what he was talking about.

Ila brought sherbert and a plateful of sweet, sticky cakes Fanny judged would be popular with her guests. She herself ate nothing, explaining she didn't want to offend them as she knew herself to be without caste. The ladies had a brief, urgent consultation amongst themselves, deciding to eat their sweetmeats well away from Fanny's contaminating presence. Oddly, she didn't feel insulted, as she would once have been. She was learning to accept that she had much to learn from these women she would once have thought naïve and silly. She could even admire them for the contentment they were able to find in their restricted lives, as well as for the loving support they gave to one another.

'Oh, look, the entertainment is going to begin!' one of them pointed out in great excitement.

'Where are we?' Fanny whispered to a wide-eyed Ila, as excited as were all the other women.

'This is Hanupur, the home of First Her Highness,' the girl answered her.

There were a number of dances performed by the professional dancing women, one of them balancing no fewer than seven dishes on the top of her head as she gyrated and bent her back almost to the floor. There was a dance with fire, clever and dangerous, and much applauded by the men outside. Fanny liked the peacock dance best of all, however, amazed how like peacocks the women could make themselves look, with tails of peacock feathers belted around their waists. They strutted, pecked, and strutted again, finally displaying their magnificent tails just as Fanny had seen the birds do in the wild. Birds or men, she thought, they all behaved in the same way, thinking themselves to be such fine fellows, showing off their fine feathers to advantage, ridiculous in their displays as they were in their power games. Even Sajjan liked his fine clothes and the power his position gave him.

Strange how familiar Hanupur sounded to her. Had Bantry ever mentioned such a place? She thought not, though if all that his women had to say about him was true, Sajjan's brother-in-law would be exactly the kind of man he would most admire and wish to associate with. Fanny had never known anything of his friends, however, and so she thought she must have heard the name elsewhere.

She turned her attention back to the dancers. In Delhi, on the rare occasions she had heard any Indian music, she had found it harsh and difficult to understand. Now, as the dances progressed, she began to find the quarter-tones and repetitive rhythms soothing. It matched the delicate movements and the uncanny sense of balance that was a part of the dance. Slowly, the colours and rhythms merged together, making her an intrinsic part of all she was witnessing, a participant rather than an onlooker. There were times when she could feel the echoing beat of the whole universe and knew herself a part of it. When it came to an end, it was like waking from a dream, the elusive memory remaining almost within one's grasp but vanishing as soon as the conscious eye is turned upon it.

The *nautch*-girls took their final bows, flirting with a vulgarity that made Fanny uncomfortable, as they caught the coins the men lavishly threw their way. She averted her face, not wanting to watch any longer, when she was brought up short to see Sajjan laughing and joking with one of the girls, uncaring that she might be looking on. She sat frozen to her seat. She would never be able to get used to his having other women and yet it came as naturally to him as breathing that he should take anything that was offered to him. 'What else are women for?' he had countered when she had berated him for looking at other women, trying to explain to him the humiliation she felt in being compared to any female who crossed his path, but he had only been amused by her strictures, refusing to take her seriously for a single minute.

It was the first night she had spent alone in the inner sanctum of his tent. She tried telling herself he was busy discussing matters of state with his brother-in-law, but she didn't believe it for a moment. Possessed of a fine Irish paddy when it was roused, her imagination ran riot, inventing more and more terms of abuse which she would hurl at his head as soon as she saw him next time. She had seen with her own eyes the open invitation of the *nautch*-girl and his far from reluctant response. The result was that she was tired and almost at breaking point by morning.

'Have our visitors gone?' she asked Ila when she came to awaken her.

'For now,' the girl answered. She yawned, smiling. 'It

was late before the men left,' she added by way of explanation.

'What about the women?'

'The ladies went home earlier, when you retired, poor things!' Ila was well aware of the unhappy fate of those who were unfortunate enough to have to live in the *zenana* of this city. 'Who knows about the others?'

'Did any of them stay the night?'

Ila shrugged. 'How would I know?'

Fanny fastened her with a baleful eye. 'I imagine you might. Where did you spend the night?'

'Asleep on the other side of the curtain.'

Fanny didn't believe her. She was accustoming herself with difficulty to the easy way Indians have of lying down and going fast asleep wherever they happen to be, regardless of comfort or privacy, but she didn't believe that anyone would dare to sleep in the Raja's tent except at his express command.

Ila only smiled at her. 'You must dress quickly, lady. His Highness wishes you to attend him in an hour's time. We're not going to break camp today.'

Fanny's temper flared. 'We're staying here another night? Why?'

Ila was bewildered by the question. 'Lady, you must dress! His Highness doesn't consult either of us before he decides to go or stay.'

'I see,' said Fanny dangerously. '*He* decides, while we meekly pack and follow!'

Poor Ila stared at her, certain she had misunderstood. 'How else would it be? In your land do the women tell the men what to do?'

If they did, they pretended they didn't. Fanny thought of the occasions when she had watched the Prince Consort being praised and flattered while his wife had looked on approvingly, apparently not minding in the least that she, the monarch, should be ignored in her own Court. No, things weren't any different in her own country!

'I wish I'd been born a man!' she declared wildly.

Ila giggled, holding out the new dress Fanny was to wear. 'His Highness wouldn't have any time for you as a man.' She twitched the dress into place, setting about the task of rearranging the headdress to her own satisfaction with busy fingers. 'Stand still, lady. If you're to accompany His Highness, you must look your best, no?'

Fanny tried to conceal her evil temper while the many ivory bangles were placed on her arms, a fine necklace was placed round her neck, and the single diamond was placed in her nose, where it caught the light, flashing as she moved, a constant reminder of the one battle she had been content to lose to Sajjan.

'Where did the necklace come from?' she asked Ila. She was sure she had never seen it before.

'His Highness.' Ila chuckled with barely suppressed excitement. 'There is more! Rings for your toes, and gold anklets – '

'I won't wear them!' Did he think he could buy her goodwill for his amorous adventures?

Ila silently held out a glass to her and, for a moment, Fanny didn't recognize herself. The full ankle-length skirt swished about her bare legs when she moved. The short bodice, tied across the back with thin cords and worn with an over-jacket, was colourful and exotic. Ila redraped the veil over her head, tucking one end firmly into her waist, leaving the other end free for Fanny to cover her face when she went out, or even if she was in the presence of other ladies senior to herself, who would be offended if she were to show them her naked face. But it was the jewellery that took her breath away. Its beauty and value would have set the gossips talking in the drawing-rooms of London for at least a week! She had been presented with a fortune, the kind of fortune with which she could have bought and sold Edwin Bantry any day she chose! Her first thought was that Sajjan was making her a highly paid whore; her second that his conscience must indeed be troubled to be so generous for so little return from her!

She was still staring at this exotic creature in the looking-glass when his summons came. His glance swept over her as she stepped forth from behind the curtain, a frown between his eyes. He walked over to her and pulled the veil over her face with impatient fingers.

'My brother-in-law, an evil man, wishes to question you himself about the British. I'm not happy that he should see you in case he talks to the wrong people. Answer only when he speaks directly to you and try to remember your manners! You're not in Delhi or London now!'

Fanny's navy eyes flashed; she disliked the tone he was taking with her.

'Where were you last night?' she hissed at him.

His astonishment that she should ask such a question was obviously genuine. 'What business is that of yours?' he shot back at her.

'I saw you with that *nautch*-girl – '

He stiffened. 'So? There have been many *nautch*-girls, and there will be many more. You have yet to tell me what business it is of yours?'

With her face covered, she found it hard to breathe. She felt smothered. Tears shimmered in her eyes. 'I waited for you,' she said.

He tilted her face up to his, letting the veil fall away. 'There'll be many nights of waiting when you can't come to me, Fanny. I have many other responsibilities besides you – other women too!'

Her lower lip caught between her teeth. 'You don't love me?'

He kissed her mouth. 'You can never be the only woman in my life, Fanny. You will have to learn to live with the way things are. If you can't, you will have your tantrums in private, where I don't have to witness your foolishness, because I don't like to see you unhappy.'

'You don't understand – ' she began.

'No, it's you who doesn't understand! You don't have the ordering of my life! Look the other way and be content with what you have! Are you pleased with the jewels I sent you?'

'I won't be bought! I'm not for sale!'

His eyes blazed. 'Enough! It's unbecoming in you to question what I do and what I am. I'll hear no more of it! I'll summon whom I please to my bed and I'm not interested in your feelings on the matter. You will never mention such things to me again! Is it understood?'

She nodded miserably, reviewing her tactics as she sought other means of getting her own way. She allowed him to cover her face again, not unpleased when he caught one of her tears on his forefinger. His mouth tightened, but he said nothing, turning away from her. Belatedly, she realized he was not going to comfort her and tell her it would never happen again because he knew it would. He wouldn't even accept it was a clash of cultures, with her as the injured party, for he knew as well as she did how frequently the most respectable of Englishmen strayed from the marital bed. She wanted to stamp her foot at him and shout it wasn't fair, but who had ever said that life was fair? Certainly not he!

'Don't forget to make your obeisance to my brother-in-law,' he reminded her brusquely. 'I've been shamed enough by you today already.'

'Sajjan – ' She met his warning glare bravely. 'I'm sorry.'

He turned on his heel and walked out of the tent without a backward glance, gesturing with a finger for her to follow. She hurried after him, anklets jangling at every painful step, for she was unaccustomed to going barefoot, and the ground was rough and the stones sharp. He made no effort to help her as he covered the distance with his usual, lithe steps, shouting a greeting to his brother-in-law, who was already seated in the shade of a tree, a short distance from the encampment.

He was careful to give no sign of the reluctance he felt in allowing Hanut to see Fanny for himself. He had felt obliged to take the man into his confidence in view of their long-standing alliance, but he had heard far too many rumours about Hanut's activities in Delhi to trust him not to betray both of them if he could thereby add to his own coffers. Most of the annoyance he had felt with Fanny was that he had wanted to warn her to say nothing that could harm her if it got back to Lord Bantry. Like all women, however, she wouldn't have listened to him while she was boiling over with her own imagined slights at his hands. He could only hope her grievances would be forgotten when Hanut deigned to notice her. She was no fool, Fanny, but had no more control over her emotions than any other woman.

It was almost too much for that lady's composure when Sajjan also flung himself down in the shade, leaving her standing awkwardly in the full sun. Was this his way of punishing her? No, that she couldn't and wouldn't believe. It was probably the way he and all his kind had been brought up to treat their womenfolk. She sighed, realizing she would have to learn to stomach more than that from him in her new life.

The heat of the day beat down on her mercilessly and

she thought she was about to faint, when he finally called her over with a careless gesture, a single, pointed look reminding her that he expected her to be on her best behaviour.

Fanny palmed her hands together as he had taught her, murmuring 'Namaste', reminding herself that it meant that the godlike in her perceived and worshipped the godlike in the other. As she touched the ground at Hanut's feet, she thought there was little that was godlike in that individual. He made the hairs rise on the back of her neck.

Sajjan relaxed visibly and she knew she had acquitted herself well. 'You may sit,' he told her in English.

Fanny found it difficult to sit on the ground as the Indians did, her feet drawn up under her skirts, and she knew she was more clumsy in her movements than the most awkward of them would have been. For an instant, her eyes met Sajjan's and she read the quick sympathetic concern in his before he blanked it out again. Her spirits rose dramatically. Perhaps he did care about her after all.

'She really is an Englishwoman!' the brother-in-law exclaimed. 'I thought all Englishwomen had yellow hair?'

'She's an Irishwoman,' Sajjan told him.

The brother-in-law had never heard of Ireland. 'I can't imagine she'd be much use to you in bed,' he commented disparagingly. 'Englishmen are always seeking elsewhere for their pleasure, anywhere but amongst their own women!'

Fanny pretended not to have heard him. Perhaps he thought she couldn't understand his own dialect. What a fool Sajjan must be to trust this man with any knowledge of his doings. He would betray his own family as easily as he would a stranger.

'Who is she?' he asked Sajjan. The woman intrigued him.

Not only did she smell sweet, but she didn't behave like any of the sweaty, red-faced Europeans he had ever met.

Sajjan shrugged. 'A woman – what more does one need to know about her? It pleased me to bring her with me for the journey, no more than that. The British have their own ways of thinking which she understands and which may be useful to me. We have need of someone to tell us what the British will do next, where they will strike and how we can best stay out of their way.'

'The British are few; we are many.'

Sajjan shook his head. 'They're no longer here just to make money.'

'What's that to me? My father signed a treaty with them years ago. We're their ally – on paper. What matters to me is that I can make use of them as they'll try to make use of me! I do business with them, nothing more.'

'Oudh, also, had a treaty with the British.'

The brother-in-law turned to Fanny. 'Is it true? Will they tear up their treaties with their established allies?'

Fanny lowered her eyes to the ground. 'The British won't be content until they rule all India, one way or another. If they don't interfere directly with the Princely States, it's because they find it easier to rule through the Rajas and Maharajas than to do without them.' She sought for the right words to explain the British sense of their destiny more clearly. 'They think it their *karma* to unite the whole sub-continent under one legal system, regardless of religious and caste differences.'

The brother-in-law gave a despising whistle. 'If it's their *karma* – As long as we can make money from them. If not, if they come here, we shall never capitulate to them!' He leaped to his feet, enjoying himself. 'We'll have a *jauhar* that'll put even the *jauhar* of Udaipur in the shade! Or, maybe only half a *jauhar*! That'd serve all those useless wives of mine right!'

'*Jauhar*?' Fanny questioned urgently, not knowing the word.

'It'll be a brave sight!' the young man enthused. 'In the evening, the women will go singing to their deaths, throwing themselves on a great funeral pyre. At Udaipur, there were thirteen thousand of them. Then, in the morning, all the men will ride out to their deaths in battle. When the conquerors take over the city there will be nothing left to them. Everyone, dressed in their wedding robes, will have gone "laughing to heaven". What do you think, brother?'

Sajjan prodded the ground with gloomy concentration. '*Jauhar* is the counsel of last resort. I prefer to come to some compromise with the British, if this woman can help me find a way.'

'You'll take a woman's advice on how you should rule your people?'

'On how to treat with the British,' Sajjan corrected him gravely. 'You and your father would do well to give up your dreaming and face up to reality also.'

'As long as I can make money from the British, why should I care what they do?'

It was Fanny who spoke. 'Do you want to end your days in exile?'

Hanut cast a startled glance in her direction. 'Does she speak to you like this?' he demanded of Sajjan.

'The British have other ways. It's taking her time to learn she's less than the dust beneath my feet. The English allow their women all kinds of liberties. When I first saw this woman at the durbar in Delhi, even the British Governor listened to her with respect.'

Hanut sat down again. 'You're welcome to her, my brother! I use my women in different ways!'

Sajjan could not disguise his distaste for his relative by marriage. He hoped Fanny couldn't guess at the perversions that were covered by that remark. 'Women talk too, brother!' he snapped.

'And advise their betters, it would seem,' Hanut smirked. 'What advice did this phenomenon give you?'

Sajjan nodded at Fanny. She saw his tense expression and had a very good idea of what he was thinking. So, he didn't like this brother-in-law of his, yet he felt obliged to warn him of the disaster he was courting if he didn't prepare for a British move against him. For someone who had given more political soirées than she could count, she could have told him then and there that Hanut wouldn't listen to anything she had to say. He and Bantry had a great deal in common besides their love for torturing women!

'If I were you,' she began, her voice low and courteous, 'I'd send to the British Governor, reminding him of the long-standing treaty you had with the East India Company and asking for his protection. Persuade him, as Jaipur has done, that he needs friends and allies in Rajputana. He may send a political adviser – '

'And British troops? To be maintained at my expense?'

'Possibly. Isn't it better to prove yourself a friend of change than just another ousted enemy, a pensioner who has to rely on their goodwill for every crust you eat?'

There was a long, appalled silence, neither man relishing the stark picture she had placed before them.

'The woman would have you play the coward, Sajjan,' Hanut said at last. 'Is that what you're going to do?'

'If I must. I am further away from the British than you are, and too small to be of much interest to them as yet. I have a little time on my side.'

'And a woman to advise you!' Hanut laughed at the

184

mere thought. 'If she's as valuable as you say, won't they come looking for her in your *zenana*?'

'All they will find is my latest wife of affection. The woman she was is dead and buried, killed by dacoits many weeks ago.'

Hanut's eyes narrowed thoughtfully. 'I prefer to rely on my own knowledge of the British. There are some who will do anything for money! Dangle a few gold coins before their eyes and they are mine! If things are made too hot for me, I can find sufficient of their men in high places to bring pressure on their government to leave me alone. There is always someone one can bribe!'

Fanny watched the two men talking together, her presence forgotten. She wondered who it was that Hanut knew amongst the British who would betray their cause for Hanut's, or more likely for a share in his money. She thought there might be quite a few. The pain of the night had disappeared for the moment as she turned her attention to Sajjan, glad that he, at least, seemed to be a man of integrity. To have even a small corner of his heart, she told herself, was worth all the changes he had wrought in her life. She gritted her teeth together, hoping she would have the strength to school herself to accept her new life on his terms. She was sufficiently realistic to know that he couldn't change things for her, even if he wanted to, but neither did she deceive herself that she was going to find it easy to become the kind of person he expected her to be.

She straightened her aching back and saw he was smiling at her, his eyes black with desire for her. She pulled her veil closer about her, glad he couldn't see her instant response. As soon as they were alone, she would thank him for all the jewels he had showered on her – and for so much more! Tonight, she vowed, was going to be quite different from the one which had gone before. Tonight, there would be no *nautch*-girls to tempt him away from her side.

Chapter Ten

Mary shrank back into the shadows, hoping her father would soon go away. Loud, angry voices resounded through the house, making her shudder. It didn't matter how brave she tried to be, she could not accustom herself to Lord Bantry's jeering speech and the screams of the women he brought home with him. Her whole life in the week since her mother had left had been acted out on the edge of a nightmare of pain and despair. Eileen was the only person she could bear to have near her, but she suspected Eileen was as frightened as she was herself.

She hadn't told Eileen that Gupta had come to her room the day her mother had disappeared. He had held her broken arm between his two hands with a gentleness that had touched her deeply.

'Don't be afraid, Miss Mary. I was asked to give you this with my own hand. Don't let anyone else ever know you have it, will you?'

Intrigued, Mary had promised that she wouldn't. She couldn't move her left arm at all, and she had some difficulty in taking the knife from his hand. 'How does it work?' she had asked him.

He had demonstrated how to press the button to release the blade. Mary had tried it for herself, a little nervous of the wickedly sharp edge.

'You be careful you don't cut yourself, Miss Mary!'

Mary had promised that she would be. She did not need to be told against whom she might need to use such a weapon.

'When I'm grown up, I'm going to find my mother,' she had informed Gupta with certainty. 'You don't believe her to be dead, do you?'

'I think her to be living somewhere,' he had agreed, 'but it is better for others to believe her dead. You will both be safer if no one looks for her for many, many years.'

Mary had nodded, her eyes wide. 'Papa would hurt her if he knew, like he hurt me. We both hate him!'

'Many people have cause to hate him,' Gupta had told her. 'Rich men have much power, however. Go softly, Miss Mary, you have many years to live yet!'

Eileen cast a worried look at her young charge as Lord Bantry's angry voice grew nearer. The child looked as if she were about to faint, so pale did she go every time she heard her father's voice. It wasn't right! If she had had her way, they would have been safely on board ship by now, but Lord Bantry wouldn't hear of his daughter leaving India for a healthier climate.

'I'm not a man who ever forgives or forgets,' his lordship had told her. 'The child stays here until I'm quite sure her mother is as dead as everyone seems to think she is. It's my belief she'll come back from the grave for that whelp of hers as soon as the hunt's off. No, until I'm sure my wife is indeed no more than a spectre, unable to be punished for her sins by mere mortals like myself, Mary will stay in my care!'

The door was flung open and Lord Bantry entered the room. He glared at his seated daughter. 'Have you no manners, chit? Stand up and curtsey to your father!'

Mary pressed her trembling lips tightly together. They both knew how difficult it was for her to stand, until her leg healed, and until she was able to move more easily. She made the effort, trying not to wince with the pain that shot up her sciatic nerve.

'Good afternoon, Papa,' she said. There was no sign of the fear she was feeling, though she could taste it on her tongue. Her mother had said it was the worst thing she could do, to show she was afraid of him, and so she wouldn't, but the effort cost her dearly.

Lord Bantry gestured to Eileen. 'Leave us, whatever your name is!'

For a long, silent moment, Eileen held her ground. She was afraid herself, however, not knowing what the man might choose to do to her if she thwarted him.

'Go!' he roared at her.

She went.

Mary took a deep breath to steady herself. 'Did you want to talk to me, Papa?'

He frowned down at her. 'I very much doubt that I am your Papa!'

It was the best news that Mary had heard for a long, long time. 'Everybody says you are,' she muttered doubtfully.

'Your mother said I am,' he corrected her.

Her face fell. 'Then you must be. Mama doesn't tell lies.'

He fastened on her use of the present tense. 'Doesn't? Hasn't anyone told you that your mother is dead?' His voice took on a sarcastic tone. 'That she was conveniently killed by dacoits with her servants, completely unharmed, looking on, servants who can't even agree about the details of the attack? You don't believe it either? Well, so much for her love for you, young lady! The truth is that's she's run off and left us – '

Mary nodded slowly. 'She hates you! She's trying not to, and she says I must too. Why do you hate us, Papa?'

'I don't think about you often enough to hate you,' he answered. 'Your mother is another matter. I bought her,

189

body and soul, yet she'd never allow me near her! I'll find her and bring her to heel if it's the last thing I do!'

'You'll never find her,' Mary said with certainty.

Her father stared at her. 'Oh? And just what do you know about it?'

Mary swallowed the lump of fear in her throat. 'If someone's dead, they're with God. How can you get her back from Heaven?'

'I doubt your mother's in Heaven, wherever else she may be!'

Mary blinked. Surely, if one was dead, one always went to Heaven? 'You mean she's in Purgatory?' she suggested. Eileen believed in Purgatory, she knew, though Agnes said it was because she didn't know any better. Mary didn't know exactly what it meant, but it sounded better to her than Limbo, which had to be a dreadful place, full of the shades of ancient Greeks and Romans and dead babies, unfortunate enough not to have been baptized.

'Superstitious nonsense!' her father derided her. 'Is that the kind of thing that Irish girl stuffs your head with?'

Mary shook her head. 'Eileen says I'm invincibly ignorant so I'll be sure to go to Heaven. God takes these things into consideration.'

'And you believe such nonsense?'

'I don't not believe it,' Mary said.

'She'll have to go!'

Mary sucked in her lower lip, perceiving she had made a mistake. 'If you don't believe it, I won't either,' she offered.

'I long ago gave up believing anything,' her father informed her. 'Religion is for women and weak fools, not for real men!'

Mary privately agreed with Eileen that her father had long ago sold his soul to the devil, so she wasn't at all surprised to know that he didn't believe in God. It was hard to see how one could believe in both.

'Everybody believes in something,' she said aloud, 'at least everyone I know does.'

'Except me.'

Mary was about to contradict him when she saw the glint in his eyes and realized it would give him the opportunity he sought to lose his temper with her again. She took a painful step away from him, wishing she could run away and hide herself somewhere, anywhere, just to escape from him.

Lord Bantry glared at his stiff-backed daughter, his eyes glazing over as he took in her resemblance to her mother. The same black hair, Irish navy eyes, and the complexion of those who lived in rain-drenched climes. God, how he hated her! How had she managed to escape him just as he'd neared the completion of his perfect plan to bring about her humiliation? The Lady Frances had a great deal to answer for, but if he couldn't have her, her daughter would do in the meanwhile.

'I don't believe in your mother's death, Mary, and nor do you! Why don't you tell me where she is?'

'Gupta said she was dead!'

'Gossiping with the servants now, are you?'

'I wanted to know,' Mary excused herself.

That was another thing for which Lord Bantry had despised his wife, the way she had treated the servants as though they were people like herself. If they looked tired, she would try to give them an early night; if in trouble, he had known her try to relieve their circumstances from her own purse. He was sure Mary would grow up to be as soft and as stupid as her mother! She was sufficiently like her in every other way!

'I believe you know where your mother is!' he said, very loudly indeed.

Mary's broken arm prevented her from covering her ears. She couldn't bear to be shouted at!

She began to cry. 'She's dead! You won't ever find her! She's dead! *She's dead!* I'm glad she is! She'll never have to see you again!'

'Do you want me to whip you again?'

His daughter shuddered.

'Then don't tell lies! Tell me where your mother is and I'll pay your passage home to your uncle in England. Eileen will go with you. You'll like that, won't you?'

Mary longed for it with all her heart. Her mouth began to work as she saw the one thing she really wanted disappearing from her grasp. Would it really matter if she were to give this devil a hint as to where her mother had gone? She thought the tall, beautiful stranger she had gone with would probably fight a whole war before he would give her up, whereas she was alone and had no defences where her father was concerned. She knew better than to expect Eileen to try to interfere if he did beat her again.

'I don't know where she is,' she whispered.

Her father lifted his arm and she was convinced he was truly about to hit her. It was then that she remembered her mother's knife. She limped to where she had hidden it, feeling it hard and unyielding in the palm of her uninjured hand. The blade flashed as she turned and faced the man she feared so much.

'Where did you get that?'

She scarcely recognized him. There was a ghastly smile on his reddened features as he reached out to grasp her wrist.

'It's mine!'

'It's your mother's!'

Mary drew back her arm, determined to cut his out-stretched hand if she could. So hard was she concentrating on this that she didn't notice him lift his other hand to bring it down with force on her outstretched arm. The knife went skimming across the floor.

'When did she give it to you, Mary? *Where is she?* I'll kill you this time if you don't tell me!'

Mary believed him. She shut her eyes tight, convinced he was going to choke the life out of her there and then.

'I'd tell you if I knew,' she said on a note of desperation. 'I'd tell you *and gladly*! She left me behind, too, didn't she? She could have taken me with her, but she didn't! She's never had any time for me!'

Lord Bantry recognized the truth of that. His own mother had complained to him that Fanny had no time for her daughter; she had used the information joyfully, sure she had a new weapon against him, but at the time, he hadn't cared a toss how Fanny felt about anyone other than himself.

'Somebody must know,' he said aloud.

Mary hunched up her shoulders. She was hurting all over, particularly where her father was holding her wrist so tightly, she was sure he meant to break that arm as well.

'Well, I don't know! I want Eileen! And I want you to go away!'

Lord Bantry released her reluctantly. He would be content if he could ever see the mother's features contorted with fear as were the daughter's now. There wasn't the same pleasure in making Mary cry, however. The child cried too much as it was; she was forever snivelling about something or other. Fanny would have stood up to him, he thought, but Mary was undoubtedly telling him the truth. He gave her a last, contemptuous look. What kind of a brat had he spawned on Fanny that day? If she had

had to produce a girl, she might at least have imparted to her some of her own courage!

Mary cried in earnest after he had gone. She went down on her hands and knees and dragged herself across the floor to where the knife had fallen. The pain was excruciating and for a long while she held the blade close against her chest, trying to will herself to pull herself to her feet. There was no strength left in her legs, not even the good one, and she cried the harder as her muscles refused to answer the commands she gave them. What would happen to her if she couldn't stand up, if she never stood again? She had a dismal picture of herself bedridden and alone, sharing this terrible house with a father who despised her, and shouted at her, and who would probably send Eileen away because she believed in God and sometimes cuddled Mary against her ample bosom, as she claimed she had always done to her younger brothers and sisters at home in Ireland.

It was Gupta who helped her up and carried her to her bed. He closed the knife, hiding it under her pillow, and he smiled at her.

'You are truly your mother's daughter!' he congratulated her.

Mary turned her face away. 'He knows she isn't dead,' she said bluntly. 'He knows we're all lying to him!'

Gupta's smile vanished. 'What did you tell him?'

'I told him I didn't know where she is.'

'Truly, you don't know. You told him no more than the truth.'

'No, I don't know,' Mary sighed. 'I'm glad I don't know.'

'It was because she loves you that she left you behind, Miss Mary. If she were ever to come back to life, she would always be dead to her own people. She wanted you to live!'

194

Mary pleated the sheet thoughtfully between her fingers. 'Papa knows she's alive,' she said again. 'He recognized her knife. Will he go and fetch her home?'

'Not while he doesn't know where she is. You must never tell him, no matter what he does to you!'

Mary's smile was bleak in the extreme. 'Next time, he'll probably kill me. I hate him!'

Gupta looked at her with concern. 'I will think about it, Miss Mary. It would be better for all of us if you were to live somewhere else away from your father.'

The little girl immediately looked more hopeful. 'Mama said I was to go to Lady Cunningham. Will you take me to see her?'

The Indian probably would have done so there and then if he had not heard Lord Bantry shouting his name with increasing impatience.

'Try to sleep,' he advised the child. 'I'll come back when I can!' He didn't like to admit to her, let alone to himself, that he also was afraid of Lord Bantry, and he knew that if he went too far, his own life, like hers, would be in danger.

Eileen smoothed her gloves over her fingers for the umpteenth time. She was hotter than she ever remembered being and she wished she hadn't come. From the moment she had entered the house, she had known that Lady Cunningham was not out of the top drawer, whatever she might pretend. The very walls shouted the information at her, with their cluttered, tawdry ornaments, and the overstuffed, mustard-coloured furniture would never have found a home with her own mistress. Eileen sniffed. She might call herself a lady, but she needn't think she could pull the wool over Eileen's eyes, because she couldn't. Lady Cunningham was no aristocrat – more likely middle-class and trying to better herself!

Eileen was just wondering what this female could possibly have had in common with Lady Frances, when Lady Cunningham came bustling into the small anteroom and Eileen knew immediately what it was. The woman might be ambitious but she was also kind-hearted.

'My word, it's too hot in here to breathe! Shall we go into another room?'

Eileen followed her well-rounded form into another room on the cooler side of the house. She noticed at once that a great effort had been made with the furnishings in here. Lady Cunningham was a quick learner! She couldn't have visited Lady Frances more than twice, but she had taken in every detail of the latter's cool elegance and had done her best to reproduce the same quality in her own household. Eileen thought the better of her for that. If she had made a mistake, in Eileen's opinion, it was because the Indian house scarcely reflected or did justice to Lady Frances's own taste, not as she had known it in London.

'Are you seeking work?' Lady Cunningham encouraged her gently.

'No, your ladyship. I'm – I was Lady Frances's personal maid.'

Lady Cunningham blanched visibly. 'Oh dear! So upsetting! I never thought to hear such an awful thing but that an English lady, going about her own business, should be set upon by those thieving devils!' Her eyes didn't quite meet Eileen's. Lady Cunningham was a bad fibber at best.

'It's her daughter, Mary, I've come to see you about,' Eileen put in quickly.

Lady Cunningham looked more uncomfortable than ever. 'Oh yes, Mary. How is the poor mite?'

Eileen clasped her hands together. 'Her father is threatening her life. He isn't after believing her ladyship is dead and he's convinced himself that Miss Mary knows more

196

than she's willing to tell him. Unfortunately, he knows she has her mother's knife – the one Father McGilligan gave me when I was setting forth to make my fortune in pagan England. Well, after Lord Bantry had raped her on the packet coming over – '

Lady Cunningham put out a protesting hand. 'My dear girl, do you think you *ought* to be telling me all this?'

'What harm can it do now?' Eileen returned pertly. 'It's Mary who must be our first concern right now, wouldn't you say? She was very badly hurt, my lady.'

Lady Cunningham was sorry to hear that. She strove, without any success, to put other stories she had heard about Lord Bantry out of her mind. She was quite sure Sir Arthur would say it was no business of hers how he chose to behave, and yet she had made that fatal promise to Lady Frances that she would look after her daughter.

'I doubt her father would be willing – ' she began hopefully.

'Her father doesn't care what happens to her, beyond hoping to use her as bait to bring Lady Frances back to him. To do that, he'd have to mistreat her shamefully, but I, for one, wouldn't put it past him!'

Nor would Lady Cunningham. She sighed, knowing herself to be beaten. 'You'd better tell me the whole,' she said with resignation. 'But, mind you, I shall never admit to anyone else that I know Lady Frances to be alive and, if you repeat one word of our conversation outside these walls, I shall deny every word of it. I have my own family to think of!'

Eileen was only too glad to unburden herself to this kindly woman and Lady Cunningham was soon intimately acquainted with Lady Frances, Father McGilligan, the puritanical Agnes, and a cast of lesser personages who took the stage and disappeared again as Eileen continued her

197

story in her soft, Irish brogue. What it amounted to was a tale of such unbelievable horror that the good woman no longer cared what her husband might say, she was determined to bring Mary to live with her. She shared one other quality with the narrator of this story, a fact which she recognized wryly as no more than she deserved for making up to the daughter of an Earl for the social advantages it might bring her. She had not known Lady Frances long, but she would gladly have lain down and died for her, Arthur or no Arthur, and she knew Eileen would have done exactly the same.

'You know that Queen Victoria is the child's godmother?'

'She is, but what use she'll be when she's thousands of miles away is beyond the likes of me!'

'Sir Arthur will have to think of something!' Lady Cunningham concluded valiantly. She smiled a wan smile. 'What plans do you have yourself, Eileen?' she asked kindly.

'I'll go wherever Miss Mary goes,' Eileen told her simply. 'Lady Frances left her in my care.'

Without a flicker of emotion, Lady Cunningham resigned herself to adding Eileen as well as Mary to her household. In for a penny, in for a pound, she told herself, hoping against hope her beloved husband was going to see this business in the same light as she herself did.

It so happened that for the first time in an age, not even their son was home for dinner that evening. Lady Cunningham was sorely tempted to speak to Sir Arthur there and then, but she knew better than to suppose it possible to have anything like a private conversation with the servants standing behind their chairs, picking up who knew what gossip to relay to their friends in the bazaars.

'My love, I have something I must discuss with you

when we are alone,' she warned him at length, unable to keep a still tongue any longer.

Sir Arthur looked at her fondly over his roast beef. 'What is it? A new dress you want my opinion on?'

Lady Cunningham didn't mind in the least that he thought her frivolous, though on this occasion she could have wished for a little more discernment on his part. He might think fashion frivolous; she knew that socially it could be a matter of life and death.

She was grateful, therefore, when it was he who brought the matter to a head when they had finally retired to their bed for the night.

'I wish it didn't distress you when those cats get their claws into you, Hetty. What's happened now?'

'It's nothing I've said or done,' she protested, not quite truthfully. 'It's Mary Bantry!'

'Ah!'

'What do you mean "Ah!"? Have you heard something too?'

Sir Arthur allowed himself a quiet, contented smile. He'd much rather hear the story from his wife than offer her some edited version of the gossip which was making the rounds all over Delhi that morning following the return of the search party, empty-handed and without a single clue as to the fate of Lady Frances. As long as his delightful Hetty didn't expect him to take up cudgels on Lady Frances's behalf, he thought he could take anything. Pity the woman had put herself quite outside the pale, but that was no skin off his nose. Even if she wasn't in fact dead and buried, nobody would ever be prepared to admit as much, not unless they wanted to join her in the half-life to which she had committed herself. He doubted there'd be so much as a murmur if that blighter should choose to marry again. They'd all be falling over themselves to accept the polite fiction that Lady Frances was dead, himself amongst them!

The daughter was another matter. 'The best thing for you to do is to invite the child on a prolonged visit. If her father don't like it, I'll go and see him myself. We can't have the Bantry women dropping like flies, can we?'

Even so, her heart was beating uncomfortably against her ribs when Lady Cunningham waited in the Bantry drawing-room for Mary and Eileen to join her, their bags packed and ready to go. Lord Bantry had been unexpectedly charming to her, raising no objection at all to her carrying off his daughter for a prolonged visit while she recovered from the untimely death of her mother. When she had first come face to face with him, she hadn't had the least idea what excuse she could offer as to why Mary should stay with her but, happily, inspiration had struck her at the last moment and she had found herself enlarging on the wonders the climate of Kashmir would do for an English-born and bred child, especially one unfortunate enough to have recently lost her Mama.

'A kindly thought, ma'am,' Lord Bantry had commended her. 'And one I shall be pleased to accept on my daughter's behalf. Her mother never took much interest in her, you know, and she's badly in need of a woman's influence on her at her age.'

'Quite so,' Lady Cunningham had agreed doubtfully. What was she getting herself into now?

'I wish I could tell you,' Lord Bantry had continued, 'that Mary is a normal child in every way, but I'm afraid she was taught all manner of fancies by her mother so that I have sometimes feared for her mind. She is with the servants too much, and always has been! She has some ridiculous notion that her mother is still alive and that only she knows where she is. Would that she were right, poor soul! However, if she should choose to confide in you, Lady Cunningham, as her mother's friend, I hope you'll see your way to telling me so that I can disabuse her once and for all.'

Lady Cunningham's jaw had dropped. Could he really believe that she would be taken in by any such nonsense? She had seen for herself the injuries he had dealt the child in the past!

'As I hope you know,' she had said in surprisingly firm tones, 'none of us has the slightest wish to forget you are the child's father. Sir Arthur has very strong views on the matter!'

When she finally took her seat next to Mary in her comfortable, well-appointed carriage, Lady Cunningham wondered why her jaw was aching, to find she had gritted her teeth together for so long that she now found it almost impossible to relax.

The sight of Mary, her useless arm dangling by her side, great livid scars down her sides, and dragging one leg as she limped across to make her curtsey, had so upset her that it had been as much as she could do to remain courteous to Lord Bantry in case he should change his mind and keep his daughter with him. The man was every bit the monster Sir Arthur had called him. Nor had she believed him when he had reminded Mary to leave her mother's knife behind, so that she couldn't threaten others as she had threatened him with its long, wicked blade! That there was such a knife she knew from Eileen, but, while she could believe that Lady Frances might have used it on him, nothing would persuade her that this poor little dab who was her daughter would have found the courage for much more than a whimper when she was confronted by her father.

Mary's small hand crept into hers as the horses pulled away from the portico that dominated the front of the Bantry house.

'You were Mama's friend, weren't you?' she said.

There was something in the look in the navy eyes that reminded Lady Cunningham of the one she had seen in Lady Frances's eyes when she had decided to visit the rose garden that fateful evening.

'I hope I was,' she said, preening herself a little on the quality of that friendship.

Mary relaxed beside her. 'I'm glad,' she said.

It was a long time before Mary would do other than shrink away from Sir Arthur every time he went near her.

'I suppose it's because I'm a man,' he sighed to his wife. 'Can't you tell her she has nothing to be afraid of from me?'

'I have, my dear,' Lady Cunningham told him, equally distressed.

Then, one day, something he said made Mary giggle, looking so much like her mother that they had both blinked at her.

'I wish you had a daughter,' the little girl had told him gravely.

He had been too wise to rush her. 'I've often wished that myself,' he had said. 'Mothers play their part of course, especially where their sons are concerned, but we men need daughters to flatter us and tell us things they can't tell anyone else in the world. Sons are all right, but I'd love to have had a daughter!'

There had been a long, a very long silence. 'I'd like to be your daughter,' Mary said.

Chapter Eleven

The fort rose high on a hill, towering over the desert land beneath. Its marvellous construction made it seem as if it had grown out of the cliffs themselves, its sides as sheer and golden as the outcrop of sandstone it crowned. The wonder was how anyone ever made their way up there, so remote and splendid was its apparent isolation.

Their procession slowed to a halt. It seemed as if the whole population had turned out to welcome their ruler home. Sajjan had dressed splendidly that morning, and mounted the elephant that had been brought out for him to ride into the city with ease and familiarity. Fanny had been doubtful of so large an animal when she had first seen it, but when she had seen Sajjan's departure, far ahead of her own, she had thought she might like a similar conveyance herself. Seated, veiled and with the curtains drawn, in the palanquin in which she was to be carried up into the Fort-Palace, she was hotter than she had ever been. Her clean clothes were soon soaked with perspiration, her scalp itched, and little rivulets of sweat ran down her back, tickling her sensitive skin.

What was holding them up now? She opened the curtains a crack, annoyed by the delay, and saw Sajjan acknowledging the acclaim of his people, accepting a multitude of garlands from one and all, until the howdah on which he was seated was piled high with flowers. She was surprised by a sense of personal pride in his progress which brought a lump to her throat. How many times in the last few days had he tried to explain to her the two-way contract between *raja* and *praja*, ruler and people, that it ill behove either side to break. And here it was, made visible before her, a genuine celebration of what they meant to each other. It was important to him that he ruled with the authority conferred on him by his people, not because some foreign power had placed and kept him on his throne. To derive his authority from the British would as surely break the spirit of the contract as the palace revolutions of old had broken the letter.

'You don't understand,' he had accused her. 'If I owed my allegiance to the British, would I still be the father and mother of my people? Would I do what was best for them, or for the British?'

'For both,' she had said.

'Can *you* do that?' he had tossed back at her. He had looked sad, almost nervous, as if her answer really mattered to him.

'Why yes, yes of course I can!' she had claimed.

'Your Queen still comes first with you?'

Her Queen was her friend. 'I don't know,' she had confessed at last.

He had shrugged his shoulders, pretending not to care. 'Tell me when she no longer commands your first allegiance. You can't pay the same loyalty to us both, Fanny.'

She had still thought she could – *then*. Queen Victoria was her Queen, as well as being her dear friend. Was it possible she had confused the friend with the personification of a people whose policies she had never been able to approve wholeheartedly? It could have been so. She wasn't sure how it had come about, but if she had to choose between the British interest and Sajjan's, her heart would choose the Raja of Kattyapur's.

At last they reached the main entrance to the Fort, the

Gate of Ganesha, the elephant-headed god who was invoked at the beginning of every venture and guarded such things as entrances and crossroads. He was also the inspiration of artists and writers, the giver of wealth and good fortune. Fanny recognized his jovial expression with relief. The Lord Ganesha was one of the more popular gods and Sajjan had told her his story. He was the son of Síva and Parvati. His father had gone away leaving a child, and had returned to find a grown man lying on the bed beside his wife Parvati. Angered by his wife's perfidy, the Lord Síva had struck off the young man's head. Parvati, hysterical with grief, had explained who the young man was. Lord Síva had promised reparation by appropriating the head of the first creature who came along, who happened to be an elephant, and, placing it on the young man's shoulders, he had restored him to life.

Fanny had laughed when she had heard the story. Unaccustomed to the endless domestic squabbles of the Indian gods, she had often been shocked by the sensual, often ignoble aspects of their stories.

'It's the inner truth of the story that matters,' Sajjan had told her.

She hadn't understood, she didn't really understand now, but she was grateful for the tuition she had hardly been aware she had been receiving. The little shrine in the Gate, bedecked with flowers and little lights, was familiar rather than strange to her as they paused for a moment beside it, gathering themselves for going up the steep slope into the heart of the Fort itself. She felt less of a stranger because she could put a name and a tale to the guardian of the city.

The procession rode on, the horses' hooves slipping on the steep grooved surfaces. A little more than halfway up they were stopped again by a barrier, where all but the

Raja had to dismount and make the rest of the way on foot. Fanny, glad to be let out of the stuffy interior, stepped down, pulling her veil more closely around her as the women crowded protectively about her. She just had time to see Sajjan turning the corner ahead of her, the elephant plodding onwards through a colourful wave of bowing men whom he totally ignored.

There was a shout of '*Bandobast!*' and a way was made for her to follow on foot, all eyes turned away from her as she struggled up the last few yards and across the open courtyard to the main entrance of the women's quarters. A small striped animal ran across her path, making her practically jump out of her skin. Later, she learned it was one of the many squirrels who ran wild all over the place, encouraged by the little piles of food that were left out for them by the people who worked around the palace. She rather hoped that other varieties of vermin weren't equally at home inside the palace, never having had to share her home with either mice or rats. It was going to be bad enough to have to share her days with a parcel of women with whom she was sure she would have very little in common.

The guards flung open the doors, their curved swords shining in the hot sunshine. Fanny suppressed a shudder at the sight of them and entered, feeling for all the world like Anne Boleyn on the way to the scaffold. How ridiculous, she thought, that she, one of the best-known hostesses in all London, should take it into her head to be nervous of a few women who had had little of her advantages in life and none of her independence, if it could be termed independence to be married off to a man like Edwin Bantry when scarcely more than a child.

Would this place ever seem to be home to her? She wished Sajjan could have been by her side the first time she entered his *zenana*. He had succeeded in frightening her earlier, holding her in his arms and telling her how she must behave when she was in the presence of his two Ranis. She wished she had listened more closely to his strictures, for one fact had been brought home to her as had no other: that whether her future home was going to prove a paradise or a place of torment would depend on the first impression she made on the senior women of Sajjan's court. She bit her lip. Would they be waiting to receive her, or would they ignore her presence, resenting her as much as she resented them?

She was led along some of the narrowest corridors she had ever seen, with so many twists and turns that she soon despaired of ever being able to find her own way about the place. Even the doors were at angles to the solid walls, making it impossible for any man to brandish an implement big enough to break down the most vulnerable part of the defences of the Palace. Then, suddenly, they came out into an open courtyard, in the centre of which was a roofed area, set with carved pillars, where Sajjan's two Ranis sat waiting for her.

Fanny's first thought was how pretty it was: the delicate arches, the lightness of the umbrella-shaped roofing, the colours of the cushions on the tiled platform, and the dresses of the women. Ila's whispered reminder to pull her veil over her face recalled her to what was now expected of her. Her hands were wet with fear and the cloth kept slipping through her fingers. It was appalling in one who had never lacked confidence in her ability to please but, for once, she was scared stiff!

She made her obeisance to both Ranis, unprepared, though she supposed she shouldn't have been, for the vacant, chilling expression in the elder woman's eyes. It was the younger Rani who got to her feet and embraced

Fanny. 'Are you the Englishwoman?' she asked her, sweeping Fanny's veil back from her face with gentle fingers.

'Yes, Second Your Highness.'

The woman was as dainty as a gazelle. 'I'm so glad you've arrived at last! It's many days since we were told of your coming and all the other wives of affection were sent away. We are all alone here now, except for the servants and the children. First Her Highness should be the one to welcome you, but you can see how she is for yourself. She's not very good company,' she ended on a wry note of complaint.

Fanny's eyes slid to the elder Rani. Tall and gaunt, she looked completely mad, with her wide, staring eyes and dribbling constantly out of the corner of her mouth.

'My name is Fanny,' Fanny said uneasily.

'Fanny,' Second Her Highness repeated. 'My personal name is Maneka, but only those who knew me as a child call me that. You must be feeling very strange. You'll feel better when you've seen your quarters. You'll always be quite private there. We never visit unless invited, and then we almost always meet out here in the courtyard. Would you like me to show you the way?'

'Thank you,' Fanny said, at her most formal.

'Don't be afraid! I shan't eat you! It's a relief you speak our language because I'm longing to hear all about your life across the Black Seas, and why you have come to live amongst us. I have been bored to death these last few days!'

Fanny swallowed. 'I don't want – ' she began. 'Sajjan told me I must always remember you are his Rani and that I'm nothing,' she confided with a small laugh. 'You must tell me if I do something outrageous. I won't mean to – '

The Rani's eyebrows rose. 'Sajjan? Does he allow you to call him that?'

'No,' Fanny admitted.

'Doesn't he get angry with you?'

Fanny squared her shoulders. 'He calls me Fanny! Not even Lady Frances!'

The Rani smothered a shocked giggle. 'Of course he does! You're his wife of affection! *I* would never dare as much!' She shook her head, marvelling at Fanny's effrontery. Then she dismissed the matter with a casual shrug, adding the warning, 'As long as you treat First Her Highness with a proper respect, I shan't complain. She, poor thing, has nothing else, not even children. His Highness treats her as a child, and sometimes I think she'd like to have more from him, for she isn't a child physically and she's very fond of him.'

Once again, Fanny was taken back by the Junior Rani's speech. She remembered Sajjan had told her that his second wife was a woman of great charm and intelligence. She could only agree with him. She found herself liking her very much, despite her reservations about the part the other woman would always play in the Raja's life. She tried to persuade herself that in the same circumstances she would have brought herself to show an equal concern for the Senior Rani's well-being, failed, and hoped instead that the other woman would never know how she really felt about both Ranis, and even the children Second Her Highness had borne to Sajjan.

'I hope you weren't hurt when you heard His Highness was bringing me with him?' she tentatively tested out the ground.

'I was sorry that all the other concubines had to be sent away,' the Junior Rani confided with a wry smile. 'It's lonely without them. They were sent to another royal house, though they're not too far away for us to visit them from time to time. They're all coming to meet you tomorrow, bringing token gifts with them to welcome you. His Highness, you see, has given instructions that although you can never really be his Third Rani, that is what he would have wished you to be. You are honoured!'

'Yes, I am,' Fanny agreed humbly.

The Junior Rani led the way up a small staircase and pushed open a door that led into a suite of rooms beyond. They were much grander than anything Fanny had expected. Somehow, the plainness of the Fort's exterior had led her to expect a similar austerity within, but these were the most luxurious apartments she had ever seen. Fine paintings in the Moghul style hung on the walls, thick hand-made carpets covered the floors, with piles of cushions here and there for her greater comfort. Several divans lined the walls for her to rest on, their embroidered covers as valuable as anything the Queen had taken with her when she had first been obliged to move into Buckingham Palace. Also, there was a marble-lined pool filled with water, for no other purpose than for her to bathe in when the mood took her, day or night. There was even a separate place for her to eat, which she would continue to do alone, with her own silver and gold dishes, and a samovar in case she should wish to serve herself with tea.

'This door leads to His Highness's own bedroom,' the Junior Rani instructed her. 'When he should send for you, you go through there and up the stairs to another door. We all have our own entrance to the staircase. It's one of the reasons we respect each other's privacy when we retire to our own rooms. As we use the staircase to visit him, so also does he sometimes choose to visit us, and he'd be less than pleased to be interrupted by another once he's made his choice.'

She said this last with such awe that Fanny concluded the Junior Rani really did see the Raja as more of a god than a man. She couldn't think it at all good for Sajjan's character and meant to tell him so when she got the opportunity. Meanwhile, she could only think how odd it was going to be to live in this society where one man's lightest whim was law for everyone else.

When Fanny was finally left on her own she flung herself on to the nearest divan, familiarizing herself with her new surroundings. It was a waste of time to be homesick, so she firmly refused to admit to any such emotion. This was the new life she had chosen for herself. No one had forced her to come here, as she had once been forced into marriage with Edwin Bantry, so if she didn't like it and wasn't happy here, there was nobody else she could blame. The only drawback she could see was what she was going to do with herself all day long with only the Junior Rani for company, delightful as she might be.

One way and another she was very pleased to see Ila when she arrived, full of excited gossip, her mind fully taken up with the unexpected dismissal of all the other concubines.

'Who were all these women?' Fanny asked her idly.

Ila stared at her, her eyes rounding in surprise. 'But, lady, you know who they were! Some of them were the daughters of *zamindars*, landowners, or *jagirdars*, those who owe their lands to the Raja's favour, even the *tehsuldar*, the Raja's tax-collector. Their fathers gave them to the Raja to gain his goodwill. Others he may have seen from time to time, and they may have found favour with him because of their beauty or charm. A man such as the Raja has many women!'

'And they were all shut in here together?' Fanny asked, scandalized.

'Where else would they live? Here, together with their servants, they had each other for company. Now they are all gone!'

'I see,' said Fanny. 'Is that my fault?'

Ila was still pouting at her. 'It's known you don't like the Raja to have other women. You want him all to yourself!'

'In my country a man has only one wife,' Fanny tried to explain.

'They have no female friends?'

'Well, they do, but they're frequently the wives of other men. We don't hide our women away as you do here. I find your customs very strange!'

Ila's easy sympathy was won. She said shyly, 'I told Second Her Highness about your house in Delhi, and all the strange clothes you wore there. She laughed a lot about how you must have looked in them. Will you show her some day?'

'I left all my old clothes behind.'

'You could draw her a picture.' Ila had been impressed during their journey by the way Fanny could capture a scene with a few lines of pencil. She hesitated, fidgeting with her fingers as she wondered if her mistress would take what she said amiss if she were to pass on the Junior Rani's warning to herself. 'Many of the women resent your coming, lady. If you're seen to be the friend of the Junior Rani, though, they won't dare to act against you.'

Fanny understood immediately. Her flesh crawled with fright. 'Could they really harm me?' she shot at Ila.

The girl nodded. 'They would like to be rid of you. You're a foreigner and a danger to them. It would be easy for one of them to bribe someone to put poison in your food as you always eat alone.'

'And how about you?' Fanny asked her.

Ila's face took on a stubborn look. 'You are my lady. The Raja himself has commanded me to look after you.'

Fanny wondered just how loyal the girl would be if she were to be tested by the kind of bribe these women would know exactly how to offer her. With sudden amusement, she realized that this society wasn't as different as she'd expected it to be from the one she had left behind. Men and women, it seemed, were much the same the whole world over, with some of them determined to scheme, lie, or cheat to climb the ladder of their own self-esteem.

Fanny leaned forward and touched Ila on the hand. 'I'll remember it was you who warned me,' she smiled at her. 'The Raja will remember also, and will see you get your reward.'

'I ask only to serve you, lady.'

It was true, though Ila couldn't have said why. She had been put out, at first, to find herself serving a foreigner, one from across the Black Seas, an outcast from her own people, and without caste in her new life. Some of those rejected women had been amongst her personal friends, some of them she had known from childhood, and yet there was something about her new mistress which more than made up for what she had lost in serving one so unworthy. She recognized in Fanny a quite different quality and had no doubt that as soon as she found her feet, the rewards of being in her service would be great indeed.

Fanny, meanwhile, was reflecting that there was rather more to living in the *zenana* than she had thought. It was becoming increasingly obvious that the key to being allowed to go her own way was to cultivate the Junior Rani's approval and devil take the rest!

Ila moved restively about the room, not yet finished with the advice she had to offer her mistress.

'I wondered why you'd been given the choker necklace that all married women wear,' she began artfully. 'Second Her Highness says you will rank next to her and must be given every respect. She also said I would be responsible if you didn't know what to do – '

'Oh lord!' said Fanny. Ila sucked in her lips in silent disapproval. Fanny grinned at her. 'Oh, very well! What do I have to do now?'

Ila looked round the room. 'You have need of many things,' she said vaguely. 'I've told Second Her Highness as much. It won't matter tonight.' She threw Fanny a meaningful glance. 'In the morning Second Her Highness is always awake at six and has her bath. Then the ingredients are prepared for her *puja*. What gods do you worship, lady? Second Her Highness says you must be allowed to worship them in your own quarters, but I have never seen you pray.'

Fanny's respect for the Junior Rani was increasing by the minute. Apparently she ran every detail of life in the *zenana* with a firm hand. She felt a corresponding guilt that she should have set such a bad example. How often had it been instilled into her that she must always be seen in church on Sundays, whether she wanted to go or not, because of the example it set to others. How often, too, had she watched her father at their daily family prayers, knowing it to be no more than a chore to him, doggedly gone through for the sake of the indoor servants. She was Lady Frances no more, but her responsibilities hadn't ceased with her change of identity. Her witness to her Christian faith should be all the more exact because there was none here to remind her.

'It says in our holy book that one should be alone when one prays,' she said firmly. 'We don't need an image of our

214

God because he's enthroned in our hearts. We talk to him in private and submit ourselves to his will for us.'

Ila nodded understandingly. 'Like the Moslems.'

'Not in the least like the Moslems!' Fanny had no idea how the Moslems prayed, but she knew theirs to be a cruel and warlike religion. 'I'm a Christian!'

That meant less than nothing to Ila. 'What will you do on special days?' she asked. 'We have such fun at Teej and at Holi. It'd be a shame for you to be left on your own.'

Fanny thought so too. She took the easy way out. 'Second Her Highness will guide me as to what I should do,' she determined.

Ila nodded her approval. She had been afraid that she, too, might have been prevented from participating in the great festivals of the year.

'The sacred horse will be returning in a few weeks. That'll be a sight to see!'

'Will it really be sacrificed when it comes home?' Fanny asked.

'It's had a glorious year. His Highness has many new lands because the rulers have submitted wherever the stallion has been. There'll be much rejoicing when it's brought home!'

So the venture had been successful, Fanny thought. She only hoped the British would never get to hear about it.

The Junior Rani sent for Fanny in the morning. It had been one of the longest nights Fanny had ever experienced. Her imagination had run riot at every noise, imagining she knew not what. She had longed to be back in the Raja's tent once more, feeling his comforting presence beside her. Instead, she had spent the night alone, twisting and turning in the humid atmosphere, wondering if she would ever survive in this strange environment.

Heavy of heart, she made her obeisance reluctantly, resenting the other woman with a return of the sharp jealousy she had known before she had even met her. Where had the Junior Rani spent the night?

'Please sit beside me,' Second Her Highness invited her.

Fanny did so, trying to make herself comfortable. Her limbs ached when she drew them up beneath her, but she was too proud to admit as much to this graceful woman. She would learn to behave as they did if it killed her! And she was beginning to think it might.

The Junior Rani watched her, her eyes shining with amusement. 'Your maid was telling me you sat on chairs in Delhi.'

'Yes,' Fanny informed her grimly. 'Only children sit on the floor!'

The Rani giggled. 'His Highness told me you had to leave your little girl behind – '

Fanny's eyes flashed. 'You've seen the Raja?'

A small hand took possession of Fanny's with a pressure surprising in one so gentle. 'Yes, I have seen His Highness. He was away from home for many weeks and there have been a few changes here he should know about. I'm his wife, Fanny.'

'So is First Her Highness!'

'Yes, but you've no cause to be jealous of her, have you? I hope so much we can be friends.' She lowered her eyes. 'His Highness wishes it to be so.'

'And that makes it all right?' Fanny demanded.

'Of course.'

Fanny leaped to her feet, unable to bear the unaccustomed strain on her muscles a moment longer. She strode about the courtyard, seeking a similar relief for her feelings. Finally, she seated herself on the very edge of the platform.

'I – I can't!'

The Junior Rani's eyes widened. 'Do you have any choice?'

Fanny smiled wryly. 'No,' she said at last. 'I wish I didn't like you, though, it would make it so much easier for me. I have the horrid suspicion that most of my happiness here is going to depend on your goodwill and I find that humiliating!'

The Junior Rani laughed. 'His Highness told me you have more courage than any other woman he's ever met. I begin to see what he means!'

'Don't you mind when he compliments me?'

The Junior Rani hesitated. 'My whole life belongs to my lord. Why should I mind?'

'I should!'

A soft sigh answered her. 'He has explained to me that my place in his life is secure. I am the mother of the Yuveraj. I am his Second Rani. I will always have a corner of his heart – '

'And then I came along and spoilt it all for you!' Fanny interrupted fiercely.

'No, no, I'm not like you. I've always known I should have to share him with others. You're taking nothing away from me.' She sighed again, hazarding gently, 'If we're seen to be friends, Fanny, others won't take sides between us, making trouble for both of us. Some of them see you only as a foreigner who can bring nothing but disaster to Kattyapur.'

Fanny gave her a sharp look. 'Ila was telling me how easy it'd be to poison my food as I always eat alone.'

'I hope it won't come to that! His Highness's revenge would be terrible and we'd all be put to death for not guarding you better! Ila's a silly girl to frighten you!'

'You mean it couldn't happen?'

Second Her Highness spread her hands in surrender. 'I

mean to see that it doesn't happen! Fanny, please, won't you make things easier for both of us?'

Fanny took a deep breath and nodded. 'I'll be honoured to be your friend.' It was one of the hardest decisions she'd ever had to make, to accept anything at this woman's hands. Yet she couldn't hate the Junior Rani as she'd like to do. On the contrary, she was afraid she might grow to like her far too much. She turned stiffly towards her. 'You're being very kind to me and you mustn't think me ungrateful.' She blinked back the tears in her eyes. 'His Highness told me about you, too. He admires you very much – and so do I.'

The Junior Rani actually blushed. 'I live to please him. As do you, Fanny.'

Fanny surrendered reluctantly in her turn. 'I suppose I must do,' she said.

Chapter Twelve

Fanny was almost asleep when the huge black eunuch of the *zenana* came to her door to summon her to Sajjan's apartments. She had only seen the gigantic guardian of the women from a distance before, and it gave her the fright of her life when this black giant, so grossly fat that he waddled rather than walked the narrow passages, was admitted by Ila and signalled to Fanny to follow him up the stairs. His costume rivalled Sajjan's own for magnificence and Fanny felt a poor dab of a thing beside him, dressed in her night clothes, with her long hair flowing down her back, unbraided and brushed until it shone.

Sajjan was alone in his bedroom. He was standing, staring out of one of the arched windows that gave him a view right over his city. Fanny joined him silently, entranced by the lights down below.

'How pretty!' she exclaimed.

Very little of the outside world could be seen from the women's quarters, as they all looked inwards, over any number of pretty courtyards, the few windows that looked outwards being locked and barred, shuttered against any unauthorized person who might be tempted to spy on the women of the ruler.

He thought she looked young and vulnerable, almost nervous of him, and was saddened by the change in her. He held out his hand to her, drawing her close against him, and was glad when she settled happily into his embrace.

'Well, Fanny, can you be happy here?'

'I mean to try to be.'

'Has everyone been kind to you?'

She nodded, not looking at him. 'Second Her Highness has been more than kind. You were right when you told me I'd like her – I do, despite the differences between us!'

'She's my Rani – '

She clutched at his nightshirt, 'I'll never get used to your having other women! Never!'

He laughed under his breath. 'I sent the *other* women away – all except Maneka. She has more right here than any other. I owe her much, my love, more than you'll ever know, and not only because she's my Rani, which you can never be. She deserves better from both of us than to be excluded from my bed and my heart. If anyone has cause to be jealous, it is she!'

Fanny smiled a wry smile. 'She's a better person than I'm ever likely to be,' she acknowledged. Her eyes lit with the teasing smile he associated with her. 'She worships you! You can do no wrong where she's concerned!'

His brief amusement died in a gusty sigh. 'And First Her Highness? How did you find her?'

'As she always is, I imagine. Sajjan, why on earth did you marry her? You must have known what she's like?'

'Politics, my dear. She comes from a family my father wished to ally himself with. You met her brother. Thank God, he has his wits, though little wisdom. He's obsessed with gold and treachery and ridiculous notions of honour. While First Her Highness lives, he remains our ally. I can only hope we're not pulled after him into some stupid enterprise that'll be the finish of us all. His honour doesn't extend as far as the protection of his people and friends.'

'I didn't like or trust him,' Fanny admitted. And poor, wretched First Her Highness! 'Poor woman!' she said gently.

He shrugged his shoulders, uncomfortable with the

memories that were conjured up by Fanny's compassion. Just so had his mother spoken of his first wife. 'We were both children when we married,' he said aloud. 'My mother would never allow the marriage to be consummated, however. She said I needed heirs who could be the mothers and fathers of my people, not idiots who couldn't be trusted even to look after themselves. She was thoroughly annoyed with my father over the match! She wouldn't speak to him for days!'

'Quite right,' Fanny approved. 'What chance of happiness did either of you have?'

'Happiness wasn't the object of the marriage,' he said dryly. 'It seldom is amongst people of our position.'

If anyone should know the truth of that, it was Fanny. However, in her experience, people seldom acknowledged that marriage could be anything less than the idealized love between a man and a woman she had been brought up to believe in. Even now she had found a man she could truly love, she wanted to put a sentimental gloss over her feelings to hide the primitive nature of her emotions from herself. She found Sajjan's realism difficult to deal with.

'Tell me about your mother,' she said, seeking a safer subject. 'Did you love her very much?'

He smiled. 'She was a very special lady. She was my father's senior wife and she ruled the *zenana* with a rod of iron. We children were spoilt rotten by all the other women, who allowed us to do exactly as we wanted. My mother was made of sterner stuff. It was she who saw to our education, who schooled me in the things I would need to know when I became Raja in my turn. She was tireless in her efforts. It was thanks to her that I learned to speak English and saw something of the world outside of Kattyapur. When my father died, it was bad enough, but I was devastated by her loss.'

'You saw her die?'

He sucked in his cheeks. 'I helped her up on to the funeral pyre before setting light to it. It's one of the duties of the eldest son, you know, to oversee the funeral rites of his father. She went gladly, with honour, saying her wedding day had been only a rehearsal for this much greater day – "loyal and loving, beloved and fair, Followed close behind him into the flames."'

Fanny felt the horror of the memory like a breath blowing over her. 'How could she do it?' she whispered.

'She wanted it that way. *Sati* means virtuous woman and is held in much honour. A widow will say, "This day is one of joy . . . our lives have passed together, how then can I leave him?" If she is left behind, she is known as the bringer of death and misfortune. She lives in the shadows for the rest of her days, unwanted by anyone.'

'At least the British are putting a stop to that! To die in such a way! How can they?'

'Our women don't lack courage or honour. My mother had her full measure of both. If you look on the wall by the Gate of Ganesha, you'll see the handprints of many of our Ranis who became *sati*, my mother's among them. I never see it without remembering that day.'

'How old were you?' Fanny asked.

'Not very old. I missed her, Fanny. I have never told anyone how much! Not only as a person, but as an adviser. With her gone, I didn't know whom I could trust. My other mothers would have preferred to have seen their own sons in my place, and who could blame them? I learned very quickly the arts any ruler requires to be successful, the first of which is to stay alive. It was only when Maneka came and took over the reins of the *zenana* that I could feel at ease again.'

'Thank God for her!'

'I do, my love, I do. In her my mother lives again!'

Fanny shuddered. There was one thing she needed to make quite clear to him, and quickly! 'Come what may, Sajjan, I shan't be flinging myself on any funeral pyre, not even yours! I haven't your faith that we have many lives on this earth. As far as I know, I have only the one, and I mean to live it to the full, until I die of old age in my bed! If you think I lack honour and courage, I can't help it. I *like* living. I always did, even when Edwin was at his worst!'

'We'll all have a better chance of living if we can keep the British away!' he began grimly. He looked at her, amusement lighting his eyes. 'Why else should I have brought you here?'

Her mood changed also. 'Was that your reason? Your only reason? Then what am I doing here, in your bedroom?'

'I don't know, since you won't die for me,' he teased her.

'I'd rather live for you,' Fanny said. 'There's too much dying in the world already. So far, we've both survived – '

'You might enjoy your next life better! You might be reborn a Raja, with many beautiful women to please you.' His laughter fell away as she spread her fingers against his naked chest. He hugged her to him possessively. 'One life won't be nearly long enough for making love to you!'

Fanny chuckled. 'No, it won't, so let's get on with it, shall we?'

Sajjan wasn't accustomed to having women laugh at him, or even with him, and he didn't like it. Fanny should be taught to treat him with some of the awe and respect a woman should have learned at her mother's knee. Then he caught sight of the warm, loving light in her eyes, and remembered all she had given up to be with him. She might not think of him as her lord, but she loved him, wanting him with an eagerness that matched his own. He remembered her fears when he had first loved her and his expression softened. If she was too bold in the liberties she took in his presence, he wouldn't really have her any other way.

The laughter left Fanny as she was thrown on to the bed, the clothes torn from her body. She wriggled away from him in protest. Always before he had cozened her into his embrace and she wasn't sure she appreciated the change. She had known him to be strong, but his arm felt like iron as he held her down, taking his time as his gaze wandered over her naked body, from her breasts to the recently shaved conjunction of her thighs. He gave a grunt of satisfaction, exploring a small, reddened patch with one finger.

'You should tell that maid of yours to be more careful of my property!'

Fanny sat up, hiding herself from him as best she could with both hands. 'D'you think I'd allow Ila – ? *Never!* Never again after that first night! I've never been more embarrassed in my whole life! I do it myself!'

He pushed her back into a lying position and continued his exploration of her. 'Don't Englishwomen shave off their body hair?'

'*No!* At least – I'm sure they don't!'

He made a gesture of distaste. 'I'm grateful you want to please me enough to shave for me. You're very beautiful, Fanny.'

'You're beautiful too!' she exclaimed, anxious to divert his attention from herself.

'How do you know?' he reproved her. 'You seldom look at me!'

The blood thundered in her veins. 'If my governess could see me now, she'd despair I'd ever learned any modesty at all! It's shameful to look at naked bodies – even more shameful to keep the lights on when – ' She swallowed, a delicious guilt creeping over her as she saw Sajjan's disbelief. 'It's true!' she insisted. 'Agnes would have had us make love through a sheet with a hole in it – and then only because children have to be born!'

'What a strange, hypocritical people the British must be,' Sajjan commented with disgust.

She was hurt. 'I seem to please you,' she pouted angrily.

'You please me when you are soft and gentle, and don't argue with me all the time,' he conceded.

Thoroughly annoyed now, she tried to push him away from her. 'And you please me best – '

His heavy-lidded gaze gave her pause. 'If I didn't please you, what would you do?' she asked him, not sure she was going to like the answer.

'Are you afraid I may beat you?'

That, certainly, hadn't occurred to her. 'Would you?'

'I'd rather teach you new ways of pleasing me – '

Her navy eyes glowed. 'Such as?'

He took her hand in his, guiding it downwards until he could feel her cool fingers trembling against the outward manifestation of his need for her. 'Now, take me into yourself,' he commanded.

If she thought it an outrageous request, she gave no sign of it. She was far too interested in what he would want her to do next. She soon found out as he took the initiative away from her, easing her body beneath his and taking over the rhythm of their coupling, with none of his usual gentleness but with a hungry, devouring power that soon had her sobbing out her own love and need for him. Even then he wasn't satisfied, not until he had forced the confession from her that she was his without any reservations, as much his as any of his Indian women would have been. Fanny held out for as long as she could, determined not to be swamped by a force over which she had no control and of which she was uncertain she approved.

'Isn't it enough that I love you?' she demanded.

'Owing your first allegiance to your English Queen?' he grunted.

She smoothed his hair away from his brow, smiling a little. 'So that's it! Do you mind my being British?'

'Not if it's I who am your true lord!'

'Sajjan, my love, you have my whole heart. Isn't that enough for you?'

'Nothing where you're concerned is enough for me! I tell myself I hold your life in my hands, and then you give me one of those cool looks of yours and I wonder what it's worth to me if there's still a part of you that thinks you can be independent of me. No Indian woman would elude me like that! A woman should submit herself to her husband.'

Fanny kissed him on the lips, unknowingly reinforcing his complaint that she lacked respect for him, a respect he was entitled to merely by being a man.

'You're more than a husband to me,' she said. 'You're my chosen lord. Isn't that enough for you?'

Sajjan suspected he was asking the impossible of her – and of himself. Their birth and upbringing had been so different. What did she know of the promises women were expected to make as they followed their husbands around the sacred fire? He had taught her much of love, surprising her with the pleasure they could give each other, so why couldn't he teach her this other thing, that a good woman's reason for living was to fulfil her husband's will, not to assert her independence from him?

He gave her a dissatisfied look. 'One day, you'll go on your knees before me and then I'll know you're mine!' he averred.

She wasn't in the least afraid of him. 'One day, maybe, you'll deserve it!' she said.

It was a relief to her, all the same, when he took her back into his arms and started to make love to her again. She thought she knew what it was he really wanted from her, and it was something she would never voluntarily give up for any man, no matter how dearly she loved him. It was her independence of mind.

The formal visit to the *zenana* of the banished women was more of an ordeal for Fanny than she had expected. The whole place was suddenly overrun by groups of sulky, depressed females and their wriggling, giggling offspring who were yet old enough to share with their mothers their suspicious dislike of the newcomer. That might have been bad enough, but what was infinitely worse was to be expected to sit still on the floor for hours together, without either fidgeting or moving about as she was wont to do.

First Her Highness had been carefully washed and dressed and sat a little apart from the others, her excitement at all the bustle and fuss knowing no bounds. For the most part her presence was ignored but, from time to time, one of the women would present her with a sweetmeat, or a drink of the sickly cordial of which she was particularly fond. A few paces to her left, and a little behind her, sat the Junior Rani, overseeing the whole affair with her customary gentle good manners. It was she who greeted the women, one by one, exclaiming over their children, and lastly introducing them to Fanny who, in turn, sat a little behind her.

It was hot and Fanny hated having her face covered. She had tried a flat refusal to conform to the custom, only to find herself met by a determination every bit the equal of her own.

'I insist you show a proper respect to First Her Highness in a way everyone will understand,' Maneka had reminded her. 'It's necessary that we should give a good example to the other women who are inclined to laugh at her. I am counting on you to behave properly, Fanny.'

Nor did she spare herself, Fanny noticed, thinking how carefully she had been rehearsed in all that was expected of her. Never, for a moment, did the Junior Rani give the slightest sign that she would rather have been talking to and playing with her own children than making much of the over-indulged, ill-tempered offspring of these women whose favourite occupation seemed to be to pick their betters and each other to pieces, with waspish tongues and a lack of goodwill that Fanny found disturbing.

Second Her Highness turned and looked critically at Fanny. 'Cover your face properly!' she frowned at her. 'And remember, say nothing, no matter what comments are passed on you! And whatever you do, don't look up when the older women look under your veil and comment on your pale looks. Accept it with humility.'

'Humility has never been my strong point!' Fanny retorted.

'Do it for His Highness. You don't want people to laugh at him, do you?'

Fanny hadn't thought they would dare. She was about to say as much when her eyes met Maneka's, dancing with amusement, and realized she had no need to tell her anything. The Junior Rani knew exactly how hard this was for her.

'Please, Fanny. My own mother is coming today, and I want so much that she should like and approve of you.'

'Of me?' Fanny was touched. 'I'll try. Who else is coming?'

Maneka sighed. 'His Highness's sisters. They're afraid

of you because you come from across the Black Seas. They say you'll bring us all bad luck.'

'Do you?' Fanny asked her abruptly.

To her surprise, the Junior Rani blushed painfully. 'His Highness has explained to me that you're necessary to Kattyapur as well as to him. His wishes are all that concern me – '

'But you'd rather he'd never brought me here?'

'No, no, I didn't know you then,' Maneka excused herself hastily. 'I thought you might not be a real woman. One hears such strange stories about the English foreigners.'

'I assure you I am a woman!' Fanny exclaimed, rather indignant.

'So Ila tells me,' Maneka returned innocently, depriving Fanny of further speech that anyone should doubt it for a moment. 'The others might not believe it though.'

She turned away again, unaware of the half-amused, half-wrathful frustration she had aroused in Fanny, who already had more than enough to distress her with the hot sun and her screaming muscles protesting at the position she was forced to take up. It was little less than torture to have one complacent female after another lift her veil and express insolent surprise that she should possess two eyes, a nose, and a mouth, just like everyone else.

The small gifts they dropped contemptuously in her lap were reluctantly given. Whether it was a jewel, a coin, or a *nazar* – a token present which was possibly all they could afford – they were all given in such a spirit of miserly dislike that Fanny could take no joy in them. In vain did she remind herself that this was an honour she was not really entitled to by her ambivalent position in the *zenana*, she longed to pin back their ears for them with one sizzling remark that would have shown them once and for all who they were dealing with. Only the occasional warning glances from the Junior Rani kept her silent, her eyes lowered, and her fists clenched into tight balls in her lap.

Consequently, she was taken by surprise when an older woman seated herself comfortably on a cushion by her side, taking her hand in hers and forcing her fingers into a more relaxed position.

'There, there, child, the worst is over and you can take your ease now. It must seem strange for you to have to sit still for such a long time. I was in Calcutta once, and I saw how the British women are never still for a moment, but must be always fluttering their fans and wriggling like children! You were brave to come all the way to Kattyapur!'

Fanny turned navy eyes on to her. There was something familiar about her gentle, restrained tones. 'You must be the Junior Rani's mother!'

'The Maharani of Jaiselmer,' the other nodded. 'I've been told so much about you by my daughter that I decided to come and see you for myself.'

Fanny looked away, realizing she was on trial. 'I admire the Junior Rani very much,' she said stiffly.

'Of course. It isn't easy for her with the Senior Rani the way she is.'

And now she has me to contend with also, Fanny finished for her, saying nothing.

The Maharani nodded gently, her eyes shrewd. 'May one ask why you came?'

'Sajjan – '

The Maharani plucked at her dress, shaking her head. 'His Highness,' she corrected. She eyed Fanny thoughtfully. 'Why shock people when there's no need to do so? You Europeans are always blind to the feelings of others, so I've been told. Let's hope your time in India will teach you we're not all to be despised, no?'

Fanny was ashamed. 'I do try to conform!' The obvious sympathy of the other woman brought a smile to her lips. 'Please don't hold my bad manners against me. My wits are completely addled from sitting in the sun for so long and, to tell the truth, my muscles are unused to your way of sitting and I doubt I'll ever walk again! How do you manage to sit for hours on the floor like this?'

The Maharani was not immune to Fanny's brand of charm and she responded accordingly. 'We do it from childhood. I expect we should find your ways equally uncomfortable. If my daughter seems to criticize over-much, she means it kindly. Your arrival here has caused a lot of talk and all the old resentments have surfaced that she herself had to contend with when she first came here. You can't possibly understand – '

'But I do!' Fanny exclaimed, laughing. So this was where the Junior Rani got her wisdom and tolerance! 'My greatest surprise was to find how alike we all are! If you ever went to the Court of Queen Victoria, you'd feel completely at home! Oh, not the clothes, or the outward things, but all the petty ambitions to move up in the world and to be noticed by all the right people, it never ends!'

The Maharani shuddered. 'I would never cross the Black Waters! Never! I'd lose an essential part of myself if I went so far away.'

'My old governess felt exactly the same way,' Fanny told her. 'Nothing would persuade her to come with me.'

'Weren't you afraid to lose caste? Is it because you have none that your people cross the Black Seas and think nothing of it? Are you so anxious to rule over foreign lands? Have you no religion?'

Fanny was amused by the thought. 'Some of us have too

much religion and feel obliged to share our Christian God with you,' she said lightly.

The Maharani's outrage made her laugh. 'As you never pray,' she accused Fanny, 'what do you know of any god?'

'Very little,' Fanny admitted. 'I do pray in my own way, but I've never been quite sure what I believe. His Highness says we each worship God in the form that makes most sense to us. I'm afraid,' she added dryly, 'that gold and making a fortune to keep them in comfort for the rest of our days seems to be the god most of us choose to worship, but there are others who genuinely want the best possible for India.'

The sharp look she received made her think she was in for another rebuke, but none was forthcoming. 'And you? Will you do your best possible for Kattyapur?'

'I shall try.'

The Maharani seemed satisfied with that. 'Then you're welcome here,' she said.

She was gone a minute later. Fanny saw her talking to her daughter and knew by the look of relief on Maneka's face that the Maharani, at least, was no longer worried that Fanny's presence in Kattyapur was nothing short of a catastrophe for them all. On the contrary, that lady understood Fanny very well and, being very fond of her youngest daughter, had been glad to find in Fanny someone on whose support Maneka could rely. She herself knew all too well the importance of having an ally in the enclosed society of the *zenana*. So did Fanny! And watching the two women together, she thought how easily she might have dismissed them as being of no importance only a few weeks before: now, despite their calm outward appearance and gentle ways, she knew that the worst thing she could ever do was to make an enemy of either of them.

She was just wondering if she dared move from her

allotted seat when a small boy escaped his nurse and came running over to her.

'Who are you?' he demanded at the top of his voice.

At the sight of him, Fanny forgot all about sitting still and not looking about her. She was enchanted by the small boy who was trying to swing on her veil and doing his best to bring her carefully arranged headdress about her ears.

'Who are you?' she countered, lifting him firmly out of harm's way on to her knee. 'You look just like Saj – !'

The hushed gasp from his nurse told her as nothing else could that she had offended badly. Instinctively, she turned to Maneka for help. She came at once, removing the child from Fanny's embrace with a smile for them both.

'This is Yadavendra,' she introduced her son. 'The Yuveraj, the next Raja of Kattyapur!'

Fanny wondered if she were expected to make some kind of obeisance to the little boy. The child himself put an end to all such formalities. Pulling himself free of his mother's restraining hand, he cast himself back on to Fanny's knee. She received him with delight, hugging him to her.

'How lucky you are to have such a son!' she said warmly.

The Junior Rani's expression warmed magically. 'You must miss your daughter,' she sympathized, 'but you'll soon have more children of your own. Do you mind his sticky fingers on your dress?'

Fanny shook her head. 'Should I – ' she began.

'No, no, Fanny. Sit *still*! And cover your face!'

The Yuveraj fetched his plateful of sweetmeats and sat beside her, leaning against her in the most engaging way, his dark eyes bright with admiration and ill-concealed curiosity. He was too young, as yet, to lose caste by associating with a foreigner.

'Are you always going to live here?' he asked.

'Always,' Fanny confirmed. She was unaccustomed to dealing with children, even with her own daughter, but she couldn't resist Sajjan's son, any more than she could resist the father.

'I'm glad. All the ladies give me cakes when they play games with me,' he added meaningfully. 'Do you make music and sing songs?'

'Never,' said Fanny.

He smiled slowly, displaying a fine row of milk teeth. 'Second Her Highness does *gurbas*, dancing with sticks, and the *ghoomar* dances, and sings *bhajans*. Why don't you?'

'I don't know how,' Fanny confessed.

He looked more like his father than ever. 'Then you must be taught!' He went over to his mother to tell her so and Second Her Highness sent Fanny an apologetic look.

'We dance for exercise,' she explained. 'You won't want to sing *bhajans* with us. They're devotional songs we sing before the Lord Krishna.' She hummed under her breath and several of the other women joined in with her. Fanny thought it a very pretty sound and said as much. 'I'll teach you the words,' Maneka offered shyly. 'Only please don't give the Yuveraj anything more to eat. His father's afraid he'll get as fat as he was as a child. All the children get too much to eat in the *zenana*. They're dreadfully spoilt!'

Fanny laughed, taking the young man's plate away from him and handing it over to his mother. 'Do you want to hear about the horses I rode as a child?' she asked him, hoping to distract him from the sweetmeats he had collected with such diligence.

He nodded eagerly. 'Then I'll tell you about my elephants!'

Fanny duly embarked on a long tale of riding to hounds.

It was more difficult than she had supposed, for her command of the language still wasn't as fluent as she could have wished. She tried to describe to him the greenness of Ireland, the 'soft' days when it hadn't actually rained but the ground had been as damp as if it had, and the many hedges, greener still than the fields they surrounded. How different was the land of her birth from the desert kingdom where she was now!

When she paused, wondering how best to describe the glorious feeling of freedom she had always experienced on the back of a horse, she found she had quite an audience.

'You mean you rode beside strange men, with your face bare for them all to see?' a woman marvelled. 'Weren't you afraid?'

'I never covered my face before I came here,' Fanny explained. 'It's not the custom in Europe. And when I rode, there always had to be some man in attendance to look after me. If my brother would take me, I'd go with him, otherwise a groom would always come with me, to see that no harm came to me.'

The women puzzled over this for a while. 'You rode completely uncovered?' they asked. 'Naked?'

'Far from it!' Fanny asked a maid to bring her paper and pencil and did a quick drawing of herself in a riding habit, followed by others of her fashionably clad for a party. The women laughed in disbelief, crowing over the drawings with increasing merriment. 'We would never wear clothes like that!' they exclaimed.

'No,' Fanny agreed. 'I was always hot and uncomfortable in Delhi dressed like that but in England, where it's often cold and wet, one's glad of one's long skirts and all the things that go with them.'

The Junior Rani smiled. 'Now we know why you find it so difficult to sit quietly amongst us,' she teased her. 'You want to be up and away, flying on the back of a magic horse!'

'At a mad gallop!' Fanny confirmed. Her navy eyes glinted with humour. 'Which was fine, unless one happened to fall off – '

It was thus that the Raja found them when he came into the courtyard to join in the fun. He had brought gifts for everyone: a pretty bauble for First Her Highness; some peacock feathers for Second Her Highness, which he handed her with an affectionate caress; and coloured balls for everyone else, some of them no more than toys, some of them filled with the sweets of which all the women were inordinately fond.

The children crawled all over him, giggling with delight as he lifted them up and swung them around his head. Only the Yuveraj made no move towards him, holding firmly on to the edge of Fanny's veil and leaning against her as he watched the others with wide eyes.

'Hey, Yadavendra, don't you want to play?' the Raja asked him.

The child declined with dignity. 'I am listening to a story about a horse. Fanny might have been killed if she hadn't clung on tight. You interrupted her.'

'Then I'll listen to the story too,' Sajjan promised. 'How was Fanny almost killed?'

'She jumped a wall too high for her horse. She didn't fall off exactly, but her mount strained a leg. She had to walk it all the way home and, as a punishment, her father made her nurse the horse better herself.'

'That sounds like Fanny,' his father said gravely.

'Yes, but she couldn't see why she couldn't have another horse to ride while hers was unwell. *You* would have given her another horse, wouldn't you?' His solemn expression broke into a blinding smile. 'I'll take you to see the *pikhanna*, Fanny. We have many elephants there. They're better than horses!'

Sajjan also smiled at Fanny. 'I see you've found yourself a friend. I hope you've told him you belong first to me?'

Fanny lowered her eyes. 'Everybody knows that,' she whispered.

He leaned forward and patted her lightly on the stomach. 'They will when you have my baby growing inside you.'

Fanny stiffened visibly, her composure gone. She could not get used to such frank speaking, especially in front of others and, although she hated to have him laugh at her by seeing how easy it was to shock her, she felt a rebuke was more than she dared essay except in the most general terms.

'You have enough children already!' she told him with some asperity.

He chuckled, poking his son in the ribs. 'Not until I have yours!'

Fanny was speechless, yet no one else seemed surprised he should say such a thing to her. The Junior Rani's mother chuckled a fat chuckle, rocking herself happily to and fro.

'It's good to see lots of healthy babies in the nursery,' she nodded to Fanny. 'Kattyapur has always bred fine babies, unlike some of the other States round about. Adopting an heir must always be second best. My first three were all girls and I thought my husband would beat me for sure if the fourth wasn't a boy, but all's well that ends well!' And she chuckled again, completely secure in herself and in her position in life.

It was Maneka who chimed in. 'Fanny should have many children, then she won't miss the little girl she had to leave behind!'

'You're right – as always,' Sajjan acknowledged, smiling at his Rani. He took her hand and raised it to his lips.

Fanny wished with all her heart she could be as generous

237

as was this extraordinary woman who had not only done all she could to welcome Fanny because it was her husband's wish that she should, but who had also added her own personal touch to that welcome with a dignity Fanny could only envy. Her admiration for her knew no bounds and, one day, she would find the courage to tell her so.

Chapter Thirteen

1860

Mary studied the address on the letter long and intently. The Honourable Miss Mary Bantry. She had never seen her name written before and she found it hard to believe that it was really addressed to her.

'May I open it?' she asked.

Lady Cunningham was quite as excited as the child. 'Of course. You do realize who it's from, don't you?'

'My godmother.'

That was true, of course, though Lady Cunningham could be forgiven if she didn't see the author of the letter first and foremost in that particular role. She watched Mary's attempt at pulling open the envelope, strongly tempted to help her. The child never would accept anyone's help, however, determined to do everything for herself despite her one practically useless arm and a slight drag in one foot when she was tired.

'What does it say?' Lady Cunningham prompted her.

Mary fingered the raised address on the single sheet of writing paper with something like awe. She could only barely remember Queen Victoria, but what she did remember was a tiny, laughing woman, with prominent eyes, who had been called away on some Very Important Business just when Mary had been about to make her curtsey.

'Doesn't she even have time for tea?' Mary had asked her mother.

'Sometimes,' Lady Frances had answered her. 'Don't feel

239

too sorry for her. It's my belief she rather enjoys the bustle and the excitement. It's the poor Prince Consort who likes to have everything done according to his own carefully prepared timetable.'

Mary hadn't understood what she was talking about. She had seldom understood her mother.

'Shall I read it to you?' she asked Lady Cunningham.

'If you will.'

Mary bent over the letter. 'Dearest Child,' she began. She liked the sound of that so she said it again:

Dearest Child, The news of your mother's disappearance is a great grief to me and, I suppose, we must conclude she is dead as your father does, though I find this difficult to believe as she was one of the most resourceful people I have ever met. Let her live on in your heart and in our memories. It is the duty of a Godmother to do all she may to replace the role of parent and I have, therefore, made it my business to find out how you are placed and what your future will be. I am pleased you are still with Sir Arthur and Lady Cunningham, for I have heard nothing but good reports of them. Lady Cunningham, in particular, will give you the guidance you need, and you must give her the love and duty you would to your mother, or even to me. I am told your father is considering finding a new Mama for you. I have written to him, telling him of my interest in you, and he assures me that for the time being he is willing for you to stay on with the Cunninghams in Kashmir, where the climate is much healthier for you. If there are any changes in your circumstances, you are to write and inform me of them at once. Meanwhile, I shall expect to hear from you on the occasions when it is your duty to send greetings to your Godmother. Affectionately, Victoria R.

'My word!' said Lady Cunningham. 'To think Her Majesty should have made enquiries about me! I never thought I'd live to see the day when the Queen herself should give me her approval! I shall be puffed up for days over such condescension – '

Mary's eyes filled with mischievous laughter. 'Of course she approves of you! A friend of her dear friend, Lady Frances – '

'Well, yes,' Lady Cunningham admitted. 'And I hope I've proved to be a good friend to her! It hasn't always been easy to keep a still tongue in my head when there was all that talk after she disappeared. As for your father marrying again, it's nothing short of disgraceful!'

'Why? Because you don't believe Mama is dead?'

Lady Cunningham couldn't accustom herself to Mary's bluntness of speaking. Young girls, she felt, should take their opinions from their elders, or, if they did happen to know more than they ought about something, have the grace to keep it to themselves.

'I have my reasons,' she said uncomfortably.

Mary's navy eyes, so very like her mother's, unnerved her. A child her age shouldn't have to worry about such things. She had done her best to protect her from the worst of her father's passions since Lady Frances's disappearance and right through the terrible ordeal of the Coroner's Court where she had finally been pronounced dead, despite the lack of a body to prove it. Lady Cunningham had done her very best for the child, though she feared that most of the damage had already been done before she had come on the scene. What kind of a man would cripple his own child? Over her dead body was Mary ever going to be returned to his care, no matter if he should marry again!

'I know she isn't dead,' Mary said.

'You *know*?'

'I've always known. She went away so that Papa wouldn't beat me again.'

Completely flustered, Lady Cunningham passionately wished the words unsaid. 'My dear, you must never, never say a word of this to anyone else!'

'Oh no,' Mary agreed.

'You shouldn't even have told me!' her mentor insisted.

'You already knew. She told you, didn't she?'

'*No!* I know *nothing*!' Lady Cunningham blew out her cheeks in exasperation at being forced into such a blatant untruth. 'Sometimes it's better not to know something, my dear. Far be it from me ever to wish you to learn to tell lies, but life has to go on as smoothly as possible. Your mother would have told you exactly the same! Her manners were always beyond reproach! If she asked one to do something for her, she would always leave room for a refusal. She would never have burdened me with the knowledge that she'd run away!' And may God forgive me for that, she added silently. What possibility of refusal had Lady Frances given her when she had asked her to keep an eye on Mary – even though she had been quite desperate at the time?

Mary just looked at her. 'It doesn't matter,' she said at last. 'Only, I thought you ought to know that as soon as I'm old enough, I'm going to go to her in case she needs anything.'

'You'd do far better to accept her death. She doesn't need anything where she is!'

'So you do know where she is?'

'And if I do, young lady,' her mentor responded with increasing exasperation, 'what makes you think I'm going to tell you?'

'Because you won't like it when I try to find out on my own,' Mary pointed out. Lady Cunningham wished she looked a little less like her mother. Whenever she came near either of them, it was like standing on shifting sand with the tide going out – she never knew what she was going to be dragged into next! Then Mary smiled, and she thought how dear the child had become to her.

'My love, don't go building up your hopes! Your mother may not want to be discovered – '

But Mary wasn't listening. 'I used to think she didn't like me, but she did really. She was afraid Papa would punish her by hurting me and then, when he did, she couldn't bear it and went away. She might need me though, one day, don't you think? She must be lonely on her own.'

Lady Cunningham's resolution collapsed about her like a pricked balloon. 'Oh, Mary love, it won't do! There now, don't fret! I expect you'll get it out of me one way or the other, but not until you're a great deal older than you are now! Now, if you please, we'll forget all about your dear Mama and think of other things! Imagine the Queen writing to you, Mary! Sir Arthur'll be ever so pleased for you! Why don't you go and show him your letter? You could show it to young Arthur too.'

'No,' said Mary. 'Your son doesn't like girls, and I don't like him either!'

Lady Cunningham sighed. She would have been less than human if she hadn't hoped her son and Mary might one day make a match of it. Imagine, if she were to be the mother-in-law of one of Queen Victoria's goddaughters – more, of the daughter of one of her best friends! No one would dare snub her then! Why, Her Majesty might even welcome them home herself when Sir Arthur took his well-deserved retirement and they settled in England. She might anyway, knowing them to have had charge of Mary with her personally expressed approval! The old, familiar panic rose within her that she wouldn't know how to behave if such a thing should happen to her. She longed for the comfortable reassurance her brief friendship with Lady Frances had provided. How good her advice had turned out to be! Always, Lady Frances had said, have a good reason for what you do, and then behave in the way most natural to yourself. It had worked, too, Lady Cunningham had discovered. It was all a bluff, of course, because she had little more idea of how to go on now than she had had before her chat with Lady Frances, but as nobody else knew that, she had managed to take her place in the social hierarchy with dignity, even with some success, and Sir Arthur had been over the moon with joy when he had been complimented on his wife by no less a person than the Governor-General's lady herself!

Arthur Cunningham barely knew his parents at all, having spent his formative years in England, in the charge of his grandparents. He had been sent to one of the lesser public schools, where his father had been before him and where he had wasted his time, learning only how to be a successful bully and the best way to ingratiate himself with anyone about him who had more money than he had himself.

His contempt for India was only outdone by his contempt for his parents. His mother he despised as being socially inferior; his father for his integrity and his obvious devotion to his beloved Hetty. He could barely conceal his dislike for every aspect of their chosen life and wouldn't have bothered with them at all if he hadn't thought his father to hold the key to the kind of life he really wanted for himself.

His parents, confronted by this stranger, were hoping against hope that he would eventually outgrow his superior attitude to themselves and their friends, though they were increasingly doubtful that he ever would. In the meantime they did their best to bribe him to keep his more unfortunate opinions to himself, and tried to hide their increasing dislike for their progeny from themselves and from each other.

Young Arthur had been less than pleased to find Mary

installed in his parents' home. It was well known Lord Bantry had acknowledged her as his child only with the greatest reluctance and in order to save his wife's face, though he had hated her for it – and in Arthur's opinion he had had every reason. It was his firmly held conviction that all females, by reason of their sex, were given to freakish whims and bouts of hysteria, which was why, very properly, they were allowed little say in the running of their own lives and none at all in the lives of other people. Lady Frances had been the antithesis of what he thought a woman should be. She had used the circumstances of her birth and her friendship with the Queen to deceive her husband and the arbiters of society and, worst of all, she had cozened his mother into being her accomplice.

Naturally, the first thing Arthur had done on meeting Mary was to share his disquiet with his father. Sir Arthur's reaction had been to tell his offspring to mind his own business.

'And if you say one word about this to your mother, you'll be sorry you were born!' the elder man had added briskly. 'She's fond of Mary! And so am I!'

Incensed, young Arthur had persevered in his self-appointed task. 'I suppose you know Lord Bantry isn't her father?'

'Did he tell you that?' Sir Arthur had grunted.

'I heard it in London. Father, everyone knows Lady Frances hated her husband – '

'She had good reason!'

'He was her husband! Wasn't that enough for her? If she didn't want to accompany him out here, she should have lived in retirement somewhere in the country. As it was, they're still talking about her parties, and the people she knew, and how she had a finger in every political pie! You'd have thought she'd have left all that to him, as a woman ought, instead of making him a laughing stock with her presumption! He was well rid of her when she disappeared!'

Sir Arthur had stared at his son, incredulous that they shared the same blood. 'I have no brief for a man who would cripple his own child. Mary stays with us!'

'My God,' Arthur had exclaimed, 'you're as big a fool as Mother is! It'll be the end of your career!'

Sir Arthur had twitched his moustaches, never a good sign with him. 'I prefer the Queen's patronage to Lord Bantry's!'

'What does she know about what goes on out here? I tell you, the sooner I get back to civilization, the better I'll be pleased!'

Sir Arthur had speeded him on his way back to Delhi, disappointed they had understood each other so little. No one, not even his dear wife, knew how much he had been looking forward to having his own flesh and blood beside him in his new appointment, someone with whom he could have talked over his problems as the representative of the British Raj in such a distant part of the globe. No, Mary was the one he found it easiest to talk to, young as she was. She shared his curiosity about the local customs; shared too, in her odd, childish way, his determination to keep this beautiful land in the hands of the Kashmiris who lived there.

'The British would spoil it if they lived here,' Mary had said when he had first taken her out with him, showing her the lakes and the marvels of the Himalayas, and the admixture of races who had come under his control.

'You think so?'

The girl had nodded solemnly. 'Mama would have loved it here!'

Sir Arthur had frequently chuckled over the memory. Mary never forgot her Mama.

Meanwhile, he had become quite friendly with the Maharaja of Kashmir and Jammu, who had been quick to agree with him that he was right to ban all Europeans from making their homes in his lands, or building there, as they did at vast profit to themselves in other States. He had none of Mary's gift for making friends with the local people, however. It was she who explained to him that the Kashmiri *pandits*, who formed the Hindu ruling minority, were called 'men of letters' in contrast to the Moslem peasants who were simple men and hardworking but who couldn't read or write.

It was Mary, too, who had explained to him why so many of the peasants, stripped to the waist in the summer sunshine, would display an array of scars all over their torsos.

'In the winter,' she had told him, 'a peasant wears a *kangri* under his coat, a wicker contraption lined with metal in which live coals are stored. They burn him as often as not, but he stays warmer than we do.'

Sir Arthur had wondered how she knew. 'Does Mary spend much of her time talking to the servants?' he had asked his wife.

'Eileen doesn't allow it.'

'Then it beats me where she gets her information from. Ask that child anything about these people and she always has the answer. She's the best travelling companion one could wish for!'

'She has some of her mother's charm,' Lady Cunningham had said with a sigh. Charm was a dangerous commodity to have these days. It mostly led to trouble, arousing envy and strife in the breasts of others. Lady Cunningham had seen it all before. She wanted better things for Mary, whom she was rapidly coming to look upon as her own daughter.

Mary was glad to see the young Arthur go back down to the heat of the plains. Even in his military uniform, she had thought him stupid and without imagination. She had borne his teasing over her awkward movements with a good grace, but she hadn't liked him any the better for it. Worst of all, she had found, was to be alone with him. He never touched her; indeed, he mostly ignored her, but there was something about him which reminded her of her father and brought back the nightmares she had been almost free of since coming to Kashmir.

Eileen had been glad to see the back of him as well. She had been unwilling to complain to the long-suffering Lady Cunningham about the way her son saw fit to treat the female servants of the household, but she had nevertheless taken the precaution of sleeping in Mary's room all the time he was with them. She had explained it away by telling the child some story about a snake she had discovered in her own bedroom, a lie she was sure both God and Father McGilligan would find it in their hearts to forgive her.

Only Sir Arthur had been in two minds about the departure. There was no good in repining, however, and he was determined to give his son's replacement on his staff the same warm welcome he had initially accorded his son. Mary was completely entranced by the new young man.

She met him first out on the verandah, his chair tipped dangerously backwards, his feet on the balustrade, and his hat over his eyes.

'How d'you do?' she greeted him formally, not knowing what else to say. His chair had gone crashing over, but he

248

himself had got calmly to his feet, bowing over her hand just as if she had been a grown-up young lady.

'You must be Miss Mary,' he said.

'Yes,' Mary acknowledged with approval.

'Walter Gilbert at your service, ma'am.'

In that moment Mary lost her heart to him. In the years ahead she never made any secret of her devotion to him, not even when she began to leave her girlhood behind her. It was completely obvious to everyone around her that Walter Gilbert was her hero and that no other man would ever count a row of beans with her. Uncertain at first of what he would come to mean to her, she met him again a few days later when she had gone to one of her favourite hideaways and had found him there before her.

He was staring across the valley at the high mountains, his soul almost out of his body as the silence surrounded him, lifting him up, far above the everyday concerns of his life below. The slight drag in Mary's walk brought him back to earth reluctantly.

She stood in silence beside him, apparently as oblivious of him as he would have liked to have been of her.

'Do you come here often?' he felt obliged to ask.

She nodded. 'It's one of my places.'

He grinned at her, recovering his usual good humour. 'May I share it with you?'

'If you don't tell Eileen about it.'

He watched her seat herself on the ground, pulling her feet up beneath her in the typical Indian position of contemplation. He noticed she had to move her left arm into position with her right hand. She looked a comic figure to him, small, her back ramrod straight, her legs folded beneath her and her arms folded across her chest. Her European dress had hardly been designed for such an exercise.

'Who is Eileen?'

'She was my mother's personal maid. She looks after me now.'

He was intrigued. 'And why mustn't she know about this place?'

Laughter lurked at the back of Mary's eyes. 'She doesn't approve of yoga, or rather she says Father McGilligan wouldn't approve. She thinks it a heathen practice. I tried to tell her about it once. She made the sign of the Cross about a hundred times and hushed me up as fast as she could. The *pandit* who taught me said it would help my arm and leg.'

'Does it?'

'It helps *me*,' Mary said.

There was silence between them after that. Mary shut her eyes, her face lifted to the pale sun. He noticed she was quite sunburned and wondered how long it would be before Lady Cunningham would insist she stayed indoors and behaved like a proper lady should. It would be a pity, he thought. He was impressed with the ease with which she seemed able to relax into some kind of a trance, going off into a world of her own.

'Can anyone do that?' he asked her.

It was a long time before she answered. 'Do you want to try?'

Walter Gilbert was a serious young man. He had his own way to make, a way in which he was handicapped enough without the possession of an active conscience that would never allow him to do anything he felt was not right. He wasn't at all sure that taking instructions in yoga from this child would be right, not if her governess, or whoever Eileen was, didn't approve. Perhaps he would be wrong to encourage her, much as he'd have liked to know more about this strange art.

Mary opened her eyes., 'You may be too old to begin at your age,' she said.

He was immediately determined to prove her wrong. 'What must I do?' he demanded.

'It's more what you don't do. The mind is like a tribe of monkeys up a tree, ideas jangling and warring with each other, never still. You have to empty your mind of everything. Look inward.'

He found it impossible. It was good, though, to sit in the sun, looking out across the valley to the snow-capped barrier of mountains beyond. The peace and beauty of the scene slowly stole into his soul. He wondered for the umpteenth time if he were cut out for a military career, or whether the powers that be would allow him to prosper in it. He had thought he would do better in the army, but now he wasn't so sure. Politics were his real passion. Sir Arthur had asked him only the day before why he didn't transfer into the Indian Civil Service. He hadn't dared tell him – he hadn't dared tell anyone! – that his chances of preferment in that service were even more remote. Once it was discovered that his mother's mother was a Parsee lady from Bombay, it was extremely unlikely they would even invite him into their houses! The strange thing was that he wouldn't have minded the girl beside him knowing. He was tempted to tell her, just to see what her reaction would be. She was quite the weirdest person he had ever met!

Mary snapped her attention back to the present moment. Mr Gilbert was nodding off, completely relaxed beside her. She poked him in the ribs, laughing at him for being such a bad pupil.

'I'll race you back to the house!' she dared him, and was away before he had a chance to pull himself together.

He could have overtaken her quite easily, for she was at her most awkward when she ran. Her skirts hid the worst of her limp when she was walking, but she hitched them up when she ran, not caring a rap that he could see her legs all the way up to her knees. As it was, he caught her up as she reached the gravel path that led back to the house.

'Why are you limping like that?' he asked her.

She was reluctant to talk about it. She turned away from him, hiding the hurt look on her face. 'It's none of your business!' she shouted at him.

It was the first time he had seen her lose her temper and he was startled by the ferocity of her anger.

'I thought you might have hurt yourself just now,' he tried to explain.

'Well, I didn't, and it's none of your business! Goodbye, Mr Gilbert.'

'Goodbye, Miss Mary.'

In the next couple of weeks he tried not to think of the child at all. He was helped in this by being kept busy with trying to explain to Delhi and Calcutta why the Maharaja wouldn't allow any Europeans into Jammu without a government permit. It wasn't enough to explain its beauty, or that it was a valued centre of the Indian arts, the Pahari painters being renowned for their dexterity and matchless colour; that would only have encouraged the British to turn it into another 'Hill Station', building houses for themselves everywhere, so that they and their families could take refuge from the merciless summer heat down below.

Instead, he had concentrated on the difficulties in getting to the place. Whole families could get lost in these valleys and would never be heard of again. In the interests of their own safety, the Maharaja was insisting it was better if they stayed away.

Sir Arthur approved this plan of campaign with remark-able ease, his mind obviously on other things. His moustaches twitched madly as he considered the papers in front of him.

'That man's getting married!' he said at last.

Walter Gilbert waited. He hoped it was the Maharaja. He would have liked to have attended an Indian wedding of some importance before his tour of duty up here came to an end.

'Mary's father!' Sir Arthur barked at him. 'Lord Bantry. Good God, the poor bride must be desperate to consider tying herself up to that man! None of our business, of course, though I don't mind telling you that Lady Cunningham thinks someone should warn the poor girl's family!'

Walter Gilbert had a very favourable opinion of Lady Cunningham, though he thought her too kind-hearted to make a good political adviser to her husband. Devoted to her as he was, Sir Arthur put too high a value on her assessment of the people he had to deal with. Not that the old girl was anybody's fool!

'Lord Bantry,' Walter repeated. 'I didn't realize Bantry is Mary's father.'

'Unsavoury story, the whole business. He beat Mary, leaving her crippled as she is now. Her mother, Lady Frances, disappeared the next day. That's how we come to have Mary with us – my wife was friendly with Lady Frances, don't you know? Well, she was there when the Indian doctor was sent for, so she knew more than most. They couldn't send for an English doctor, not if they wanted to keep the whole business hushed up, so they sent for this Raja's *hakim*.'

'Which Raja?'

'Kattyapur.'

Walter Gilbert frowned, turning the story over in his

mind. 'Why did Bantry beat up his daughter? Seems an odd thing to do.'

'Queer fellow! He wants an heir, naturally enough, but Lady Frances wasn't willing. Lady Cunningham said he beat Mary to make her mother change her mind. Fond of the child and all that!'

'I thought Lady Frances was killed by dacoits?' Gilbert remembered suddenly.

'She was, my dear fellow, she was! She was declared dead at that inquest they held! The fellow still has no right to start all over again with some other poor female! Can't expect Mary to be there, can he? Not while she's still in mourning for her Mama? Don't want her upset again. Don't want her having nightmares again either! She had one when my boy was up here. I think Arthur reminded her in some way of Lord Bantry. I don't mind telling you that boy is a bitter disappointment to me! Anyway, Mary will never hear a word against her mother and all Arthur's talk of how badly done by her father had been set her off again. My wife had a terrible time with her before we came away from Delhi, what with all the ladies trying to pump her for information, and Hetty worrying all the time as to whether she was doing the right thing. I was glad when we came away!'

'Mary seems happy enough now,' Walter offered.

'She's a good little thing,' Sir Arthur said gloomily. 'Didn't deserve to be dealt a hand like that! Got devilish fond of her since she's been living with us, she's never any trouble. Can't help wondering what her future will be though.'

'Isn't she a bit young to be worrying about that?'

'Never too early!' Sir Arthur thought of something else and his face cleared as if by magic. 'Her mother left her a fine legacy though, by George! Queen Victoria is the

254

child's godmother and she takes a personal interest in her, too. Her father won't dare harm her again if he thinks Her Majesty might get to hear of it! Mary had a letter from her just the other day, written in her own hand, and beginning "Dearest Child". She couldn't ask for more than that, could she?'

'No, sir,' Walter agreed hastily.

He was glad, though, that he didn't have to make the decision as to whether Mary should attend her father's wedding. When his own invitation arrived he made sure he was visiting the Dewan of the Maharaja, the leading adviser of the Prince, a man so subtle and mysterious in his thinking that Walter was convinced he was running rings round them all. He was courtesy itself towards the British resident, even towards Walter himself, but he would never answer a question directly, preferring to speak in riddles, elaborating with endless quotations from the old myths of India, deliberately confusing his listeners.

Tonight, the Dewan had asked Walter if it was possible to have sunlight without shadows, as the British seemed to think. Can you have Parvati the beautiful, without her other identity of Durga the terrible? Walter had known Parvati to be the god Síva's consort, but otherwise he had never heard of her. What had the fellow been talking about?

The riddle was still in his mind when he came across Mary all alone on the verandah in the moonlight.

'I'll never understand Indians!' he exclaimed. He went on to tell her what the Dewan had said. 'Does that make sense to you?'

'Oh yes,' Mary said. 'If you don't know sorrow, you can't recognize joy, or appreciate life if there wasn't any death.'

Walter Gilbert stared at her, resenting the ease with

which she had grasped such a difficult, abstract piece of thinking.

'Who taught you that?'

Mary shrugged. 'I don't know.'

'Because if you've been talking to the servants again – '

'I talk to everybody,' she claimed.

'Well, you shouldn't! You ought to be learning other things – '

'What other things?'

'The sort of thing young ladies of quality do learn! Even if you don't attend your father's wedding, you ought to remember you are his daughter, a member of the British aristocracy!'

Mary shook her head. 'You wouldn't think that if you knew him,' she said. Her eyes swept up to his face and she smiled very slowly at him. 'I wouldn't be seen dead at his wedding – nor alive either!'

He found himself shocked by her attitude and spoke more sharply than he meant to. 'And what does Lady Cunningham say to that?'

'Oh, she doesn't approve of the marriage either!' Mary said blandly. 'My father is a bad man,' she added carefully. 'A very bad man! She doesn't like him any more than I do.'

'But he's your father!' Walter Gilbert protested.

'I hate him!' Mary said simply. 'I try not to, but I always have!'

Chapter Fourteen

The whole of Kattyapur throbbed with excitement. For days now the visiting princelings from round about had been arriving, their retinues like exotic, moving flower-beds, stretching out as far as the eye could see. Brahmins chanted from the Vedic psalms without ceasing; astrologers drew up their complicated charts and argued endlessly; and Sajjan, the centre of all this activity, began to prepare himself for the return of the white stallion with endless rituals and an ascetic routine that precluded him from ever seeing Fanny.

Nor were things any calmer in the *zenana*. Non-stop visitors left the ladies exhausted and tearful from the petty quarrels that resulted, a feature of life that was usually nipped in the bud by the ever-vigilant Second Her Highness, who could tell harrowing tales of the palace coups that had been brought about by politically minded women who often worked to further the aims of their home State rather than the one into which they had married and had been made miserable by the circumstances in which they found themselves. But the Junior Rani hadn't been herself these last few days. She had dragged herself about, her face an unattractive putty colour and with dark circles under her eyes.

'It's the heat,' she had told Fanny in weary tones.

'Is that all?' Fanny had soon made it her business to discover that there was no one who took the least interest in the Junior Rani's health or happiness, while taking it for granted that she was always there to listen to their complaints and to smooth their way for them.

The Junior Rani had managed a tired smile. 'No, it isn't all, but you needn't imagine I'm going to tell you all about it. You still show me no respect, bursting in here and demanding answers to questions you have no right to ask –'

'Who does have the right?'

'His Highness. First Her Highness –'

'Much use that is!' Fanny fumed. 'I've a good mind to send a message to your mother!'

A chuckle answered her. 'You're impertinent! I'm a grown woman, Fanny!'

'So am I, but you don't scruple to tell me what to do!'

Second Her Highness would have liked to deny it. 'You're my responsibility,' she replied at last. 'I'm not yours.'

'Well, I'm making you mine. His Highness is too busy getting ready for that poor, wretched animal to come near us. All right, all right, I'm not saying he *neglects* us, but he does have other things on his mind at the moment and these fools we live amongst aren't slow to take advantage. Now tell me, what's the matter?'

'I had a miscarriage,' Maneka confessed. 'I've felt tired ever since.'

The world whirled about Fanny's ears. *Sajjan's baby!* She thought she had come to terms with her jealousy. It was clear to her now she had not and it was tearing her apart.

'A miscarriage?'

Second Her Highness looked concerned. 'It happens, Fanny. It wasn't the right time for its spirit to be reborn. Don't be too sad!' A wise look came into her eyes. 'I shouldn't have told you!' she sighed. 'It'd be different if you had your own children. You should have been expecting long since! But there, I'm always forgetting you're not really one of us.'

Fanny recovered herself with difficulty. It was like Maneka that she should offer her the cover of being upset over the death of a child, but they both knew better. Nothing could reconcile her to the fact that Sajjan should summon another woman to his bed besides herself! She pinned a jaunty smile to her lips.

'Never mind about me, it's *you* we have to worry about now. There's no chance of any change in my circumstances until they've finished murdering that horse of Sajjan's!' she added gloomily.

Truly shocked, Second Her Highness turned reproachful eyes on her. 'I do beg of you to be more careful, Fanny! Already my maid is saying that it's because of you that I had a miscarriage. Neither His Highness nor I can protect you from the wagging tongues of those who resent your presence here if you make no effort to help yourself!'

Fanny saw that she had offended badly. 'I'm sorry,' she said.

'You're as annoying as a small child! I can't think why I put up with you!'

'Nor can I,' Fanny agreed gently. She wondered if she would ever be as nice a person as the Junior Rani of Kattyapur. She wouldn't, of course, but how she wished she had at least made more effort to guard her tongue to please her. 'You wouldn't have anything to do with me if His Highness hadn't asked you to, would you?'

Maneka laughed. 'Oh yes,' she assured her. 'I'm like the Yuveraj! I like to listen to your funny stories. I've always been glad you came to live here.'

Humbled, Fanny vowed to do better in the future. It took all her tact to persuade the Junior Rani to have more vegetables in her diet, more of everything that would provide the iron she so plainly lacked. She longed to set about her, ordering up this and that, as she would have done in England, but here, anything to do with food was kept severely away from her except where the children were concerned. She was in no doubt that her very presence could contaminate the food on the plate, with evil resulting if so much as her shadow were to fall on the dish.

'No more fasting! No more picking at your food!' Fanny threatened the Junior Rani. 'Leave it to the holy men for a change!'

Second Her Highness looked down her nose. 'What would you know about pleasing the gods? We must all play our part in helping His Highness to vanquish his enemies and acquire more lands.'

'Not if it means I have to live with a pack of quarrelling women!' Fanny told her severely. 'I have an interest in getting you back to normal as fast as possible!'

Second Her Highness shook her head at her. 'You'd do better to help him with your prayers,' she said primly, and she quoted from the Bhagavad Gita, the most popular book of the Hindu scriptures: ' "If any worshipper do reverence to any god whatever, I make his faith firm, and in that faith he reverences his gods, And gains his desires, for it is I who bestows them." It worries me you have no respect for such things.'

'You fast more than enough for both of us!' Fanny responded blithely. 'If you don't eat properly until you're quite well again, I'll find some way of getting His Highness to make you take care! And don't think I can't do it! The fact is that neither he nor I can do without you!'

The Junior Rani coloured up like a young girl. 'You do me too much honour,' she murmured.

'On the contrary, I don't do you nearly enough!' Fanny retorted. 'I know you to be a better person than I – '

'No, no. I may be an older soul, but we each have our own destiny to fulfil. I'm glad we can be friends, Fanny. His Highness hopes for that, I know.'

'I'm glad, too,' said Fanny.

There were many times when Fanny was to be glad of that friendship. If Maneka told her to wear a special colour, or made a face at her choice of jewellery, Fanny would always go and change, knowing she was fortunate to receive such gentle and considered advice from such a source. She soon learned that just as Rajput brides always wore saffron or red, those being the colours of the sacred flames of the fire around which they would follow their husbands in the marriage ceremony, so were other colours deemed appropriate to other festivals. At Diwali, all the ladies would dress in dark blue; at another time, everyone would appear in green; and Fanny, who did her best to conform and to draw as little unfavourable attention to herself as possible, would follow suit, making the graceful Junior Rani her model as to how she should behave on every public occasion.

Apart from her children, Maneka's great interest was in fostering the local arts and crafts. Often the reception courtyard of the *zenana* would be filled with samples of the embroidery and clever designs of the local women, or with samples of the miniatures that were painted at the school she had personally brought into being within the city of Kattyapur. When it came to such things, Second Her Highness's patronage was sought far and wide, her deep knowledge of the subject being respected by all and sundry. All manner of aspiring artists would visit her, never actually seeing her face to face because she always remained behind screens, but the discussions on their work would be fast and furious, the sound of her laughter ringing out if she scored a valid point and persuaded someone to her own point of view. Fanny was interested to notice that Sajjan did everything he could to encourage her in all this activity and concluded that she, too, would be given similar freedoms if she ever discovered anything of a comparable nature that she wanted to do. In some ways, she discovered, the women in the *zenana* were far freer to pursue their avocations than their counterparts were in Europe. Sajjan seemed infinitely more generous towards the women in his life when they sought his approval for their works.

In some ways, but not in all. It annoyed her intensely that when he deigned to visit the *zenana* to play the board games that were popular with them all, the other women would invariably allow him to win, congratulating him on his brilliance of play with every appearance of sincerity. Fanny, who had played chess several times with Second Her Highness and been soundly beaten for her pains, poured scorn on the Raja for accepting his victories so easily. She was amused that he should be hurt by her teasing, and wished she had left well alone when he chided Maneka for cheating to please him.

'It's sad how everyone indulges you! Why don't you take your losses like a man?' Fanny had said with disapproval.

'But, Fanny,' a tearful Maneka had remonstrated with her, 'I much prefer it when His Highness enjoys his games with me. He doesn't like to lose!'

'What about you?' Fanny had insisted. 'Don't you like to win sometimes?'

'I prefer to lose to His Highness!' Maneka had maintained stubbornly.

'You see,' said Sajjan, glad to have everything back to normal, 'we're all quite happy as we are!'

Fanny, however, never allowed him, or anyone else, to beat her if she could help it. She had a quite unfeminine

262

urge to excel at whatever she should turn her hand to. On the rare occasions she managed to achieve victory over either of the other two, she would gloat over it for days.

'Why does it matter to you so much?' Maneka asked her once, amused. 'You and His Highness can't both win, and you both get so angry when you lose to the other!'

Fanny had laughed. 'But when we win, it puts us in a good temper for days together! The only difference between us,' she had added with a frown, 'is that I like to win fair and square!'

Maneka was unimpressed. 'You should enjoy His Highness's victories more than your own.'

It was at times like those that Fanny felt the overwhelming cultural divide between them. And yet – and yet, she was constantly teased by the memory of friends of hers in London getting their own way only by pretending to lose to their husbands. She had thought then, as she thought now, that it was the men who had come off worse in these exchanges by allowing themselves to be patronized by those they were convinced were less able than themselves. When she had tried to say as much to Sajjan and Maneka, however, neither of them had understood why such a little thing should worry her.

That had all been before they had known the sacred stallion was on his way home to Kattyapur. Now, all such entertainments had ceased. There was nothing but muddle and huddled forms of people praying in every corner of the palace. Fanny would have been bored out of her mind if it hadn't been for her concern for the Junior Rani who, at last, was beginning to look more like her usual self.

'When will all this fuss be over?' Fanny asked her when she returned to her usual duties.

'Soon. Has it been so terrible?'

'Without you to tell everyone how to go on, it's been a madhouse!' Fanny told her.

Maneka immediately looked worried. 'I hope First Her Highness hasn't been upset by anyone. She hates being ignored. She's the Senior Rani – '

'Nobody ignored her,' Fanny assured her. 'We're much too frightened of your disapproval not to see she's treated as she should be. She's rather enjoyed all the fuss, though there was one day when she didn't leave her room. Her maid told me she was having one of her fits, but I may have misunderstood her?'

'No, she is given to fits.' The Junior Rani laughed suddenly. 'Since when were you afraid of my displeasure, or of anyone, Fanny?'

'I was once.'

'But never of anyone here.' Maneka drew a small packet from behind her back. 'I have a small gift for you, to thank you. No, no, don't say anything. You may not like it, but it is a fine example of our Rajput art. I chose it specially for you.'

Fanny unwrapped the piece of ivory, on which had been painted a noblewoman having her toenails painted by her maid. It was a pretty domestic scene, similar to the ones she saw every day in her new home. Probably it was the most valuable gift she had ever received, but it was the thought behind it that made the tears sting at the back of her eyes. Impulsively, she flung her arms around the dainty woman, kissing her warmly on the cheek, all thoughts of etiquette forgotten.

'You're a darling! May I show it to Sajjan?'

'His Highness,' Second Her Highness corrected her automatically.

'May I show it to him?'

'Of course.'

'It's the most beautiful thing I've ever been given! I've never seen anything like it. Our paintings are quite different in Europe.'

Maneka's enthusiasm flared into life. 'Like the portrait of the old Raja? Painted in oils on canvas. It makes his face look dirty on one side where it's supposed to be in shadow.'

There were no shadows on the small miniature, only a series of bright, clear colours, outlined in fine lines of black ink. If it lacked something in perspective, it more than made up for it in detail.

It had been days since Fanny had seen anything of Sajjan. She was overjoyed, therefore, when she received a message from him inviting her to accompany him outside the Fort to see the special enclosure that was being built to receive the sacred stallion.

'It has to be completed today,' he told her. 'The astrologers have finally agreed that tomorrow is the most propitious day for the ceremony.' His lips twisted into a wry smile. 'You still don't approve, do you?'

'Does it matter what I think?' she challenged him.

He shrugged. 'It's too late to change our fate.' He smiled again, seeking to bring her round. 'The British are far away, Fanny. They won't care what we do here, not for a while yet.'

'You think not? They'll have lists made of everyone who attends tomorrow. They probably know better than you do what is going on here. The British aren't fools! The best we can hope for is that they don't see you as a danger to their own plans for the unification of India.'

Sajjan's sulky look told her that he agreed with her, but didn't want to admit it. 'It's true enough that they have their spies everywhere – even among my own people.' He shrugged off his concern. 'When we come back to the Fort,

I have something to show you.' He gave her a sidelong glance, full of amusement. 'It'll make up for all the neglect you've suffered recently. How have you managed to keep yourself occupied?'

'Second Her Highness had a miscarriage.'

The pain on his face reminded her that he had been the father of the lost child. 'I know,' he said at last.

'You never came to see her.'

'I couldn't. She, at least, will understand that. You were kind to her, Fanny?'

'I was hurt by it too,' she said.

He nodded, accepting that that was so. 'Will you never be content with what you have?' he asked her.

'I try to be. At least she and I are friends. Second Her Highness gave me a present of a miniature painted on ivory. I brought it with me to show you.'

He whistled under his breath when he saw it. 'You're fortunate!' He handed it back to her. 'I am pleased you're friends.'

They continued down the corridors in silence for a while, Fanny enjoying her moment of freedom. She frowned when she saw the palanquin he had had brought round to the entrance. She would have liked to have ridden out beside him, to walk and run in the sunlight with him. She found it very hard to be confined morning, evening, noon, and night.

'After the ceremonies tomorrow, my advisers and I are going to meet and decide how best we can knit the new lands into the present State. It'll be a difficult meeting at best, with everyone resenting each other, and me especially. There's a small room, screened off the main chamber, where I want you to sit and listen to all that's said.' He frowned fiercely at her. 'Woe betide you if you say a single word, or otherwise betray your presence there! Afterwards, you can give me your impressions.'

'Yes, Your Highness.'

He turned away, satisfied she would obey him. 'Shall we go?'

But still Fanny lingered. 'What makes you think these other rulers will meekly submit to you just because the sacred stallion crossed their lands?' she asked. 'Won't any of them stand up and fight for what is theirs?'

'Custom and religion say they must submit.' He heaved a deep sigh. 'That's what the British never understand. Our own ways mean much to us and they work when they're allowed to! These petty rulers were so many tyrants, using their people as slaves and worse! It is right to bring them to order, and what better way is there than this, when the will of the gods is made known to the highest and the least in the land, that they must submit their methods to my judgement? One fights other men, but it's a brave man who fights the gods as well. As Raja, the welfare of my people is my destiny – otherwise the contract between us is broken. The sacred stallion is only making manifest what has already happened between these men and their peoples. What I want the British to know is that I have reason, custom and religion all on my side. I am not a land-hungry felon, trying to snatch what isn't mine!'

Fanny had her own doubts that the British would understand that. Experience had taught her that her own people saw their presence in India as a civilizing mission, bringing law and order to a benighted people whose own customs were unsavoury to say the least. They would move slowly, however, informing themselves of everything that was going on all over the land, even to those furthest corners where their writ didn't yet run. She had no doubt there would be someone already here in Kattyapur, carrying tales back to his British masters.

'It will be at the durbar that the British will plant their spy,' she said with sudden certainty. 'It would be the best place to judge the mood of both peoples and rulers – and your intentions!' She eyed him thoughtfully. 'Sajjan, I think you should tell your people who I am – '

'You're my woman!' he interrupted her roughly.

'I was also the Lady Frances Bantry, confidante of the Queen of England. Tell them that. If the right people were to know I'm here, the British will think twice before they do anything to bring you down.'

He didn't like to tell her that she had been declared dead by the British in their Coroner's Court on the evidence he had arranged for them to find. 'Are women so important to the British?' he asked instead.

Not in her experience! Something in his expression told her he was hiding something from her and it wasn't difficult to guess what it was. So Edwin had had her declared dead already, had he? She wasn't surprised.

'It's nothing to do with me as a person,' she said aloud. 'They couldn't care less about me, or what's happened to me! No, it isn't me who worries them, it's the Queen. They know how close we were, though heaven knows, she'd be shocked into a fit if she were to see me now! What they can't be quite certain of, however, is that I may take it into my head to write to her and tell her why I ran off to Kattyapur. Poor soul, as if I'd do anything to cut up her comfort so! She already takes a great interest in India and likes to hear every detail about her new domains. And she's a great one for Causes, bless her! No, you can take it from me, they want her to hear only good things from India. Besides, she was fond of me and she's a very loyal friend. If she ever decides to make it her business to find out why I left Delhi and came to Kattyapur, there are a lot of people who would come out of it badly.'

Sajjan didn't answer at first. He helped her into the palanquin, drawing the curtains tightly shut with his own hands.

Then he said, 'Some of my nobles have never heard of Queen Victoria.'

Fanny opened the curtains a crack. 'I know.'

Sajjan shook his head. 'You frighten me. In Delhi, I wondered how the British meant to impose themselves on us who are so many when they are so few. They dress up in their unsuitable clothes, and march up and down, and seem content if we do the same – '

'I know!' Fanny agreed. 'They strut about like peacocks! Don't underrate the British though, Sajjan. They've been in India for a long time now, slowly increasing their possessions. If you make them think you're their enemy, we'll have a disaster on our hands.'

He pursed up his lips. 'A *jauhar*?'

She shivered, thinking of the women who were now her friends who would be the first to don their best clothes and go singing to their deaths, to be followed the next day by the men, determined to die honourably on the battle-field. Her mouth closed with determination.

'I won't allow it!'

'You won't?' He sighed heavily. 'Nor will I!' He pulled the curtains shut again and signalled to her bearers to lift the palanquin on to their shoulders. 'Let's do our best to enjoy ourselves while we still may!'

Fanny was more interested than she had thought she would be to see the enclosure that had been built to receive the sacred stallion. It was built of twenty-one octagonal pillars, covered with golden plates and hung about with magnificent materials and garlands. It was hard to believe the macabre ceremony that would be enacted there, harder still to think that those rulers who had lost their lands to Sajjan would be awed by it into submitting to his sovereignty. The Rajputs were a proud people, who valued their independence. No matter how lightly he held the reins, she could imagine any number of rebellions brewing beneath the calm surface. He was going to have his hands full bringing them all to heel.

'I'll have religion and custom on my side,' he reminded her, reading her mind as easily as if she had spoken her thoughts aloud.

'You do want to be a Maharaja!' she teased him.

'The title isn't important to me. My people will give it to me when they think I deserve it. Many of these smaller landowners are tyrants to their people and unpopular because of it. They execute both men and women on a whim and take their children into slavery. That's their business. But when they raid my lands and do the same to my people, then it becomes my business. Will the British take that into consideration? Will they know of it?'

'They will if you tell them why you're acting against the landowners.'

He turned towards her, grasping her by the upper arm. 'Fanny, why are you so sure they know all that goes on inside the inner courts of my palace? Are you one of their spies?'

'I'm sure, my dear man, because I've heard them talking in the drawing-rooms of Delhi. You forget that there we women mix freely with the men and, although they may think they never discuss anything of importance in front of us, there's not a woman there who can't find out what's going on if she's interested. Besides, their husbands confide in them when they're alone, if they're on speaking terms at all. And then there is the servants' gossip. If one pays heed to all their chatter, one can soon find out what's going on in every household of importance in Delhi!'

He jerked his head sideways and upwards in the characteristic gesture of his people. 'Are you sure you're not the British spy in my court? Would they dare to send a woman?'

'No to both questions.' Her smile mocked him. 'You taught me where my allegiance lies on a certain night not far from Delhi. Have you forgotten so soon?'

He smiled briefly. 'Maneka says you have no religion to keep you to your vows!' he fretted.

'I have my love for you.'

'And your jealousy for my Junior Rani. It's well known that many wives will further the interests of their father's State before those of their husband's. It's been the downfall of many a princely family.'

Fanny wondered what she could say to convince him. 'Sajjan, it isn't true I have no religion. I thought Maneka understood that. Besides, I don't exist any longer for my people and even if I did, I much prefer being with you!'

'And you're impertinent with it!' He smiled, satisfied with her answers. 'How often must I tell you not to call me Sajjan? Do you ever hear Second Her Highness taking such liberties?'

'She wouldn't dare!' Fanny smiled back. 'But I have your promise that you'll never do anything to hurt me. You see how much I trust you? More, it seems, than you trust me,' she added dryly.

'I'm trusting you with the future of Kattyapur and my people.'

Startled, her amusement fell away. 'Me?'

'You think me foolish, when you have been the friend and confidante of my greatest enemy – '

'Queen Victoria is no enemy of yours!'

'Her government is.'

'I suppose so,' she conceded unhappily. 'The whole world seems to be beset by greedy men and women itching to get their fingers on somebody else's wealth. But be warned, Sajjan, the *sahib-log* aren't your only enemies. There'll always be those amongst your own people prepared to sell Kattyapur for a few pieces of silver.'

His eyes narrowed. 'Where did you learn such things?' he demanded.

'In London,' she began. Then she chuckled, her eyes full of laughter. 'It's one of the things I learned from the Holy Book of my religion,' she said loftily. 'If the Son of God can be betrayed for thirty pieces of silver, what price the rest of us? Spies are only as dangerous as you allow them to be! Find out who they are and give them the information you want them to carry back to the British. Make them work for you!' She leaned back against the cushions. 'Now, I'm tired of politics! Tell me what's going to happen here tomorrow!'

He leaned back as well, grinning at her. 'Tomorrow, I'm going to become a great man!'

She prayed that it would be so, and that all his dreams would come true for him.

Chapter Fifteen

Fanny watched from the seclusion of her conveyance as the Raja checked all the arrangements for the morrow. She was fiercely proud of him, knowing him to be a better man than many of those of her own people who thought it their duty to civilize him in their own image. It was going to be a hard task to keep Kattyapur free and independent for him, even without this business with the horse. Her face set in thoughtful lines. The British had the rest of India to play with; surely they could spare Kattyapur to her and Sajjan!

When he came back to her, he looked hot and tired. 'It's difficult to get anyone to think of more than one thing at a time in this heat,' he complained. 'Something is bound to go wrong tomorrow!'

'It won't be your fault if it does,' she comforted him.

'That's not the point.' He shrugged, hoping to dismiss his worries. 'If the sacrifice isn't carried out to the last detail, it would have been better never to have started on it. If they find fault in any particular, my new subjects will be quick to excuse themselves from the rest of the contract. First Her Highness – ' He broke off, thinking better of what he had been about to say. 'Fanny, what do you say we go out into the desert and watch the sun go down. There's no finer sight in Kattyapur than the *chhatris*, the cenotaphs of our Ranis, against the setting sun.' He looked embarrassed for a moment. 'I feel very close to my mother there,' he added.

'You have Second Her Highness now,' Fanny pointed

out. It cost her dearly to remind him, but there was no denying that the Junior Rani was an asset to him.

He nodded. 'I have, haven't I? But she'll only tell me what she thinks will be pleasing to me – as my mother did my father! Maneka didn't know me as a boy who had to be led by the hand and taught to take my first steps in this life.'

Fanny was touched he should include her in his private pilgrimage. 'I never knew my mother,' she told him. 'She died when I was born.'

'Your father had no other wife? Who brought you up?'

'The servants mostly. I had a governess – and two older sisters, as well as a brother.'

'So that was where you learned to listen to servants' gossip!'

She laughed with him, her mood lightening with his. 'It's surprising what one can learn from servants and unsuspecting wives. Even in the *zenana* we hear a great deal of what is going on in the outside world. Many of the women were born far away and are often homesick for their childhood homes.' She straightened her shoulders, putting the *zenana* out of her mind for the time being. She smiled at her own pleasure in her moment of freedom. 'I thought a *chhatri* meant an umbrella?'

'It does. The cenotaphs are like delicate umbrellas of stone, raised by pillars over a plinth. They're very beautiful.'

The *chhatris* were like nothing else she had ever seen. Fanny was allowed to get out of the palanquin and walk around for a while, the bearers moving away to a discreet distance. She took her own path amongst the pretty red sandstone structures, marvelling at the way they had caught something of the grace of the women they were meant to represent. Sajjan went straight to the one which was dedicated to the memory of his mother, while Fanny deliberately went another way, leaving him alone with his memories of her. After a while, he called her over to where he was standing.

'Look, over there is the "tank", the reservoir, that was built at my mother's suggestion, so that the women wouldn't have to walk so far to fetch water. The waters of the monsoon are caught there in a small, artificial lake. You see the shrine of thanksgiving beside the *ghats* where the women do the washing and come at evening time to collect the water. We need more water in this dry land. I suppose you British would see we had it?'

'You don't need the British to do it for you,' she said. 'Why don't you build another reservoir yourself?'

'Perhaps I will – if I don't have to put all our energies into making our defences secure instead.'

The bearers had disappeared from sight, keeping well below the line of the horizon so as not to offend by glimpsing the features of their ruler's woman. From time to time, Fanny had seen one of their colourful turbans bobbing along. Sajjan had told her when they had travelled through Rajputana from Delhi that one of the reasons his people wore such bright colours was so they could be more easily found if they were to get lost in the desert. The only other creatures around were the wild peacocks – and the chattering monkeys, taking full advantage of the food that had been put out for them.

'They're not at all afraid of us, are they?' Fanny commented.

'No, monkeys know they have a special place in the hearts of men. Rama, one of the incarnations of the god Vishnu, married a woman called Sita. She was stolen away from him and carried off to Lanka. Rama got her back in the end, with the help of Hanuman, the Monkey God. The monkeys formed a bridge with their bodies and Rama crossed over the sea to the island of Ceylon to regain his consort. Sita was the first woman to become *sati* in a final act of purification because Rama thought she might have been defiled by her abductor.'

'Had she been?'

'No.'

'What a cruel story!'

'You must find your own meaning in it. We all seek an ideal in our lives. The story of your own God is cruel too.'

Fanny's first reaction was to reject such an extraordinary idea. Her second was to wonder where he had heard the story of Jesus's death on the Cross. She was constantly surprised by the width of his interests.

She put her hand in his. 'You don't need to wait for tomorrow, Sajjan, you're a great man now! How Queen Victoria would love you!'

'No, no,' he protested. 'I'm sure the Blighty Rani would never call me friend!'

They climbed slowly to the top of another hill, looking back to the Fort and the encampments of the visiting nobles gathered about it. The sky took on an orange tint and a thousand birds came flocking home to roost, swooping over the water for their last drink of the day.

A procession of women came to the *ghat* below them, as graceful and as colourful as tropical flowers, their bronze pots swaying gently as they walked, their veils floating out behind them in the light evening breeze.

'They make me wish I were beautiful!' Fanny sighed. 'Even the peacocks look dull beside them! And as for the peahens –'

'You have eyes the colour of the sky at night,' he remarked unexpectedly. 'Wasn't the Lady Frances considered beautiful in London?'

'No, she had style instead – and I was an excellent hostess.'

'And what worried you in those days?'

'What would happen when my husband came home from India. I felt only moderately safe even when there were several thousands of miles between us.'

'Do you still worry about him?'

'About what he may do to Mary, yes. I can't help it. He's a truly evil man!'

'I wish you would forget Mary. She belongs to the past.' He hesitated, then he went on, 'Were you always unhappy, married to him?'

'Always. I didn't realize at the time how unhappy I was, but it was with me every minute of every day. If something pleasant happened to me, I was grateful, but I never allowed myself to feel content, not for a moment. I was far too busy surviving. That was the most important thing in my life.'

He put his hand on her arm, fingering her bracelets. 'I was told in Delhi that everyone would try to get themselves invited to one of your parties in London. I wondered how this could be, when you were a woman living alone. I understand it better now. Even Maneka's mother found you charming. You understand and manage people very well. I am pleased you feel safe and happy in my *zenana*.'

She wondered if she were completely happy. At least she was learning the meaning of contentment. And there was always Sajjan! It still astonished her how he could reduce her to a blushing, quivering need for him merely by looking at her. Shyly, she looked up at him through her lashes, her fingers meeting his, pulling the ivory bangle out of his grasp.

'Why ivory?' she asked, to give herself something to say.

'It means your husband is brave enough to fight an

elephant – and win. Do you want to know what your other jewellery signifies?'

She smiled. 'Yes, please.' Everything in her new home seemed to have a meaning.

She was glad, too, to see that the break away from the Fort had made him less agitated and worried. She would keep him out there for as long as she could, she decided. There would be time enough for him to finish his preparations and start receiving his guests after they had seen the sunset together.

He touched her forehead with his finger, tracing backwards up the parting in her hair. 'You have a *tikka* for your forehead, worn in the parting of the hair, to warn you "to walk on the straight path". Your earrings – ' he touched the lobes of her ears – 'remind you not to listen to gossip and idle chatter.'

'They do?' Her eyes filled with laughter.

'Indeed.'

'I'm afraid I don't deserve to wear them. I'm far too fond of gossip to want to give it up!'

'All part of your insatiable curiosity about other people?'

She thought about it, her head on one side and her lips twitching into a smile. 'Maybe.'

He passed on to her neck. 'The necklace means your head should always be bowed in humility. The bangles remind you of the charity you owe the poor, and the anklets that you must put your best foot forward.'

'All that?' She wriggled her toes, amused. 'And the nose-ring?'

'Ah, that's to remind you not to spend more than your husband can afford.' He grinned at her. 'It suits you.'

'Could I spend more than you can afford?'

He captured one foot, rubbing it gently between his two hands. 'It was more to remind you not to seek more than I have to give. In some ways, the Raja of Kattyapur is the poorest man in his kingdom.'

She didn't pretend to misunderstand him. She knew he wasn't talking about money, but then she hadn't been either. 'I try not to mind,' she said. 'It helps that I like Maneka very much – '

'Second Her Highness,' he corrected her gravely.

She twisted her bangles round her wrist. 'If she were the only one – '

'She is now, sweetheart.'

She flung both arms about his neck, drawing him down on top of her. 'What about the *nautch*-girl you bedded when we camped close to your brother-in-law?'

He laughed at the memory. 'She was a figment of your imagination! I spent a very boring night playing games with a lot of stupid men. My brother-in-law is a very vain man. He has bad blood from his mother. Most of his children are as vacuous as First Her Highness. His father is dying and leaves everything to others these days. He's ready to shed this body and move on. His son, as you may have gathered, thinks he can take on the British and win. It will be a terrible time for us all when his father departs.'

'As long as you keep out of it! You will, won't you?' The urgency in her voice made him look away.

'He is my brother-in-law, Fanny, and who can read the future?'

Sajjan's kiss was hard, tempting her to respond in kind. She made a play at biting his tongue, allowing the now familiar excitement of his touch to sweep over her. She would always remember him like this, she thought, with the orange sky as background, the last of the sun picking out the jewels in his *sarpech*, the ornament he wore in his turban. His shoulder muscles were hard and smooth beneath her fingers, covered by the silk of the knee-length coat he was wearing. She breathed in the scent of him, making the most of the moment. She would have liked to have made love with him, but she knew he would never forgive himself if he broke the rules of his sacrifice just when he was bringing it to a triumphant conclusion.

'I thought we came to see the sun go down,' she reminded him.

He groaned, pulling away from her reluctantly. 'I shouldn't be here at all. We shouldn't have anything to do with each other until it's all over. I should be preparing myself for what I must do tomorrow, not dallying with a mere female who can set my blood on fire with a look! See what you do to me?'

She laughed softly. 'I'm glad I do!'

He groaned. 'Don't tempt me, Fanny!' He spread his hands, pointing to the emptiness all about them. 'There isn't even a peacock to see us!'

Fanny sat up, immediately spotting one of the strutting birds only a few yards from their feet. '*You* would know,' she said soberly. She began to laugh. 'When I think how you're always lecturing me on what's proper and what's not – ' she went on with mock severity.

His kiss cut her off. 'Enough! Enough! We must be getting back. Would that I could send for you to while away the night by my side, but there's no hope of that. I shall have to spend the night doing *puja* to the gods – you ought to be doing the same!' He stood up, pulling her up on to her feet. 'This is very important to me, Fanny.'

'And to Kattyapur,' she conceded. 'Don't worry so much, Sajjan. We'll make sure the British are told only what we want them to hear. Trust me, darling! I'm an excellent campaigner when it comes to British politics!'

'Darling,' he repeated. 'What is darling?'

Her eyes lit with laughter. 'It's an English endearment.

280

I've never used it to anyone before. Ridiculous, isn't it, that I had to wait for someone who doesn't even know what it means?'

She had thought he would laugh with her, but he was entirely serious as he answered her, 'You may call me darling. I like it. It'll shock people less than when you call me Sajjan, and that'll please Maneka also.'

Fanny took a last look round the scene of her moment of freedom, reluctant to go back to the Fort.

'Darling is much worse than Sajjan!' she murmured.

'But only you and I will know that!'

His expression changed as he turned away from her and she realized he was no longer thinking about her, or anything else but the events of the morrow. In his mind, he was already considering the ordeal that lay ahead of him, the grand sacrifice that would force these lesser rulers to bow their knee to him. She wished she were entitled to take her place by his side, could share it all with him, but as things were, there was little enough she could do. It felt as though she were being led back into prison as she followed the giant black eunuch down the corridors, and it seemed to her irritated imagination that he was fatter than ever as he waddled along in front of her.

Female patience had worn thin by the next morning, with everyone trying to get ready at the same time and all the maids tripping over each other in their anxiety to be first with everything for their own mistresses. Fanny longed for the peace of the *zenana* before they had been invaded by all these visitors, shrill in their demands and united in their dislike for herself.

It had always been a matter of wonder to Fanny that it took so long to dress and perform one's toilette even on a normal day. Today, with Ila pernickety and bad-tempered, and taking offence at the slightest thing, she was driven to desperation point. If she could accept that she was of less importance than almost anyone else there, why couldn't her maid?

She had grown used to doing without soap. Instead, there were three different oils that came in three silver bowls, one for the face, one for her body, and one for her hair. Four copper bowls were filled with four different kinds of fragrant water. There was *thali* paste, made from freshly plucked leaves, which was used to wash one's hair; powdered *gram* (chick peas) which was applied to one's body and removed with a piece of fibrous bark called *incha*. After that, one was washed all over again in a bright red substance made from boiling the bark of forty different varieties of trees. Nor was one finished then, for the oiling of one's skin had still to be done.

'Be careful you don't get the face oil on your hair,' Ila instructed Fanny. 'The saffron in it will stop your hair growing properly.' Ila thought poorly of Fanny's hair anyway, comparing it with the thick, lustrous growth of Second Her Highness, and wishing that her mistress would just this once submit to her ministrations with patience.

'Does it matter what I look like?' Fanny tried to tease her, bored by the whole process.

'It'll matter to you when His Highness's interest passes on to some other woman!' Ila sniffed.

Fanny felt cold at the thought. 'Perhaps my interest will stray first!' she retorted proudly.

Ila's only response was a renewed onslaught on the tangles that had got into Fanny's hair during the night. After a while, the maid ventured in softer tones, 'Lady, did you cause Second Her Highness to lose her baby?'

'Certainly not,' said Fanny. 'Who says I did?'

'It's known you resent her place in His Highness's life.'

Fanny knew better than to deny it. What was the point, when everyone knew all the other concubines had been sent away because of her jealousy? 'Where I come from, the men only have one wife,' she tried to explain. 'Ila, you know I couldn't do anything to harm Second Her Highness! She's the best friend I have here!'

'You come from across the Black Seas. You bring bad influences with you, whatever you do here.'

'Is that what the Brahmin priests say?'

Ila hesitated before replying. 'They don't dare! Second Her Highness insists your coming here is a good omen for Kattyapur, and the priests have nothing to say about it.'

'Second Her Highness is an old soul,' Fanny said slowly, a little uncomfortable with the concept. Ila, on the other hand, was completely at home with it.

'She is a noble lady, as you say,' she agreed.

She finished the task of teasing out Fanny's hair over the *karandi*, a pot of live coals on which handfuls of fragrant herbs had been thrown. She went on to apply yet another powdered herb along the line of Fanny's parting which was supposed to prevent her from catching colds.

'Another moment and you'll be ready,' she promised, recognizing the signs of her mistress's growing impatience with the proceedings.

'Thank goodness for that!'

Fanny stood up to take a look at herself in the glass, trying to reconcile the barbaric stranger she saw there with the Lady Frances she had been accustomed to seeing. The two images seemed to have remarkably little in common with each other.

'Fanny!'

She turned quickly at the imperious tone of voice, to behold the Yuveraj in the doorway of her bedroom, uninvited and unannounced. She made her obeisance before the rigid, small form.

'You know you shouldn't be here,' she rebuked him. 'They'll be looking for you. I must say, you look splendid!' she added, taking in the magnificence of his dress in which he looked more like a miniature version of Sajjan than ever.

He pulled at her clothes. 'Fanny, do come! Second Her Highness is in tears!'

This was unusual enough to have Fanny's whole attention. 'Second Her Highness? What on earth's happened?'

'It's First Her Highness. She won't get dressed. Please come, Fanny.'

'Your mother may not like it.'

The small frame stiffened. '*I* am telling you to go!'

Fanny gave him exactly the same mocking smile she would have given his father. 'Oh well, in that case, by all means! I hasten to obey!'

He grinned back at her. He had lost one of his front teeth since she had last seen her, giving him an endearing, gappy look.

She followed him meekly to the suite of rooms where First Her Highness was waited on by her own maids. She could already recognize Maneka's voice, for once raised in anger, uttering the most fearsome threats to the women who were supposed to be getting First Her Highness ready for the day. Behind the anger was a note of panic Fanny had never heard before. The Yuveraj was right to be anxious. Something had happened to have such an effect on the Junior Rani, something disturbing that she was afraid she wouldn't be able to deal with. Fanny's instinct was to rush to her help, happily remembering to pull her veil over her face before Maneka could accuse her of any lack of respect for the Senior Rani.

Fanny had never been invited to First Her Highness's

rooms before. They were a little larger than her own, similarly furnished except for the collection of brightly coloured baubles that were kept for the woman to play with. The Senior Rani herself was lying face down on the floor, drubbing her clenched fists on the carpet.

'I won't! I won't!' she wailed.

Maneka was standing over her, trying to pull her to her feet. 'You have to! You're the Senior Rani! His Highness will be very angry – '

'She has to do what?' Fanny asked.

The sound of her voice, cool, calm, and indifferent, had a marvellous effect on the assembled ladies. They stopped their wailing and turned to stare at her with hostile eyes, astonished she should have dared to burst in on them unasked.

Fanny turned her attention to First Her Highness. 'What's the matter with her?' she asked.

Maneka sniffed. 'First Her Highness has a leading role in today's proceedings. She won't get dressed, ready for her part.'

Fanny was nonplussed. She couldn't remember that First Her Highness had ever been expected to do anything before. Nor could she think she would be a reliable participant in anything of importance. 'Is she – well enough?' she asked delicately.

Maneka's shoulders sagged in despair. 'She was born for this! I thought she'd enjoy being the centre of things for once. *I don't want to take her place!* It would invalidate the whole sacrifice if I were to – presume to do it for her. *She's* the Senior Rani, not I!'

There was more to it than that, Fanny thought shrewdly. She had never seen Second Her Highness in such a state, her hair falling over her face and her veil coming loose from the jewelled hairpiece that should have held it in place. Fanny looked at her with real affection.

'The Yuveraj was quite right to order me to come and help First Her Highness,' she said gently, but with a firmness that instantly commanded respect.

'It's got nothing to do with you!' Maneka rebuked her wearily.

'The Yuveraj – '

'The Yuveraj may think you can walk on water, I do not! This is something you don't understand and can't help with. I'll speak to you, *and the Yuveraj*, when I'm finished here. Wait for me in the courtyard.'

'If the Senior Rani's role is so important to His Highness and to Kattyapur, naturally she's upset you might be forced to take her place. You're always telling me that she's the most important person in the *zenana*.' She sat on the floor beside the snivelling woman. 'First Your Highness, take pity on my nothingness and my ignorance, and tell me why you won't get dressed?'

Fanny had never been called upon to deal with the handicapped before, but she had dealt with hysterics and she couldn't think the Senior Rani was doing herself any good by rolling about on the floor and chewing the cushions. She bent over her, taking a firm hold on her wrists, and brought her to a sitting position, smiling kindly at her.

'Fanny, veil your face!' Maneka hissed at her.

Fanny waved a dismissive hand in her direction, her eyes never leaving First Her Highness's face. 'Now, tell me why you don't want to get dressed,' she encouraged her. 'Are you ill?'

'His Highness doesn't like me! Why should I do anything for him?'

Watching a globule of spit run down the other woman's

chin, Fanny doubted that many people could find it in their hearts to like her, but it was unfortunate that she should know it.

'You're his Senior Rani – '

'I'm not a real wife!' the woman complained. First Her Highness mostly lived apart in a world of her own. How unfortunate that she should have one of her occasional shafts of reason just now.

Fanny patted her hand. 'You're still the Senior Rani! Ever since I came here, everyone has warned me that I must always treat you with the respect that is your due. Like all of us, you must fulfil your destiny. You don't want Second Her Highness to take your place, do you?'

First Her Highness gazed about her with wild eyes. 'You're a foreigner from across the Black Seas. You understand nothing!'

'I'm looking to you to teach me,' Fanny said humbly. 'You understand what you have to do, don't you? Isn't this the day when everyone will publicly acknowledge how important the Senior Rani is to Kattyapur?'

First Her Highness stared into space, her mind clouding again. 'Want to do it!' she declared at last. '*I'm* the Senior Rani! Second Her Highness can't do it because she isn't as important as I am!'

'I'm unworthy of such an honour,' Second Her Highness chimed in with a marked lack of enthusiasm. 'Only the Senior Rani is worthy of it!'

First Her Highness clapped her hands together. 'Yes, yes, only I can do it because I'm the Senior Rani! And afterwards we'll play games together. We'll play with my new coloured balls and none of you will make jokes I don't understand!'

Her maids breathed a collective sigh of relief, starting to dress her quickly before she should change her mind. They shouldered Fanny out of the way, glad to be rid of her doubtful presence. Fanny was glad to go. The Yuveraj was waiting for her in the courtyard below.

'Is it all right now?' he asked her.

'I think so. Your mother isn't very pleased with either of us, however – '

Second Her Highness came rushing into the courtyard, swinging her son up into her arms. Her eyes were bright with unshed tears. 'You shouldn't have bothered Fanny,' she told him.

The child wriggled out of her clasp. 'Fanny wanted to help,' he informed her. 'She likes me. She likes you too!'

'Does she?' For once, Maneka looked less than sure of herself. 'Do you like us, Fanny?'

Their eyes met over the boy's head. 'I thought you knew,' Fanny said. 'You're a very remarkable woman.'

The tears brimmed over and ran down Second Her Highness's cheeks. 'First Her Highness is getting harder and harder to manage. Yesterday, she threw live coals over her maids' heads. The day before that, she upset all the oils and threatened to have them whipped for their clumsiness. It can't go on!'

'What was it all about today?' Fanny asked.

Maneka managed the ghost of a smile. 'You'll see,' she said wryly, 'if she goes through with it. I thought she'd enjoy it – all the fuss and excitement, and herself in the centre of things. I thought the poor thing was coming into her own at last!'

'Besides, you didn't want to do it,' Fanny remarked. 'Whatever *it* is?'

Maneka coloured up fiercely. 'No,' she admitted, 'but that hasn't anything to do with it! If it were my destiny, I'd do it gladly!'

At least she would do it with dignity, Fanny acknowledged, no matter how much she disliked it. Her eyes danced with sudden amusement as she took in the picture the Junior Rani presented.

'You should see yourself!' she teased. 'Next time you tell me to tidy myself, and so on, and so on, I'll remind you of today!' She lifted Maneka's headdress off her brow, readjusting it with gentle fingers and pulling her veil across her face. 'There, that looks much better!' she said.

Chapter Sixteen

Fanny had little idea of what to expect from the day's ceremonies. She had hoped Second Her Highness would find the time to explain what was going on to her, but she knew that any such idea was completely unrealistic when she saw the crowds who had gathered to see the end of the sacred horse. It was not something she really had the least ambition to witness herself. In vain did she shut her eyes and try to repeat the saying from the Bhagavad Gita Maneka had taught her; it did no good, she felt sick to her stomach at the thought of anyone slaughtering the magnificent animal that was the sacred white stallion. She tried the prayer again; 'Whatever man gives me in true devotion, fruit or water, a leaf, a flower, I will accept it, that gift is love, his heart's offering.' There was no mention in that of using an animal in sacrifice, let alone such a fine horse as this one.

She couldn't see very much of what was going on from where she sat. She had chosen the seat, a little apart from the other women, so as not to offend any of their visitors with her lack of caste. It had the other advantage of giving her a little space to herself, for it was appallingly hot in the women's pavilion where the *chik* curtains that surrounded the makeshift building kept out what little breeze there was as the crowds pressed in all round them, patient and silent in the uncanny way of Indian crowds, where even the children seldom cry.

'May I sit beside you?' a gentle voice asked her.

Fanny started, miles away in her own thoughts. She

looked up to see the Maharani of Jaiselmer settling herself on the multicoloured cushions beside her.

'I am honoured,' Fanny murmured. She pulled her veil more closely across her face, wondering if she should do anything more to greet Second Her Highness's mother. No doubt she would hear about it later if she took too many liberties.

'My dear Fanny,' the older woman said, 'I hear we're all in your debt since this morning's episode. Maneka was still upset by it all when I saw her this morning. I wonder how much longer First Her Highness will be able to live unrestrained. She seems madder every time I see her.'

Fanny chuckled. 'It was worth it to see your dignified daughter on the verge of hysterics!' she said.

'She had cause,' the Maharani defended her daughter. 'That woman has always been a thorn in her flesh!'

The two women exchanged meaningful, resigned glances, knowing they would never get Maneka to admit as much.

Fanny's amusement left her. 'I hope to God the British will understand what His Highness is doing!'

'There's little they don't hear about, one way and another,' the Maharani said bitterly. 'But why should you care when they're your own people, Fanny?'

'My allegiance belongs to the Raja of Kattyapur!' Fine words, Fanny mocked herself. She wished she was one half as single-minded as she pretended. She made a gesture with her hand. 'I just wish I understood all this better! I know you all think it's important for Kattyapur, and it must be so, but if I don't understand it, neither will the British!'

The Maharani smiled kindly at her. 'You won't ever understand it with your mind, Fanny. None of us do. We glimpse the meaning in our spirits and are enriched by it.

Which one of us can ever encompass the whole meaning of reality?'

Fanny would have been content to have understood just a small part of it, but everything, even the massed humanity outside, seemed strange and deplorable to her that day. The colour from the men's turbans and the women's dresses hurt her eyes. She should have been accustomed to the saffrons, golds, pinks and reds by now. Even the blues had a depth of colour that would have seemed unnatural back home. Nor could she condone the unkempt priests and ascetics, their hair matted and their flesh, what there was of it, barely covered by their white robes. Others, who were monks, she supposed, wore a saffron that lit their progress as they wandered through the ranks of their brethren. Watching them, she was startled to see yet another ascetic without a stitch on go striding past their pavilion. His forehead was striped with some symbolic markings, his body emaciated to the point of death. Fanny felt herself less and less in sympathy with the whole business.

'I shouldn't have come!' she muttered under her breath.

The Maharani patted her hand. 'One day you'll understand – '

'Never! Why do holy men have to be so dirty?'

The Maharani didn't understand what she was talking about. 'Fanny, dear, will you take some tea?'

Fanny shook her head automatically. Seeing the maid with a silver tray full of gleaming glasses of the beverage coming towards them, she made to move away. To her surprise, Maneka's mother stopped her.

'If anyone moves, it'll be me. But you are right to refuse. There are some here who would be deeply upset to have you use the same vessel as themselves. Maneka will see you have something later. It's too hot today to go for long without drinking. We're not like those ascetics you see outside, who can go for days without food and drink, even sleep, no matter how hot it is!'

Fanny thanked her for her kindness. There was a hush outside, followed by a ripple of anticipation. And then, suddenly, everything seemed to happen at once. No one stirred as the white stallion was ritually suffocated. Fanny, feeling slightly sick, was glad she didn't have to witness its last death throes. The heat engulfed her in a momentary spasm of acute discomfort, the sweat breaking out on her brow. She wished herself anywhere else but there.

Nothing, however, had prepared her for what was to follow. The dead horse lay on the ground, its coat gleaming in the sunshine. Fanny saw First Her Highness being led out to it and leaned forward with interest, wondering what part the woman was expected to play in the horse's death. With shocked outrage, amounting to disbelief, she saw her lie down beside the horse as if she were about to mate with it. Indeed, it was soon clear she was as excited as if she were in the throes of coupling, her cry of triumph mixing with the sonorous tones of Sajjan as he began an endless prayer over the symbolic writhings of his Senior Rani, asking that the stallion should lay his seed well in the channel of the one who had opened her thighs to him.

Fanny sat, stunned, barely aware of where she was. No wonder no one had explained the ceremony to her – they were too ashamed! She turned angry eyes on Second Her Highness.

Intercepting her look, Maneka took her mother's place beside Fanny.

'If I'd known, I'd have helped the poor woman not to dress this morning!' Fanny shot at her.

Maneka's eyes filled with tears. 'It's a great honour for her, Fanny.'

'It wasn't an honour you wanted!'

'I'm not the Senior Rani. It has to be the chief queen! You helped this morning and you saw that First Her Highness wanted to do it in the end. It's part of the ceremony. She had to do it if His Highness is to succeed in his plans for Kattyapur.'

Fanny turned her back on her, lowering her veil over her face, refusing to witness any more of this so-called ceremony. Never in her life had she felt more humiliated for anyone else. Was she the only one with any sense of decency? How could Sajjan permit such a thing – more, how could he order it in the first place? She felt as though she had never known him, never shared an intimacy with the terrible, exotic creature in front of her who was finally coming to the end of his barbaric prayer.

Had she been mad to think she had ever understood him? Worse, would she go tamely to his bed again when he sent for her, knowing he was capable of something like this? Her tongue felt like a lump of wood in her mouth as she realized that she would. Too honest with herself to deny it, she began to wonder what kind of a human being she could be. She couldn't fall back on the excuse, as could everyone else present, that their religion demanded such excesses. She couldn't believe hers did anything of the kind! Her sole reason for being there was her unsanctified, outrageous love for Sajjan that had already separated her from all that had been familiar and dear to her in the past. Was that an excuse with which she could eventually come to terms?

Maneka took Fanny's hand in hers. 'Don't condemn us, Fanny. Don't condemn His Highness. He values your opinion.'

Fanny shook off the contact, uncaring whom she hurt. 'I condemn myself,' she said. 'I have no business being here.'

There was no way she could avoid First Her Highness's triumphant return to the pavilion. The woman seemed to have grown at least a foot taller, so exultant had she been made by her experience. Fanny realized she had never seen her with a straightened back before. She was always hunched up, drooling over her own secret thoughts. Now, as she crowed over Maneka for not being worthy of such a mighty destiny, she looked almost handsome.

'I'm the mother of all Kattyapur! The sacred horse and I are one! And I didn't make any mistakes! I'm not as stupid as you think! Only I could match his strength! None of you were worthy!'

The woman cackled with laughter as she said the same thing, over and over again, as if she had learned it like a parrot. Fanny suspected that she had, and she thought she knew who had taught her so well. She shuddered with renewed disgust at the whole proceedings.

'You'd better warn me what happens next?' she whispered to Second Her Highness, who was still sitting beside her, reduced to a stricken silence as she watched the Senior Rani. Fanny couldn't guess what was passing through her mind, nor did she care, so intent was she with her own disgust.

'The horse is quartered and cooked. The marrow is taken to His Highness for him to eat. He eats the "spirit" of the horse and acquires its powers, just as – just as First Her Highness was absorbed into his male potency.'

Fanny received this information in silence, unable even to pretend that she felt anything other than a vast repugnance for the madwoman, the horse, and even for Sajjan. Nor could she understand how anyone like Second Her Highness could believe that the ceremony held a power that was beyond question, nor why the petty rulers and nobles who had come to witness it would submit themselves and their lands to Sajjan because of it. She would never, never understand what drove these people!

Second Her Highness touched her gently on the arm. 'It's time to go back to the Fort. There's going to be a programme of dance and song to entertain our visitors. Do you wish to be excused, Fanny?'

'It might be better.'

Maneka's dark eyes filled with a tearful sympathy. 'Please don't upset yourself so! It's only that you don't understand – '

'No, I don't!' Fanny agreed. She was glad she didn't.

'Long, long ago, before the Rajputs lived in India, our ancestors worshipped the horse, the white horse. It's a memory with us, as old as our beginnings as a people, and we respect that. The Aryan people were a noble tribe.'

Fanny could appreciate that. She knew that they, or a people very like them, had come to England also. She remembered seeing the ancient white horse that had been carved into the hillside in Wiltshire, nobody knew by whom, and the rampant white horse had also become the badge of the County of Kent. But she was not English, she was Irish! Nobody, but nobody, had ever worshipped horses in Ireland so far as she knew. She shut her eyes, hysterical laughter rising within her. *Everybody* in Ireland worshipped the horse! Oh, not in the same way, to be sure, but there, as here, whole communities gathered together for no better reason than the pleasure they took in their horses!

'First Her Highness – '

'It's her destiny.' Maneka sought to appease her. 'A ruler doesn't only govern. He's the *ma-baap*, the mother and father of his people. In a sense he is his people. First Her Highness knows that. It was for today that she was born.'

Fanny glanced across at the unfortunate woman, who

296

was still repeating the story of her triumph to anyone who would listen. 'Do you think so?'

Second Her Highness's eyes didn't quite meet hers. 'She knows, Fanny. Inside, she knows. She knows she did a great thing for Kattyapur and her lord, her husband, today. Don't take her moment away from her – even in your own mind! She deserves your respect, as she always has, because she's achieved the purpose of her life.'

Fanny sniffed. 'Have I denied it?'

Maneka looked at her with gentle reproach. 'Haven't you? Aren't you trying to deny her the dignity of fulfilling her destiny with honour?'

'I'm not denying it!' Fanny snapped, exasperated.

She resented being put in the wrong when, for once, she had made up her mind that she was on the side of the angels. She sniffed again. If the British could put an end to extravagant rituals such as these – and *sati*, and *jauhar* – perhaps they should be welcomed with open arms?

Second Her Highness's look contradicted her, making Fanny feel as if she had failed in some way and, consequently, angrier than ever.

'You are being arrogant,' Maneka reproved her sadly. 'You think yourself better than she. You think it's nothing that she's the Senior Rani of Kattyapur. You see her only as a drooling idiot you feel sorry for. You won't admit that today she was the Senior Rani in fact, as well as in name. You don't want to give her the respect that's her due.'

Fanny was chastened into silence. There was justice in what the Junior Rani was saying, little as she wanted to admit it. First Her Highness was entitled to her moment of triumph, all the more because she knew, in her own muddled way, why it was that Sajjan had never summoned her to be his wife in fact as well as in name. She probably also knew that she could never have managed all the duties that the Junior Rani performed in her name. Today must have been the first real fulfilment she had ever known.

'I'm not as genereous as you seem to be,' Fanny conceded at last. 'If I were you, I'd resent having to take second place to an idiot all the time!' she added irritably.

'Yes, I know.' Maneka smiled, her eyes alight with mocking laughter. 'You resent me too! Why can't you learn to be content with what you have? Don't British husbands ever enjoy themselves with other women?'

'Frequently,' Fanny acknowledged dryly. 'I'm not in love with them, however.'

Even as she spoke, though, she knew that Maneka would have no conception of what she was talking about. She had no notion of the possessive side of loving another person, of wanting exclusive rights that were denied to all others, the rights of an acknowledged ownership. Did Maneka never think of the nights Fanny spent with Sajjan as something stolen from herself?

Maneka squeezed her hand. 'He loves you too! I'm sure he must tell you so!'

Fanny didn't answer, not wanting to break down completely in public. At times she could school herself to accept Sajjan's deep affection for his Junior Rani, and his willingness to provide her with the large family she wanted, but at others she only survived at all by putting all thought of such matters firmly out of her mind. Just now, she wanted to be free of all of them, even of Sajjan, and indulge herself in a fit of homesickness to which she felt she was quite entitled!

Second Her Highness organized the journey back to the *zenana* with all her usual tact and charm. Fanny had to linger behind longer than most of the other women as few wanted to travel with her, but that held an unexpected reward in that she was able to witness the first of the elephant fights, something she had never seen before, and a display of horsemanship that had her cheering out loud when Sajjan succeeded in spearing a tent-peg as easily as if he'd been seated in an armchair. She couldn't help shaking her head at herself, after all the years she had spent acquiring a proper sophistication, that she should be reduced to an enthusiastic schoolgirl by a display of skill that would have left most of her acquaintance quite unmoved.

She was still at odds with herself when it came to her turn to move. She had never had cause to doubt her own political judgements before, but up till now the choices open to her had never been clouded by her own emotions. She had been quite clear as to what she was doing from the first moment she had arrived in London and had set about achieving her ambition of reaching the very pinnacle of a society she had been brought up to take for granted. She had known then, in a way she could only envy now, that the British way of life was superior to anything else anywhere in the world. She ought to have been equally sure of that today, but somehow she wasn't. Maneka, of the gentle ways and a wisdom that Fanny knew would never be hers, had put paid to all her certainties. She could still wonder, however, what the society she had left behind her would make of today's events. *She* might have learned to have doubts that her way was always the right one: the British had no such doubts and never would have. It wasn't a lesson that any of them had any intention of learning.

Fanny was in her own rooms when the black eunuch came to summon her into Sajjan's presence.

'Tell him I can't come just now,' she said.

The huge, mountainous man shook a pudgy finger at her. 'Your lord demands your presence. Come, lady.'

'No.'

A silent battle of wills ended with the eunuch bowing slightly and going back the way he had come. Fanny sighed with relief. She couldn't face Sajjan until she had sorted out her tangled emotions. Nothing, she felt, would ever cleanse her memory of First Her Highness writhing on the ground in the full sight of everyone there. In time, she hoped, the image would be blunted by other more pleasing ones and she would be able to take up her life again. Sajjan would have to wait.

She was not left on her own for long, however. She was trying to distract herself by studying the strange letters of her new language, determined to learn to read and write as well as did Second Her Highness. The book was taken from her grasp and a harsh hand hauled her to her feet.

'You have much to learn, Fanny, if you think you can rebel against my express wishes!'

Startled and confused by Sajjan's unexpected presence, she was overcome by the magnificence of his dress. How very splendid he was! How right she had been to think he looked like a god when she had first seen him!

'Sajjan – '

'Say nothing!' he cut her off. 'You're unworthy to have an opinion I wish to hear! You're nothing more than the dust beneath my feet!'

She swallowed, not knowing him in this mood. Pride made her straighten her back and lift her chin, defiance written large on her face.

'Make your obeisance,' he commanded quietly.

Almost she defied him – almost, but not quite. She sensed a desperation about him that was as real as her own. She stooped to place her hand on the ground where he was standing and was surprised when he held it there, a prisoner to his foot.

Then he bent also, taking her two hands in both of his, his eyes never leaving her shadowed face.

'Now, tell me what's the matter! Why do you refuse to do my bidding?'

Fanny caught a sob in the back of her throat. 'It was horrible!'

'You'd made up your mind to that long ago. No one forced you to watch.'

'If I'm to live here, I have to take part in the life here. Today, I saw you with new eyes. You're all strangers to me. I want no part of you! I don't even know what I'm doing here! I need time to think, Sajjan. I can't just go on as I did before.'

'How much time?'

She hadn't expected the question. If he had shown her any sympathy, she would have broken down and cried in earnest. She had thought that sympathy would be the method he would have chosen to undermine her hard-won resolve to be free from pressure when she made up her mind to help him, not to insist on her loyalty as if it was his by right.

'I don't know.'

'Of course you don't. You're no different from any other woman, Fanny. Men have causes, women must follow the path their lords choose for them! Must I remind you it was your choice to follow me?'

'I chose not to stay in Delhi!'

'You chose to come with me!'

'Yes,' she admitted at last, hoping he would be satisfied with that.

He threw himself down on one of the divans, looking about him with a moody expression darkening his handsome features. She longed to go to him, to throw herself into his arms, forgetting everything else, but she wouldn't allow herself to be so spineless.

'Are you missing your daughter?' he shot at her.

'Sometimes.' She stood before him, her head meekly bowed, trying to hide her seething thoughts from his observant eyes.

'There will be other children.'

'Yes, and what kind of a life will they have? Will any of them be expected to pretend to copulate with a dead horse?'

To her indignation he began to laugh. 'I'm afraid not. Your children, like yourself, will never be important enough for that!'

Fanny's lips trembled, though whether with tears or laughter she couldn't tell. 'I'll never get the picture of that poor woman out of my mind! I want no part of it! It was disgusting!'

'Only in your own mind.'

His comment shocked her quite as much as anything which had gone before. 'I don't want any child of mine to be made to witness any such scene! I'm not even sure if I want to have any of your children!'

He stood, towering above her, as assured as she was dubious. 'That is my choice, not yours. When I say come, you will come; and when I say go, you will go. You're my woman by your own choice and, as such, it's time you learned what that means. If I send for you to come to my bed, you won't refuse me a second time. Is it understood?'

She shivered. 'Would you rape me too, Sajjan?'

His glance filled with contempt. 'Is that what you truly believe? When has it ever been rape between you and me?'

Surprisingly, it was she who looked away, ashamed. 'I'm sorry.' She took a deep breath. 'I can't help it if I'm different from your other women!'

A muscle jerked in his cheek. 'What really bothers you, my love, is that you're not as different as you'd like to be! However, it wasn't to have you in my bed that I sent for you just now. I wanted to remind you of the Council tonight.'

Her eyes widened as she realized she had completely forgotten all about it. 'I'm not sure I ought to be helping you against my own people,' she said uncomfortably. 'I felt very British out there, this afternoon.'

He put a hand beneath her chin, turning her face to his. 'You may be British, but you are also my woman! I have your promise to help me.' His thumb parted her lips, sharpening the desire that flooded through her body at his touch. She could have wept with humiliation when she realized that he knew it too, reading the message that was clearly written in her eyes. 'Are you a less honourable woman than my poor Senior Rani?' he asked her deliberately.

She shut her eyes, wanting his kiss. 'Perhaps we have different ideas of honour!' she said proudly.

'What is more honourable than to serve your lord?'

She couldn't answer him. The pain in her heart brought the tears flooding into her eyes, but she refused to cry in front of him.

'I can't condone the murdering of horses!' she claimed. 'You don't deserve that I should help you!'

His kiss was hard, the kiss of a man who meant to have his own way. 'You put your life in my hands, darling. You can't complain if you find yourself overruled from time to time, when you try to escape me.'

It was his use of the word darling that did it. She flung her arms about his neck, opening her mouth to his.

'If I didn't love you as much as I do, I think I'd hate you right now!' she said.

Chapter Seventeen

First Her Highness was still holding court when the massive form of the black eunuch came once more for Fanny. Maneka, for once, was unable to contain her curiosity at this unexpected turn of events.

'His Highness is entertaining,' she said. 'What does he want with you now?'

Fanny shrugged her shoulders. She would have told her – as much as she knew – but she thought it better not in such a public place. She had been sitting in the courtyard for long enough to know of the resentment amongst many of Sajjan's new nobles at their loss of power, a grievance shared in good measure by their wives. Fanny could sympathize with their reluctance to acknowledge First Her Highness's rightful place, but their belittling of the Junior Rani aroused her anger and she was glad to see Maneka's mother move into action on her daughter's behalf. In fact she was sorry when that lady departed at a fairly early hour, professing herself to be exhausted by the comings and goings of the day.

When the eunuch came, however, Fanny's mind was on other things and it was only Maneka's gentle reminder that made her cover her face and make her obeisance to the excited woman before she withdrew in the wake of the giant black. She would have preferred everyone to have believed she was merely retiring to her own rooms to eat her lonely meal, but there was no chance of that with Sayed rolling his eyes and bellowing her name at the top of his voice. This time he didn't mean to be met by her refusal, as was obvious by the way he kept looking towards the Junior Rani for her support. Amused, Fanny followed him down the rabbits' warren of corridors to the public rooms down below.

The room behind the hall of audience was airless and dark. Fanny peered through the lattice curtain of marble that separated her from the brightly lit enclosure where the men were about to take their places. She could clearly see the *gadi*, or throne, at one end, where Sajjan would sit, and marvelled at its beauty. It appeared to be fashioned wholly of gold, with scarlet and yellow cushions. Every inch of the metal had been worked with the devices of Sajjan's family: the sun; peacocks with jewelled eyes in their tails; and a variety of swords and shields which were more difficult to distinguish from where she was sitting.

Sajjan looked very fine as he took up his position on the *gadi*, drawing his feet up under him. One by one, his advisers and nobles came in, half-drawing their swords for him to touch, before going to their allotted places. Precedence here was every bit as important as it was to the English, Fanny noted, as she saw their jealous regard for their neighbours, checking to see that nobody had taken advantage of their rank. To Fanny, who had never bothered with such things, largely because, if she were honest, she had never had to, they appeared more like quarrelling peacocks than ever, each one guarding his territory with flashing eyes and determined, jutting chin.

She enjoyed the sight, however, of Sajjan's dignified acceptance of their tribute. He might be a barbarian, but he was a magnificent barbarian! She made a conscious attempt to dismiss the events of the day from her mind. She had work to do and if she were to accomplish anything, she would have to think the way the British thought, weighing up every detail to see if it would work to their advantage, their minds uncluttered by personal concerns. This came hard, when she seemed to have been on the edge of tears all day. She had been far too emotional altogether recently – even Maneka had noticed, watching her with that thoughtful look she had when she saw a potential threat to her smooth running of the women's quarters.

Fanny was surprised to discover she could understand the speech of the men better than she could their wives, until she realized they all spoke the Rajput dialect as their mother tongue, while many of their wives came from as far away as Maratha or Bengal, chosen as a means of forming alliances halfway across the sub-continent in a forlorn hope of keeping the British out of their concerns. Such marriages were seldom a success. Betrayals were frequent, fired by the jealousies between the various wives and the fierce pride of the Rajput men who, twirling their moustaches, would launch themselves into thoughtless battles at the least provocation, presenting the British with the very opportunities they sought to deny them.

Fanny studied their faces, one by one, wondering how many of them were already in the pay of the British. Many of the newcomers had the surly expression of the vanquished. Many more didn't like Sajjan's references to 'responsible government'. While they didn't interrupt their new master, it was obvious, when their own turn came to speak, that they wanted to go on exactly as before, in their old despotic way, with little concern for the sufferings of their peoples. Hadn't they been born to work and suffer, as their lords had been born to benefit from their labour? Fanny found herself hoping that the worst of them would be reborn as a beast of burden with someone like themselves for a master, and caught herself up, aghast. Where was that glow of European superiority now that had fuelled her all through the sacrifice of the horse, even through her quarrel with Sajjan? Was it going to desert her now when she needed it most?

She turned her attention back to the endless talk, glad to find there were also some who took their responsibilities as seriously as did Sajjan, running their tiny States as if they were indeed the father and the mother of their subjects. It was this idea, she knew, that was the key to Sajjan's reason why they had to retain their independence at all costs. It was this contract between *raja* and *praja*, ruler and people, that had to be rescued from the greedy depredations of a foreign rule, which might keep the princes in place, but would destroy their reliance on their own peoples' goodwill for the privileges they enjoyed. Under the British Raj they would rule with the consent of the Paramount Power, not their own people, and would be destroyed in the end because of it.

'The British are destined to be the overlords of India, as were the Moghuls before them. We have no choice but to prove to them that we are determined to be their loyal allies, as we were to the Moslems they replace. We will go to Delhi and Calcutta and bow the knee to them, but we don't need them here, telling us what we may or may not do in our own lands!'

There was a murmur of assent to this. The East India Company had already acquired most of India for Britain, but since the government had been transferred to the Crown, who knew what further demands the Queen might make of her vassals?

Sajjan cleared his throat. To anyone who knew him he was plainly nervous, and yet he sat on the *gadi* without moving a muscle, apparently sure of his right to lead and to know that the rest would follow. The sacrifice of the horse must be powerful magic indeed to tame this band of autocrats to his will, Fanny thought wryly, but as far as she was concerned, magic it remained.

'I brought back from Delhi a British woman, one of the nobility, a friend of the one who wears the crown far away in England. She is present tonight at our deliberations, behind the lattice so as not to embarrass her. Despite being a woman, she is wise in the ways of our new masters. Even the great men amongst them have listened to her words in the past. I saw this with my own eyes. She has advised me to make my peace with the British and to assure them of my loyalty as their ally. That way, they will allow me to keep what I hold, providing I rule justly and do nothing to disturb the peace. Other States, greater than mine, were quick to prove themselves reliable friends to the British and have been rewarded accordingly.'

There was a flutter of dismay amongst his hearers. Sajjan's stillness contrasted vividly with the restlessness of his nobles. The Rajputs were a proud people, who did not relish bowing the knee to anyone. Many of them, Fanny knew, would have preferred to fight and die, rather than compromise and stay alive.

'Who is this woman?'

The speaker was a man in a green coat and turban, one of the lesser nobles, judging by his position in the hall. He had a thin, clever face and the bearing of a military man. Had he once served with the troops of the East India Company?

'The Lady Frances Bantry.'

Fanny admired the indifferent way Sajjan brought out her name. He was playing with high stakes, but he gave no sign of it. The look on the face of the man in the green turban showed that he knew it too.

'The Lady Frances was killed by dacoits. Or was it that you brought her here by force?'

For the first time Sajjan was in danger of betraying his emotions. The look of terror on Fanny's face on that memorable day could still rouse his anger against the man who had caused it.

'The Lady Frances came to me for sanctuary when her husband half-killed her little girl in a jealous rage. She was afraid for them both had she stayed a moment longer under his roof. She has chosen to make her home in my *zenana*.'

'And you trust this woman?' The man in the green turban shot a look at the darkened area behind the lattice screen. 'Women are notoriously devious,' he added disparagingly.

Sajjan waited for him to continue, a polite look of interest the only sign that he was listening.

'Lord Bantry is well known for his evil temper,' the man confirmed, as if the words were being dragged out of him. 'The woman could still be working for the British. They know no laws of hospitality, betraying their friends as easily as their foes. What makes you think it'll be you she'll serve when your objectives clash with theirs?'

Sajjan permitted himself a small smile of triumph. 'Naturally, Lady Frances chooses to remain a loyal subject of her friend, the English Queen, and also to make me what service she may in return for my protection. I have promised her that nothing will be done in Kattyapur that will conflict with the Paramount Power's interests in India. The British need have no fears that we will renege on our decision to seek an alliance with them on a mutually agreed basis.'

If the man in the green turban was satisfied with this statement, many others were not. Added to their previous resentments was the new one that the Raja of Kattyapur should submit himself to the advice of a woman, and she a foreigner from across the Black Seas at that.

'Remember the siege of Chitor!' one of them reminded him. 'Did Rawal Ratan give in to the demands of Alauddin when he lusted after the Rani Padmini? No, his twelve sons mounted the *gadi* in turn and, after three days, went forth to die as the goddess Kali demanded. That is the honourable way! To declare *jauhar*! Padmini and thirteen thousand women died! Ratan himself was the twelfth king to be sacrificed. Only his son, Alaisi, was saved. That's the way of the Rajputs! The woman will make you the toy of the British! Send her back to them before they learn of her presence here and come to rescue her!'

'You'd rather die, when we might live and prosper?' Sajjan returned dryly.

'Rather die than be taken in by the beauty of a woman!'

'The British won't lay siege to us because of Lady Frances's presence here,' Sajjan said carefully. 'It would be inconvenient to them if she were to return to life when they have thankfully declared her to be dead.'

'She is a spy come among us! What if they demand to have her back? Will you send her?'

Fanny found herself waiting for his answer with bated breath. It had never occurred to her before that he might send her back to the British one day.

'No,' Sajjan said with finality.

'You'll declare *jauhar* for the woman, but not for your honour?'

'I will never declare *jauhar*,' Sajjan bit out. 'The woman stays because it's my will she should. She is a woman like any other and must obey her lord. The only difference is that she was brought up among the *sahib-log* and knows their ways. They'll be content to have her here, a friend of their Queen's watching over their interests. If we were to fight the British, we should lose everything, lands and people, and gain nothing – '

'You call honour nothing?'

Sajjan's contempt was riveting. Fanny was glad it was not being turned on her. He looked formidable and very much in control. At that moment she would not have cared to exhaust his patience, as she had so nearly done that afternoon.

He spoke again. 'I have already declared myself a friend to the British. I cannot in honour withdraw that friendship, nor would I want to. There is no cause for *jauhar*, nor will there ever be here again. The woman advises, and I command, that we live in peace with the British, and become great men under their tutelage. That is the honourable way forward, gentlemen, and that is Kattyapur's official policy from now on.'

When everyone was gone, Fanny became more conscious than ever of the airlessness of the cubbyhole where she was seated. She hoped, anxiously, that she wasn't going to faint. She felt decidedly odd and that annoyed her. She had always prided herself on her tolerance of heat and cold and anything else that came her way. Yet today she had been tearful, nauseated, and hot and cold by turns. She hoped she hadn't caught a fever, as she had been warned would happen to her sooner or later in India.

She sat on in the darkness, deep in thought. The British would be satisfied for the time being, she was sure of that. Those whose business it was would be intrigued to discover what had happened to her, but she doubted if they would officially acknowledge that she might be still alive. That would be far too awkward for them to stomach, especially if they were also informed that she was living in Kattyapur as Sajjan's wife of affection. None of them would want her back if that was to come to light! But that wouldn't stop them from making use of her presence in Sajjan's court to keep him in line at no effort to themselves. Altogether, it was an arrangement that would satisfy both sides, she thought, if Sajjan could control his nobles and stop them from making more trouble for him than they were worth. Some of them would bow the knee to him for religious reasons, accepting the sacrifice of the horse, but it was often those who were outwardly the most devout who wouldn't be too nice in their methods of regaining their independence from him, no matter what the cost.

The door opened and she looked up, expecting to see Sayed come to take her back to the women's quarters. It was Sajjan himself, holding out his hand to her. 'Well?' he challenged her.

She looked down her nose. She was feeling more and more light-headed. 'I haven't made up my mind yet that I want to be on your side!' she told him.

The look he gave her reminded her who was the ruler there. 'We'll argue about that later,' he dismissed her complaint, ' – if we must! I've only a few moments now before I must go back to my guests. Did it go as you'd hoped, Fanny?'

He had more faith in her than she had in herself, it seemed.

'I think so,' she answered. 'Who was the man in the green turban?'

His eyes narrowed. 'A lesser noble. He comes from Jaipur originally. He's the adopted son and *kumar* of one of the chiefs here today.'

'He looks a military man.'

'You think him to be our British spy?'

She nodded. 'He knows too much about what's going on in Delhi. He even knew who I was.'

Sajjan picked on that like a cat pouncing on a mouse. '*Was*, Fanny? Past tense?'

She gave in with a long sigh. 'Was,' she repeated.

He pushed her veil back from her face, running his hand down the line of her cheek. 'You weren't sure earlier what you had become,' he reminded her.

'No, and I'm not sure now. Don't rush me, Sajjan. I'm still upset about today. I was beginning to feel at home here; now I wonder if I ever will! I'm a stranger, a foreigner from across the Black Waters. I don't understand you. Perhaps I never will!'

He, too, looked exhausted. 'We'll always understand one another, even when we wish we didn't.'

She smiled at that, caught up in memories of other moments when they had been completely at one with each other. Had she known so much happiness that she could afford to be profligate with the bounty this man had brought her?

'True, but what do you really want from me, Sajjan? Does it matter to you if I can't approve of everything you do?'

He touched her lips. 'I admire you when you think as man,' he said, 'but it's the woman I want beside me all my days. I want to hear the woman admit she's beneath the heel of the Raja of Kattyapur!'

Her smile mocked him. 'Would that really make you happy?'

'To know myself seated on the *gadi* of your heart? Yes, that would make me happy. Is it too much to ask of you?'

Her navy eyes lifted to his. 'Yesterday, I'd have said not. Today, I don't really know. I was *shocked*, Sajjan.'

'Will you get over it?'

'I don't know.'

His expression hardened. 'You belong with me now. You must accept me as I am!'

'Do you accept me as I am?' she countered.

'I put up with more from you than I would from any

other woman. If you were other than who you are, we would not be having such a conversation. Think on that, Fanny. There are things I can't change, no matter how they rub against the grain with you. You are one person, Kattyapur is many.'

Fanny sighed. 'Maneka tells me I shouldn't criticize what I don't understand. This wasn't criticism, though, this was revulsion!'

She would have liked it if he had put an end to her doubts by taking her in his arms. She wanted to be swept off her feet and taken to bed by him, so she wouldn't be able to think any more. His hand fell away from her and she knew his mind had already left her, as he was about to leave her physically.

'I must go,' he said with a frown. 'And so must you. Tell nobody anything. Politics don't stop at the door of the *zenana*. Sometimes I think they begin there as often as not. If you need to escape their questions, ask Second Her Highness to suggest you withdraw to your own rooms.'

Fanny's eyebrows rose. 'She won't want to oblige me today –'

Sajjan jerked his head. 'Haven't you realized yet what a valuable friend you have in her? Listen to her when she tells you what to do, Fanny. She understands my people as you understand yours. When it comes to the other women, Maneka can, and will, protect you, as even I can't.'

Fanny recognized the truth of that. 'I still love you,' she said tearfully.

'Then do as I tell you! Goodnight, Fanny *Bai*!'

'Goodnight, Your Highness,' she whispered back. She wished she could keep him by her side for a while longer, putting off the moment when she would have to return to the other women. What he had said about the Junior Rani reminded her of how alone and exposed she was here, though there was nothing new in that. When hadn't she been just as alone amongst her own people? More alone, because she hadn't known Sajjan then. 'Goodnight,' she said again in stronger tones.

She thought she was about to cry again. She wiped the tears from her eyes impatiently. Whatever could be the matter with her that nobody could speak to her without her wanting to burst into tears? She was given to far too much weeping these days, she told herself sternly. She couldn't remember that she had ever been such a crybaby in her life before.

Second Her Highness gave her permission for Fanny to withdraw almost immediately. It was easy to see she was still curious as to where Fanny had been and she made a point of accompanying her to the foot of the stair to her rooms.

'Is all well?' she asked in her gentle way.

'I hope so.'

'I instructed Ila to leave your food ready for you.' She caught the look of distaste on Fanny's face. 'You must eat, Fanny! You haven't eaten properly for days, only picking at this and that.' And how did she know that? Fanny wondered. The young Rani turned on her, a bright sparkle in her eyes. 'And don't tell me it's the ceremonies of today which have put you off your food, because I know better!'

Fanny managed a smile. 'The truth is that I long for a good plate of roast beef and Yorkshire pudding, with vegetables that have never seen a spice – '

'Beef?' Maneka blinked. 'Beef is *cow*!'

She looked as shocked as Fanny had felt earlier. Fanny cursed herself for her tactlessness. She should have known by now that to Maneka it was the one unforgivable sin to

315

kill and eat the cow she worshipped as the mother-symbol of all things.

'I just meant I long for some English food,' Fanny tried to explain. 'I've had a lot of fancies recently about the things I want to eat.' She noted the shadows under the other woman's eyes and thought the day couldn't have been easy for her either. 'When will you get to your own bed?' she asked.

Maneka made a face. 'Not for a long time yet. I managed to persuade First Her Highness to retire about an hour ago, so the rest of the evening should pass more pleasantly. I think all the attention has gone to her head – like the child she is!' She put a hand on Fanny's arm. 'I can say that, but I'm not going to apologize for rebuking your disparagement of her earlier. I was right, and you know it!'

Fanny saw that far from receiving an apology, one was expected from her. For a moment she didn't see why she should, but a little reflection on Maneka's many kindnesses made her more generous. She said, in the open way she had, 'Then I'll apologize instead. I won't pretend I wasn't shocked, because I was, and I don't think I was the only one to be made uncomfortable by it. However, I will concede I was also suffering from that terrible affliction of all the British: that we are always right about all things, and that it's our mission in life to convert everyone else to our point of view. I doubt I shall ever quite lose the habit, not even with you to tell me how silly I'm being, so you'll have to put up with me the way I am!'

Laughter filled Maneka's eyes. She put up a hand to cover her mouth in case Fanny should think she was laughing at her and be offended because of it. 'That's what His Highness says the British are like too,' she confided. 'He says they strut about like peacocks – '

'And the Rajputs don't?' Fanny interrupted.

Maneka laughed again. 'You're so funny, Fanny. The Rajputs are a beautiful people!'

'Even the women!' Fanny acknowledged gloomily. 'I know just how the poor peahen feels as she follows her mate and is dazzled by his magnificence! What else can I do but caw in admiration amongst all these beautiful people?'

Maneka slanted a questioning glance, unsure whether Fanny was serious or not. 'His Highness thinks you beautiful,' she hastened to assure her. 'When he first told me about you, he said you were both beautiful and clever.'

Fanny was completely disarmed. 'Oh, Maneka, I hope he didn't hurt your feelings. You weren't upset, were you?'

'I was – dismayed,' Maneka admitted. She took a step over Fanny's threshold. 'May I come in for a moment? You don't mind? You see, it wasn't because he had fallen in love with you and was bringing you back here as his favourite that I minded your coming. That I can live with! No one can take my position as the Junior Rani away from me, and I'm fortunate that His Highness has an affection for me also.' Maneka sat down beside Fanny on the divan. 'No, it was because I didn't know if you were a woman like the rest of us. You might have been another kind of being, mixing with men all the time, and running away from your husband, instead of giving your life for his. I didn't think we'd have anything to say to one another. I – I thought you'd overrule me, and laugh at me, even though I am the Junior Rani!'

Fanny stared at her, open-mouthed. 'What made you think that I could?'

'I didn't know what to expect. It was a great relief when Ila said you had the same functions as other women and that you'd been afraid when His Highness had taken you into his bed. I was afraid that first time, too.'

317

It was silly, but Fanny felt herself to be on the verge of tears again. 'He brought me here because I could be useful to him –'

'No, no, he wanted you as a man wants a woman! You could have been useful to him in Delhi! If it had only been that, he wouldn't have brought you here, upsetting us all, and making even his most loyal courtiers wonder if he weren't losing his wits! He would have kept you somewhere else and visited you there, if you weren't necessary to him to be part of his real life.'

'I could kiss you for that!' Fanny declared.

'But, Fanny, you must have known –'

Fanny shook her head. 'I only thought of it as being a great change in my own life. I never thought about it from your point of view. Forgive me, Maneka –'

'Second Your Highness,' Maneka rebuked her automatically.

Fanny clutched at her stomach. 'You'd better stay away from me,' she warned. 'I've been feeling all day as if I'm sickening for something. I don't want you to catch it too.'

Maneka was unperturbed. She gave Fanny an amused look. 'I could have told you any time this past week what's the matter with you! Don't British ladies know when they're with child?'

'Of course they do!' Fanny's indignation died away as she made a quick calculation in her mind, feeling more foolish by the moment. 'Whatever am I going to do?' she moaned.

Maneka's soft glance wrapped her in a cosy cocoon of feminine sympathy. 'Was it very bad last time? Sometimes it can be like that with a first child, especially if the midwife is a stupid person, knowing nothing of how to ease things along. This time, it'll be much better.' She smiled, patting Fanny on the arm. 'I'll be with you, and so will the wise woman who attended me at the birth of all my children. Tomorrow, or perhaps the next day, we'll consult the astrologers, and then we can make plans. His Highness will be delighted!'

Fanny bit her lip until it hurt. 'I don't want His Highness to know!'

Maneka was bewildered. 'If you don't want to tell him, I must!' she insisted, with a touch of indignation.

Fanny shook her head violently. 'I don't want to be a mother again!'

Maneka ignored that. 'I'll tell His Highness in the morning. *He* won't allow you to feel sorry for yourself for long, not with his child growing inside you! This must be a happy time for you, Fanny. You wait and see!'

But Fanny wouldn't, couldn't believe her. For a long time after the Junior Rani had left her, she sat and brooded on her memories of her last pregnancy and of the man who had changed her whole life in the space of a few minutes. Most of all she remembered her hatred for that man, some of which she had transferred on to her own child throughout her early life. Was she going to have to go through all that guilt and despair once again?

She had thought she would lie awake remembering all night long, and she could hardly believe it when Ila shook her awake the next morning, already excited by her mistress's news.

'When will the baby come?'

Fanny shrugged. Why hadn't she left the bearing of the children to Maneka? And then, even as Ila began to speak again, she felt herself blushing like a young girl and a new exaltation brought a glow of happiness to her features. This was Sajjan's baby, not Edwin's! And nobody, not even the gentle Maneka, was going to take it away from her!

Chapter Eighteen

For the next three months, Fanny lived in an aura of contentment that nothing was able to disturb, not even the knowledge that Maneka was also expecting a child of Sajjan's. She was absorbed in her own fecundity and the marvel of having a baby she wanted growing within her. It was almost as if she were incapable of worrying about anything. It was one of the happiest times she had ever known. Only Maneka dared to laugh at her new placidity.

'I'm sure your baby will be a girl,' she said once. 'She'll be as lazy and as self-indulgent as her mother!'

Fanny threw a cushion at her. 'Yours will be a warrior-king, I suppose?'

'He'll be a Rajput!'

That made Fanny thoughtful. Her child would be a Rajput too, descended from the sun, as were all Sajjan's children.

'I wish I knew what it all meant,' she said.

'It means to me "a river of beauty and love is flooding my heart With an exquisite joy" . . .'

'That's beautiful! Are you descended from the sun, Maneka?'

'The moon. Sri Krishna, the leader of the Yadus, was one of my ancestors.'

'Krishna? The incarnation of Vishnu?'

'Is that so difficult to believe?'

'No,' Fanny said. 'I'm impressed. No wonder you're such a superior person!'

'Oh, Fanny! You have no respect for anything! Aren't you proud to be your father's daughter?'

'He's a mere Earl, not a god! The two can't be compared!'

'You're not to laugh at me!' Maneka commanded her. ' I don't know why I put up with you!'

'Nor do I,' Fanny agreed, suddenly serious. 'What does it mean to be descended from the sun – or the moon?'

'It means in Jaiselmer that the Princes have as their title "the Lord of Yadava", and are protected by the divine umbrella which was given to Krishna by Yadava. The royal howdah is silver, because that's the colour of the moon, rather than the gold which most princes have. Actually, my family have ruled only in name for many years now. The Prime Minister's family hold all the power, though my father is the Maharaja. And now we have to put up with Colonel Tod as well, the British political agent. He's a good man in his way, but he'll never be one of us! We don't need the *sahib-log* to tell us what to do!'

Fanny hadn't realized the British had come so close. She wondered if Colonel Tod ever had an audience with the Maharani and, if so, whether he knew about her. It seemed likely that he would have been told something about her, if not the whole story.

'I suppose Sajjan can't claim descent from Krishna too?'

'No, he's of the Suryavansh, clans claiming descent from Rama, an incarnation of the sun. I remember my father stressing this when it was first decided I should become his Junior Rani.'

'Is that why you married him? Did you like him?'

'I'd never seen him. He was very kind. I respected him for that. I'd heard such stories from other women about what they had to put up with from their husbands, I didn't know what to expect. I was afraid. I didn't know then that

321

his mother had taught him not to despise our sex, as so many men do. He was very fond of her.'

'How old were you?' Fanny asked.

'Nearly fourteen. I had been going to be married before, but the man died. My father wasn't happy about my coming here because of First Her Highness. She and His Highness had been married as children.'

Fanny had never thought of the Junior Rani as being much younger than herself, certainly not that there were ten years between them. At thirteen, Fanny hadn't begun to think of marriage. Far from it, her life had been divided between the schoolroom and her horses. She thought about Maneka at the same age, coming to Kattyapur and taking up the reins of Sajjan's *zenana*, and wondered again if there wasn't something in this notion that some people were born older than others.

'Who looked after First Her Highness before you came?' she asked with interest.

Maneka's eyes flashed with indignation. 'No one! She had any number of her own women from Hanupur who were supposed to attend her. They claimed to be afraid of her and she can be very violent when she's unhappy, but the truth is they were far too busy seeding rebellions against His Highness to have time for her. When I first saw her, her hair hadn't been brushed for weeks; she was unwashed and her clothes hadn't been changed for more than a week. It was a disgrace!'

'Which you put an end to?'

'Even an insensible stone demands respect, and First Her Highness is far from that! She feels things very deeply. It was my duty to care for her!'

And to protect Sajjan by doing so? Fanny was thoughtful as she went back to her own rooms. All the time Maneka had been speaking she had been priding herself on the civilized nature of her own people, who never would have believed in any such nonsense as being descended from the sun or the moon, yet she doubted that many of them, herself included, would have tackled, at the age of fourteen, a whole army of strange women out of pity for First Her Highness, or seen to her needs with the same care as the Junior Rani had done ever since. No wonder Sajjan thought her a blessing from the gods!

Fanny threw herself on her bed for her afternoon nap. Daily, she vowed to herself she would spend the time studying her letters and, daily, she allowed the book to slip from her hands and drowsed the hours away instead. It was as if all her strength had gone into the only part of her that mattered for the moment, leaving her with no energy for anything else, no matter how hard she tried to concentrate.

A knock on the private door leading to Sajjan's apartments brought her to her feet. An instant later, Sajjan stood before her, his hands on his hips.

'The British are coming! What are we going to do?'

Fanny was startled out of her lethargy. 'The British are coming? *Here?*'

'They're sending a platoon of soldiers to find out what our intentions are towards the Raj.'

'Is that all?' She sank back down on to the divan. 'Surely, you're not worried about one platoon of redcoats?'

'I've never stopped worrying about the *sahib-log*!' He glared at her. 'If I'd known what being pregnant would do to your wits, Fanny, I'd have kept you out of my bed until the danger was past!'

Fanny smothered a laugh. She batted her lashes at him. 'Could you have resisted me?'

He pulled her up into his arms. 'No. I can't have enough of you! Tell me what to do!'

She spread her fingers against his embroidered coat, deliberately tempting him. 'Well,' she said slowly, 'we could take advantage of a long, hot afternoon, when nobody ever comes near – '

'If you tell me what the British intend first!' He put her away from him, eyeing her with wry amusement. 'Then we'd better go to my rooms, because I have it on the very best authority that you seldom spend your afternoons alone these days.'

'True,' she acknowledged. 'The Yuveraj honours me with his presence from time to time. Amongst other things, he's teaching me to read and write.' She put her head on one side, a little daring, for she knew he still resented the fact that she had known another lover before him – if Edwin could be termed a lover! 'Are you jealous?'

'Not of my own son. I give thanks daily, however, that I can keep you close in my *zenana*, without having to rescue you from the attentions of other men!'

Her eyes were clear and innocent. 'There never was any other man for me. Don't you know that yet?'

His mouth tightened in painful memory. 'I thought I'd lost you the day of the Asvamedha, the sacrifice of the royal stallion.'

Some of the shock she had felt then struck her anew. 'It was a bad moment,' she agreed. 'Maneka saved us from making it any worse – '

'She explained it to you?'

'I don't think even she could do that! Nor will I ever understand why First Her Highness had to do what she did! No, Maneka taught me I could respect something, even if I don't understand it.' She smiled at him. 'And to respect your Junior Rani more each day! And even to have some compassion for the Senior Rani, poor soul! You see

324

before you a woman who's growing in all the virtues every day.'

He laughed. 'Oh yes? Does that mean you prefer to study your books rather than spend time with me?'

A touch of mischief lit up her face. 'It's sad how we can't keep our hands off each other, isn't it? Oh dear, I'm afraid I still have much to learn! I love you so much!'

He began to undress her, his reason for coming to her room forgotten for the moment. The slight heaviness which was all that was visible of her impending motherhood excited him beyond belief, knowing that it was his baby that was causing these changes, a completion of their union that she had accepted as eagerly as he. Once the child was born, he told himself, she would forget the loss of her daughter and be wholly his.

Not since that first time had she felt any distress in being naked with him. If she thought about it at all, she was saddened that so many women of her own kind knew nothing of the joys of loving their husbands without any guilt or reluctance. She sighed softly, enjoying his experienced, exploring hands on her flesh. His thumb stroked her nipples, making them spring into life.

'I shall enjoy seeing you feeding my child,' he murmured. 'Will you mind if I watch you?'

Her answer was to put her lips to his, pulling his head down to hers. Almost before she was ready, he had carried her to the bed, thrusting himself into her with an urgency that brought her to life beneath him, the mounting storm within her matching his and carrying them both into that exclusive world of their very own.

Afterwards, leaning up on one elbow, he stroked her stomach with a possessive hand. His body was as golden as hers was pale; Fanny relished the contrast between them, enjoying the aftermath of their love-making as never before. Everything seemed possible to her when there were only the two of them together. But real life had other people in it. She pulled away from him, knowing herself to be greedy where he was concerned. He would resent the ease with which she had distracted him if she didn't bring him back to the point of his visit.

'Tell me more about this British platoon?' she invited him. 'How soon will they be here?'

'A couple of weeks. Maybe three.'

'Then we've got plenty of time to prepare for them. A platoon is hardly an army. At a guess, I'd say they've been sent to find out if I'm really here and, if I am, whether my presence here will work to their advantage.'

'I can work that out for myself!' he grumbled. 'What I want to know is what to do about them? It would serve them right to disappear without trace.'

She shook her head. 'You must welcome them with open arms, my love! They'd enjoy one of your displays of horsemanship, and riding your elephants! It's a pity I can't be by your side to receive them – ' She withstood his glare of disapproval with equanimity – 'but they'll quite understand if I were to receive them in private away from the Fort – and alone.'

Sajjan stiffened. 'Why alone? I don't like you to be seen by other men!'

She was tempted to remind him of the many times he had insisted she conform out of respect for his customs; this time, it would be he who would have to conform to her customs and she could see it wouldn't be easy for him.

'Darling,' she said, very gently, 'they'll need to know if you're holding me a prisoner here. If I go out and meet them alone, they'll know I'm here by my own choice, and they'll be far more inclined to listen to me. It'd spoil everything if some foolish young lieutenant took it into his head to effect my rescue and carry me off back to Delhi!'

He looked as cross as his young son did when she refused him anything. Perhaps, she thought, the same methods would work to restore his good humour. She ruffled her fingers through his hair, smiling at him.

'It isn't practical for me to meet them as an English lady in the *zenana*,' she began, 'though that might be arranged later. If I ride out to meet them – '

'You're not riding anywhere!'

Fanny felt the sting of disappointment. It was so long since she had sat on a horse, riding hell for leather with the wind in her hair. She wasn't an Irishwoman for nothing. She rode well, better than any of her siblings, and she would have loved to have known again the sensation of controlling a spirited animal with only the lightest of reins and the force of her own will. She abandoned the idea with reluctance.

'Then I'll have to be carried out – by men you can trust not to gossip about what they see. I shan't be veiled when I talk to our visitors and we don't want that little item to be the talk of the marketplace, do we?'

'I mind that less than the thought of your being with those men on your own. I should go with you, to protect you!'

'Sajjan, I'm meeting them as your trusted adviser, not as your woman!'

He rose up, pacing about the room without a thought for his naked state. 'They may persuade you to return to Delhi,' he said at last, as sulky as ever the Yuveraj could be.

She wondered how he could possibly think that any young British soldier would find anything to admire in her at that moment, made pregnant by a native ruler and with a diamond in her nose? She almost laughed, but she knew too well what it was to feel the sharp wounds that jealousy could inflict. She went to him at once, putting her arms about him.

'Nothing could ever make me leave you!'

'You don't know what they might offer you! What if they promised you a passage back to London and your old life there? Your Queen could keep you safe from your husband as well as I! Wouldn't that tempt you to go with them?'

'Not without you.'

He looked gloomier than ever. 'That's what you say now. Only I know how much you miss your daughter. I've heard you crying for her in your sleep! If you didn't love her, you'd have forgotten her by now.'

'I was a very bad mother to her. I'm hoping to do better this time, with your baby.'

Sajjan put an arm about her shoulders. 'Are you looking forward to mothering my baby?'

She nodded, unable to put her feelings into words. How could she possibly make him understand how half of her longed to hold his baby in her arms, while the other half cringed away from the thought of giving birth again, remembering the agony of her labour the last time.

'And you'll forget Mary?'

How did one ever forget one's own child? She compromised. 'I try not to think about her,' she said. 'There's nothing I can do to help her now.'

He found himself wishing it didn't have to be like that. If he could have done, he would have had the child brought to Kattyapur just to please her. There was no other woman in the world whom he would have considered indulging to such a ridiculous extent. How was it that this woman, with eyes the colour of an evening sky, could turn him, who'd been born to command, into her humblest supplicant?

Fanny's thoughts had gone on to a different track. She wondered if she could ever explain to him that there was no way she could ever go back to her own people. There was no one now who would dare to receive her, not even the Queen, even if she should be so minded. Victorian society did not forgive those who offended against its sexual mores. She knew as well as anyone that victims were considered as guilty as the perpetrators of most sins, especially if they were women, and the worst sin of all was to 'go native', as it was euphemistically called. Even her dearest friends would rather she were dead than that!

Sajjan's fingers kneaded her shoulders, feeling the strain of her thoughts in her taut muscles. 'Fanny, are you afraid for your daughter? Will you put her in jeopardy by having it known you're here?'

Fanny attempted a laugh, but it was more like a sob. 'How could it be otherwise? She *is* my daughter, Sajjan.'

He took a deep breath, chewing on his lower lip. 'Very well, it'll be as you say. You can meet them alone the first time, taking with you the Seal of Kattyapur to show you have my trust. Later, Second Her Highness and you can receive them together in the *zenana* in my presence. That way, they'll understand your position here as my wife of affection.'

She wondered if he thought he was doing her a favour. 'You don't like my coming out from behind the curtain, even for a moment, do you? You don't have to worry, you know, as soon as they've gone, I'll be glad to get back to concentrating on being a mother-to-be.'

His touch was possessive and his kiss even more so. He had understood what she had told him, but he still had his doubts that she was truly satisfied with her new life, no

329

matter how much she insisted she could never go back to her own people. He knew she had been brought up in ways that weren't his and often chafed against the restrictions of the *zenana*. How many times in the past had she mocked the custom of purdah to him? He was frequently afraid he wouldn't be able to keep her beside him for the rest of their days, that one day she would escape him and try to find all she had lost when he had brought her here. He had always been taught that women were his to be enjoyed and forgotten, yet this one threatened to make herself as indispensable to him as the air he breathed. If she ever chose to leave him, he wouldn't want to live without her. He knew better than to tell her as much, however. There was no woman living who wouldn't use such knowledge for her own ends. Not even his mother, not even Second Her Highness, would resist overturning his decisions if they thought they had the power to do so. He couldn't believe that Fanny, despite her European origins, would be any different. As it was, she frequently trespassed on his good nature, showing no sign that it was the man who was born to rule and the woman to follow where he led. No, he was determined she should never know the full extent of what she meant to him.

Two days later, First Her Highness had a fit in the night and was found dead by her maids in the morning.

Fanny was awakened by the sound of wailing women and wondered what on earth had happened. There was no sign of Ila, despite the lateness of the hour, which added to the mystery. Ila was a great believer in keeping to a regular routine, whatever Fanny might choose to do, and as Fanny had long ago discovered that servants were the true tyrants of this world, she now found herself quite upset at being allowed to oversleep for a couple of hours.

'What's going on?' she demanded without ceremony, when the maid finally made an appearance.

'It's First Her Highness!'

'What's the matter with her this time?'

'She's dead.'

'Dead!' Fanny thrust her feet out of bed, shocked out of the pleasant waking dream she had been indulging in. 'What did she die of?'

Ila merely looked puzzled. 'It was her time,' she shrugged.

The courtyard down below was humming with activity when Fanny descended the narrow steps that led to her private rooms.

'Is there anything I can do?' she asked uncertainly.

Maneka, who alone amongst the mêlée of women showed genuine signs of grief, gave Fanny a distracted look. 'Nothing. Yes, there is one thing. Keep Yadavendra with you, and do what you can to distract his attention, will you? His Highness says he must attend the funeral tomorrow as First Her Highness had no sons of her own and, in a way, was entitled to think of him as her own. I know he's the Yuveraj, and has to learn his responsibilities, but, oh Fanny, he's only just six years old!'

'He'll be all right,' Fanny tried to comfort her.

'How can you say so? His Highness will have other things to do besides keeping an eye on him. What am I to do?'

Fanny wanted to take the small, delicate woman into her arms, but she knew Maneka wouldn't welcome such a display in public. She was always very conscious of her dignity.

'It's a good thing he is so young,' she said instead. 'He won't understand much of what's going on and, if he does, Sajjan will make time for him, no matter how many other things he has to do. You don't have to worry about that child! With you for his mother and Sajjan for his father, he'll know by instinct exactly what to do!'

Maneka summoned up a weak smile. 'I suppose it's no good reminding you to call the Raja of Kattyapur His Highness when you speak of him? Really, Fanny, I despair of you!'

Unrepentant, Fanny captured the Yuveraj and bore him away, promising him a game of 'Fox and Geese' which she had been teaching him in exchange for his lessons in reading and writing in Hindi, skills in which he was improving daily in order to keep himself ahead of her.

'What's the matter with First Her Highness?' he asked her.

'She died,' Fanny answered, as if it were an everyday occurrence of not much interest.

In the distance they could hear the prayers being said, the atmosphere of surcharged emotion following them up the stairs to Fanny's rooms.

'I don't want to play a silly game, I want to see what's going on!' the small boy declared. 'Fanny, let's go and help Second Her Highness?'

'She sent us away. She'll be angry if we don't do what she says.'

'Fanny, you have to do what *I* say! I'm the Yuveraj!'

'I seldom do what anyone says,' Fanny returned calmly. 'You ought to know that by now. Ask your mother!'

He giggled, delighted to find a fellow miscreant. 'All right,' he consented. 'I'll stay with you.'

The atmosphere in the *zenana* was stifling all day. While no one was going to admit as much, the death of the Senior Rani had come as a relief to everyone. Her violence had become more unmanageable each day, especially after the sacrifice of the royal stallion. Her women were afraid of her, and the other women avoided her as much as they could. Fanny had tried to visit her occasionally, more to please Maneka's sense of propriety than for the Senior Rani's own sake. She had never found it easy to tolerate the weaknesses of others and, while the Senior Rani's mental state had aroused her pity, it had also revolted her if she was exposed to her undiluted society for longer than a few minutes.

By evening, Second Her Highness looked completely exhausted. She had spent the whole day in prayer and fasting, and then with her own hands prepared the Senior Rani's body for cremation.

'Do you have to do it all yourself?' Fanny demanded, taking a critical look at her. 'Why can't her maids do it?'

Second Her Highness looked more weary than ever. 'She was the First Wife, the Senior Rani of Kattyapur. She didn't inspire much love when she was alive, poor thing, and it's little enough to do for her now.'

'What you mean is, you couldn't trust anyone else not to skimp the preparations,' Fanny said. 'What a good woman you are! You ought to be dancing with joy that you're the *only* Rani of Kattyapur now. I would be!'

'I am – a little relieved,' Maneka confessed. 'I was wondering what to do when she became more violent than she was already. She might have hurt one of the children. You've no idea what a worry it was to me! His Highness wouldn't have heard of her being put under restraint because she'd suffered so much already.'

Harming a child, thought Fanny, was the one thing Maneka would never have been able to forgive her.

'Her time had come,' Fanny said, quoting what Ila had told her earlier.

Maneka's brow cleared as if by magic, confirming that

she had said the right thing. 'Yes, I was right when I told you she'd fulfilled her life as the Senior Rani. There was nothing left for her to do.'

'Oh, you're always right!' Fanny agreed in rallying tones.

Maneka gave her an outraged look, followed by an unwilling laugh. 'Is nothing sacred to you? You have no respect for anything!'

But Fanny wouldn't have that. 'I respect you,' she said. 'I often wish I were more like you.' And she was rewarded by the look of complete astonishment on the Junior Rani's face.

The Yuveraj enjoyed the cremation every bit as much as Fanny had predicted. Dressed in white, with a khaki turban he had some difficulty keeping in place, he was full of the great fire his father had lit. He even showed a gruesome interest in the moment when the Senior Rani's skull had been shattered to allow her soul to escape. He had had a fine time, he assured his mother, throwing ghee and a few chips of sandalwood on to the pyre when it came to his turn to do so, quite obviously never once connecting the garlanded figure in the flames with the woman who had sometimes played noisy and rather frightening games with him in the *zenana*.

Sajjan's mood had been considerably less exultant. 'With her death, the treaty with her father is broken. I hope that brother of hers doesn't take it into his head to attack me to divert his people's attention from the British.'

Fanny felt his anxiety like her own. 'The British won't allow it!' she insisted, her fingers crossed behind her back. She smiled slowly at him. 'The *sahib-log* does have other uses besides warming your bed for you!'

He grinned back, his mood lightening. 'I forget you're

one of them these days! You're far more beautiful dressed as one of us than you were in that ridiculous crinoline!'

She made a face at him. 'I'll have you know it was all the crack! The very latest fashion. All the ladies in Delhi were green with envy!'

'I like you better without,' he maintained. 'Better still when you have only your ivory skin to cover you!' He was amused he could still embarrass her so easily. Reluctantly, he began to take his leave of her. 'I must go to Her Highness. This has been a difficult time for her. Be kind to her, Fanny, especially when the British arrive. She often feels inadequate beside you, especially when you argue with her. I sympathize with her! You have a ready tongue!'

Fanny laughed. 'Don't you believe it! When Maneka and I argue, I'm the one deserving of your sympathy. She makes me feel like a naughty schoolgirl and I'm all of ten years older than she!'

'Would you change places with her?'

'Never!' Fanny was quite decided about that. 'She was born to be the Rani of Kattyapur. You're lucky to have her!'

'Yes, I am,' he acknowledged. 'I didn't think to hear you admit it, however!'

Fanny frowned. 'I know, but you see, I *like* Maneka. I'll never have a better friend.'

The Raja stooped and kissed her. 'Nor she either, I think,' he said.

Chapter Nineteen

They had plenty of warning of the British platoon's arrival. Sajjan followed their progress day by day, fighting the temptation to ride out and meet them himself. He trusted Fanny – with his life as well as his kingdom – but he couldn't reconcile himself to the idea that she should go out to meet these strangers alone and unprotected. True, they were her people and he had seen how easily she had handled even the most important of the *sahib-log* in Delhi, but she had changed a great deal recently. Ever since she had learned she was with child, she had had a calm, contented look, which he hoped meant she had accepted that Kattyapur, and he, was her future and that there was to be no turning back. He didn't want any British soldier, no matter how well intentioned, reminding her of old allegiances and old friendships that were better forgotten.

Fanny was busy making her own preparations for the meeting. When Sajjan questioned her as to what she was going to say to them, she refused to answer, making light of his anxieties. The truth was that she had no idea herself, but nothing would have induced her to admit this to him, knowing he was still seeking any excuse he could find to go with her, and that, she knew, would never do.

When the platoon was camped a mere two miles from the Fort, she had Sajjan send a message to say she was coming. The answer came back immediately, signed by a Lieutenant Walter Gilbert. The name meant nothing to her.

'I won't go all that way in a *doolie*,' she insisted. 'You'll have to allow me to ride some of the way.'

'You'll lose the baby. If you won't go by palanquin, or walk, we'll have to find some other way.'

Her face lit up with anticipation. 'By elephant? In your howdah? That'll make them sit up and take notice!'

'But discreetly, Fanny! I don't want the whole world knowing that I am ruled by a woman!'

She danced about him, delighted by this new plan. 'I've always wanted to ride on an elephant! Oh Sajjan, how kind you are to me!'

He knew he was mad to allow it but, as usual, he couldn't refuse her such a harmless treat. He smuggled her out of the rear entrance to the palace himself, however, leading her by the hand to the mounting block and leaning across to settle her himself into the howdah, pushing yet more cushions behind her back, and finally unfurling a golden parasol over her head.

'I'm coming with you as far as the first ravine,' he insisted.

Fanny only nodded. Truth to tell, she was glad to have his company.

At the Gate of Ganesha, she found herself whispering, '*Sri-Ganesaya Namah*. Reverence to Lord Ganesha!' It was Maneka who had told her that this elephant-headed god should be invoked at the beginning of any enterprise. The invocation no longer sounded in the least bit strange to her.

As soon as she judged she was sufficiently far away from the Fort-Palace, she put aside her veil, enjoying the sense of freedom the action gave her. The rhythm of the elephant's comfortable gait was soporific and, had it not been for the constant delight of the beautiful birds and the anxiety of her thoughts, she would have been fast asleep by the time they arrived outside the Bisnoi village where the British were camped.

Her first sight of the village was the herd of deer that lingered on the outskirts, unharmed by the humans amongst whom they lived. The Bisnoi were renowned for their particular respect for both animal and plant life. Fanny looked about her with interest, noting the pure white clothes of the men and the bright colours of the women's dress, with their heavy bangles covering the whole length of their arms.

Fanny had left most of her own jewellery behind her, all except for the choker necklace that betokened her relationship with Sajjan, and the diamond she wore in her nose because it never failed to bring his presence very close to her. Without him, she felt as though she were going naked to her doom. Indeed, she was more than half afraid the young British officers would think her naked anyway, dressed as she was according to Rajput customs. She hoped they wouldn't be so shocked by her appearance as to be unable to listen to anything she had to tell them.

There were two young officers who came out to meet her. They had made her the compliment of donning full dress uniform, their swords carefully held at their sides. As the elephant approached, they both saluted smartly, their white gloves gleaming in the hot sun.

The leader, his complexion dark for any Englishman she had known, solved the problem of her dismounting by edging her mount towards a small escarpment and bidding her climb out of the howdah and on to the top.

'Very well managed, Lady Frances!' he congratulated her. 'You've no idea what a pleasure it is to meet you. May I present the son of a good friend of yours, Mr Arthur Cunningham?' He bowed over her hand. 'Lieutenant Gilbert at your service!'

338

The impossibility of making an answering curtsey came upon Fanny with the suddenness of a thunderbolt. Instead, she palmed her hands together and bowed in her turn, relieved to see the young man was merely amused by her difficulty.

The same could not be said for Mr Cunningham. He was deeply shocked by her appearance, his eyes fastening on the diamond in her nose. His Adam's apple quivered several times before he could bring himself to acknowledge her salutation.

'I hope you bring me good news of your mother?' Fanny said kindly.

He goggled at her for a few seconds longer. 'I should have thought it would be your daughter you'd enquire after first! Good God, it would be the end of her if she knew what had become of you!'

Fanny's eyes met his. 'I see no need for her to know, do you?'

He coloured up angrily. 'I was against my parents taking her in! Her place is with her father!'

But Fanny was no longer listening. 'Mary is with your mother! Oh, I'm so glad! I liked her much better than anyone else I met in Delhi! Your father would never have achieved such a high position without her, don't you think? Such luck for him when he persuaded her to marry him!'

Lieutenant Gilbert gave his young companion a sardonic glance. 'I see you haven't lost your touch, Lady Frances,' he said with appreciation. 'I've had a chair put out for you in the shade over there.'

She smiled at him. 'What I'm really looking forward to is a proper English meal, full of forbidden things! Would that be possible?'

Brown eyes twinkled into navy. 'I'm sure it can be managed.'

'Yes, well,' Fanny confided easily, 'I think it must be because I'm in the family way that I can think of nothing else but food that's never looked at a spice even across the kitchen table! I love the food here in the normal way but, just recently, I've been afflicted by visions of great joints of beef, and all the pies and things we enjoy back home.'

Mr Cunningham's Adam's apple lurched up and down again. Finally, he walked away in disgust, unable to contain his dislike for her any longer.

'He must be a sad disappointment to his parents,' Fanny sighed. 'Is he really so easily shocked?'

'I'm afraid so. He's also one of Lord Bantry's hangers-on, which did little to recommend him to his father. Sir Arthur regards Mary as his adopted daughter and woe betide anyone who dares to make things more difficult for her than they are already!'

Lieutenant Gilbert handed Fanny into the comfortable camp chair he had had put out for her use. It was difficult for him to regard her as a total stranger, so much did she resemble her daughter.

Fanny, on the other hand, was perturbed to find herself wondering if she wouldn't be more comfortable on the ground. It had been a long and painful process learning to sit on her feet like an Indian and now, when she should have been able to enjoy the luxury, she found it impossible to sit in the chair with any degree of comfort.

'It was tactless of me to upset Mr Cunningham,' she said aloud. 'I hope I haven't made things more awkward for you than they are already?'

Lieutenant Gilbert sat down beside her. 'You're very like your daughter, ma'am.'

Fanny looked away. 'How is Mary? How is she really?'

'She was well enough when I last saw her. I'm attached to Sir Arthur Cunningham's staff, so I see her fairly frequently. It was he who recommended me for the task of coming here to meet you. His son was an afterthought. It was felt that the fewer people knew about you being in Kattyapur, the better it would be all round. Arthur doesn't like it, but he won't betray his own father because of his friendship with Lord Bantry.'

Fanny hoped he was right. She knew, as nobody else did, the dangers to herself and Kattyapur if Edwin Bantry were to discover her whereabouts. He would go to any lengths to punish her for evading his plans for her. No matter how much time elapsed, she had no hope he would forget his hatred for her.

'Do you like my daughter?' she asked the young man beside her.

'Me?' She was even more like her daughter than he'd thought! Her questions were every bit as able to disconcert him! 'Yes, I do,' he replied honestly. 'She's different from . . . other girls of her age. I take care not to argue with her as I invariably lose. Sir Arthur and Lady Cunningham are devoted to her.'

'Does she limp badly?'

'Not badly. She does limp, but it was her arm that took the brunt of the beating. She wouldn't go to her father's wedding. Not even Lady Cunningham could persuade her it was her duty. She's very loyal to your memory.'

He flicked his fingers for the bearer to bring them a tray of pressed lemon juice. Fanny was unsurprised to recognize the features of the man in the green turban as he placed a glass by her side. She nodded to him, sitting up very straight, wishing she had her veil to pull across her face.

'We make contact again,' she said.

'Indeed, lady.' He spoke in the Rajput dialect. 'Your lord allowed you to come here without him?'

'I'm here as Lady Frances,' she answered him.

341

He jerked his head upwards and sideways. 'You must have a very persuasive tongue, lady. His Highness won't rest until he has you safely returned to him!'

She smiled with him, liking the man. 'He is my lord,' she said simply.

She became conscious of Lieutenant Gilbert watching this exchange with interest. She stirred uneasily in her seat, hoping he hadn't understood what she had said. It wasn't as Sajjan's wife of affection that she sought to impress him.

'Are you quite comfortable, Lady Frances?' the young man asked her.

'Thank you, yes,' she said grimly. Nothing would have induced her to give Mr Cunningham the satisfaction of finding her sitting on the ground like a native woman when he returned.

Mr Gilbert had the temerity to grin at her. 'Nevertheless, I'll fetch some of the cushions from the howdah in case you prefer another position. It might be more fun to have our picnic on the ground.'

'*Quel tacte!*' Fanny drawled after him.

He laughed. 'On the contrary, I'm hoping you'll teach me how you do it. Mary will sit on her feet by the hour!'

He seemed to know a great deal about Mary, Fanny found herself thinking. 'I thought at first I'd never learn!' she confided. 'Every muscle rebelled after the first few moments. I had a very good teacher though. You'll meet her when you visit us in the *zenana*.'

'The Junior Rani?' he hazarded.

He was very well informed. Better than she had expected. 'The only Rani. The Senior Rani died a week or so ago.'

He shot a quick look at her. 'Does her brother know yet?'

342

'We're hoping you British will stop him from making any trouble.'

His eyebrows rose. 'Is that how you think of us?'

She caught herself up short, wondering if she had made a mistake. She chose to be honest. 'Not really, not all the time. I want to do my best for Kattyapur. You do believe that, don't you?' At his quick nod, she breathed a sigh of relief. 'I can promise you that Kattyapur will make a good ally as long as I'm here. That's what you came to find out, wasn't it?'

'More or less. The Raja values you as a political adviser, I'm sure.'

'It's the main reason he brought me here.'

He couldn't prevent himself from allowing his gaze to drop to where the first signs of her pregnancy were only just visible. 'I think he may have had other reasons too, Lady Frances?'

'If he sees me as a woman first, it's because that's the way women are here. He does listen to me, too, though. He's a very enlightened man, Mr Gilbert.'

'I suppose he knows of your friendship with Queen Victoria?'

Fanny smiled. 'I made sure of it. I hope you'll remind your superiors of the affection in which she has always held me?'

Mr Gilbert smiled back. 'I shan't have to. Your daughter writes to her godmother on all the proper occasions, and Lady Cunningham does the rest. Lady Frances, I won't play games with you. Sir Arthur and I discussed your circumstances very thoroughly before I came away. It didn't surprise me to know you were a noted hostess in London before Lord Bantry brought you out to India. Did you miss the life?'

Fanny put her head on one side. 'I expect it'll be hard

for you to believe, Mr Gilbert, but I've never been happier than I have been since coming to Kattyapur. I was bitterly unhappy with Lord Bantry – '

'You don't have to tell me anything you don't want to!' he cut her off. 'I've met Lord Bantry,' he added grimly.

Fanny hadn't expected to receive any sympathy from her compatriots. She found herself liking the young man very much.

'Tell me more about my daughter,' she invited him. 'My one regret was having to leave her behind.'

'You did everything possible to protect her future, or so it seems to me. Sir Arthur has even forgiven you for making such shameless use of his wife! They're both devoted to Mary. She has something of your famous charm – and of your understanding of political matters. She goes about with Sir Arthur a great deal, telling him all manner of things about the Indians he wouldn't ever hear otherwise. We all wonder how she finds out about these things. I don't mind telling you, I've learned a great deal from her myself. You have no cause to worry unduly about her, ma'am. She won't go anywhere near her father and he's the only person who might harm her. Lady Cunningham has done a good job in reminding everyone who matters that Mary is the Queen's goddaughter. The Queen herself has done the rest by taking a personal interest in her circumstances. Both ladies have proved themselves good friends to you!'

'I know it,' Fanny acknowledged softly. 'I tell myself that we won't go far wrong in India while Queen Victoria is on the throne. Remarkable times like these produce remarkable people to deal with them, as often as not. I've been fortunate to know more than one of them.'

Mr Gilbert thought his guest rather remarkable herself. He might not have understood her so well if he had not known Mary, he thought. As it was, he had a glimmer of understanding as to why Lady Cunningham had taken on the task of raising her daughter on a few days' acquaintance and, more to his purpose, why the Raja of Kattyapur would do anything sooner than compromise his relationship with her by attacking the Paramount Power. She might be dressed in a costume that would bring a blush to the cheek of any other lady of his acquaintance; she was nevertheless completely assured and unrepentant about her present mode of life, just as if it were the most ordinary thing in the world.

He met her eyes squarely and was astonished to see she wasn't as sure of herself as she would have him believe. More, she was acutely uncomfortable sitting, ramrod straight, on her chair. He thought again of Mary and found himself smiling. There was something about their very vulnerability, which both would deny with horror, that made him want to protect them both. It was unlikely, though, that young Cunningham could ever be brought to see either of them in quite the same way.

He half-rose as the junior officer came back to them. 'Is lunch ready?' he asked him.

Arthur Cunningham did his best to put a civil expression on his face. He had never wanted to come on this assignment, but his father had overruled him, telling him that his whole career depended on how he acquitted himself. He had certainly made it plain enough that if he ever breathed a word to anyone else of Lady Frances's whereabouts, or anything else about her that he might discover while he was away, he would answer for it with his career and future prospects. Young Arthur might wish he had the courage to defy his father, but he knew he would not, which only added to his hatred for Lady Frances. He had a strong dislike for those who consorted with the local people, unless it was on business, and that excuse was not one any proper woman would seek to use. Anyone of Lady Frances's breeding should know the importance of keeping the pure blood strain, yet she was completely brazen about living with this Raja fellow, joking about the child she was bearing, when she wouldn't give Lord Bantry the heir he'd wanted. Death would have been too good for her! The whole business made him shudder. He doubted he could bring himself to sit down to a meal with her. Like calls to like, he thought contemptuously, noting the understanding the other two had struck up in his absence. He hated Walter Gilbert almost as much as he hated and resented the Bantry women.

He bowed, bringing his heels together with a sharp click. 'Have to ask you to forgive me for leaving you,' he said, his mouth settling into sulky lines. 'Not feeling quite the thing. I'm sure you understand!'

Fanny did. She knew better than to think it was anything other than her presence which had upset him, whatever he might profess. She wished there was something she could do to win Lady Cunningham's son round, but she could see by his set expression that Edwin had done his work well where this young man was concerned. Perhaps, if she had met him under other circumstances . . .

'Have you been in India long, Mr Cunningham?' she asked him.

'Long enough to hate it. I spent a few months with my parents in Kashmir, but I'm settled now in Delhi. At least there is some kind of social life there, though I believe you didn't fancy it much, Lady Frances?'

'It seemed quiet – after London.'

'Where you entertained without a host? That must have been awkward for you?'

'Not really. Both my father and my brother live in London most of the time.'

'Not in Ireland?'

'They have homes there too. I think most people who want to be in the centre of things end up in London these days, no matter where in the British Isles they come from. There are even one or two English people who thronged the kind of parties I used to give,' she added on a light laugh.

'With the English paying for everything!' Mr Cunningham retorted bitterly.

'Do they?' Fanny knew better than to contradict him. 'The Irish have been too hungry to pay many taxes recently, and the Scots have had to make way for their landowners' sheep; does that make them less British?'

Mr Cunningham thought it wholly unbecoming for a woman to talk politics. His dislike of Fanny increased with every word she said.

'Your husband doesn't like to see women busybodying in public affairs!' he muttered. 'I agree with him!'

It was a relief when he took himself off to find out what was delaying their luncheon. 'I wish I could like him better!' she said to Lieutenant Gilbert. 'He won't tell Bantry where I am, will he?'

'Not if he values his career.' Mr Gilbert plumped up some cushions and gestured towards them, inviting her to make herself comfortable. 'His mother vouched for him not to say a word to anyone. I think we may trust her, don't you?'

Fanny seated herself with relief on the cushions, pulling her feet up under her. 'He doesn't like me,' she said, adding, 'at one time that would have upset me for days. I *enjoyed* being the Lady Frances most of the time. It amused me to have everyone falling over themselves to gain my approval. How the mighty are fallen!'

'What about the Raja? Doesn't he seek your approval?'

She shook her head. 'The Raja of Kattyapur rules alone. If he listens to me, it's because he wants to understand the mind of the British. His decisions are his alone. He wants only the good of his people – '

'What about that business with the horse?' Mr Gilbert shot at her. 'Did you agree with him over that?'

'The horse had been turned loose long before I left Delhi. Was it such a bad thing?'

'Not according to the reports we received from Colonel Tod of Jaiselmer. According to him, the *zamindars* he replaced were mostly idle good-for-nothings, spending most of their time thieving from one another. The Colonel was beginning to think he'd have to do something about them himself if your Raja hadn't acted when he did. Ah, here's lunch!'

Walter Gilbert watched as Lady Frances served herself a selection of roast meat and the vegetables she craved, amused by her gleeful anticipation of the meal ahead of her. He wondered if she always had such a zest for everything she tackled, and was again reminded strongly of her daughter Mary. There was no sign of Mr Cunningham joining them, he noticed, and hoped Lady Frances wouldn't take offence. The Raja of Kattyapur could be useful to the British one day.

'I'm looking forward to meeting the Raja,' he said aloud.

Fanny eyed her plate greedily. 'He wants to meet you too. He didn't like me coming out here by myself.' She took a mouthful of beef, savouring the taste of it. It wasn't nearly as good as she'd thought it was going to be and she was hard put to it to hide her disappointment. Worse, she felt *guilty*, eating Maneka's sacred animal. She felt like a cannibal, eating death into herself.

'Why should he mind your spying out the land for him?' Mr Gilbert enquired. 'Isn't that what political advisers are for?'

Fanny hesitated, another piece of meat halfway to her mouth. 'I'm also his wife of affection,' she reminded him.

Walter Gilbert carefully avoided looking at her. 'I had thought you might be,' he said carefully at last.

'But you're shocked nevertheless?'

'No.' His eyes finally met hers. 'There are those who will be, but I'm not one of them, Lady Frances.' He smiled wryly. 'I have a Parsee grandmother. I'm not at all ashamed of her either, but I don't tell everyone about her because these things are frowned upon these days and I have to think of my career.'

'Then why tell me?'

He laughed shortly. 'I was once tempted to tell your daughter too. I may do so yet one day. I'm not sure why. It's a kind of thank you for being honest with me.'

'I see,' said Fanny. 'When you do, will you also tell her about me and teach her not to be ashamed of me?'

'If that's what you want.' He leaned forward, putting his hand on hers. 'You don't have to worry about Mary understanding why you did it, Lady Frances. She's probably the one person in the world who'll always understand. You're very alike, the two of you.'

'Are we?' Fanny was more doubtful about that.

'Very alike,' he affirmed. 'Do you want to eat any more of that meat?'

Fanny shook her head. 'Perhaps if it were curried – given a little taste – ' She broke off, laughing at her own inconsistency.

When Mr Cunningham came back to do his duty by

Lord Bantry's runaway wife, they were still laughing together. Mr Cunningham's temper curled inside him, wishing he could deliver her back to Lord Bantry there and then. That would stop her laughing! Probably for ever!

Maneka was verging on a state of rebellion, held in check only by her fierce sense of the duty she owed to her husband.

'What have these people to do with us?' she demanded of Fanny. 'Why do they come to the *zenana*? His Highness could have arranged for you to see them downstairs if it's necessary for you to speak with them!'

'Talking isn't enough,' Fanny told her. 'His Highness wants them to see how I live now under his protection. Men and women mix much more socially in England than you do here. You'll find them quite accustomed to talking to women – even other men's wives.'

Maneka presented a white face. 'But, Fanny, are you sure they're really men? I've heard it said the *sahib-log* –'

Fanny bit back her laughter. 'They're men, just as I'm an ordinary woman like yourself,' she assured the little Rani. 'Remember, it's you who are honouring them by receiving them, not the other way round!'

Maneka clutched at her. 'You're sure, Fanny?'

'Absolutely. Remember how you used to worry about me?'

Maneka managed a weak smile. 'You were never a strange man from the *sahib-log*!'

Fanny wished she could think of something which would put her at her ease, but nothing came to mind. 'They're only people,' she said again. 'You're the Rani of Kattyapur!'

Even so, she could feel her tension as Maneka sat, a heavily veiled little figure, in the place where First Her

350

Highness used to sit, her back as straight as a plank of wood, her fingers twisted together in her lap.

Fanny sat a little behind her, looking forward to the change in their usual routine. It would have been fun to have discussed the two men with the Rani, telling her her own impressions of them, but Maneka was deaf and blind to everything but her own agony of shyness. Fanny noted the frightened panic in her eyes as she enclosed herself in an armour of aloof dignity, refusing to be comforted.

The men, when they arrived, looked as ill at ease as their hostess. Fanny stood up as they entered and introduced them carefully to the Rani, first in English and then in her own language. Her eyes narrowed dangerously as Mr Cunningham did no more than sketch a salute, his contempt for everyone present written clearly in every line of his body. She cast a quick, warning look at Walter Gilbert, who stepped into the breach as easily as she had hoped he would.

'You do us a great honour, Your Highness,' he murmured in a travesty of the Rajput dialect.

Some of Maneka's fright left her at the formal, mispronounced words. Plainly this was, indeed, only a man! She made a suitable response, waving Fanny to take her own place again behind her. Thereafter, Fanny was merely required to translate until the maids brought in the refreshments that were to be served to the three Britons.

With a hint from her, Mr Gilbert embarked on a series of well-chosen questions about Maneka's speciality, the miniature paintings in which she took such an interest. Arthur Cunningham said nothing at all. He peered at the beverage he was offered as if he suspected it might be poisoned, then he turned to Fanny.

'Gilbert would have me believe you still owe your

allegiance to Queen Victoria despite living here, Lady Frances. I find that hard to believe.'

Fanny's look mocked him. 'Her Majesty has always been one of my dearest friends. You don't have to doubt my loyalty to her.'

'What about the Raja? His way of life can never be yours!'

Fanny swallowed down her anger. 'It took a little getting used to,' she admitted calmly. 'However, I've met only kindness here, from the Rani most of all. When I think of the alternative of being murdered at my husband's hands, I assure you I'm more than contented with my lot.'

'Lord Bantry is much respected – '

'You mean his money is!' Lieutenant Gilbert broke in dryly.

Fanny edged a little forward. She would have loved to have handed out young Arthur Cunningham one of her famous snubs. Her tongue had always been her best weapon and, anyway, Mr Cunningham deserved no better of her. She opened her mouth, enjoying the thought of his conceit in his own opinions wilting before her. She edged forward a little more. Belatedly, she realized she had other responsibilities that evening besides taking Arthur Cunningham down a peg or two!

She turned apologetically to Maneka, seeing she had somehow managed to move her seat until she was seated in the first place, her back almost to the Rani, intent only on the revenge she had wanted. Would she never learn?

She put out a hand to her, her head bent. 'Your Highness, I'm sorry. I forgot for the moment what an ordeal this is for you. Why didn't you order me back behind you?'

'You're amongst your own people, Fanny.'

'A poor excuse for bad manners!'

'No, no,' Maneka protested. 'Truly, I don't mind! Why does the red one make you angry? You like the other one, don't you?'

'Yes, I do. He brought me news of my daughter. The red-faced one doesn't approve of me.' She smothered a giggle. 'I'm very much afraid he thinks me a barbarian!'

Maneka giggled happily also. She was at last beginning to enjoy herself. 'He's a fool! But the other one is a good man.' The beginnings of an idea came to her and she was immediately brimming over with excitement. 'Fanny, go and get the miniature I gave you and this man will take it to your daughter so she'll know you haven't forgotten her! I'll give you another one sometime, when I see one that's good enough. Please, Fanny, it'll give your Mary so much pleasure!'

Fanny did as she was bidden, touched as always by Maneka's thoughtfulness. It took her some time to find the miniature and pack it up into some kind of a parcel for Mr Gilbert to take with him. By the time she returned to the courtyard, Sajjan had joined them, holding the Yuveraj by the hand.

For a long, desperate moment, Fanny stood at the top of the small flight of steps and wished that she were dead. She knew that this was the moment when she had come to the crossroads of her life, not that anybody would know it but her! It was worse, far worse, than the time when she had decided to leave Delhi. Her mouth felt dry with fright, and she longed to cut and run, and not have to go back to the assembled people below.

She had probably knelt before the Raja of Kattyapur tens of hundreds of times by now, but it had always held an element of play-acting before; this time there was none, not with the two British gentlemen looking on in an appalled silence while she made her obeisance to her new lord. She knew well what they would think of her, the Lady Frances, doing such a thing. A curtsey they might have understood, though even curtseys were few and disdainfully offered to the native princes. There could be no more final declaration of where she stood in the future than what she had to do now.

Taking a deep breath, she straightened her back and slowly descended the stairs, her head held high. It seemed to her they were all staring at her as she crossed the courtyard, pausing in front of Sajjan to make a full obeisance, putting out her hand to touch the ground at his feet. Rising, she bowed low to the Yuveraj, who grinned at her, and then before Maneka, taking her place behind her with a slowly expelled sigh of relief.

Unaware of the drama that had just been enacted before her, Maneka turned impulsively to her. 'Is that the painting? Ask Mr Gilbert to deliver it for you now, Fanny!'

The young man came forward at once. She could feel his sympathy as he bent to receive the package and it was as much as she could do not to blush as she wondered what he must be thinking of her.

'That was very bravely done, Lady Frances.' His fingers pressed hers. 'It convinced me as nothing else could have done that Kattyapur is safe in your hands. That's the message I'll take back with me to Delhi – and your present for Mary, of course!'

She looked up at him uncertainly. 'Yes, I think you do understand,' she said at last. 'I am not Lady Frances Bantry any longer. Here, I'm the Raja of Kattyapur's concubine, his wife of affection, less than the dust beneath his feet. If I can keep the peace between him and the British, I'll do it, and gladly, but because that's what he wants and I won't pretend it is for any other reason. I can tell you this though, you'll never have a better ally than the Raja!'

He took the wrapped miniature from her, putting it carefully away in his pocket. 'If Sir Arthur doesn't completely understand that, Mary will explain it to him,' he promised.

'I hope she may!' She bit her lip. 'Mr Gilbert, I'd rather Mary doesn't know the miniature comes from me. Tell her – oh, tell her anything you choose, but not that! Not as I am now!'

'I will do my best to hold my own counsel, but it isn't always easy where your daughter is concerned. I doubt she will ever entirely conform to the society that bred her. Her ambitions lie elsewhere.'

And with that she had to be content.

The Yuveraj came and sat beside her, bored by the conversation of the men. Only Maneka seemed perfectly content to sit in silence with her own thoughts. She didn't miss much though, darting glances at the strangers from behind her veil. Finally, she put a trembling hand on Fanny's knee.

'You were right, they are only men!' she said disparagingly. She slanted a bubbly smile at Fanny. 'Do they all dress like that, in those tight trousers? No wonder you ran away from them! His Highness looks much more splendid!'

Fanny found herself laughing. She could have hugged Maneka for her wisdom! How strange, she thought, that she could have changed so much in such a short time, from the elegant Lady Frances to Sajjan's wife of affection. Stranger still, she wouldn't have changed places with her former self for anything in the world! She had finally come home.

BOOK THREE
Wife of Affection

Chapter Twenty

1875–6

'Your Blighty Rani has been declared Empress of India.
There is to be a huge durbar in Delhi – '

'Not in Calcutta?'

'Delhi is more central. Everybody is going.'

Fanny's eyes shone. 'You are going to Delhi?' she asked
in carefully neutral tones.

Sajjan was not deceived. 'Yes, dear heart, I am going.'

'Take me with you!'

He shook his head sadly. 'Much as I'd like you with me
on the journey, it's too dangerous for you to be seen in
Delhi. However careful we were, someone would talk. I'll
have a large entourage with me.'

'Please, Sajjan.'

He looked at her askance. She made a pleasant picture,
her latest child, a daughter, on her lap; Krishna, her second
son, playing by her side.

'Haven't you enough to keep you occupied here?'

Fanny tried not to look as guilty as she felt. 'I might see
Mary,' she said at last.

She had expected his wrath to explode all about her, but
he was only sad, as she was, that her daughter should mean
so much to her after all this time. He still had nightmares
that this woman would one day return to her previous life
and that nothing he could do would be enough to keep her
by his side.

'And if you do see her, what then?' he asked.

'I only want to see her,' Fanny answered. 'I won't even speak to her unless you say I may! It would mean so much to me to see with my own eyes how she's grown up!'

'What makes you think you will see her?'

She shrugged her shoulders. 'I'm sure the Queen will suggest her goddaughter should be one of the Vicereine's attendants. I'll be able to see her then. Everybody will be far too busy to notice one more native woman in your retine! Do I look English any more?'

He grinned. 'You look like the Irishwoman you claim to be sometimes, not cold like the English are.'

She smiled back. 'Only when we're alone together.'

Watching her playing with her children, he wondered if he couldn't agree to her request after all. She never ceased to surprise him, this woman of his. He remembered how jealous the Yuveraj had been when she had first produced a son of her own, yet she had soon seen to it that the two boys were friends, never hesitating to explain to the uncomprehending Ganesha that it wasn't only his extra years that should command his respect for the Yuveraj. 'One day he'll be Raja,' she would say. 'You must always be ready to lay down your life for him.'

'Yes, Mama,' the small boy would agree.

She always spoke English to her children, and mostly to the Yuveraj as well, gracefully asking him if he would permit her to use her own language in his presence as she felt more at home in it still. Sajjan wondered if his sons realized how important she thought it for them all to be completely at their ease in the language of the Paramount Power, as she was now in theirs, switching from one to the other with an ease that even he couldn't emulate.

'It may reopen old wounds for you,' he said now, still mulling over her request.

'I only want to see her. I want to know if she still limps –

if Lady Cunningham did a good job at teaching her how to behave in society. Oh dear, I can never explain to you what I mean! But it wasn't as though the poor woman had much of a start herself and I'd like to think Mary can hold her own in a world that's power hungry – and a little puffed up in its own conceit besides!'

'You will have to stay behind the curtain every moment we are away!'

She rose to her feet, balancing her baby on one hip. 'That won't be any hardship to me,' she promised. 'I'll be with you!'

Still he hesitated. 'You must ask Her Highness's permission. If she raises no objection – '

Fanny hugged him, pushing the baby into his ready arms. 'I'll ask her at once!'

She was away, calling the Rani's name as she went. Sajjan stayed where he was, looking at her retreating figure, knowing as well as Fanny did that Maneka's consent would be readily forthcoming, lonely as she'd be without his wife of affection's company during the long weeks when they would be away.

It had never occurred to Fanny that her baby would be a boy. When Maneka, in the last stages of pregnancy herself, had announced she had a son, Fanny had thought for a moment she must have made a mistake.

'He's a fine boy. Do you want me to suggest a name to His Highness?'

'Tell him Ganesha,' Fanny had said. 'I want to call him after the god of new beginnings. He'll understand that.'

Maneka, too, had understood well enough that Fanny had been thinking of Mary, but she'd been wise enough not to encourage memories that had to be painful to the newly delivered mother.

Maneka had been as delighted with the new arrival as if it had been her own. 'There now,' she had crooned, ' it wasn't nearly as bad as you thought it was going to be, was it?'

Nor had it been. Nor had it been with any of her other children. Instead of a doctor, she had had Maneka's calming presence, very much in command of the situation, her wise women as gentle and as able as the London midwife had been ham-fisted and incompetent. The birthing had been over almost before it had begun, with only the constant drone of prayers and the smoke of incense to disturb her, as she had briefly wondered what would be the state of her baby's soul without the benefit of Christianity.

Ganesha had grown rapidly. He was something of a miracle to his mother, whose memories of Mary at the same age were of a screaming bundle of fury, constantly ailing, and without any of the charm of this placid, greedy creature, who wriggled with joy from head to foot every time he saw her. She hardly remembered Mary as a baby though, for most of the time she had seen very little of her at that age. She recalled her best as she had been when she had last seen her, hurt and afraid and forced by her father's abuse into a knowledge of brutality that Fanny would have done anything to have kept away from her. She had never known Mary, her first-born, as she had known the children she had borne to Sajjan. In some ways Mary had always been a stranger to her.

Thinking of Mary led naturally to thinking of Mary's godmother. What a long time she had been away from them both. In the intervening years, Victoria had been widowed and had withdrawn from the world as much as her position would allow. And Mary? Mary must be about the age she had been herself when she had first come to

Kattyapur. Oh, perhaps a year or two younger, but a woman in her own right and very likely married too, though Sajjan had never told her that she was and Fanny had never liked to ask.

She could have told Sajjan any time these last years that there had been no chance of her being received back into her own life, no matter what she wanted, no matter what the Queen wanted, after that day when they had received the two British officers in the *zenana*. She would take to her grave the memory of that awful moment when she had realized she would have to make her obeisance to Sajjan in front of them both. She could still go cold at the memory of it, with the same astonishment that neither Sajjan nor Maneka had had the slightest idea of what the gesture had cost her. Only Walter Gilbert had understood. He was a young man she considered should go far – if the British didn't discount him because of the Parsee blood that ran in his veins. Sometimes she despaired of her own people, with their ingrained conviction of their own superiority and their consequent lack of interest in the customs and habits of their subject peoples.

Maneka's consent to Fanny going to Delhi was given with only half her mind on the matter. Of far greater concern to her at that moment was the coming ceremony when her youngest son would receive the sacred thread, the symbol of his caste.

'I am so proud, Fanny,' Maneka confessed, sighing a little, 'though I think mothers must always consider their sons too young to have such a fuss made of them! Do you remember how it was with the Yuveraj?'

'I hadn't seen my own son receive the sacred thread in those days,' Fanny remembered, smiling. 'I had no idea what it meant. I was inclined to think my children to be outcasts like their mother!'

Maneka clicked her tongue in annoyance. 'They are the Raja's sons, Fanny, long before they are yours!'

'Maybe. But they grow away from one after they've been born again. It hurts me not to be able to eat with my own children.' She sighed. 'The Yuveraj was always in my company before – '

'Children grow up, Fanny. Surely, you don't need me to tell you that?'

Fanny thought back to the Yuveraj's great day. His brothers had had a much quieter time of it, without all the public ceremonies, the feasts, and the crowds of people. To Fanny, the whole ceremony had been a mystery. Maneka had tried to explain it to her as a boy's formal initiation into his caste and religion: that, ritually, the Yuveraj had been about to be born again, and given the thread to wear as proof of his position in life.

Fanny smiled down at Maneka's bent head. 'Wouldn't you like to go to Delhi?' she enquired.

The Rani's astonishment at the very idea made her want to laugh. 'I see you wouldn't! Think of all the new things you'd see, though. I could show you – '

Maneka shook her head, horrified by the idea. 'I could never leave the children! And there must be a hundred other things I have to do! No, no, why should I want to go away to Delhi? You go, Fanny, and enjoy the heat and the dust and the flies, and all the other trials of the road!' She gave Fanny a long, considered look, a hint of amusement at the back of her eyes. 'You probably will! I should hate every moment of it!'

'I have to admit it's more comfortable here,' Fanny agreed. 'I've come to love it!'

'But Mary isn't here?'

Fanny sighed. 'I only want to see for myself that she's

all right. My other children are here – my whole life is here! – but – '

'I have said you may go. His Highness has agreed you should go. Why are you still arguing about it?'

Fanny didn't know. She could only think she was arguing with herself, half of her wanting to see the woman Mary had grown into, the other half afraid she wouldn't like what she saw. It was always with her that Mary was Edwin's daughter and that she must have inherited some of Edwin's characteristics as well as her own!

Fanny winced away from that old, old worry of hers. 'I'll miss you,' she said abruptly. 'What shall I bring you back from Delhi?'

Maneka rose to her feet. 'Come back safely, that's all I ask! When are you to leave?'

'As soon as possible after your son's ceremony.'

Maneka pursed her lips together. 'So soon? I don't know how we shall get everything ready in time! Fanny, can you manage to make your own arrangements? If you were going later on – '

'Of course I can!' Fanny averred. 'Don't fuss so! You've got your hands more than full with your own affairs! I can manage quite well to pack up my own things. Don't worry about it, Your Highness!'

Fanny's excitement grew as she laid her plans for the journey to Delhi. It was an excitement she could only share with Ila, who would go with her, and who was as eager as she to leave Kattyapur behind her for a few weeks. Besides, Ila had visited Delhi once or twice before, and had many friends there. Fanny had often wondered if there were not also some man she had known there and whom she was hoping to see again. It was strange that Ila had never responded to her clumsy overtures that she might like to marry one of Sajjan's courtiers who would provide her with the best of everything. It was rare for an Indian woman to prefer the single state.

'I am better as I am,' she would say. 'Who would marry me at my age? Why do you want to see me married to a man I know nothing about? You're not my father to try and gain some advantage from my marriage!'

'Good heavens, no!' Fanny had agreed, much struck. 'Only you can't go unmarried all your days! To tell the truth, I'd miss you terribly!'

Fanny remembered it had been Ila's marriage she and her maid had been discussing the day before the Yuveraj had received the sacred thread, a day which had been a landmark in her life in Kattyapur for some reason she could never quite explain to herself. Perhaps it was that she had learned to understand the Rani a little better that day.

She and Ila had been interrupted by the Rani, harassed by all the things she had yet to do before the morrow, who had come to tell Fanny to expect a visit from the young Yuveraj that afternoon. She had frowned at Fanny. 'I shan't pretend I didn't try to persuade him to stay away from you,' she had confessed. 'He ought to be preparing himself for tomorrow, with which you certainly won't be able to help him, but he says he's missed his conversations with you recently!'

'And I with him. Will you come with him for the visit?'

Maneka had looked quite shocked at the idea. 'I have my own preparations to make. Don't keep him too long, will you, Fanny?' And she had hurried away again.

When the Yuveraj had come to her rooms, however, Fanny had been so pleased to see him, she had forgotten her best intentions to chase him away as his mother would have wished.

'My, but you're a welcome sight!' she had told him. 'I'd almost forgotten what you look like!'

'Haven't you seen His Highness to remind you?' the lad had retorted. It had always been a joke between them that he looked so like his father.

'That's none of your business!' Fanny had protested.

'Everything is my business in Kattyapur.' He had sounded serious and quite unlike himself. 'After tomorrow, Fanny, I shan't be able to visit you as often – '

Fanny had sniffed. She had been expecting this. 'Because I have no caste, I suppose. Well, let me tell you I think very poorly of a religion that tears up old friendships as if they were of no account!'

The Yuveraj had taken her hand in his. 'Tomorrow I shall be a man, Fanny. I have to start to live like a man. My mother will see less of me also. As for that other nonsense, the longer you live amongst us, the less people care about things like that. My mother has always been on your side, you know, no matter how prickly you can be, but no ruler can afford to offend his people's religious sensibilities, as she would be the first to tell you.'

Fanny had sniffed again. 'I suppose it is thanks to her that my children are accepted as your brothers just as much as any of her own children?'

'Indeed. She has always been your friend.'

Fanny had acknowledged the justice of that. 'I hope I have been a good friend to her too. If I could only forget that she is your father's wife – and with far more rights than I can ever have – ' She had broken off. 'I suppose you will be getting married yourself soon?' she had changed the subject.

The Yuveraj had smiled and nodded. 'I hope to marry someone just like you!' he had teased her.

'You'd do better to find someone like your mother!' she had answered seriously.

His face had softened, the laughter dying away. 'You are right, Fanny. I am very lucky in both my mothers!'

She had been flattered and hadn't minded in the least that he should know it. She had enjoyed their chats as much as he had, and so it was with some reluctance that she had brought the visit to a halt, shooing him out of the door, and bidding him to enjoy himself as much as would be possible on the morrow.

'Will you be praying for me, Fanny?' he had asked her.

'In my own way,' she had promised. 'Not that I know the first thing about it.' She had put her head on one side. 'I wish you a very long and happy life, my dear!' And she had been touched when he had kissed her lightly on the cheek. They had always understood each other, these two, and not even Ganesha was closer to her.

He had stood in the entrance for a moment, a sudden smile coming into his eyes. 'Tell me something, Fanny, do you ever lose on purpose nowadays to my father when you play chess together?'

'Never!' she had averred. But it hadn't been quite true and they both had known it. 'What makes you ask?'

He had chuckled, raising his brows in exact imitation of his father. 'Oh, something my mother said recently!'

Which, Fanny thought, had put her in her place! Though how Maneka could possibly have known such a thing was completely beyond her!

The women hadn't had much of a view the next day. The rituals had been performed in the main audience chamber of the palace, the women, as always, behind a screen to protect them from the curiosity of the male guests. Fanny had thought it would never end. Interested, at first, to see that the Yuveraj was every bit as solemn as was his mother when she went about her religious duties, she had watched as his head was shaved by a man with a wicked-looking knife and had been rather glad that her little daughter, at least, would be spared undergoing any such ceremony. Her stamina had taken a battering by the time four or five hours had passed, and she would have sought some way of removing herself from the rest of it, if she hadn't caught sight of the tears of pride in Maneka's eyes and glimpsed a little of what the occasion meant to the other woman. After that, there was no way she would have revealed to her the boredom that was assailing her. In that moment she had realized a little of what the other woman meant to the whole of Kattyapur as well as to her husband and, even, to her.

The Yuveraj had worn only a small strip of material about his waist. He had looked younger and more vulnerable in his naked state than he had when he was fully dressed. The thread had been hung diagonally from his left shoulder, not the simple thread a poor boy of his caste might have expected, but one of thick, solid gold. He had worn a necklace of rubies about his neck and rings on his fingers, which he had twisted from time to time, betraying that he was not yet accustomed to their presence on his hands.

It hadn't ended even when the rituals were completed. A vast reception had been prepared in the durbar hall, where the boy had been once again the centre of attention as he had begged for the alms that were supposed to support his existence. Family and friends had responded by presenting him with symbolic items of money and jewellery, while the Brahmin priests had given grain. Fanny had been glad she had gone to the trouble of having some of the shop-keepers come to the *zenana* with their wares, and had chosen an ivory chess set, beautifully carved by hand, which had been placed amongst the other gifts and which she knew would be very much to his taste.

The whole of Kattyapur had been *en fête* for the next few days. Luxurious tents had been set up in every available space for the many guests and free meals had been supplied for all the townspeople. The best part for the Yuveraj himself had been the ceremonial procession through the town, great handfuls of rose petals being showered on him by his father's people. Fanny had only been able to get a glimpse of the decorations, of the flowers, the banana palms, the brass lampstands and the hanging glass lights that were hung in profusion at every corner, but she, too, had felt proud that Kattyapur could produce such a spectacle and that she had become a very small part of the life of Kattyapur.

It had been a busy few days for the Rani. If Fanny had had any illusions left about a boring, secluded life in the *zenana*, Maneka had been a striking example of how busy and varied it could be. People of all kinds poured in and out for the privilege of having a word with her, many of them connected with the school she herself had founded to train the local people in the art of miniatures, often finding the bursaries needed for the poorer students herself.

Fanny had taken no part in any of these activities, as she had taken no part in the lesser ceremonies her own two elder sons had undergone. She had spent a great deal of her time in her rooms, playing with Ganesha and nursing the second child she had borne to Sajjan, her daughter Indira.

She was remembering these things, between commanding Ila what she was to pack up for the journey to Delhi and which things were to be left behind, when another maid came to tell her the Yuveraj was below in the courtyard, wishing to see her.

She jumped to her feet with alacrity, going to the top of the small flight of steps that led up to her rooms.

'Oh, how glad I am to see you!' she greeted him. He

was a good-looking man, very like his father, but with the easier manners of a younger, less formal generation. 'What did you think of England?'

'Ganesha was more at home there than I shall ever be!' He hesitated. 'I hear you're to come to Delhi with us?'

Fanny took a deep breath of sheer excitement. 'Yes. It'll be like going on a second honeymoon!'

Despite his recent visit to Europe, she still had to explain to him what a honeymoon was, let alone a second one. When she had finished, he was laughing at her in much the same way as Maneka did. It wasn't only his father he resembled, she observed.

'It means a great deal to me!' she defended herself, going straight into the attack, just as she always had in the days when they had played chess together. 'I don't like to leave your mother alone, however. She fasts too much and prays too often when I am not there to divert her. Sometimes I think she finds the other women as boring as I do!'

'The children will fill her time – as we always did,' he answered comfortably, leaving Fanny to wonder if he had any idea of his mother's strength of character and her many interests, let alone the frightening sense of duty that made her suffer the dullest of her companions with an appearance of interest and delight.

The stars hung heavy in a sky as dark a blue as Fanny's eyes.

'Oh, Sajjan, thank you for bringing me! Doesn't this bring back the most delightful memories?'

'A second honeymoon,' he brought out slowly.

'Oho! Who's been talking?'

'I'm not telling you, but be grateful that he did. I've told him to make himself scarce – to go hunting with his friends! – whatever he likes – to give me time to be alone

371

with you in the evenings. It brings back many memories for me too.'

Fanny rubbed her hands over his shoulders. She never failed to be affected by their width and strength, the hardness of his body, and the pleasure it gave her even when they didn't make love, but just took time to talk together, as any other couple of her acquaintance might have done.

'Sajjan, I'll never reach the bottom of my love for you. Sometimes, I think it'll never be as good between us as it was this last time, but it always is, and often it's even better! I was afraid of you, and then I was afraid of having your babies, but I always loved you better than anything else in the world!'

He wondered how she could make such a claim, missing her daughter Mary as much as she still did. Did she never wish herself back in her old role of Lady Frances Bantry, friend of the Queen-Empress herself? He put the thought to the back of his mind, determined to enjoy the present moment with her by his side, willing him to crave the release only her body could bring him.

'Between here and Delhi, we have all the time in the world to make another baby!' he suggested slyly.

She relaxed beneath him, laughing. 'How delightful!' she responded in kind. 'I'm a much better mother than I ever thought I would be, though I'm getting too old to have many more children.' She veiled her eyes from him, her lashes casting shadows on her pale cheeks. 'I love all your children, Sajjan, but I love you much, much more! Will you still love me when I can't have any more babies?'

A shaft of triumph lit his eyes. 'Until death,' he promised her.

'Until death and beyond!' she responded happily.

Chapter Twenty-one

Mary stared at her father across the table in a way which he particularly disliked. The only reason he put up with her presence at all was because he was still convinced that, in one way or another, she would one day lead him to her mother and a glorious revenge. She was far too like the first girl he had married, who had eluded his grasp for so many years. There had never been another woman who had appealed so much to him, none other he had wanted so badly to plunder and bring to ruin. She had thought herself different from others of her sex who could be quickly taught to submit to their masters and he still longed to teach her the place of any woman in his life. How dared she run off and leave him in that way, if that is what she had done, or, worse still, how could she have left him for another world?

Mary's navy, mocking eyes reminded him of all he had lost. Sometimes, when he was in the same room with his daughter, he could feel his hatred for them both churning in his stomach. She knew it too, damn her to hell! Yet he had never been able to persuade her to betray her mother's memory, no matter how afraid of him she was! Yes, he had only to look at Fanny's daughter to hate her, almost as much as he had hated her mother!

He hated Mary most of all, he thought, when he saw her beside his sad, tired, defeated wife and his puny, sickly son whom he doubted would ever achieve his majority, even if he were to send them both to England, as the poor woman constantly begged him to do. It was obvious that Mary was never ill. Apart from the effects of the beating he had given her, she was the very picture of good health, embracing the heat and dust of India with all the zest her mother had brought to life. If he hadn't known that all European women suffered in the atrocious climate, he would have had to conclude that she found India the perfect place to live and enjoy herself.

'I suppose the Queen wrote to you in person to tell you of her new title?' he asked the girl sarcastically.

'The Queen-Empress, Papa,' Mary rebuked him.

'Piddling woman! We shouldn't be saddled with a woman on the throne in the first place!'

'I think she does rather well!' Mary retorted. 'And she does all in her power to reconcile all the peoples of the Empire to British rule, which is more than the politicians are able to do! I think she particularly loves all things Indian! I know for a fact she has repeated some of the things I have told her to Mr Disraeli!'

'Damned foreigner!' her father grunted. 'It shows she doesn't know what she's doing that she created him Earl of Beaconsfield. One might almost think he was an Englishman. It was probably he who decided to send out Lord Lytton as Governor General of India. He's a great deal too easy with the natives, if you ask me. Nothing but laws and regulations nowadays – all in their favour, needless to say! It's a wonder anyone can still make any money at all!'

Mary had heard it all before. 'The Empress of India. One can't help being pleased about it because at least she loves her Indian subjects, which is more than you can say for some of her representatives! Did you hear that she wrote to Lord Lytton saying, "In their prosperity will be our strength; in their contentment, our security." I wish others would show the same good sense instead of trying to pretend they were at Home, living in their own suburbs all the time! If we want to keep India, we'll have to learn as much from them as we can ever hope to teach them!'

'And what do you know about it, Miss? Females should be taught to mind their own business – even when they call themselves the Queen of England, Scotland and Ireland, or even the Empress of India!'

It had been years since Mary had first marvelled at the blinkered fear in which most of her compatriots regarded the Indians. It was all of a piece that her father should add to that the sadistic cruelty he brought to his relations with women. She had been very young when he had first taught her to wonder if stupidity and cruelty weren't somehow linked, the one leading inevitably to the other. Not that Walter Gilbert agreed with her about that. He thought people had to be taught to be cruel, and that the public schools of England were the ideal breeding ground to tutor the English ruling classes in the arts of torture, hypocrisy and contempt for others. Mary didn't blame him for his opinions, though she didn't entirely share them. She thought he was biased by the fuss that had been made when it had come out he had a Parsee grandmother, ruining him overnight in the eyes of most of those who officered the British Raj in India. Of course, if young Arthur Cunningham had been the only product of a public school she had ever known, she might have been as damning of them as Mr Gilbert was. Fortunately, she knew of one or two others who seemed to have come to no harm through that particular experience.

She put her head on one side, regarding her father thoughtfully. 'Why do so many of us go on living here, when we hate everything Indian and different to ourselves? It doesn't seem very sensible to me! It's their country after all!'

'Nonsense! It doesn't belong to them – never did! A lot

of warring peoples, never agreeing about anything, doesn't add up to a proper nation. India belongs to the British and always will because we understand government and don't stand any nonsense! The Indians aren't fitted to rule themselves, and never were! They even found the Moghuls better than their own princes! Look at the bribes I used to have to pay out to get the simplest things done! You can't trust any one of them! See a black man with an angelic look on his face and you can be sure he's laying plans as to the best way to do down his neighbour!'

Mary clenched her fists. 'The Queen made Lord Salisbury apologize for calling Indians black men.'

'Shows how little she understands about them! She'll be receiving their so-called wives, as well as the native princes, at Court next! They know better than that out here! Know better than to recognize black and white marriages at all! Which reminds me, Mary, you can tell Lady Cunningham from me that I'll take you away from her if I hear you've been seen in the company of young Walter Gilbert again! I'm giving her the benefit of the doubt that she hasn't yet heard he has a touch of the tarbrush! Parsee grandmother, I'm told! I'll not have him coming anywhere near you!'

He saw with pleasure the hurt he had dealt her. Her wince of distaste raised her a trifle in his estimation. It never occurred to him that it was he who had caused the wince, not Gilbert's grandmother, about whom Mary held the most romantic notions.

'What else did the Queen have to say to you?' He barked out the question, furious that he needed to ask. Many times he had demanded his daughter should turn all her letters over to him, unopened and unread, but she had never done so. If circumstances had been different, he would have made her obey him, but a fear that he might go too far lingered somewhere in the back of his mind. It had been a long time before he had recovered from the first interview he had held with Lady Cunningham over Mary's future, to find that Mary's mother had not only made Queen Victoria godmother to the child behind his back, but that apparently everyone but him had been quite conversant with the honour. Oh, the woman had agreed that Mary's injuries should be blamed on the dacoits who had killed her mother – if indeed they had! – but she had made it quite clear that, if such a thing were to happen again, it would be the Queen herself who would be asking about his activities in India and he had no ambition to be drummed out of the society where he longed to be a leader, a truly respected man of money.

'She suggested I should be a Maid of Honour at the durbar to be held in Delhi in her honour. Lady Lytton has already agreed – '

'You? A maid of honour? Don't be ridiculous!'

Mary shrugged, a new idea beginning to form in her mind. 'If you want me to refuse, what excuse am I to give?'

Lord Bantry's face turned a mottled red. 'You were only asked as an insult to me, you stupid girl! Everyone knows your mother foisted her bastard on to me and that I was obliged to acknowledge you because I could never produce any proof! I'll not have you taking a higher place than my wife and heir at any durbar! I don't care what excuse you give, you're not to be there at all! Pack yourself off back to Kashmir! Lady Cunningham can go with you – '

'Oh, I don't think so, Papa. She's been bidden to attend in her own right, not just because she's Sir Arthur's wife. The Queen never forgets how kind she's been to me all these years.'

'If she's as fond of you as you say, she won't mind staying home with you! No one will miss her! A common woman like that can't expect to be fêted as if she were – '

'The daughter of an Earl, Papa?'

The mocking words broke the last control he had over his temper. His clenched fist pounded on the table and a vase fell to the floor, shattering into a dozen pieces.

'Leave the room, Mary!'

Mary did so, dropping him a small curtsey made awkward by the protesting nerve in her leg. The smile she used to cover the gaucheness caused by the injuries he himself had inflicted on her was the last straw. He picked up the heavy base of the vase and hurled it after her, striking her on the head. Mary didn't so much as hasten her pace as she walked away from him, her back ramrod straight and her head held high, the blood pouring down her face from her scalp. God, how he hated her, hated her for her self-control which reminded him so much of the Lady Frances. Indeed, often, these days, he couldn't tell the mother from the daughter, now that Mary was a fully grown and independent-minded woman, and he hated them both, as he hated their whole sex.

Eileen was waiting for Mary in the hall, as she did whenever her mistress visited her father. As the years had gone by, she had become more and more afraid for Mary in case her father should force her into marriage with a man of his own kidney. The fact that Lord Bantry seemed supremely unaware that Mary was rapidly approaching an age when she could look forward not to marriage but a lifetime of spinsterdom did nothing to relieve the Irishwoman's anxieties for her.

'Mother of God, what happened this time?' she demanded.

'I'm not to attend the durbar.'

'Well, you won't be sorry for that, will you? Haven't you been saying for days you'd be the awkward one up there for all to see, and you expected to arrange Lady Lytton's train with the other girls?'

Mary dabbed a clean kerchief to her head. On the rare occasions when she saw her father she always tried to persuade herself she wasn't afraid of him any longer. The truth was that she was afraid of all men inside, where it didn't show, and of her father most of all! Only Sir Arthur and Walter Gilbert had ever been able to break through her defences; the one because even she had never doubted his obvious devotion for her, the other because there had always been something about him which had commanded her respect. He had never once laughed at the more outrageous ideas she had come out with, taking them all as seriously as she did, and never once had he dismissed her as being of no account in a man's world.

Most of her time, she had felt more comfortable amongst the *gurus* and holy men of Kashmir than amongst her own kind. Walter Gilbert had been the one person who had understood when she had retailed their teaching to him. She would discuss with him by the hour what it meant to be no more than a bubble of consciousness, contrasting that with the notion of the Christian soul. More, since they had told her that one day she would have grown out of her present body; as a snake sloughs off one skin to reveal another of equal beauty underneath, she would leave this body behind and continue her life in another, that everything was a part of everything else and thus worthy of respect, she had thought the two faiths to be totally incompatible. But Walter Gilbert had seemed to understand their teaching even better than she did herself.

'Quite right,' he had approved. 'Nothing is alien to us, no place and no person, if we know ourselves to be at one with the whole universe.'

'Do Christians believe that too?' Mary had asked him

doubtfully. Lady Cunningham's Christianity was apt to be as confused and as respectable as her own, with very little idea of the transcendence of the Other.

'Oh yes,' Walter had assured her. 'Christians believe that the whole of life is summed up in the person of Jesus Christ – all life! Can one part of your body be a stranger to another?'

Mary had thought not. She had missed talking to Walter Gilbert since he had left Sir Arthur's staff, though both men had promised he would return as soon as it could be arranged. Her devotion to him had increased if anything since she had come of age.

She dabbed at her head again, wishing she had stayed behind in Kashmir and not come to Delhi with an excited Lady Cunningham, who would never understand why Mary should have been forbidden to attend the durbar. Mary disliked practically everything about Delhi, but most of all she was bored by the endless gossip and chitchat about the latest London fashions that none of them had seen.

'Has it stopped bleeding?' she enquired of Eileen.

Eileen examined the gash. 'It has – for the moment.' She wrung her hands together. 'You shouldn't have gone in alone, Miss Mary! I told you how it'd be! Let's hope Lady Cunningham will collect us before he finds out you're still here!'

They didn't have long to wait before Lady Cunningham drove up at a spanking pace in a brand new carriage, her delight in her purchase making her overlook for the moment the ashen face of her young friend.

'Sir Arthur said I was to buy the very best! What do you think, Mary? Have I been too extravagant?'

Mary laughed. 'Sir Arthur thinks everything you do is marvellous. He won't think it extravagant at all, but just the setting to show off the jewel he married and make himself the envy of every other man there!'

Lady Cunningham lowered modest eyes. 'Well, yes,' she admitted, 'I think he may feel a little like that. I must be the most fortunate woman in all India!'

Mary chuckled. 'If you tell Sir Arthur that, he'll think it money very well spent!'

'How well you know us both!' Lady Cunningham sighed happily. She took a closer look at Mary and was shocked by her appearance. 'My dear, climb in at once. Must your father quarrel with you *every* time you visit him?'

Mary twisted her fingers together. 'There's nothing new about it, Aunt Hetty. We've always known he hates me as much as he used to hate Mama. I suppose he really is my father?'

'Of course he's your father!' Lady Cunningham clicked her tongue against her teeth in exasperation. 'What bee have you got in your bonnet now?'

'He said everybody knows I'm my mother's bastard, foisted on to him – '

Lady Cunningham's mouth tightened into a straight line of disapproval. 'He had no right to say anything of the sort to you! And I'd rather not hear such language on your lips either!'

'But if it's true, Aunt Hetty, I shouldn't mind at all! I'd rather have anyone else for a father!'

'Nevertheless, he *is* your father, whether you like it or not!' Lady Cunningham said, with all her usual good sense. Then she went and spoilt it all by adding with a bitterness seldom heard from her, 'One doesn't *choose* one's parents, or one's children either!' And Mary knew she was thinking about Arthur, who was rumoured to have struck up the oddest friendship with the ruler of Hanupur, a man who had been said to have had the breasts of his favourite concubine transformed into elephant's trunks on an idle fancy. Naturally, Arthur, and very likely her father too, found much to admire in such dissipation. They were three of a kind.

'Oh dear,' Lady Cunningham went on quickly, her pleasure in her new conveyance quite ruined as she drove off down Lord Bantry's grand driveway, 'how difficult life can be sometimes! We must just give thanks, Mary, that you don't take after your father, but your mother, poor soul. You've grown as like her as two peas in a pod and no mistake!'

Mary laughed. 'I wish I could believe you meant that as a compliment, Aunt Hetty! She took the most shameful advantage of your good nature! And I must confess I'm glad she did, for no child could have had better parents than you and Sir Arthur have been to me.'

'And very fond we are of you too! Which reminds me, Sir Arthur said I was to be sure and see you were as well rigged out as any of the other maids of honour are likely to be! Now, not a word, young lady, he's very pleased to do it. As I've told you before, taking you in was the best thing we ever did where his career is concerned. Her Majesty never fails to enquire after him, no matter whom she's writing to in India. Ever so attached to your mother she must have been,' she added reflectively, 'and it wasn't all because she was the daughter of an Earl either!' She kept to herself her doubts that no matter what Mary chose to wear, nothing would disguise her lack of any suitors for her hand in marriage! And now she had quarrelled with her father again and looked more like a prizefighter than the well-brought-up young lady she should have been.

Mary turned away, not knowing how to say it. 'I won't be going to the durbar!'

Poor Lady Cunningham couldn't believe her ears. 'Of course you're going! My dear child, what's the Queen going to think if you don't?'

Mary dabbed at her throbbing head, which had started to bleed again. With difficulty, Lady Cunningham managed to keep her hands off her and concentrate on her driving. Rightly or wrongly, she couldn't help blaming Mary a little for getting herself in such a state just when she most wanted her to look her best! She must have said *something* to have put her father in such a taking!

'Papa's forbidden it. He doesn't like my taking precedence over his wife – '

'But my dear, you're the Queen's goddaughter!'

'Yes, I know. And I know what it means to you and Sir Arthur. But the truth is, Aunt Hetty, that I'd much rather not be a maid of honour and this is the perfect excuse for me not to have to go through with it. Just imagine what a freak I should look, with only one good arm and dragging one leg. And standing all day in the hot sun is not my idea of having a good time, kind though Lady Lytton is. No, I have another plan, but I thought I'd discuss it with you first, if you don't mind – and with Sir Arthur of course!' She swallowed nervously, knowing how disappointed Lady Cunningham was not to be on intimate terms with one of the maids of honour after all. How much the older woman would have been looking forward to the hustle and bustle of being someone really important for a change, for she had never been able to think of herself as such, no matter to what dizzy heights her husband climbed! 'I'm going to write to Her Majesty and tell her I'll be in Bombay at the time of the durbar – '

'In *Bombay*? My love, do you know anyone in Bombay?'

'Not personally, no. I thought I might propose myself

for a visit to Walter Gilbert's grandmother. I know you may not like it, and I don't want to do anything you truly think I should not, but I can't think of anyone else who would welcome me into their home. I haven't many friends.'

No, Mary didn't have many friends. The truth was that society didn't know what to make of her, what with the rumours about her mother and the far more serious allegations that people made about her father from time to time. Irrationally, Lady Cunningham felt she had failed Lady Frances in some way by maintaining the contact between Mary and her father. There was always trouble, every time she visited him. Mary had a way of withdrawing into herself when anything disturbed her, and that tendency had become more exaggerated by her contacts with all those holy men in Kashmir – whom Lady Cunningham didn't consider to be holy at all, but downright shocking in the extraordinary things they asked of their bodies and tiresome with it! Oh, she had wanted to put a stop to Mary's gadding about the countryside, without anyone giving a thought to her future, years ago, but Sir Arthur wouldn't hear of it, vowing that Mary was the best eyes and ears he had in the whole of his territory. Well, for once he had been wrong and now the pigeons were coming home to roost, or whatever the expression was. Something had to be done! If Mary was ever to find a husband she had to stop consorting with natives as if they were her dearest friends and, above all, she had to be stopped from going to Bombay to visit that Parsee grandmother of Mr Gilbert's! If anyone were ever to hear of it! Lady Cunningham felt quite faint at the thought.

One thing she prided herself on, however, was knowing her duty when she saw it and she never flinched from performing it. She flicked a meaningful glance at Eileen

384

and, opening her purse, she suggested that she and the *ayah* whom she herself had employed to look after Mary's every waking moment and most of her sleeping ones as well should go and buy a selection of sweets from the *mithai-wallah* who had set up a stall a little way back from the street they were passing through.

'You never know how much English these people understand,' she muttered to Mary, 'and it's better if even Eileen doesn't hear our conversation. There's been far too much gossip already!'

'That's because nobody really believes Mama to be dead. It's just more çonvenient to pretend they do!'

Lady Cunningham couldn't deny this, much as she would have liked to do so. She wondered how it was that in a single moment Mary could manage to strip away the convenient assumptions of life and expose them for the hypocrisy they were. What did she expect them to do? Pretend that if Lady Frances was found alive and well she wouldn't be shown the door of every respectable household in Delhi and Calcutta? One had to have rules and one had to live by them. Much good it would do to try to explain that to the stubborn creature beside her, however. Mary was as unbending towards society as she was to her own father.

And that led her to even more uncomfortable thoughts. In her own mind, Lady Cunningham was convinced that Lord Bantry was mad and couldn't be held responsible for the terrible stories that circulated through the bazaars about him. Best to say nothing of *that*, she decided. One did not discuss such things with unmarried ladies, not even with Mary, all of which made it much more difficult to find the right words to tell her the few home truths she felt were fitted for her state of life.

Her horror would have been all the greater had she

known that Mary had long known all about her father. If she had ever had any doubts on the subject after her mother's departure, the few nights she had spent under his roof since then had destroyed any illusions she might have had left. She knew all about her stepmother's bruises and endless complaints as to what life held in store for her. Worse, she had heard the screams of the Indian girls he bought and brought home with him; screams that were all the more vivid because of her fluency in their dialects, which she understood quite as well as she did her own. Lady Cunningham's kitchen Hindustani might have concealed the worst of these happenings from her. Mary knew exactly what was happening to those girls – she even knew that it wasn't unusual in that terrible household for their pathetic, broken bodies to be put out with the rubbish in the early morning, for Lord Bantry's servants had made no effort to hide from her how they felt about their master.

Lady Cunningham sighed. 'If your father would only allow you to go home to England, your uncle could have charge of you, introduce you to some suitable young men, and all our problems would be solved. You'd make an excellent match, no doubt, and would have a very happy life – '

'I wouldn't!' Mary objected with a shudder.

Lady Cunningham sighed again. 'Mary, you must try to overcome your fear of men. Look how happy I am with Sir Arthur – '

'There's another reason,' Mary went on, just as if she hadn't spoken. 'I'd be bored stiff in England before the first year was out. Mama may have made an excellent hostess: I'd be a disaster! No, Aunt Hetty, I think we shall both have to resign ourselves to my never marrying.'

Lady Cunningham began to see that she should never have started on this conversation after all. Her dewlaps quivered helplessly as she wondered what to say next. What would Lady Frances have said? Inspiration struck her.

'That's all very well, my dear,' she began in firm tones, 'but there's precious little else in this world for a woman but marriage! One doesn't wish to appear worldly and ambitious – such dreadful qualities in any female! – but the importance of making a good marriage can hardly be exaggerated. You may *think* you don't want to have anything to do with a man, but the lot of a spinster is the dreariest imaginable, *everybody* looks down on her, and that's something I wouldn't like you to have to experience!'

'If I do marry, darling Aunt Hetty, you know you won't approve my choice of a husband. You know there's only one person I have ever wanted to marry.'

Lady Cunningham closed her eyes, fanning herself with a lace handkerchief. The difficulties of having to find a socially acceptable husband for Mary had been worrying her for years! She knew, without his having told her, that Lord Bantry wasn't going to settle a penny piece on the girl, even supposing she could bring any young man up to scratch in the first place! Mary was disinclined to allow any member of the opposite sex to get close enough to her to see the flashes of charm that were so like her mother's, or the sparkle of humour that filled her navy eyes with mirth at the slightest opportunity. No, faced with a young man, she pokered up, looking straight through the unfortunate as if he didn't exist for her, limping away from him as fast as she could, deliberately stressing her crippled state in a manner Lady Cunningham could only deplore. Only with Mr Gilbert had she ever been known to laugh and flirt and joke like any other young lady of her age, and she certainly couldn't marry him, not now that it was known he had black blood!

387

'Before you can marry anyone, he has to know you well enough to ask you!' she exclaimed with some asperity.

Mary laughed. 'If Walter Gilbert doesn't know me well enough to ask me, I'll ask him!'

'Mary! It doesn't matter what you say to me, but I do beg of you never to say such a thing to anyone else!'

Mary laughed again. 'What odd things you worry about, Aunt Hetty! Why should he mind who does the asking? But if you prefer it, I won't actually ask him, I'll make myself obviously available instead, as I have no doubt you did with Sir Arthur!'

'That's all very well, my dear, but your father will never allow you to marry Mr Gilbert and neither will I! It would be much worse for you than it ever was for me and, you may believe me, I know all about such unequal marriages! I knew I wasn't good enough for Sir Arthur from the very beginning and I was very hard to convince that I was the right person for him, let me tell you, mightily flattered by his interest though I was! Sir Arthur could have had his pick – '

'And would have been perfectly miserable with anyone else!'

Lady Cunningham preened herself. 'I have made him happy, haven't I? It proves what I was saying, my dear. Not all men are like your father!' Which wasn't the point she had been trying to make at all but one look at Mary, her cheeks a very pretty shade of pink despite the gash on her head, made her hope, despite herself, that she might be persuaded to look at someone other than Mr Gilbert after all. She would have looked prettier still, Lady Cunningham considered, if she hadn't become so terribly sun-burned! It was more than time she was curbed from walking out without a parasol. Nor should she be allowed any longer to talk to all and sundry in their own tongues, poking her nose into things she should know nothing about. Why, the other day Lady Cunningham had actually heard her apologizing to a servant for having caused him trouble! Whilst it was an excellent maxim that a young lady should be seen to behave as such, that did not include speaking to, or even noticing, one's inferiors as they flitted about the house fulfilling their functions.

Mary, never cast down for long, turned impulsively towards her mentor. 'But if I don't go to Bombay, Aunt Hetty, how shall I ever see Walter Gilbert's grandmother for myself and make up my own mind about her?'

'Your father will never allow it!' At least she hoped he would not!

'My father won't care where I am as long as I'm not in Delhi taking the shine out of my poor stepmama!'

Her tone was so dry that Lady Cunningham was reduced to silence. It was all too true! If she weren't so fond of Mary – But there, none of this tangle was of her making, which made it all the more imperative to take steps now to prevent her from ruining her whole life!

'Mary, dear, if I speak frankly, it's only because I'm afraid you'll get hurt. Most young girls fancy themselves in love, often with quite unsuitable young men, before Mr Right comes along! It was like that with you and Mr Gilbert. You *thought* you liked him better than all the others, but the fact is you'll never be able to marry him and the sooner you face up to that the better! There are many other admirable young men in the world who would be honoured to ask you to marry them if you were to give them the slightest encouragement. *Nice* young men, who would never dream of hurting you – '

The *ayah* came running back to the carriage, her mouth full of sweets, and Eileen in hot pursuit. The Indian woman dropped the carefully folded packages on to Mary's lap, making some laughing comment. Mary answered her, laughing also. Lady Cunningham had no idea what either of them said, but she couldn't help noticing their mutual regard, just as if they were bosom friends indeed! It all brought back that time when Lady Frances had curtseyed to that romantic-looking Raja, and look what had come of that!

Mary sat back in her seat. 'Tell me why I can't marry Mr Gilbert?'

'Isn't it enough that his grandmother is a Parsee?'

Mary's eyes rounded with suppressed indignation. Lady Cunningham cursed herself for her lack of tact. She might have known that Mary would take it amiss.

'Do *you* like Mr Gilbert less because of his grandmother?' Mary asked in dangerously quiet tones.

'No, of course not!' Lady Cunningham denied irritably, because of course everyone had their reservations about mixing the races. 'One regrets it, naturally, because it's always sad when someone of talent is held back by something they can't help, but one has to face facts, and one of them is that he'll never be as socially acceptable as he would have been without her. I daresay nobody thought anything of it when his grandfather took up with her. It was quite common in those days, I believe, as there were so few European women out here then. It's a cross poor Mr Gilbert will carry to his grave, but that doesn't mean that you have to help him carry it! Dearest child, you've no idea how unkind even the most broadminded people can be if you're the least bit different from the way they are themselves! Things will be difficult enough for you – ' She broke off, her pale eyes filling with tears. How was it that it was always left to her to explain these things, which anyone in their right mind would understand by instinct! Why couldn't Sir Arthur, just this once, be the one to tell

Mary that if she set herself up against the prevailing ways of the world, that world would turn and rend her without the slightest compunction?

Mary must have known something of what the older woman was thinking, for she put a hand on hers. 'Dear Aunt Hetty, please don't worry about me! You have to live in society for Sir Arthur's sake, and very well you do it! I don't and I hope I never have to! I offend practically everyone sooner or later without even trying and, to tell you the truth, I despise them almost as much as they do me. I'm much happier without them!'

'That's easy for you to say, but you've never made the least effort to make yourself acceptable in society, or to anyone who really matters! Most young women would give their eye-teeth to be a maid of honour to Lady Lytton!'

Mary rolled her eyes heavenward. 'Exactly! Doesn't that say it all, Aunt Hetty? Most young women would want that; I'd only feel awkward and out of place! What I do want to do is go to Bombay! Please, won't you give me your blessing?'

Thus appealed to, Lady Cunningham knew she couldn't refuse her. 'Oh, Mary love, I wish you wouldn't! But I won't stop you if you're sure that's what you want to do; you're old enough to make your own decisions. The best I can do is to pass on to you the advice your Mama once gave me and leave you to make what you will of it. I was giving my first very formal dinner party and I was very fussed about all the arrangements because I knew most people were coming for no better reason than that they wanted to pick holes in everything I did! She told me that giving a dinner party, like life itself, was all a matter of mastering the rules, just as we had to in the silly games we used to play as children. Then, if we need to break the rules, always to have an excellent reason for doing so. She knew the rules better than anyone I've ever known and, when she chose to break them, she had an excellent reason for doing so. I couldn't have done it in a million years, but I admired her for it! I always admired her! The thing is, do you know the rules well enough to break them by going to Bombay? Be very sure you know what you're doing before you cock a snook at your own kind. There may come a time when you'll need them and then it'll be too late for you!'

Mary gave her an unhappy look. 'Would you and Sir Arthur ever cast me off?'

'Certainly not! The very idea! Besides, I promised your mother, and I never go back on a promise! All I'm asking is that you take a long look at what you're doing! I only want you to be happy, my love!'

'I know, Aunt Hetty. I will be happy with Mr Gilbert, as I shouldn't be with any other man. I'm always afraid with other men – that they might turn out to be like Papa. Not even you can ever understand what *he's* like, yet he's perfectly acceptable to your precious society, even though they know he's slowly killing that poor creature he married in my mother's place. He likes young girls the best, girls younger than I am – '

'My dear child!' Lady Cunningham didn't want to hear any more. Even Indian girls had their feelings, she supposed. It was all too horrible to contemplate!

'Yes,' Mary continued calmly, 'but, you see, he cuts a very fine figure in society, doesn't he? How many other seemingly respectable gentlemen do the same as he does? Nobody wants to know, and so nobody does know! If I can't marry Mr Gilbert, I shan't marry anyone!'

Lady Cunningham took one of the sweets from the packet on Mary's lap, unwrapped it, and popped it into her mouth. She felt quite exhausted and at least ten years older than she had when she had started out that morning.

'Very well then, my dear, you have my blessing to go to Bombay – and let's hope your father never gets to hear about it! And *you* can write and explain it all to Her Majesty, because I'm quite sure that I wouldn't know where to begin.'

Mary raised her face, her eyes shining with sudden laughter. 'Oh, that's easy! I'll send her my Indian miniature to show her that we're not all barbarians out here, and I'm sure she'll understand! She isn't nearly as frightening as you make her out to be! Besides, she knows I hate having to appear in public more than is absolutely necessary. She won't mind my disappearing to Bombay!'

Lady Cunningham could only hope she was right. It wasn't only the Queen she had to worry about! She felt positively ill at the thought of explaining what Mary had decided to Sir Arthur. He wasn't going to like it any better than she did. Oh dear, why did everything that had to do with Mary have to be so difficult?

Chapter Twenty-two

Mary had never been anywhere by train before. She and
Eileen were in a state of high excitement as they watched
their luggage being stowed away and finally climbed
aboard themselves to inspect the reserved compartment
they would have to themselves. It was completely safe, for
there are no corridors on Indian trains, and they had the
whole carriage, with only a cubbyhole at one end for the
servant who would bring them their meals and see to their
every need.

'My word! Did you ever?' Eileen marvelled. 'I never
thought I'd live to see the day when I'd travel in a
monstrous contraption such as this! They were building
railways everywhere when we left England – I don't
suppose you remember? Do you think they're entirely
safe, Miss Mary?'

'I hope so.' Eileen had proved herself a noble ally over
this excursion, ever since she had learned Walter Gilbert
was at the bottom of it. Of him she approved wholeheartedly, as she attended the same church as she did herself.
To everyone else it was another black mark against him, as
it was very rarely that a Catholic could be considered as
'one of us', with their Papist religion and worship of the
Virgin Mary. Mary grinned. 'Whatever would Father
McGilligan say if he could see you now?'

Eileen was offended. 'You may laugh all you like, Miss
Mary, but I'm telling you I'd not set foot on this thing if I
didn't know that he'll be praying for the two of us this
whole night long! You never met him, but there's many a

poor soul who'd never have seen the inside of heaven if it hadn't been for the powerful prayers of that lovely man!'

Mary relented. 'It's certainly kind of him to put me in his prayers,' she acknowledged, 'as I'm not one of his flock.'

'Ah well, he'd be knowing you have no say in that! Invincibly ignorant, that's what he says you are, my dear, and there's special arrangements made for those!' She sighed heavily. 'It's lucky you are, if you ask me, for it's a terrible responsibility being of the True Faith, with only a pack of heathens all about one!'

Mary knew Eileen had never really come to terms with the Spanish or Portuguese priests who ran the parish where she worshipped. She missed having Father McGilligan on hand much more than she missed her constantly expanding family, fond as she seemed to be of each and every one of them. The Spanish priests lisped so badly she could hardly understand them and, worse, they gave outrageous penances when she confessed her sins, asking her to say a whole rosary as often as not, when everyone knew a couple of Hail Marys were all that would be asked of one back home.

Mary enjoyed travelling on the train. She had thought she might be too excited to sleep much, but as soon as the bedclothes were turned down and she put her head on the pillow, she knew nothing more until morning. By the time they reached the outskirts of Bombay, she felt as though she'd lived on a train for the greater part of her life, so familiar had its sights and sounds become. It had also proved to her, as nothing else had, that India was a vast place with an endless variety of peoples and architecture.

It took all her courage, though, to step down off the train at Bombay. The platform was crowded with more people than could have reasonably fitted into twice the space – and that was without the animals! It was one thing to look out on such scenes from the safety of the train, quite another to be a part of them herself. People everywhere stood and stared at the train open-mouthed, quite unaware that if they could see the alighting passengers, so could those passengers see them! For the first time since she had made up her mind to come, Mary began to doubt the wisdom of making such a long journey by herself, to a place where she was not known by anyone and where nobody who would know her was expecting her.

And then she saw Mr Gilbert and she could have been alone on the platform. She saw nothing, felt nothing, smelt nothing, while she drank in the unexpected vision of him, the colour flooding up into her pale cheeks, all her usual self-possession deserting her.

'I didn't know you'd be here,' she confided shyly.

He wished she were less vulnerable. He knew only too well how easy it was to hurt her. He raised his hat to Eileen, and then took Mary's arm firmly in his, leading her unerringly through the throng of people and animals and piles of luggage that were strewn everywhere across the platform.

'My grandmother, Kulfi, told me of your visit. I was able to get a week off – but more of that later! I wanted to see you.'

Mary stood still. 'Why?'

He was used to her abrupt ways by now. 'We'll have plenty of time to talk later. I thought we might make an excursion to visit the Hindu temple caves on Elephanta Island, if you'd like it? Kulfi doesn't enjoy little boats,' he added meaningfully.

'Nor does Eileen,' she said, not giving anything away.

'Splendid! It sounds as if it'll be just the two of us!'

Mary looked up at him and as hastily away. 'Lady

Cunningham wouldn't approve of my going with you without a chaperon,' she ventured.

'Isn't that why you came?'

She shook her head. 'I wanted to meet your grandmother.' She spread her fingers against the cloth of his coat. 'I'll go anywhere with you, but I don't want you to regret anything, in case anyone should get to know about it.'

He laughed out loud at that. 'You're stealing all my lines!' he accused her, and then, seeing the doubtful look at the back of her eyes, added, 'I shall never regret anything I do with you.'

Mary knew the instant she set eyes on Mr Gilbert's grandmother that she had found a kindred spirit. Seated in the tiny woman's sitting-room, crammed full of carved blackwood cabinets displaying all manner of porcelain and glass, Mary began to relax and enjoy herself. The terrors caused by her father and all her anxieties began to slip away from her. She felt truly happy.

'I thought Kulfi to be a frozen dessert?' she said to the diminutive Parsee lady.

'So it is, flavoured with pistachio nuts and cardamoms, like me! It's what I'm called by everyone nowadays. You see, we Parsees never marry outside of our own community and so I'm an outcast to my own people. My husband bought this house on Malabar Hill and I've lived here ever since. When I pass my own family in the street, we bow and exchange polite little greetings, but it can never be the same. Of course things are much worse now than they were at first! When we first married, the British found me amusing and unusual. Now I'm designated a native person and not amusing at all! I'm not complaining, Miss Bantry, I've had a very happy life; I'm telling you how things are because you're so young and have your whole life before you. It's rather like having a contagious disease; one contracts it by contact with the bearer. It won't escape people's notice that you're visiting me here.'

'I hope it is noticed!' Mary said.

'There speaks the bravery of the very young! Or is it foolhardiness?' Kulfi teased her, showing neat, even teeth that were cleaner than any other person's that Mary had seen.

'It's neither!' Mary said in that odd, abrupt way of hers. 'I have something to tell you, too. I don't have any native blood, but I do have bad blood in my veins, which is much worse! I hope I take after my mother, but one can't be quite sure, can one? People say my mother is dead, but I have never been certain that she is. She ran away when my father tried to punish her by beating me. That's why I have a weak arm and limp a bit, especially when I'm tired. I've always thought of her as someone rather special. She must have made a very good friend, because my godmother has never forgotten her, and Lady Cunningham had only met her a couple of times when she took me into her own family and brought me up as her own daughter.'

Kulfi and her grandson exchanged glances. 'Who is your godmother, child?' Kulfi asked. 'Does she live in India?'

'She's the Queen-Empress,' Mr Gilbert supplied in strangled tones.

'The Queen-Empress!' Kulfi's worship of the British sovereign was clear for all to see. 'She actually writes letters to you? How wonderful for you! But why aren't you at the durbar? Surely, you must have wanted to help celebrate her being made the Empress of India?'

'My father forbade it,' Mary explained.

'And so you came to visit Walter's grandmother? How interesting!' A smile broke over her features. 'Imagine you being on those sort of terms with the Queen-Empress!'

She bounced excitedly up and down on the overstuffed sofa she was sitting on. 'How lucky you are! It could be, I suppose,' she added in more sober tones, 'that if your father were ever to threaten your happiness, you could apply to her to overrule him?'

Mary smiled, looking the very picture of innocence. 'Exactly,' she said.

Kulfi was as proud of her Parsee heritage as she would have been if she had never had to leave the community. Over tea, and in between plying Mary with a variety of sandwiches, delicious fried curry-puffs, and iced cakes in such vivid colours they made Mary blink, she happily recounted the history of her own people.

'We came first from Pars in Persia, where we followed our own prophet, Zoroaster. We fled from the Moslem persecution because, you know, they won't allow any prophet other than their own. Sometimes one can live in peace with them, but then something will stir them up and they go crazy for a while, especially those who live in Persia, not that I know anything about them, because we Parsees never mix much with the other communities, even if they happen to have lived next door to us for centuries!'

'That's true of practically everybody!' Mary observed.

'Not of you,' Mr Gilbert said fondly. He went on, turning to his grandmother, 'In Kashmir, if Sir Arthur or I ever wanted to know anything about the local people we always asked Mary. She knew more about them than did their own ruler.'

'Not very surprising,' Mary said dryly, 'as he's of a different faith to most of his subjects.'

'And you're not?'

'Who knows what I am! How did the Parsees come to Bombay?'

'They went first to a remote island in the Arabian Sea, but later they moved on to Gujerat where, at first, the king denied them entry. It's a lovely story! The king sent for a *chatti* of milk to demonstrate how well populated his kingdom was. However, one of the Parsees present slipped a small coin into the milk without displacing a single drop. It was a gold coin, so they say, and the king was most impressed, thinking that these strangers might well bring great wealth with them. Nowadays, most of us live in Bombay, following the path of "Asha", of goodness, in the most hospitable city in all India! There, now you know all about us!'

Mary smiled at her. 'I hope I will one day,' she said.

The little lady smiled back, her eyes as bright as a bird's. 'I wish more British people felt the same. It would make things much easier for Walter! Did he tell you he's transferring from the army to the political side?'

Mr Gilbert gave Mary a quizzical look. 'Your godmother insists on equality in the political service! I'm afraid it's impossible for me to get any further in the army. They don't really want half-castes, spoiling things for the rest of them!'

'But you're as British as any one of them!' Mary exclaimed.

'Of course he is!' Kulfi chimed in.

'I used to think so,' Mr Gilbert admitted. 'I've learned better. Even young Arthur Cunningham cuts me dead these days.'

'I'd have thought you'd be glad of that!' Mary said stoutly. 'However did such fine people produce such a monster?'

Mr Gilbert put a hand on her arm, making sure of her full attention. 'He isn't a monster because he won't speak to me, Mary. He isn't even unusual in that. Most people

400

these days react as he does. All sorts of excuses are made, but the fact is the British don't want to be reminded they ever consorted with other women before they brought their own wives out here. The women object even more than the men! It was bad enough at the time of the Mutiny, when the officers had no inkling of what their men were thinking because there were no social contacts between them. Heaven help us if anything like that were to happen again! We're already all drawn up on opposite sides!' A closed look, familiar to him from the past, was the only response he got from Mary. He tried again. 'Arthur isn't a bad man, Mary. He's been taught to believe the European is innately superior to the Indian, that's all.'

'Just as my father says one has to have coloured blood to run amok?' Mary retorted in withering tones. 'You don't know Arthur Cunningham, so you don't know what kind of a man he is. Wait until he marries, and then ask his wife what sort of person he is! I don't suppose he's much different from my father!'

Somehow – Mary never knew quite how it happened – she found herself gathered into Kulfi's loving embrace, the only sign of Walter Gilbert being the door closing behind him. Mary couldn't remember the last time she had been hugged by anyone, or shown any physical sign of affection. She was embarrassed to discover she liked the warm feeling it gave her. She wanted to burrow her face deep into Kulfi's bosom and let the world go by without her for a while.

After a few minutes, however, she thought it time to resume her usual iron-clad composure. How dreadful that she should repay this woman's kindness with such a display of emotion!

'I'm sorry,' she apologized. 'That was unforgivable of me. Poor Mr Gilbert! Whatever will he be thinking of me?'

'What should he think?' Kulfi soothed her. 'He's told

me something of your father. It worries him you might think he could be violent to any woman also?'

Mary was astonished. 'Mr Gilbert? He isn't at all like my father!'

Kulfi patted her hand. 'He's a man – but I think you've noticed that for yourself, no?'

Shattered, Mary tried to recover herself. 'Yes, I have,' she admitted.

'What about Mr Cunningham?'

Mary shivered.'He's friendly with my father. Neither of them likes women. I don't really know if he's violent or not, but I feel that he could be. I don't like going near him!'

Kulfi smiled gently. 'What worries my grandson, little one, is that you'll blame his whole sex for what your father did to you. There are good men as well as bad ones in this world.'

Mary was once more in control of herself. 'If I didn't know that, I wouldn't be here,' she said with dignity.

During the next few days, Mary realized there was a family affection between grandmother and grandson that was new in her experience. They were forever laughing and joking together without resentment and without the slightest care of what they said to each other. It made her feel good to listen to them, though she seldom joined in, just in case they should feel she was presuming on the welcome they had given her.

She had heard all about Kulfi's attempts to persuade Walter Gilbert to give up his military career many years before, wanting him to take over the family's cotton business in Bombay.

'Years ago there were fortunes to be made!' she insisted to Mary. 'The American Civil War meant that all the

Confederacy ports were blockaded and Manchester's supplies in England were cut off at a stroke! For four years they had to depend on us for their cotton. Prices soared! I can remember drinking champagne out of a pint mug when my husband made a particularly good deal! However, maybe Walter was wise to choose his own career for, as soon as the Civil War was over, Manchester resumed trading with the Americans and we were forgotten, and he was still a very young man then. There were many bankruptcies over here amongst those who thought it would go on for ever, and young men are not always very wise. They're in too much of a hurry, often, to make good decisions.'

'But you survived?'

Kulfi jerked her head. 'We saved ourselves by paring our prices to the bone, though even then, most of the old cotton kings went back to their old partners. It didn't matter!' Her eyes twinkled with laughter. 'My husband knew it couldn't last. Four years was long enough for him to make his fortune. Walter will never have to worry where his next crust of bread is coming from.'

Mary hastened to assure the little woman it didn't matter to her how long Walter's purse was. It was important to her to be honest with Kulfi and she was being completely truthful about that. Money was never something that would matter much to her.

Kulfi poked her in the ribs with an affectionate finger. Unaccustomed to being touched, Mary nearly jumped out of her skin. She wasn't at all sure she appreciated having her dignity ruffled, but nor did she complain, and it wasn't wholly because she knew the little woman would laugh at her for minding.

'I'm not interested in money!' she reiterated sulkily.

'Just in my grandson?'

'At twenty-five I haven't much time left to think of marriage,' Mary told her in muffled tones. 'If I'm not to be left on the shelf – '

Kulfi poked at her again. 'I was already married at fifteen! You go with Walter to Elephanta Island, my dear, and see what that brings, yes?'

'Yes,' said Mary.

On the appointed day, when Walter Gilbert came out from the kitchen, their picnic in a wicker basket in one hand, he found Mary studying the brash, Europeanized paintings Kulfi hung with more enthusiasm than taste on her walls. Mary had listened to her explanation that they were exactly what the Queen-Empress was known to have on her own walls, finding it difficult to believe. She certainly hoped not, not when she had taken such trouble to send her the delightful Indian miniature at no little sacrifice to herself.

Seeing her doubtful expression, Walter asked, 'What kind of paintings do you like?'

Mary blushed. 'Oh – oh, these are very nice, I'm sure.'

Walter grinned. 'They're not, they're quite awful! But Kulfi likes them, bless her! You haven't answered my question.'

Mary's enthusiasm for her subject lit her up from the inside in the most remarkable way. 'I have a passion for miniatures! Do you remember the one you brought me home, refusing to say where you'd got it from, but that it was a present from somebody close to me?'

'I do.'

'Well, that started me off on making a small collection of my own. I don't have very many – and none as good as that one, which is why I chose it to send to the Queen.' She paused for breath. 'I don't think the – the person would have minded my parting with it, do you?'

'No,' he agreed. 'I don't suppose she would.'

She smiled radiantly at him. 'So she did send it!' she whispered. 'Oh, don't worry, I shan't tease you to tell me where she is – at least, not now! I won't promise never to make you tell me, because – because I've always thought she might *need* to be found one day. You wouldn't refuse me then, would you?'

'Probably not,' he confirmed.

It was the beginning of a lovely day, caught out of time, the kind of day that transforms the whole meaning of one's life, lending a glow to the future that perhaps it doesn't always deserve.

Mary stepped with some trepidation into the small boat that was to take them out to Elephanta Island. She had been greatly looking forward to being totally alone with Walter Gilbert, but she felt less sure she was doing the right thing as she watched the shore fade into the distance behind them. She wasn't any use to him when it came to sailing the boat, with only one arm and a leg which gave way just when she needed it most. She was afraid Mr Gilbert might think her a poor sort of companion for the expedition and became lost in a gloomy reverie, convinced that he didn't really like her at all.

It was no better when they finally arrived and Mr Gilbert would barely allow her to look round, he was in such a hurry to get to the temples. He wants to go home already, Mary thought mournfully, and began to wish herself anywhere but there, alone on the island with him. She couldn't think that anyone she knew would approve of her being there and she became more fearful of his intentions by the minute. When they came up to the cave-temples, she took one look at the damaged statues and refused, point blank, to take one step further inside.

'I shouldn't have come!' she said unhappily, shutting her eyes tight.

Walter Gilbert didn't notice her distress. 'They're beautiful!' he gasped. 'I suppose it was the Portuguese who damaged them – '

Mary cleared her throat, peeping at the statues through her lashes. 'What were the Portuguese doing here?' To her, they seemed a much safer subject than these lewd statues which he should never, *never* have shown her!

Walter turned his head to look at her, taking in her rigid stance and averted eyes. It wasn't the reaction he had expected from her, not his Mary! He'd been so sure that she would understand what the temples signified to those who had eyes to see.

'The Portuguese were everywhere,' he told her, giving himself time to think. 'Catherine of Braganza brought Bombay as part of her dowry when she married Charles II in 1622. Mary, what's the matter?'

'I think your statues are disgusting!'

He came close to her, putting his arms around her. 'I thought you, of all people, would appreciate them,' he tried to rally her. 'What were you expecting? You've seen the lingam, the symbol of male potency, the source of life, in a hundred temples dedicated to Lord Síva, and you didn't mind! Is this any worse?'

Mary's attention was successfully diverted from herself. 'I never knew that's what it meant!' she exclaimed in complete disbelief. 'Are you sure?'

Walter made an effort not to laugh. He thought back to the time she had sat on the hillside, overlooking that valley in Kashmir, lost to everything and everyone. She had been so young then, yet he had thought she knew everything, that her spirit had been as old as time itself. Now, it seemed, there was something he could teach her.

'Quite sure. Open your eyes and look, Mary. It isn't like you to be missish about anything that matters! Forget what they seem to mean at first sight and let their true meaning seep into your consciousness as you taught me in Kashmir. Turn round now, and take a good look! They represent the creative principle that regenerates the whole universe. See the strength of them, the spiritual power, the unity of things which ought to have nothing in common with each other. Can't you feel the power that comes to you from them?'

Mary was much more conscious of the feel of his arms about her than she was of any statue. Reluctantly, she forced her attention to the new panel Mr Gilbert was pointing out to her. She recognized the central panel, the Mahesamurti, the Great Lord, the eighteen-foot-high triple image, as representing the Hindu Trinity, and knew she was seeing in stone the monotheistic tendency in Hinduism which she had been told about before, but had never really understood. Brahman the creator was on the right; Síva the destroyer on the left; and in the centre Vishnu, the preserver of all things. The three aspects of life in one.

She was about to share her discovery with Mr Gilbert when that individual finally lost patience with her. He turned her round to face him, giving her a shake, and kissed her hard on the mouth. She felt his anger and made the mistake of trying to reason with him.

'Mr Gilbert – '

He kissed her again. He couldn't bear it that Mary, of all people, should trivialize something that meant a great deal to him. Then he felt her come to life in his arms and everything else was forgotten! This was the Mary he had always known and loved!

Mary herself was quite simply overwhelmed by the moment. No sooner had she come to terms with the darkness all about them, the erotic figures coming out of the wall at her, and a new knowledge of herself as the eternal female, than he had kissed her, the same intent look on his face that was on Síva's stony features as he stared eternally at his consort Parvati. In that moment she felt herself and the core of all reality to be one and the same.

Walter's arms fell away from her and, much flustered, she made a play of rearranging her skirts, not daring to look at him.

'I've wanted to do that for a long, long time,' he told her.

'I'm glad you did.' She could feel her heart drumming against her ribs and belatedly realized she was still clutching his hand to steady herself.

'I thought you were disappointed in me,' she said.

'You've never disappointed me, not since that first day we met and you taught me to sit like an Indian.'

'I've grown up since then,' she pointed out.

'In years, not in other ways.'

She nodded gravely. 'Haven't you noticed?'

He moved a little further away from her. 'I'm trying to remember how inexperienced you really are. I've always had difficulty remembering that where you're concerned.'

She leaned against him happily, not at all afraid of him. 'I know. I'm sorry I didn't understand your statues at first. Please kiss me again!'

'No!'

She smiled. 'Why not?'

'Because we're alone here and it wouldn't stop with one kiss. I shouldn't have kissed you before. My only excuse is that I wanted you to wake up and feel the genius and the magic of this place, not dismiss it out of hand because you don't understand it. I've always admired the way you see life as a whole, and not bits of good and bits of bad which don't fit together. But you did feel it in the end, didn't you?'

'Yes, I did.'

'Then let's go outside again and find a good place to eat our picnic.'

Mary readily assented to this plan. She had a great deal to think about and most of it she didn't think she should discuss with him. At another time, she might have taken a further look at the giant frieze because she had very little idea of what it was that men and women did together, though she had guessed some of it from the talk she had heard around her father's house. What was completely new to her was that any woman might enjoy it, but she thought that she might – with Walter. It made her all the keener to put her plan into effect, just as soon as she had his consent to it.

He found a shady grove and spread the rug out under the trees. Mary opened the basket and peered inside it, wondering which of the good things Kulfi had packed with her own hands to bring out first.

'Mr Gilbert – '

'Don't you think you might call me Walter?'

She licked her lips, eyeing him from beneath her lashes. 'Do you know why I really came to Bombay?'

'To escape the durbar, wasn't it?'

'Partly. The Queen did suggest to Lady Lytton I might be one of her maids of honour, but Papa wouldn't hear of it. That wasn't why I came though.'

Walter flung himself down beside her, putting a hand on hers as she fingered the clasp on the basket in a renewed attack of nerves.

'I flattered myself you might have come to Bombay to see me?' he suggested. 'Was that it?'

Mary didn't answer. She chewed on her lip. 'Parvati

meditated for a thousand years when she decided to marry Síva. I'd want the man I married to notice me quicker than that!'

For once he knew exactly what she was talking about. He took her other hand in his, pulling her down beside him, the picnic forgotten.

'It didn't take me a thousand minutes to notice you, my sweet Mary!'

'Didn't it? Walter, will you marry me?'

He lay completely still. For a moment she thought he hadn't heard her, then he opened one eye and looked at her. 'Ask me again when you've had time to think about what it would mean to be married to someone like me,' he said with a touch of bitterness.

She pulled her feet up under her, exactly as she would have done as a child. He thought how like her mother she looked, with the same indomitable lift to her chin, the same stubborn set to her mouth, as she considered what to say next.

'I need to know your answer now,' she said at last. 'Because, if you will marry me, it won't be the slightest use trying to get my father's consent. I shall have to go to England and ask the Queen to intervene on my behalf, and that'll take a great deal of time to arrange. I can't wish myself on her with only a few weeks' notice!'

Walter blinked. 'The Queen?' he repeated faintly.

'Don't you want to marry me?' she asked him.

Didn't he want to! He pulled her into his arms and kissed her to show her just how much he wanted her, forgetting that until today, she had never been kissed by anyone before. He felt her responses and marvelled she should trust him enough to put herself so completely in his hands. He felt an ache in his groin and reluctantly put her away from him before he lost his head entirely. There was very little of the prude she had been earlier, or the child, in the woman he had held in his arms.

'Darling Mary, I'll never marry anyone else!'

'Good,' she said. And she smiled. 'I hope you mean that because the Queen may want to see you too before she gives her consent, and she much prefers a man who knows his own mind! I love you too!'

And she bent her head and kissed him full on the lips, as if it were the most ordinary thing in all the world to be talking this way. 'Do you love me?'

'You know I do,' he said.

Chapter Twenty-three

Fanny awoke in an utterly contented frame of mind. She had loved every moment of the freedom their travels had brought her. Even here, in Delhi, they still slept in their own encampment, with herself kept well out of sight of any except her own women. But the thing she loved most of all was having Sajjan to herself for hours together as he slept the nights away beside her. She wouldn't have minded if it had gone on for ever.

They had been fortunate to be allowed to pitch their tents in the grounds of Humayun's Tomb, an edifice raised by Haji Begum, wife of the second Moghul Emperor, and dedicated to his memory. People said the design of a low building, lightened by arches and crowned by a bulbous dome, had been the inspiration for the later, and more famous, Taj Mahal at Agra. Fanny, who had never seen the Taj Mahal, was sufficiently overcome by the beauty of the monument and its surrounding gardens to think it the most beautiful place in the world.

From where she was lying, she could hear the little green parrots quarrelling in the trees and the small, striped squirrels of India pattered a path over the tents looking for the food they knew would be provided for them sooner or later. Fanny would probably put out some crumbs for them herself, for she had long ago caught the habit of providing a small proportion of one's plenty for every living creature. Sometimes she would smile to herself that Maneka's influence should stretch all the way to Delhi, for Fanny wouldn't have dreamed of disobeying any of her injunctions, no matter where she was. Where things of the spirit were concerned, the Rani ruled supreme, and Fanny seldom rebelled as she would once have done, knowing that her own wisdom lay elsewhere, where Maneka never dreamed of interfering.

It was very early but there were already people everywhere. As far as Fanny knew, Delhi never slept. The streets were forever crowded with throngs of people with nowhere else to go. Thousands of them lived all their lives in the public view of their neighbours and, in some parts of the city, the smell was a dreadful advertisement of how far there was to go before Indian hygiene was brought up to the lowest standards at home, though there too, cholera could wipe out whole villages and the children died like flies of smallpox and other such diseases. It was the heat and the perennial lack of water that made everything seem so much worse in India.

Sajjan stirred beside her. 'Are you up and dressed already?' he asked her.

She flung herself down beside him. 'It's such a lovely day – ' she began.

He laughed at her enthusiasm. 'When isn't it with you? What did you expect? One of your Irish "soft" mornings to make you feel more at home in the crowded city?'

'At least we have fewer flies!'

He lay on his back, pulling her down on top of him. 'What a pity you put all that effort into getting up, my love, when I have every intention of undressing you again!'

She made a pretence at unwillingness that wouldn't have deceived anyone, certainly not the man beneath her. 'I don't know how you can,' she protested. 'You ought to be out and about, finding out all that's going on, not wasting your time with me!'

'True!'

'Then why aren't you?'

'Because,' he said soberly, 'I not only want to make love to you, I have some questions to which you may know the answers.'

Some of the joy went out of her. 'We can never leave Kattyapur behind us, no matter how far we travel, can we ?'

'I am Kattyapur.'

'To me, you are Sajjan, my lover!'

He shook his head. 'Your lord, Fanny. I can't afford to forget, even if you do!'

Who cared what he called himself? She knew him intimately in her own body and that would always be his prime importance to her. He was the man she loved, and that meant more to her than any other role he cared to assume.

She bent her head to his and allowed the foreplay of passion to build between them. No matter how often she took her place in his arms, her joy in him was renewed as if it were their first coming together and they still had a hundred different discoveries to make about each other. Perhaps they did, no matter how well they knew the other's body, and the little, unfailing ways of making their partner's pleasure the more complete.

Sajjan caressed her breasts, marvelling that they should still be as firm as a young girl's despite her children. He touched his lips to her nipples, smiling at the shudder of pleasure that passed through her frame. This pale woman excited him as no other could. The ivory of her skin smelt of rose-water, reminding him that her maid would soon be interrupting them, unless Fanny had already told her not to make an appearance until she was sent for.

'What time is Ila attending you?' he asked.

Fanny frowned, her concentration disturbed. 'She hasn't

414

been herself since we arrived in Delhi.' She laughed, abandoning herself more comfortably to his touch. 'I think she has a lover here.'

Sajjan was doubtful. 'Whom does she know in Delhi?'

'I don't know. She lived here years ago, didn't she?'

Sajjan said nothing more, but he stored up the information in his mind. He wished he had looked more carefully at Fanny's maid, but she had never meant more to him than another pair of hands who served him indirectly and whom he seldom saw other than as a shadow in Fanny's wake. There were hundreds of women attached to the *zenana* and he couldn't keep up with each and every one of them. Not for the first time, he wished Maneka was with them. She would have known exactly where Ila was and with whom!

The maid was forgotten by them both, however, as soon as he reversed their positions on the pillows and began to make love to her in earnest, thrusting himself into her willing body with an intensity that made her yielding response the more delightful to them both.

The patter of footsteps in the public part of the tent brought them back to the present. Fanny's reluctance to bring their loving to an end was rewarded by a last, loving pat from Sajjan.

'Your maid?' he asked her.

She smiled. 'I'll have to speak to her about her timing. Shall I send her away?'

'No. Find out where she's been all night. And, Fanny – '

'Yes?'

'See if anyone followed her back here! Not that she'll know if they did or not, but she may have noticed something.'

Fanny was startled by this last instruction. 'Does it matter?' she asked.

415

'Yes, my love, it does. I've been hearing rumours that Bantry has been trying to find you. With all this fuss going on,' he added dryly, 'I'm not the only Raja in town. First Her Highness's brother is setting Delhi alight with his activities. Have you forgotten that I once made the mistake of introducing you to him?'

'Hanut.' She said the name so softly that he had to strain to hear her.

'Have you been wondering about him too?'

'Not him, no,' she answered uneasily. 'I was wondering if young Arthur Cunningham was still in Delhi. He won't have forgotten where I am either. I know he swore to his father he'd never tell anyone, but I wonder how much his honour is worth. I'd feel safer if Walter Gilbert were on hand to keep him in check. Have you seen him at all?'

'He's visiting his grandmother in Bombay.'

'I wish he were here.'

'He wouldn't be much use to you if he were. You know his grandmother is a Parsee? Once that was out, most British doors were shut against him. I'm told Arthur Cunningham was the first to cut him dead.'

Assuring herself that Sajjan was decently covered, Fanny pulled back the curtain and seized Ila by the hand, drawing her into the private part of the tent. The maid's eyes widened as she realized that the Raja was still abed.

'I'll come back, lady!'

'No, you won't! You'll tell us where you've been!'

Ila's frightened eyes went straight to the makeshift bed. 'Her Highness said I was to tell no one my lady is in Delhi.' She lowered her eyes modestly. 'I would die sooner than betray my mistress!'

'If that's so,' the Raja said, 'you won't mind telling us where you were?'

'I was with Gupta,' the maid said sulkily.

'Gupta!' Fanny repeated. 'The Gupta who works for my husband?'

Ila nodded. 'He was in Kattyapur on holiday last year,' she muttered. 'He's an honest man, Your Highness!' she appealed to the Raja. 'You remember how well he helped with your plans when you abducted my lady? Why should he want to betray her now?'

The Raja laughed shortly under his breath. 'That Gupta! You'd better bring him to see me, girl, and we'll find out how honest he is.'

'Yes, Your Highness.'

The Raja looked at her sternly. 'What news has Gupta given you of the Bantry household?'

'Why should he tell me anything?' She hesitated, chewing on the inside of her cheek. 'It's a bad place! My lady was fortunate to escape when she did. Things have gone from bad to worse – '

Fanny went as white as a sheet. 'Mary?'

'She's well. Her father forbade her to attend the durbar so she's gone away – Gupta wouldn't tell me where! It's the new wife who's suffering now, and that poor little boy of hers! Gupta says he'll be in his grave before long, that his father is already trying to corrupt him with his evil ways.'

Fanny shuddered. 'How can people allow it?' she demanded.

Sajjan sat up, holding out an arm to her. He nodded to Ila to leave them before holding Fanny close against him.

'Be thankful that Mary is far away from him,' he consoled her. 'When Gupta comes, we'll find out where she is – '

'If he knows!' she wailed. 'Oh, Sajjan, I wanted to see her so badly! It's been such a long time – '

'And you've never forgotten, have you?'

She shook her head. 'I'll never forget her. I can't! I'm sorry, because I know how much you'd like me to, but I can't. She's still my daughter!'

'Fanny, my love, it would be better for *you* if you were to forget her. What can you do for her now? Were you ever able to protect her from her father despite all you tried to do for her? You gave her life – it is enough! Do you think I don't wish daily that it could be otherwise, that I could have been the first man in your life? We have to accept life as it is.'

'Even the Raja of Kattyapur?'

'Even I! Even you! You have your other children to fuss over.'

She knew he was right but she couldn't bring herself to admit it. 'I've always felt guilty about Mary!' she said instead.

'And what about your other children? Do you feel guilty about them too?'

She threw herself on her knees beside him. 'I don't have to. They'll never lack for love in their lives, not with you as their father. But what has Mary ever had? You know what kind of a man she has for a father, and I was always so afraid that she might grow up to be like him, I wouldn't allow myself to get close to her until it was too late. I was the most abominable mother imaginable, never petting her, or telling her how pretty she was. Nobody ever loved or had time for Mary.'

Sajjan frowned thoughtfully. It was at moments like this that he was forced to recognize that Fanny was a European, driven by the same, mysterious forces that drove the rest of them. They would trample over whole nations and think it no more than their duty, yet some small personal thing that no sane person would think to be more than their passing responsibility and they would hug their guilt to themselves as closely as a lover! Yet, in a way, he could understand it! He remembered the moment when he had put out his hand and helped his mother up on to his father's funeral pyre. It was an agony that returned to haunt him frequently in his dreams. Was it something like that that Fanny had suffered when she had left her battered child behind in Delhi?

'She's gone to Bombay,' he told her abruptly. 'She's gone to visit Mr Gilbert's grandmother. She probably arranged it with the young man when her father wouldn't allow her to attend the durbar. Your Blighty Rani's wishes don't count for much with either her or her father.'

Fanny stared at him. 'How could she have done such a stupid thing? Oh, Sajjan, why didn't you tell me before when we could have done something about it?'

'I knew you would be disappointed, though it is probably best for you not to see her. She is no longer the child you left behind!'

Fanny stroked his arm, but her mind was elsewhere. Watching her, the Raja was amused to see her transformed back into the society hostess he had first known. More and more, he thought of Fanny as being one of themselves but here in Delhi, he was reminded she was still the daughter of an Earl.

'Who allowed her to go?' Fanny fumed. 'She'll be ruined!'

He shrugged his shoulders. 'There's nothing you can do about it.'

Fanny glanced his way with unseeing eyes. 'But don't you see what it'll mean to her future? She deserves better than that!'

Sajjan became impatient. 'It's none of your business any longer, Fanny! I brought you here against my better judgement so that you might catch a glimpse of her, and maybe see for yourself how she has grown up, but nothing more! She isn't in Delhi and that's that!'

Fanny knew there was sense in what he said but, all the same, she couldn't help brooding on what she'd been told. Surely Mary must have known better than to travel all that way on her own – and to see a Parsee grandmother! She wasn't prepared to play up that aspect of things to Sajjan, but anyone with an ounce of sense could have seen how British society would respond to a prank like that! Obviously, there was nothing she could do about it – she didn't need Sajjan to tell her that! – but it didn't stop her wishing she were in the position to wring someone's neck, Lady Cunningham's if none other presented itself, for allowing her daughter to do anything so socially inept and foolish besides!

As more and more people poured into Delhi, Fanny was left increasingly on her own. She didn't mind this as much as she had expected. During her time in the *zenana* she had learned how to reserve her energies in the heat of the day and the trick of doing nothing in particular for hours together. Sajjan, with his usual kindness where she was concerned, had arranged for many of the latest novels to be brought to her and this was a treat indeed for one who had been starved of much of the latest English literature for years.

'I'll make arrangements for books to be sent to you at Kattyapur every month,' he promised her.

'Have them sent to Maneka,' she suggested. 'It would be better not to have my name attached to anything like that.'

He was satisfied that her good sense was restored to her. 'Much better!' he agreed. 'I'm glad you see it that way.'

Fanny only looked at him. When he was dressed in silks and satins, he still looked like a god to her. She considered telling him so, knowing his delighted laughter would fill the tent and that it would be hard to get his mind back on to the social event he was attending that day. It was a temptation she enjoyed, glad she still had the power to move him as he moved her. It made her feel like a young girl again.

Fanny was lying on her stomach on the cushions that served as a bed, her attention focused on a novel by Charles Dickens, whose description of the scenes of poverty in London conjured up a great many memories for her. Was it some good deed she had done in an earlier life that had saved her from having to sweep the streets of a large city for a living, or from starving to death with her child beside her, friendless and alone? Perhaps. She knew enough about the mechanics of government to know it was about the pursuit of power and not about alleviating the misery of ordinary people. Human nature being what it was, she doubted if it would ever change either.

Ila came running in, interrupting her thoughts. 'Lady, Gupta is here, wanting to see you.'

Fanny looked up with a frown. 'Can't you see to him, Ila?' she asked dryly.

'He has a message for you, lady.'

'For me?' Fanny's puzzlement was clearly written on her face.

Ila nodded enthusiastically. 'It's from an Englishwoman. Will you see him, lady?'

'How did she know I was in Delhi?'

'I don't know,' Ila admitted. 'Why don't you ask Gupta?'

'I will.'

Gupta was exactly as she remembered him. She pulled her veil over her face to hide herself as best as she could from him but, even so, she could feel his shock as he took in the very different creature she had become from the mistress he had served so briefly while she had been in Delhi.

'It's good to see you again, Gupta,' Fanny greeted him.

He put his hand over his heart. 'My lady prospers in her new life!' He failed to suppress his delighted smile. 'You have become one of us! How very well you look!'

'I am well,' Fanny smiled back at him. She had always liked Gupta. 'What have you come so see me about?' Seeing her old butler and Ila together, she thought she knew. They made a handsome couple.

'A servant came with a message this morning, lady. He said he came from Lady Cunningham, or I should have sent him about his business there and then. I questioned him very closely and he certainly knows the Cunningham household as if he did work there. It seems Lady Cunningham is concerned about your daughter Mary's future. She needs your advice!'

Fanny's ire of the morning revived at his words. Of course Lady Cunningham needed her advice! The poor woman probably hadn't known how to stop Mary undertaking such an ill-judged venture. She remembered her as she had known her, at odds with society and vulnerable to any criticism. She must be very upset to ask for Lady Frances's help under the circumstances.

'Where is she?'

Gupta looked increasingly uncomfortable. 'The message said she would meet you at the Qutab Minar, at five o'clock this afternoon.'

'Then I must hurry!' Fanny exclaimed.

Gupta studied the ground at her feet. 'I was hoping to have audience with His Highness, my lady, to see what should be done about this message. If it is from Lady

Cunningham, she could be brought here to see you without any danger to yourself.'

'What danger could there possibly be?' Fanny retorted.

'Messages can be sent by anyone in another's name,' Gupta pointed out.

'But only Lady Cunningham would know I might be with His Highness – and she only because she saw us together! Who else could have sent it?'

'His Highness will know what to do.'

'His Highness isn't here! I'll miss her if I dally until he gets back! No, Gupta, you and Ila must come with me, and perhaps another strong man to see we don't have any trouble! Wait outside and I'll get ready as fast as I can!'

Fanny grew increasingly impatient as everything seemed to conspire to make her late for the appointment. 'Will you please hurry!' she begged them, wishing she could have stepped out of her conveyance and made the rest of the way on her own feet.

'His Highness – ' the hapless Gupta began.

'Forget His Highness! I have a great deal I want to say to Lady Cunningham, and it's probably much better if he never knows anything about it!'

The Qutab Minar is a five-storey tower in the Afghan style, commemorating the defeat of the last Hindu kingdom in Delhi. It dates from 1193 and is built mostly of red sandstone, though the top two storeys are made of marble and sandstone, that and the surrounding balconies being the main decoration of the slightly tilting edifice. At the foot of the tower stands what is left of the first mosque to be built in India. In the courtyard of the mosque stands a seven-metre-high iron pillar that was originally erected there in the fifth century by the Hindu king Chandra Varman, though a Sanskrit inscription suggests it may be even older and was probably brought to Delhi from elsewhere. No one knows how the iron was made. It must have some miraculous quality, not to have rusted down in the two thousand years of its existence. Fanny was unsurprised when Ila giggled and told her that if she could encircle the pillar with her arms, her fingers meeting, she would surely gain her heart's desire.

'I already have mine,' she said with a slight smile. 'Why don't you try it?'

Ila was only too willing. Fanny and Gupta stood close by, watching her as she strove to gain the necessary inches that would bring her happiness.

'You'd better help her,' Fanny advised, seeing the expression on the butler's face. How faithful these two had been to one another through the separation of so many years. It was not a usual Indian trait.

Left alone for a moment, she looked about her, interested as always in her surroundings. Squirrels ran back and forth here too, their little striped bodies practically invisible in the dappled shadows under the trees. A mongoose, in the care of a scrubby small boy, was being touted as the answer to anyone who was trying to get rid of snakes from their vegetable plots and gardens. Fanny laughed at its antics, thinking what a good pet one would make for her young sons, if she could persuade Maneka to allow one inside the *zenana*.

She was hardly aware when the touts, selling bangles, religious souvenirs, fans made of peacock feathers, and any amount of other articles, were shoved to one side by a red-faced young Englishman, his pith helmet pushed down over his brow.

'Lady Frances?'

She should have known better than to have turned at the sound of her name. No one possibly could have recognized her, closely veiled as she was, unless she had given herself away. She was shocked to recognize young Arthur Cunningham.

'What do you want?'

Arthur Cunningham savoured the moment. Before, when he had seen Lady Frances in the *zenana*, it had been more than his future career had been worth to betray her. There were no parents on hand to restrain him now. The excitement of thinking of how Bantry would take his revenge on her made him sweat more than ever. He felt hot and sticky all over. For a moment he thought he might vomit, so intense was his pleasure but, to his relief, that sensation soon passed.

'Well, well,' he said slowly. 'It is you, isn't it? I've come, Lady Frances, to restore you to the loving embrace of your husband!' He laughed shortly. 'I didn't think you'd be so easily taken in! What a simpleton you've become! That's what comes of not having to live by your wits for a while – it's made you slow, *stupid*, or were you always like that?'

Fanny glanced about her for help. Out of the corner of her eye she saw Gupta, his hand raised, and she shut her eyes tight before she could see the blow fall on the back of Arthur Cunningham's head. The helmet went spinning to one side and she bent and picked it up, her heart hammering against her ribs.

'It's Lady Cunningham's son,' she said. 'Have you killed him?'

'I hope not,' Gupta said grimly. He looked about him for Ila, summoning her to his side. 'Take your mistress home, woman, as quickly as possible!'

Ila rebelled, far more afraid for Gupta than she was for Fanny. 'What are you going to do?'

Gupta pushed at Arthur Cunningham's body with a naked foot. 'I'm going to rob him of everything he has in his pockets and leave him here. Please go, my lady, and take Ila with you!'

Fanny needed no second bidding. What a fool she had been for coming here on her own! Good God, her wits must have been addled to have considered doing such a thing! Worst of all, Sajjan would be extremely angry and she had to admit he had every right to be.

Mayhem was the only word to describe the scene when Fanny got back to their encampment. She hurried into Sajjan's tent, scuttling behind the curtain as quickly as she could manage it. Her clothes were dusty from the streets and she knew the traces of her tears could be seen on her cheeks. He would know she had been crying and he couldn't fail to notice the evidence of her adventure, even if Gupta didn't tell him about it. Slowly, she came to the conclusion that she would do better to make a clean breast to him and throw herself on his mercy. Whatever his feelings on the matter, Sajjan would never be unjust.

She went straight to him when he came in, falling on her knees before him. 'Sajjan, I've done the most awful thing,' she began unhappily.

He brushed her words aside. 'I know. I'm sending you, Gupta and Ila back to Kattyapur before anyone else guesses you are here. Oh, Fanny, Fanny, I warned you never to leave the sanctuary of my tent – '

'I thought it was a message from Lady Cunningham – '

'You didn't think at all!' he blazed at her.

She bit her lip. 'I'm so sorry, Sajjan. I've spoilt things for us both, haven't I? Please don't send me away.'

'I have no choice. Do you imagine young Cunningham will keep quiet about this?'

'He can't be certain I'm with you. I was standing apart

426

from Gupta when he came up to me, and I'm sure he didn't know it was Gupta who hit him.'

'I'm not prepared to take the risk. Gupta must disappear as well, just in case. Mr Cunningham is a friend of Lord Bantry's and will have seen him performing his duties in that household. I'm not having him hauled up before the justices because of you!'

'But must I go also?' Fanny pleaded.

Sajjan straightened his shoulders. There were tears in his eyes, but she had no means of reading his thoughts, concealed as they were behind his tight expression of disapproval.

'How can I keep you here? You'll go back to Kattyapur and that's that. I can't allow you and your daughter's welfare to endanger my people, Fanny. Go home and consider if Kattyapur isn't more important to you also than the life you used to live here in Delhi!'

Fanny bowed her head. 'You must know – '

'You could have been killed!' he groaned in response. 'For your own sake you must go quickly! You are the wife of my heart, Fanny! I don't want to have to live without you! But you can't stay here! You made your choice many years ago. I told you then there could be no going back and I thought you accepted that. Mary is the daughter of your body, but she can never mean anything more to you than that! She must live her own life apart from you!'

Fanny raised her chin. 'You won't blame Mary, will you?' she asked him. 'I've often thought you resent her.'

He shrugged. 'My other women all came to my bed untouched!' Then he saw the expression on her face and immediately wished the words unsaid. 'Oh Fanny, how do you expect me to feel about her? If you want to please me, go home to Kattyapur and learn from my Rani the virtues I expect to find in my women! She has more understanding

427

than you and I put together – and she won't be inclined to blame you for something you can't help: that no matter how hard we both try to believe otherwise, you are still an Englishwoman only pretending to be one of us!'

Fanny plumbed the depths of misery and despair during the long journey back to Kattyapur. She had Ila to talk to, but she wasn't hard-hearted enough to stop her maid from enjoying her time with Gupta. It was easy to see she was very much in love with him and when Fanny's permission was sought for them to marry, she gave her consent gladly, even while it added to her own sense of isolation. To be home once more at Kattyapur and to see Maneka again was the only joy that was left to her, for who knew how many months it would be before the Raja would be home again.

Maneka took one look at her and was shocked by the change in her. She did what she could to divert Fanny's attention on to a hundred other things, but Fanny continued to lose weight and her unhappiness was plain for all to see. As the weeks went by and still Sajjan didn't arrive, the little Rani decided that it was more than time Fanny told her what had gone wrong in Delhi. She listened to Fanny's halting story with alarm.

'If you had been discovered the whole British army might have come down upon us!' she exclaimed.

'And it would have been my fault!' Fanny wailed. 'I can never forgive myself for that! I wanted so badly to save Mary from herself, I never stopped to consider I was putting myself in danger, let alone Sajjan and all Kattyapur!'

'It is done, Fanny. His Highness will soon be home and then we shall have you laughing and enjoying life again!'

Fanny shook her head. 'It can never be the same. How can he ever trust me again? How can I ever trust myself?'

Maneka managed not to laugh. 'After all these years, and you still think yourself the most important person in the kingdom!' she teased. 'Why not leave it to His Highness to make these decisions? Isn't it enough for you that he loves you? If he was angry, it was probably because he was imagining you dead and bleeding and alone, and him unable to protect you from your own folly!'

But when Sajjan finally came, he still didn't send for her immediately, not until the Rani confessed to him her anxieties over Fanny's health.

'Has Fanny been complaining?' he asked.

Maneka's eyes flashed. 'You know better than that. Fanny never complains! The truth is that I don't think she can live without your love.'

The Raja gave her a sharp glance. 'Nor I without hers. Have I made too much of this incident, Maneka? I thought she would be killed!'

She gave him look for look. 'So I told her! I don't believe either of you gave a thought for Kattyapur, but that I did *not* tell her!'

Fanny, when she was sent for, ran straight into Sajjan's arms. 'It isn't enough for me to tell you how sorry I am! Can you ever forgive me?'

He was alarmed to see how thin she was. 'I was afraid for you!' The admission was torn from him, despite himself. 'I must forgive you if I am to forgive myself!'

'I shall never think of Mary again!' Fanny promised. 'You were right and I was wrong.' She gave him a playful prod in the ribs. 'And I didn't need all those weeks without you to work that out for myself, my love!'

He smiled slowly. 'Maneka says I should have guarded you better, that you're only a woman after all and not a politician.'

429

Fanny found herself smiling also. 'Do you know,' she said, 'that coming from Maneka, I think that may be a compliment!'

'I'm sure it is,' he agreed.

'And you, my lord, what do you think?' she tempted him.

'As long as you know yourself to be *my* woman, that's all I ask,' he said.

Chapter Twenty-four

It was the time of Holi, the festival of spring and the common people. Maneka took an innocent pleasure in the preparations, going to endless trouble to make sure that nobody was overlooked and that, come the day, all the ladies were armed with suitable ammunition to throw at one another.

'I'd love to visit Mathura at Holi time,' she confided to Fanny. 'It must be lovely to see all the processions and dances in honour of Krishna. It's said that if one is very holy one can catch a glimpse of Krishna dancing with the Gopis in the fields of Vrindavan.'

'I don't think His Highness would care to have you witness such a sight,' Fanny retorted. 'You might leave him to become Krishna's sixteen thousand and ninth wife.'

Maneka giggled, pleased by the compliment. 'I think it's you who'd want Krishna as your husband,' she said slyly. 'Perhaps he would satisfy you as even His Highness cannot?'

Fanny actually blushed. She could only wonder at how well the Rani knew her, which was all the more surprising for, despite Maneka's present heavily pregnant condition, Fanny suspected the younger woman had never found the same joy she did herself in Sajjan's bed.

Fanny gave the mixture Maneka was preparing a poke of distaste with an idle finger. Unlike Maneka, Holi was not her favourite time of year. Some of the ladies had too good an aim and too much dislike for her to be gentle when they threw the wax balls of coloured powders, or the silver and leather containers of coloured water that stung on delivery and left indelible stains that no amount of washing would remove. 'Why does everything have to have its hurtful side?' she sighed.

'Without pain we wouldn't know joy,' Maneka answered simply. 'One is the other side of the other. If you haven't learned that, Fanny, you're still a child.'

Fanny grinned. 'I'm not an "old soul" like you,' she acknowledged. 'Look out, though, I'm learning fast!'

Maneka shook her head, laughing. 'It isn't a competition.' She moved her swollen body carefully. 'There's something else I wish to tell you. This is to be my last baby – '

'Nonsense!' Fanny cut in. 'Who says it'll be your last? You're young enough – '

'No, no, I've no wish for any more. The Raja and I are agreed – '

'Since when?'

Maneka jerked her head. 'I don't require your permission, Fanny!' She relaxed a little, embarrassed. 'I thought you'd be pleased. What's the matter with you? Isn't this what you've always wanted?'

'I thought so once,' Fanny admitted. 'I can't ask you to give up so much, though. I wouldn't do it for you!'

Maneka's eyes filled with compassion. 'I know. But, you see, you don't come into this at all. I have my children. Now it's time for me to move on to the next stage in life.'

'But it isn't just the children!' Fanny objected.

'For you, Fanny, for you! I never expected more. I always knew His Highness would have other women for his pleasure. He might have considered he had done his duty after the Yuveraj was born, but he knew I longed for other children, and he has always been kind – '

'He needs you!' Fanny blurted out.

'Yes, but not in his bed. I'm giving up nothing I don't wish to give up. I wish you'd believe me – this is what I want!'

Fanny did believe her, even while she couldn't understand her motives. She knew the Rani well enough to realize how important her religious duties were to her and that many Hindus divided their lives up into different ages, following the appropriate customs for each age. With Maneka being younger than herself, however, she couldn't believe she was ready to make such a sacrifice. She herself needed the physical expression of her love for Sajjan, and his for her, as she needed the air to breathe and the waters of the earth to drink.

'Sajjan may still have something to say about this!' she warned.

But Maneka only smiled lazily at her. 'He knew many moons ago, Fanny. I am still his Chief Wife and Rani.'

'The *only* Rani of Kattyapur!' Fanny said at once. 'I knew that when I first saw you!' She was silent for a moment. 'In all my life there have only been two women whose approval really mattered to me, and yours even more than the other's.'

Maneka leaned forward, shaking her head. 'Three women, Fanny. The Queen-Empress, me, and your daughter Mary.'

For once, Fanny was rendered speechless. She knew Maneka had perceived a truth she had long denied to herself, even more since that time in Delhi.

'I gave her so little,' she said at last. 'I want her to be happy.'

'You gave her life. She has her own destiny which she must fulfil in her own way, as you must yours.' Maneka put back her head and laughed. 'You must forever be thinking you can change things to suit you, mustn't you?

433

In the end, though, it doesn't matter what we say or do. We must, each of us, do our duty as we perceive it, though probably nothing will be changed by it in the end. You make too much of what happens on the personal level, and you miss the grand forces of good and evil that move all mankind. Once, you told me your God was killed and rose again to save us all. Surely, his death meant more than a blotting out of the petty misdeeds of his followers?'

Fanny tried to hide her irritation at this exposition of her own faith, knowing that she was not deceiving the Rani one whit. Had it come to this, that she had to learn the meaning of her own religion from one of the very idol-worshippers her co-religionists were determined to convert to better things?

Her irritation gave way to a shared amusement as she caught the lurking twinkle in the back of Maneka's eyes. 'You're probably right,' she said. 'I never did pretend to understand such things. I'm sure we can change things, however. All it takes is a little thought and a great deal of perseverance!'

'Oh? And what are you going to change now?' Maneka asked innocently.

'I'd like to change the Holi custom of inviting that pack of women to visit us for the pleasure of having things thrown at us all evening!'

Maneka was much amused. Her eyes snapped with suppressed laughter. 'They've never forgiven you for having them sent away. Most of them were given to His Highness for political reasons, to push him in one direction or another. With your coming, they lost all their influence with him. Never forget that, Fanny!'

'And what's their excuse where you're concerned?'

'What other day can they throw things at me and get

away with it?' the Rani countered without rancour. 'They mean no harm.'

'They hurt!' Fanny retorted.

'A little, a very little. Poor Fanny, what a pity you don't know how to throw them back with equal vigour! These women have been playing the game since childhood – '

'Haven't you?'

'Yes, but it wouldn't do for the Rani to show more skill than the other ladies, would it?'

'I'd teach them a lesson they wouldn't forget in a hurry!' Fanny growled. 'Teach me how!'

Maneka slapped at Fanny's fingers. 'No, I will not! And if you don't see why not, that's why I'm the Rani of Kattyapur and you – '

'Merely a wife of affection!' Fanny finished for her.

Maneka laughed with her. 'Never mind! Perhaps in another life you'll have everything you want and I won't be there to share it with you!'

Which would have been fine if Fanny had ever known what it was that she really wanted. All she knew was that she would have had a hard time surviving these last years in Kattyapur without Maneka's care and friendship.

'It sounds a very dull prospect!' she said aloud, and was surprised when the little Rani looked as pleased as if she had given her a bunch of flowers.

'It would have been dull for me also,' the Rani said.

The celebrations for Holi began early. The Raja and the Yuveraj travelled through the streets of the city, seated on their state elephants, joining in the laughter and the excitement of their subjects. They came home exhausted, making much of the bruises they had received from the wax pellets that had been thrown at them, exploding against their clothes or naked skin to deposit their load of coloured powder. Some of these containers were the size of tennis balls and could land with a thump that could easily unbalance the unwary.

The women waited with ill-concealed impatience for the men to come into the *zenana*, their public duties fulfilled. It may have been a gentler game they then played round the fountain in the courtyard, but Fanny thought it must have been wearisome for those who had already suffered the ordeal of the streets. The women, as always, took a vicious pleasure in plastering Fanny with colour, both dry and liquid. Fanny's temper, never very certain under this treatment, was about to give way when the Yuveraj came to her rescue. With a few well-judged balls of his own, he had the women running in all directions to get away from them.

Sajjan grinned at Fanny's cross face. 'I'd have thought you'd be resigned to being hit a few times by now!'

'Resignation isn't my long suit!'

He wiped her face for her, displaying an appalling mixture of reds, yellows, greens and purples to her critical eye.

'You could keep to your own rooms for the occasion,' he suggested gently.

'And leave Her Highness to their mercy all on her own?'

'She enjoys it. You don't,' he pointed out.

'Nobody enjoys being bruised from head to foot! She may have enjoyed it as a child, because I suspect she was a crack shot with those things at one time, but she wouldn't dream of giving as good as she gets nowadays!'

Sajjan turned to watch his Rani for himself, just in time to see one of the women land a wax ball on the side of her face. He saw her wince and, in a flash, retaliate with a ball of her own, with a stinging force he would have been hard put to emulate himself.

'She looks as if she can manage,' he commented.

436

Fanny gave a delighted cheer in English, forgetting Maneka wouldn't be able to understand her. 'Splendid!' she yelled. 'Do it again, Maneka!'

Sajjan put a hand over her mouth, effectively silencing her. 'I thought you'd resigned from the game?' he teased her.

Fanny clenched her fists. 'I'd give anything to be able to throw like that!' she mourned.

'The Yuveraj would teach you if you asked him to,' Sajjan said dryly, knowing what a favourite Fanny was with his son.

Fanny looked down her nose. 'What would be the use? Her Highness demands we suffer in the name of *noblesse oblige* – most of the time,' she added as Maneka got in another telling shot at one of the more persistent pests of the *zenana*.

Sajjan didn't understand the French words, but he understood what was meant by them. He laughed out loud. 'You ought to understand that, Lady Frances!' he teased her. Then he sobered, looking sad, as he often did when he looked at her these days.

'I haven't been Lady Frances for a long time now,' she tried to soften his mood.

'No, but tonight you must try to think like Lady Frances again – if you will?'

'Has anything happened?' she asked him uneasily.

'The old Raja has died in Hanupur. Hanut is supposed to succeed him, but the British have heard enough about him to think they may be forced to take over Hanupur themselves.'

Fanny bit her lower lip. 'Is that anything to do with us? I can't tell you what the British may do about anything these days. I don't want to know! Please don't ask it of me.'

437

Sajjan looked at her long and hard. 'You never used to be afraid of your own people! You begin to think like a woman, Fanny!'

'I am a woman!'

'But you used not to think like one.' He brushed his forefinger down her cheek. 'Another day I would approve the change,' he said sadly. 'Tonight, though, I need you to think like a man, a man of courage and honour!'

'I'm afraid of being swayed by old memories again,' she murmured, not looking at him. 'I'd never forgive myself if I let you down once more!'

'Me, or Kattyapur?'

She tried to smile, knowing he was trying to comfort her. 'You're always telling me you're one and the same thing, but you never will be for me. It's the man I love!'

'Then tell me what I must do to pacify the British and keep them away from Kattyapur. Hanut was my brother-in-law. I don't like the British being so close to us here.'

She nodded helplessly. 'We can't keep them away for ever! The time is coming when you'll have to compromise with them – and you'll get a better deal from them as their proven ally than anything I can do for you after all this time. Hanut is nothing to you, after all. His women are terrified of him!'

Sajjan rubbed his chin thoughtfully. 'Listen in tonight and then tell me what to do!' he instructed. 'You will know better than I if they are genuine in wanting my friendship, or if they mean to use me for their own ends.'

It was with a heavy heart that she took her place late that night behind the marble lattice work. The British came in full uniform, their swords dangling by their sides. Hearing their clipped accents, Fanny thought how foreign her own people had become to her. These men were strangers to her, as if she had never known their ways at

438

all and, if they were ever to meet face to face, she knew they'd dismiss her as the barbarian she had become. They no longer had anything to say to each other.

Nor had they much to say to Sajjan. They may have come as allies to pick his brains about what he knew of the new Raja of Hanupur, but they treated him as a servant who had no independent existence of his own. Things must have changed a great deal since she had left Delhi. It was obvious that all government had become bogged down in the red tape that surrounded every communication between London and Calcutta. It was as if they no longer trusted anyone, and it showed. Their questions were cautious, suspicious and couched in such condescending tones that Fanny longed to give them a piece of her mind on Sajjan's behalf. It was obvious that while they disliked Hanut, Sajjan, as his brother-in-law, was equally under suspicion. They no more believed his protestations of friendship than he did theirs. Was this crass mismanagement of men and affairs a common feature of the new British government, she wondered, with its lack of respect for the men and manners of the sub-continent?

She felt weary and disillusioned by the time she was taken back to her own rooms. With enormous care, she washed herself from head to foot, for she still had some of the colourful stains from the women's courtyard 'game' all over her clothes and body and she was hopeful of ridding herself of at least the worst of them, along with the feeling of distaste the British had left behind them. It was only when she had finished that she acknowledged to herself that she was afraid of what the future would bring to Kattyapur.

By the time Sajjan sent for her, her fears had put her in a very bad temper indeed.

'I'll tell you one thing,' she said as soon as she saw him. 'They don't trust you any more than they do Hanut!'

Sajjan smiled at her furious face. 'You didn't like them?'

'When they spent all their time patronizing you, the Rajputs, and everything you've tried to do here?'

He raised an eyebrow. 'As bad as that?'

Fanny sat down abruptly. 'I thought them bad-mannered and stupid! Were the British always like that?'

'I believe not. Some of them are still quite likeable!'

'I'm relieved to hear it!'

He took her hands in his. 'Is that all you have to tell me? That they don't trust me as an ally?'

She took a deep breath. 'No, I have one more piece of advice to give you.' Her eyes glimmered with tears. 'It's best I should be nothing more than your wife of affection from now on. The British are on the march and there is nothing I can do to protect you from them. I don't understand why they are doing this, but it's clear they can see no difference between you and Hanut, or any other native Prince!'

He caught a single tear on his forefinger. 'I never thought to see you cry over what you used to laugh at and call the Dance of the Peacocks,' he smiled at her. 'You never used to cry!'

'Because I always thought I could save you from them!'

'Hush, my love. India can do with their Pax Britannica, as you well know. We go to war with each other far too often and without any care for the well-being of our peoples. Hanut isn't the only one of his kind. That's why I must play my part in the dance. I don't want the British laying siege to my gates. They make far too good soldiers. I shall always need you, Fanny, to explain their ways to me. Is that too much to ask of you?'

Fanny sighed. She was silent for a long, long time. 'I

can't advise you any more. You must deal with them yourself and make a new treaty with them. Go to the very top – to Sir Arthur Cunningham, if he'll listen. These men who came here tonight know little and care even less!' She put a hand on his arm. 'I haven't been of as much use to you as you hoped, have I?'

His fingers brushed her naked flesh, eliciting an immediate response. He kissed her on the lips, his tongue making a play for hers. 'Your advice wasn't the only reason I brought you to Kattyapur,' he reminded her. 'Aren't your children enough of a hint of what I want – will always want! – from you?'

She laughed, successfully distracted from her own dark thoughts. 'Tell me about it?' she invited him.

'Aren't the children enough for you?' he countered.

'Not nearly enough!' She put her head on one side. 'And to think I used to wonder why the Queen-Empress had so many children!' she mocked herself. 'She tried to explain it to me one day, but I didn't know what she was talking about! Poor thing, she must be so unhappy without her Albert!'

Their love-making was slow and satisfactory. She was hardly aware when he lifted her and carried her to his bed, for the familiar waves of desire were already breaking against the sandbanks of control she had over herself. Higher and higher he took her, raising her from one peak to another until, satisfied, they fell back to reality, warmed and contented in the glow of happiness they never failed to find in each other. She would always have this moment, she thought, until the day she died. She had loved, and she had been loved. A smile curved her lips. She had certainly been loved today, loved as the woman she had always been, despite Maneka's initial doubts on the subject. Sajjan's wife of affection was all she ever wanted to be

441

from now on. Henceforth politics would have to take care of themselves, leaving her to fulfil the only real ambition she had ever had in life – to be the woman of the Raja of Kattyapur!

Chapter Twenty-five

Mary had never been as cold as she was at Osborne. The Queen, she was told, didn't like rooms to be overheated, which meant that most people went about with perpetual colds in their heads and noses like beacons, made worse by Her Majesty's own imperviousness to the virus. She showed no sign whatsoever of knowing how ill one could feel with a raging cold and nothing to comfort one but rallying commands to pull oneself together. Mary had been flattered to be asked to spend the Christmas season with her godmother. What was even better was that Walter Gilbert had been invited to accompany her, not that she had seen anything of him, for he was being put up at Barton Manor, whereas she had the doubtful pleasure of sharing the Princess Beatrice's rooms, the Queen's youngest child, married for two-and-a-half years, but still living at home as her mother was still as possessive of her children as ever; indeed, probably more so as she was so much alone these days except for the chosen few who did their best to keep her from brooding over the welfare of her subjects. Princess Beatrice couldn't have been more welcoming, though she plainly thought Mary to be rather an odd guest to be invited for the festivities.

Waiting for the Queen in her own private sitting-room, Mary spent the time looking out of the wide, curving bay window to the sea beyond. Members of the royal family were arriving from all over Europe and sounds of laughter sounded through the house that the Prince Consort had first bought and then practically rebuilt so that he and his wife should occasionally have moments of privacy, away from the prying eyes of her subjects. There was no doubt that it was this which made it Queen Victoria's favourite place. Her love of the Isle of Wight was well known and she was always there at least twice in every year.

Shivering with cold, Mary turned away from the window, wondering if she dared sit down. Two desks stood in the room, one of them with a whole lot of bell-pulls by the knee-hole. Mary went closer to read the legends that were imprinted on them and was surprised to notice, amongst the many pictures of the Queen's family, a portrait that she thought at first was of herself. It was small and, without thought, she picked it up to study it more closely. The clothes the sitter wore dated it to about the time when Mary had been born. There was no doubt about it, it was a portrait of her mother.

'You're very like her to look at, my dear.'

Mary whirled about, the portrait falling from her fingers. She made a valiant attempt to catch it before it hit the floor, but her crippled arm refused to move quickly enough and it landed with a crash at her feet.

Scarlet with humiliation, Mary made her curtsey. 'I'm so sorry to be so clumsy!'

'I startled you,' the Queen said kindly. She watched as Mary stooped and retrieved her mother's picture, pushing her left arm into position with her right hand. 'I hadn't realized you were so badly injured that terrible day,' the Queen went on. She took the portrait from Mary. 'You're very like her!'

'Only in my looks,' Mary answered. 'I could never be a London hostess, or do half the things she did.'

The Queen seated herself in front of the desk. 'She was one of my dearest friends. I can't count the number of times she stood where you're standing now, telling us all

444

the latest gossip. My dear Prince Albert thought very highly of her! This was his desk, you know, where he would sit and explain all the State papers to me.' She pointed to the desk on the left of her own. 'I miss those days!' Tears came into her eyes. 'And it isn't the least use telling me life must go on, it doesn't help in the slightest!'

'No, it doesn't,' Mary agreed in her odd, outspoken way. 'I never admit my mother's dead, Your Majesty.'

The Queen's face softened momentarily. 'She must be dead as far as I'm concerned,' she said with gentle emphasis. 'I won't listen to you if you tell me otherwise.'

'No, ma'am.'

'But that isn't why you came here, is it?'

Mary took a deep breath. 'I came to tell you about the man I want to marry!'

'Did you, indeed? And what has your father got to say about it?'

Mischief lit Mary's eyes, making her hearer gasp at the likeness between her and her mother. Just so had Lady Frances looked when she had been about to say something outrageous – and that had usually been about Lord Bantry also!

'Lord Bantry has the gravest doubts that he is my father, ma'am. I have to respect his opinion – as you are always telling me I ought! – and so I did exactly as he asked and haven't bothered him since with my own affairs. It seemed to me that your consent was much more important to me! If the Queen-Empress says her goddaughter may marry, who will dare gainsay her?'

'Very like your mother!'

Mary went on her knees beside the Queen's chair. 'May I tell you a little about how I feel about him?'

'Perhaps you'd better. You can begin by telling me what's wrong with this young man of yours?'

'There's nothing wrong with him. If he doesn't go about much in Calcutta and Delhi, it's because he has an Indian grandmother, who absolutely worships you and has pictures of you in every room of her house in Bombay!'

'You won't flatter me into liking him!' the Queen told her.

'I wouldn't dare!' Mary declared, laughing. 'If your daughters can't flatter you into thinking their way, who am I to try?'

'That sounds like Princess Beatrice!' The Queen was silent for a long moment, her indignation growing visibly. 'What does it matter if his grandmother is an Indian?'

'It matters in India a great deal these days, ma'am.'

'Well, *I* shan't hold it against him!'

'I'm glad. You see, ma'am, when I was so badly injured as a child, it wasn't by the dacoits who killed my mother. It was Lord Bantry who whipped me within an inch of my life. After that, I was afraid of every man I met. A man, *any* man, can seem perfectly respectable and be accepted everywhere, and yet he may still be a monster to his own family. I want to marry Walter Gilbert because I'm not at all afraid of him.'

The Queen sighed. 'Your father was always the same! But men have some rights in this world which women don't. He was entitled to take your mother to India with him – she was his wife! And he's entitled to veto your marriage, my dear, if he's a mind to!'

'If he is my father!'

'Yes, well, as to that I won't venture an opinion. I've often thought I was wrong in not asking him to leave your mother in London as one of my ladies-in-waiting.'

'Ma'am, I'll be for ever in your debt – '

'Yes, but are you the best judge of what will make you happy, child? I'm not going to promise anything! However, I will see Mr Gilbert for myself and, if I like him, we'll see what can be done. Meanwhile, we have Christmas to celebrate. It's one of the best times of year, don't you think? Everything's so pretty at this time of year! Of course, it was my dear Albert who brought the Christmas tree to this country and it makes such a lovely focus for our present-giving and for all the family parties!'

Mary did her best to look enthusiastic. Her own impression was one of universal greyness. The sky was grey, the sea was grey, even the bare trees were grey. Looking out of the window, there wasn't a single flower to be seen. She longed for the burning plains, the brilliant sunsets, and the colour of the people she increasingly thought of as her own. A few splodges of what was half-snow and half-rain landed on the windowpanes. How often had Lady Cunningham told her of the joys of a snowy day in England! She thought the grey sleet a poor thing beside the snows of the Himalayas, especially with the damp cold that went with it.

The Queen, watching her, saw the girl shiver and determined there and then to look kindly on the young man she wanted to marry. When she thought of the time and care she had lavished on her own children, the Swiss Cottage that had been built for them, the model farm where they had played, and the Fort Albert where her sons had learned the first rudiments of military matters, by comparison Mary's childhood had been bleak indeed.

'Have you taken any exercise yet today?' she asked her goddaughter. 'You may walk out with me, if you wish. We may even go across to Barton Manor and I'll show you the grove of cork-oaks the Prince Consort and I planted together. I expect your Mr Gilbert will be pleased to receive a visit from you?'

'Oh *yes*, Your Majesty! I'll just change my shoes – '

'And a warm coat! Take one of Beatrice's, yours weren't meant for this climate! And if you see any of the grandchildren with their nurses, they may come with us. I see little enough of them these days, they're all so far away!'

The children were all pleased to be going out with 'Gan-Gan', as they called her. Nursery tea, consisting of a piece of brown bread and butter, followed by another smeared with a light coating of jam, was plain by any standards. Mary had been shocked at first, until she had discovered that, washed and brushed, they were taken down to their grandmother immediately after tea, and she shamelessly fed them sweet biscuits while she tried to balance the younger ones on her extremely slippery knee. She loved them all and they all loved her, even while their nurses threatened them with her ire every time they stepped out of line.

The Queen rode in a dog-cart, graciously acknowledging the greetings of everyone they met. Everyone else walked. Mary wandered through the cork-oaks, thinking how dreary they were, dripping water on to everyone. No matter how hard she tried to avoid the puddles, her shoes were soon damp and rubbed her ankles. Then she saw Walter coming towards them and everything in her world was made right again.

She ran towards him, her whole face alight with joy. 'The Queen is going to see you! Oh, Walter, isn't it marvellous!'

He saw she was limping badly from the long walk from Osborne to Barton Manor and wondered if he dared ask the Queen to take her up with her for the return journey. The Queen, her sharp eyes missing nothing of their reunion, came suddenly to life.

'Mr Gilbert!'

He made his bow, colouring at the implied rebuke in her voice. 'Your Majesty.'

'My goddaughter has walked further than she is able. Be good enough to see her home.' The dog-cart pulled away, before halting again. 'Oh, and Mr Gilbert, we're expecting you to join us for the festivities tomorrow.'

'Thank you, ma'am.'

The Queen nodded, satisfied. 'Don't be late for supper, either of you! I can't bear to be kept waiting for my meals!'

It was a very pretty scene with all the colourful packages heaped up under the elaborately decorated Christmas tree. It did something to alleviate Mary's hunger for sunshine, heat and dust, and above all for some of the strong colours of India.

'I thought there'd be flowers in the gardens,' she confided to Walter Gilbert. 'Aunt Hetty always said – '

'Not in winter.'

'Why can't there be flowers all the year round?'

'Perhaps one appreciates them more if one only has them part of the time,' he suggested.

She shook her head, quite definite about it. 'I love flowers all the year round. And another thing! Aunt Hetty said English birds sang better than Indian ones. When they sing at all, they sound much the same to me, and they're not half so pretty!'

'It's winter, love. Spring and summer is the time for birds.'

Mary thought it was more likely that it had been a long time since Aunt Hetty had seen her native land and that, in the way people have, she had remembered only the sunny days and forgotten all about the endless weeks of rain and cold.

She turned her attention on to the Duke of Connaught,

Arthur, the Queen's seventh child, a young man a couple of years older than she was herself, whose annual task it was to hand out the gifts from the tree. It made a pleasing pattern to watch each recipient take his or her parcel, open it, and then rush across the floor to Gan-Gan to show her what they had found inside. It was not like anything she had ever experienced before.

And then her own name was called and Connaught was thrusting a small package into her hand. Completely overcome that anyone should have remembered her, she took it back to Walter and opened it on his knee, her excitement at having a present all of her own visible to everyone. Beneath the wrappings a small, painted miniature fell out into her hands. She knew at once it wasn't one of the Moghul ones which had previously been all that had come her way. This one was finer, with purer colours, a magnificent work of art that rendered her completely speechless.

'It's beautiful!' she whispered.

'You'd better go and show it to the Queen as everyone else does,' Walter prompted her.

She went at once. 'It isn't Indian, is it?' she asked, the words tripping over each other.

'No, child, that one is Persian. I thought you might like it as you obviously have some knowledge of oriental art. It will grace your collection, as the miniature you sent me graces mine! You have very good taste! I'm told the one you sent me is a museum piece – not that I plan to part with it! I have it close by me in my bedroom!'

Nor was that the only present that Mary received. No one was forgotten, not even Walter Gilbert, who received a set of coins to commemorate the new Empress of India, and a pocket watch that had once belonged to the Prince Consort. Nothing could have indicated the Queen's approval more completely than this last gift, for her mourning for her husband was as genuine now as it had been on the day of his death. To him, and to him alone, she had surrendered her whole being and she had been stricken with the loss of his support, not only in her private life, but in her role of sovereign. She had quite simply not known how she could go on without him and, even now, she felt herself a lesser being without him to tell her what to do on every occasion. It was a feeling that Mary understood very well. It was exactly how she felt about Walter Gilbert.

To meet his sovereign alone and face to face was the most nerve-racking ordeal that Walter Gilbert had ever undertaken. His collar felt at least two sizes too small for him and his gloves didn't seem to fit his hands. He managed a very smart bow, however, and stood to attention, his military cap under his left arm.

'You sent for me, ma'am!'

'Yes, Mr Gilbert, I did. I am not, however, a military parade, so perhaps you will stand at ease and allow me to get to know you. You should learn something from my goddaughter, who isn't in the least bit afraid of me! I'm your Queen, Mr Gilbert, not your judge and jury!'

A reluctant smile lightened his scowling features. Now that he allowed himself to look at her properly, he was surprised to discover that Queen Victoria was every bit as small as his own grandmother. And she seemed to have a genuine affection for Mary.

'If I'm nervous, ma'am, it's because I'm afraid you'll think me impertinent to aspire to Mary's hand in marriage. She could look much higher – '

'Yes, I expect she could. To tell you the truth, I'd like to keep her here with me for a year or two, and I had planned to do exactly that, but she would be like a caged butterfly, don't you think?'

'Yes, ma'am, I do.'

'You know, Mr Gilbert, Lady Frances Bantry asked me, before she went to India, if I would take an interest in her daughter's future should anything happen to her. It didn't take much imagination to know that she, my dearest friend, was bitterly unhappy in her marriage to an unscrupulous man who was very unkind to her. I'm telling you this because, as a man of the world, you will know that there is nothing any outsider can do if a husband chooses to abuse his wife and children; not even I can do anything about that! It distressed me beyond measure when she told me she was afraid she was going to her death in India, but it was my duty to let her go, and hers to obey her husband's wishes.'

She fell silent for a long moment. Mr Gilbert cleared his throat. 'I am acquainted with Lord Bantry.'

The claim was met by a sharp look. 'Is it true that he told Mary he wasn't her father?'

'Yes, ma'am. Nobody takes him at all seriously when he says things like that. Mary chose to take notice this time – '

'Yes,' the Queen cut him off. 'I understand exactly why Mary decided to apply to me for consent to her marriage! What I want to know from you is, will I be doing right if I give it?'

Walter rocked back on his feet. 'If I may say so, ma'am, I think the sooner Mary leaves her father's control the better. One hesitates to speak of the past, but she owes him little in my opinion. She has known very little happiness in her life.'

'What about Sir Arthur and Lady Cunningham?'

'They brought her up as their own daughter. But they, too, especially Lady Cunningham, are afraid of Lord Bantry. If she ever has to return to live under his roof, I fear for her life, ma'am.'

'You may be right. Very well, Mr Gilbert, tell me about yourself. Mary has already told me you have an Indian grandmother. She seems to think you find her something of a handicap to your career?'

'She is a Parsee, ma'am. Even if it were to put an end to my career, I wouldn't change her for anyone else! I can't wait until I tell her that you actually received me in your own private room! She's your most loyal subject!'

'So Mary told me,' the Queen said dryly. 'If she can find the space on her walls for yet another picture of the Queen-Empress, I shall give you a signed picture to take back with you for her. Others may feel themselves to be superior to those who live in other parts of the world, Mr Gilbert, I do not! One of these days, I mean to have an Indian secretary to help me understand better all that is happening in the sub-continent. More, I mean to build an Indian durbar room here, at Osborne, so that we can become more accustomed to each other's culture. People are forever telling me that women are particularly badly treated out there. Would you agree with that?'

Mr Gilbert swallowed. 'They are,' he began. 'It's the same with them as it is for women anywhere, ma'am. Their lives depend far too much on the whims of the men of their household. It's my belief it'll always be the same until women have control over their own property and have a legal entity other than being the chattels of their husbands.'

'You're a radical, Mr Gilbert!' the Queen accused him. 'I prefer a more conservative approach myself. Women shouldn't have too much power – it's against everything I believe in, like this new Married Women's Property Act!'

She looked up, catching the amusement on his face. It wasn't often that anyone dared laugh at her, but she had never minded someone holding an opinion that was contrary to her own. She didn't think it would do him any harm to be brought down a peg or two, however.

'Do you have money, Mr Gilbert?'

'My grandparents made their fortune in cotton during the American Civil War. Kulfi, that is my grandmother, controls the family business at the moment, but eventually it'll come to me.'

'Your grandmother is a good businesswoman? No doubt you get your radical views from her?'

'And from Mary.'

The Queen was thrown off-balance by that answer. She didn't quite know what to make of it. 'That's all very well, but if you can't advance any further in the army, things being as they are, what do you plan to do with your life?'

'I've applied to transfer to the political side, ma'am. I'm fortunate in having worked on Sir Arthur Cunningham's staff and he has promised to put in a word for me in all the right places.'

The Queen was thoughtful. She nodded. 'We need good political agents to represent us in the Princely States. I think you'd do very well pursuing such a course, don't you? What languages do you speak?'

Walter Gilbert told her, impressed by her intimate knowledge of India. 'I rather fancy being sent to Kattyapur,' he added, knowing he was treading on dangerous ground.

The merest flicker of an eyelid was all there was to betray the fact that the name was familiar to the Queen. 'Why there?' she asked, in smooth, neutral tones.

Mr Gilbert was tempted to pull at his too-tight collar, restrained himself with an effort, and waited for some inspiration to strike him. It did. 'You already know of Mary's great interest in Indian art, ma'am. The Rani of Kattyapur is the acknowledged expert in Indian miniatures in the whole sub-continent. People travel from all over the world to seek her opinion on their work. She has founded a school in Kattyapur, so that the old methods can be rediscovered and passed on to the succeeding generations. It would give Mary a great interest when I am away from her. She may even care to try her hand at learning the technique herself.'

'Lucky girl!' Queen Victoria was something of an artist herself and she knew the value of proper teaching. It was one of the things she and Prince Albert had prided themselves on providing for their children. She thought it was a future that should suit her goddaughter very well. She gave the young man in front of her a look of complete approval.

'Mr Gilbert, I shall be very glad to give my consent to my goddaughter becoming your wife. I shall write at once to Lord Bantry informing him as much, and also that you will be married in my presence in the church at Whippingham before you return to India. If you are to travel out together, it will be much better if you do so as man and wife, quite apart from the fact that it will relieve us of the necessity of having to explain why none of your parents on either side has chosen to be present!'

Mr Gilbert blushed scarlet. He longed to embrace the smiling woman in front of him and he would have done, too, if she hadn't held him off with an imperious hand.

'The Church of St Mildred at Whippingham is where I myself worship on Sundays when I am at Osborne. It was largely rebuilt to the design of my husband. Even the rose windows in the north and south transepts were made to his designs, adapted from the much larger rose window in Notre Dame Cathedral in Paris. Princess Louise will make all the arrangements! She has a great feeling for all such things, I promise you. Well, young man, what are you waiting for? I haven't the least doubt that Mary is waiting outside for you to tell her what the verdict is. All I ask of you is that you be kind to her!'

'I will, ma'am.' He turned to leave, thought better of it, and came back to face her. He licked his lips, sweating profusely. 'After what her father did to her, Mary is afraid of most men,' he said awkwardly. 'She isn't afraid of me.'

The Queen smiled up at him. 'And have you ever thought why that might be so?' she asked him.

'No, Your Majesty, I haven't.'

'Then I shall tell you. You liked her before you loved her. Mary has known very little of either emotion. You'll do very well together, Mr Gilbert, but do try to remember that women expect a lead from the men they marry! Don't let those radical ideas of yours create any unhappiness between you!'

'No, ma'am!' he said. And bowing formally to her, he left her, almost running in his eagerness to get back to Mary.

Chapter Twenty-six

1878

Mary sat in the middle of the huge bed, dressed in a plain calico nightdress that was the best one she possessed. She hadn't previously allowed herself to think beyond the wedding ceremony and now that it was all over, she had little zest for the night ahead. It was cold in the hotel room, colder even than it had been at Osborne. Outside, a few flakes of snow were the forerunners of the wintry storm that was coming. Mary had been frozen all day. She had been chilled through in the bedroom she had shared with Princess Beatrice's personal maid even before she had been allowed to get up and dress in the exquisite lace wedding-dress the Queen had given her. In the church she had been shivering so badly, she had found it quite difficult to concentrate on her vows, or to look at Walter, feeling him only as a threatening shadow by her side. It had only been by making her mind a blank and concentrating on Her Majesty's generosity to her that she had got through the service at all.

Nor had the reception been much better. Mary had always felt awkward in company, feeling that everyone was remarking on her limp and the uselessness of her left arm. Mostly, neither bothered her much these days, but when she felt herself the centre of attention, her old self-consciousness returned to her and she wanted nothing more than to run away and hide. Walter hadn't been as much help to her as she had hoped. Surrounded by the royal children, he had proved himself a great favourite with everyone, especially the Duke of Connaught, who had been kind enough to support him through the ceremony, and who had put himself out to be pleasant in the most affable manner.

Mary had been more concerned with the Queen's reactions. She was still surprised that such an important person should actually like her, and she had been overcome by Her Majesty's generosity, herself paying for everything she felt Mary could possibly need in her new life. She had even taken it upon herself to speak to Mary on the evening before her wedding day, as if she were indeed taking the place of the girl's mother. Mary, accustomed to plain speech, hadn't had the least notion what she was talking about. Seeing this, the Queen had backed away with one last warning that Mary should always obey her husband in everything.

'It comes to all women, my dearest child, and to some few of us is given True Love and that makes all the rest worthwhile! I hope you find it with your young man!'

Mary had curtseyed, longing to make her escape. Now, she rather wished she had stayed to listen to more. The Queen might have given her some clue as to what was expected of her now that she was alone with her new husband.

Shivering, she forced herself to reflect on her visit to Osborne, congratulating herself on its success. She had achieved everything she had set out to do, so it was strange that she didn't feel more triumphant, as she had during the Christmas charades, for instance, when even the critical eyes of Princess Louise, the Duchess of Argyle, had been pleased by her ingenuity in working up the scenes that had given the clue to each syllable of the word they were portraying for the other side to guess. She had forgotten for a while both the cold and herself and had thrown herself into the game with the zest for life she had inherited from her mother. She wished she had more of it now, instead of the lowering feeling in the pit of her stomach that something quite dreadful was about to happen to her, and that she would never be able to feel quite the same about Walter thereafter.

They had crossed the Solent to the mainland on the Queen's own private yacht, standing side by side on deck in the snow, Mary in the coat she had first borrowed and had then been given by the Princess Beatrice. Almost she wished herself back again on the heaving deck – anywhere but here!

The door opened and Walter stood there, looking strangely unlike himself in his nightclothes. Mary shivered again and in a flash he was beside her, pulling her close against the heat of his body.

'Poor love, you are cold, aren't you? Did you long to run away to your secret place and sit on your feet for a while in total silence, after shaking the chattering monkeys out of your mind and heart?'

Mary nodded, unable to speak. She buried her face in his shoulder, a little bit reassured by the familiar male smell of him, now mixed with soap and water as a legacy from his ablutions.

'From now on,' he went on more tentatively, 'I'm hoping you'll run to me and not away from me.'

Mary tried in vain to stop her teeth chattering. 'You won't always want to be bothered with me,' she said, determined to be practical, 'and I have many interests of my own. I shall try not to be a nuisance to you.' She gulped. 'The thing is, I'm not sure what you want – '

'I want to make you warm,' he comforted her. 'Come, lie down under the bedclothes and hug me until you stop shivering! You'd think they'd have taken the time to warm the bed for us, wouldn't you?'

Mary did as she was bidden. 'I don't expect to feel warm again until I get back to India!' she sighed. 'Everybody speaks of England as Home, but I long to be really at home again, don't you?'

He rubbed a hand up and down her back. 'We'll always be at home with each other! That's what marriage means, my Mary.'

The last place Mary felt at home in was that enormous bed with him, but she didn't dare say so. She waited for him to lie down and go to sleep, hoping she would be able to do likewise, but sleep seemed to be the last thing on his mind. She wondered if she should tell him that the cold made her arm and leg ache even more than usual. In her experience, however, gentlemen didn't really want to hear such things. She supposed it was because they were injured so frequently in battle themselves that they seldom offered sympathy to one another as women did – not that she knew very many men, but she well knew that Sir Arthur Cunningham, when faced with his wife's petty ailments, would only hum and haw and look the other way, even while he might tell her that his poor Hetty was feeling a bit under the weather, don't you know?

Her thoughts were interrupted by Walter lifting the hem of her nightdress and drawing it up. She pushed his hand away indignantly.

'Don't!' she said crossly.

'My love, don't you realize I want to see you?'

She eyed him thoughtfully. 'Why?' she asked at last.

He laughed shortly. 'Haven't you heard the expression about never giving a man the right to dress you if you don't also give him the right to undress you?'

Her eyes widened. Memories of the Elephanta caves came back to her. 'Are you going to do *that* to me now?'

He might have known she would mention the unmentionable with all her usual bluntness. Her inability to dissemble was a constant delight to him.

'One of the reasons I married you was to make love to you,' he confirmed gently.

Mary managed a fleeting smile. 'I'm not beautiful like the statues,' she told him.

'You are to me!'

She thought it must be true if he said it. She wondered if she should tell him she found him beautiful too. Every time she had seen him at Osborne she had thought how handsome he was, looking fit and tanned amonst all the other pale courtiers. With a sudden, impatient movement she helped him remove her nightdress, wishing she was as voluptuous as the female statues had been.

'You know,' she said, because words were the last weapon she was going to throw away until she knew exactly what he intended by her, 'I don't think your advice about dressing and undressing is meant for married ladies. It probably isn't proper at all.'

'Probably not,' he agreed gravely.

A frown creased her brow. 'Is it – is it as much fun if you're married?'

He grinned. 'I'll tell you tomorrow.'

'But you're undressing me now!' she objected.

'Oh, that! Darling Mary, you're a constant delight to me!' He chuckled, putting his arms right round her and hugging her close to him beneath the bedclothes. She had seldom been completely naked when she had been alone and her consciousness of him beside her in the bed brought a light flush to her face. For the first time since coming to England she felt truly warm! 'Mary, my love, I love you very much! If I didn't, I wouldn't have asked you to marry me!'

'You didn't,' she reminded him. 'I asked you!'

He chuckled again. 'Because you love me?'

As always, she took the question perfectly seriously. 'I'm not sure I know what that means. I *like* you better than anyone else I've ever met. I know they say perfect love casts out fear, but I've always been afraid when I've loved anyone. I loved Mama, but until the last few days I never felt comfortable with her – '

'Loving me will be quite different from loving your mother!'

'Because of what you're going to do to me?'

'Amongst other things. Loving someone means finding a delight in them, thinking them beautiful, being glad when they come into a room, laughing together, maybe quarrelling once in a while for the joy of making up!'

Mary was entranced. 'Then I do love you!' she claimed. 'You make me feel warm all over – '

'I mean to make you feel other things besides that!'

Mary had thought her moment of triumph had been when she had gained the Queen's consent to her marriage to this man. Now, she knew it was nothing compared to this moment. If this was what being a woman meant, how glad she was that she was one!

She turned happily into Walter's arms, as eager to make her own discoveries about him as to receive the caresses he plied her with. It never for a moment occurred to her to hide her pleasure in the effect of his body on hers. She was equally proud and pleased that she should arouse him and, once the initial burning sensation was past when he first entered her, she rode the heights of the experience with him, never once holding back as he had supposed she

462

might, inexperienced as she was and with the example of her father ever before her.

When, at last, they fell apart and settled themselves for sleep, he inwardly applauded her courage. In the past, he had known her to be many things, all of which he had admired, but he had never suspected she could be as passionate or as physically generous as she had just been with him.

He pulled her sleepy form closer against him. 'If anything ever happens to me, love, you must promise me to find another husband who'll love you as you deserve!'

Mary grunted against his shoulder.

'You hear me?' he demanded with increased urgency. He couldn't bear to think of this glorious creature, unknown to anyone but him, being stunted and unloved ever again for as long as she lived.

'I shan't want to marry anyone else,' she said. 'I've always known that, haven't you?'

'There are other men – '

Her fingers found his mouth and silenced him, smoothing his lips in a gentle caress.

'Not for me,' she said. 'They wouldn't understand Síva and his Dance of Life. You were the only one who was in the temple that day. You and me. Síva and Parvati. It's because you understand that that I've never been afraid of you. We don't really matter at all, do we?'

'Don't we?'

'No, it's life that matters.' Her hand strayed down his body and found its target. She smiled slowly as his muscles tensed against her. 'You've taught me so much tonight!' she said. She moved her useless arm out of her way and began to kiss him as he had her. 'I'll worship the life force in you any time, my love! How about you?'

* * *

Sir Arthur Cunningham's moustaches twitched angrily. Lord Bantry's very name was enough to put him in a bad temper these days. If he had had his way, Lord Bantry would have been forced to leave India a long time ago. He could have told anyone who cared to listen that one monster would inevitably seek out others of his own sort, but this particular trio could bring nothing but pain to him. Lord Bantry, the new Raja of Hanupur, and his own son. Poor Hetty would say their son was misled and that he wasn't as bad as the other two, but Sir Arthur had always maintained you could tell a man by his friends, and that said it all as far as young Arthur was concerned.

Poor Hetty! Sir Arthur had known as well as did everybody else that she had hoped Mary would look favourably on a marriage with their son. Who could blame her if she had preened herself a little at the thought of being the mother-in-law of a goddaughter of the Queen-Empress herself! Women were given to their foolish dreams. Sir Arthur cleared his throat, congratulating himself on his greater realism. Mary was as dear as any daughter could have been to him and he was glad she had married her Walter Gilbert, though how she had talked the Queen into permitting it was beyond him! He'd always thought the old girl was a realistic person, awake to everything that was going on around her, yet it was frequently said she despised social pretensions. Perhaps she had thought the disapproval of young Gilbert by his superiors to be something similar. She couldn't know how much it had come to matter if one had a touch of the tarbrush these days! Women, even the best of them, like his Hetty, would always try to change facts to suit themselves when it came to their dreams of romance, filling their lives with a lot of nonsense they'd be better off without!

And now he had learned that Lord Bantry had been invited to the new Raja's festivities in honour of his accession and was already on his way to pay an extended visit to Hanupur where, no doubt, he would be provided with enough female flesh to sate even his perverted tastes. Sir Arthur wondered if the time hadn't come to deal with that nest of vipers. That was something he wanted to consult Walter Gilbert about as soon as possible. He valued that young man's advice more than that of his aides these days.

He sorted further through the messages that had been left on his desk and his eye was caught by another one that dealt with Walter Gilbert personally. Sir Arthur's eyebrows shot up with astonishment when he saw the boy had been appointed Political Agent to Kattyapur – and on the request of the Queen-Empress herself! Slowly, he whistled under his breath. The sly dog! But he couldn't think of anyone he would rather have down in that part of the world! It was the best piece of news he'd had for a long time!

Lady Cunningham was pink with excitement when her husband finally got home that evening from his temporary office in Delhi.

'They're home, my love! And ever so happy!'

'Where are they?'

He stepped back to watch Mary's approach, disappointed to see her limping worse than ever. Did that mean she was something less than happy with her new husband?

'Well,' he harrumphed, 'how was England?'

'Colder than you'd believe,' she told him in that odd, abrupt way of hers. 'It was snowing when we left – and please don't tell me any more stories about how beautiful it is! It's nothing of the kind!'

'Isn't it?'

Mary's eyes danced. 'Aunt Hetty seemed to remember it that way!'

'Aunt Hetty is a romantic, my dear!'

Mary reached up and kissed him warmly on the cheek. 'So is the Queen-Empress – and sentimental with it! Her welcome was as warm and loving as the climate was chill and grey.' She held out her left hand to him. 'What do you think of the new Mrs Gilbert?'

'She looks a great deal grander than Miss Bantry used to do,' he commented.

'I'm still the same person inside.'

'Are you, Mary? You weren't tempted to stay with your godmother for a while at Osborne as she wanted?'

'Mr Gilbert talked her out of it. She didn't care who his grandmother is! I liked her very much, Uncle Arthur. She and Aunt Hetty would understand each other very well.'

'Tell that to your Aunt Hetty,' he advised her. 'Between the two of us, my dear, she isn't best pleased you've married Walter Gilbert. She had such high hopes for you!'

Mary smiled knowingly. 'Not Arthur again!'

Sir Arthur's moustaches twitched in sympathy. 'Never did like him, did you? Nor did I! Always told her it was unrealistic to think you'd look his way, but you know what women are!'

'I'm beginning to,' she said gravely.

The moustaches twitched, followed by a guffaw of laughter. 'You are, are you? Perhaps that Gilbert is a better choice for you than we realized!'

'I think he is, Uncle Arthur.'

Sir Arthur had rather more to say to Walter when he managed to get him on his own, away from the ladies. 'Want to talk to you, my boy!'

'If it's about Mary – '

'It isn't! Thing is, I heard today you're being sent to

Kattyapur by personal request of the Queen. What's the meaning of this, that's what I want to know? You know very well who else is down there!'

Walter looked thoughtful. 'Do you know, sir, I could have sworn the Queen herself had a personal interest in Kattyapur. She covered it up mighty quickly but, just for a moment, when I told her that's where I wanted to go, there was a flash in her eyes as if it wasn't the first time somebody had mentioned it to her. I could have sworn she knows a great deal more than she's given credit for. And another thing, she keeps a portrait of Lady Frances on her desk, in amongst a whole collection of family pictures. I thought it was Mary at first – they're very alike, aren't they?'

'Did you *ask* to go to Kattyapur?' the older man asked, aghast.

'I thought Mary would like it.'

'You must be mad! What tale did you spin to the Queen?'

Walter Gilbert fired up indignantly. He bit down his anger, however, knowing how much they both owed this man. 'The Queen knows about Mary's interest in Indian miniatures. She shares it, as a matter of fact. She gave Mary a beautiful Persian miniature for her Christmas present. I told her the Rani of Kattyapur is a recognized authority on Indian art and that it would give Mary something to do, to learn the techniques in the Rani's own school. Her Majesty thought it a jolly good idea. You should see some of her watercolours! They're as good as any I've seen anywhere!'

Sir Arthur looked at him shrewdly. 'Mary liked her too. I'm not criticizing you, boy, for taking her to Kattyapur. Know your own business best, I daresay. To tell you the truth, I'll be devilish glad to have someone sound there. You can both accompany me for the shenanigans at

467

Hanupur on your way there. Did I tell you I'd been chosen to represent the Crown for the occasion?'

Walter was delighted. 'Congratulations, sir!'

The two men shook hands, the understanding they had always shared renewed and strengthened by their common devotion to Mary and their love for India.

Lady Cunningham made the most of her small moment of glory. She insisted Mary went everywhere with her to retail all the latest gossip from London in general and of Osborne and the Queen-Empress in particular. Nothing went as she had anticipated, however. Mary would talk happily about her uncle, now regularly attending the House of Lords and claiming he had been put out to grass and was being kept away from the Commons where the real political life of the country was carried on as they now held the purse strings. She would talk about her cousins, the latest fashions, and made an effort to restrain herself when the beauties of the English winter were extolled in her presence. The one thing she would flatly refuse to speak of was the one thing that everyone wanted to hear: how the Queen looked, what she had said, and who her favourites were these days.

'Dear child, I wouldn't ask it of you if it weren't for your own good!' poor Lady Cunningham pleaded with her.

'I know, Aunt Hetty. I won't use the Queen, however, no matter how much you want me to! What she did for me, she did for the sake of her friendship with Mama. She even paid for my wedding gown, and for my trousseau – the wedding, everything! She became a person to me, not a peepshow!'

Lady Cunningham sat down on the nearest chair, her plump face quivering with emotion. 'You always did hit hard, Mary! But, dear child, I didn't mean you to turn Her Majesty into a peepshow!' She gave the younger woman a despairing look. 'You don't know how they talk! I thought that if we talked about the Queen enough, they might overlook – they might be prepared to forget – '

'That Kulfi is my husband's grandmother?'

'Well, yes, dear.'

'But I don't want anyone to overlook Kulfi.'

'You may not, but you won't be asked anywhere. You might as well be a fallen – '

Mary put a hand over her mouth, stifling her laughter. 'Me, Aunt Hetty? Is that what we've come to? That to be married to someone with black blood is as bad as fornicating with a white man?'

'*Mary!*'

'I'm sorry, Aunt Hetty.' Mary played with the ring on her finger. 'Don't you ever think we're rather a ridiculous people?' She saw that Lady Cunningham did not. She had fought her way to the top and that was where she meant to stay. Mary sighed. 'Don't worry, they'll soon forget all about me and my marriage when I've gone to Kattyapur – '

Lady Cunningham clutched at Mary's knee, her face pale. 'Kattyapur? Why are you going to Kattyapur?'

Mary's eyes narrowed thoughtfully. 'Mainly because I prefer to live where my husband is going to live and he's being sent to Kattyapur.' She paused significantly. 'What does Kattyapur mean to you, Aunt Hetty?'

'To me, my dear? Nothing. Absolutely nothing! All these little States sound exactly the same to me! Oh Mary, whatever shall I do without you?'

Mary embraced her gently. 'Aunt Hetty, you've always treated me like your own daughter and, believe me, I shall never be able to repay you for all you've done for me, but even your own daughter would have left you one day and gone to live with her own husband – '

'Oh that, my dear! It isn't that! I could bear that, as long as I knew you to be happy with Mr Gilbert, but I shall be afraid for you every day in Kattyapur! I wish you were going anywhere but there! Even to Bombay, to that Kulfi, or whatever she's called. But Kattyapur! *Anything* could happen to you there! I'll be worried to death night and day until you come back to Delhi!'

Mary withdrew, a mask falling over her face. 'There must be more to it than that!' she said abruptly. 'Aunt Hetty, is Kattyapur where you think my mother is?'

Lady Cunningham nodded, the tears falling down her plump cheeks. 'Yes, I'm sure she is! But Mary, there's nothing you can do for her, and what good will it do getting yourself involved with her again? She'll blame me for allowing it, I know she will! And it isn't my fault! It's Mr Gilbert's fault for wanting to take you there!'

'Nobody will blame you for anything, Aunt Hetty! If my mother's there, it's up to her to make herself known to me, don't you think? It's the Rani I'm interested in! Did you know she's quite famous for her collection of miniatures? I mean to learn all I can from her – if she'll receive me, though why she should want to receive anyone from the British Raj is quite beyond me! Now, please don't cry, Aunt Hetty, or Uncle Arthur will never forgive me!'

Lady Cunningham cried all the harder. Mary threw her an exasperated look from time to time, wondering why people had to take on so about nothing at all. It was thus that Walter Gilbert found them and, taking in the situation at a glance, he set himself out to entertain them both with stories of their adventures on the ship out. In a few moments, Lady Cunningham was laughing with him, exclaiming over Mary's refusal to sit at the Captain's table for her meals, and wishing she could have been with them when they had visited such places as Cape Town.

'Don't you long to be going back again?' she sighed happily to Mary in an agony of nostalgia.

Mary was about to tell her she wouldn't mind if she never saw England again, when she caught her husband's eye. She blushed instead, looking suddenly very young and modest.

'I shall always remember my English wedding night,' she said instead, and was rewarded by the look of warm laughter in his dark brown eyes. It was a remark which met with Lady Cunningham's complete approval also.

'I'm sure you always will, my love, as I do mine! So much nicer than these hot, sticky nights we have out here, with never a breeze to make one feel in the least bit romantic!' She paused, shaking her head. 'If only it weren't Kattyapur!'

Mary, her patience exhausted, raised an eyebrow at her husband. 'Why didn't you tell me Mama is living in Kattyapur? Did you think I'd make a scene, or something? Well, I won't, not unless *she* wants to see *me*. Do try to explain to Aunt Hetty that it won't matter where we live, Mama doesn't have to see us if she doesn't wish to.' Her eyes filled and she looked away. 'She probably won't want to see me after all this time, and I don't blame her, not if she thinks I may have turned out anything like my father!'

Lady Cunningham blinked mournfully at her. 'But, my love, you always said you meant to find her one day and, although I couldn't approve of your doing so, I can't let it pass that she wouldn't be delighted to see you, grown up and a married lady. She would be every bit as proud of you as Sir Arthur and I are, of that I'm quite certain!'

She would have liked to have said a great deal more, but Mary's face bore that shut-in look that she knew well of old. She didn't envy Mr Gilbert having to deal with Mary in one of those moods of hers. She looked to him for help and, to her astonishment, he gave his wife a poke in the ribs, smiling down at her, and said,

'What Mary means is that it'll all be the same in a hundred years, ma'am. Surely you know better by now than to let her philosophizing worry you?'

'Oh well, if that's all it is,' she began, and was even more surprised when Mary gave a delighted giggle and, taking her husband's hand to her lips, kissed it for everyone to see, just as if they were alone together! And she watched as they laughed together like a couple of children, holding hands in the most unaffected way. They were still laughing when Sir Arthur came to join them, a broad smile on his face.

'I haven't heard anyone laugh like that since Mary went away!' he said. 'How thankful I am, *we are*, to have you home again! Aren't we, my dear?'

Seeing her husband looking so happy, Lady Cunningham thought things couldn't be so bad after all. 'Indeed we are,' she said warmly, and wished she had the courage to hold her Arthur's hand in public, just as Mary was doing. 'And what's more, I'm *glad* the Queen gave her consent to your marriage, no matter what anybody else says! I hope you'll be as happy as Sir Arthur and I have always been!'

'And still are!' Sir Arthur chimed in, looking at his wife in just the way that she liked best. 'And still are, my love!' he repeated gruffly.

Chapter Twenty-seven

Fanny was learning something of Maneka's interests and duties the hard way. She grew increasingly concerned about the Rani, who had been withdrawn and more subdued recently than she ever remembered. Maneka herself said it was only her pregnancy that was making her so listless. 'Besides, Fanny, it's good for you to have something to occupy your time!' she would tease her friend.

Something? Fanny had been completely overwhelmed by all that was being asked of her. She hadn't been entirely surprised to find that Maneka kept lists of all the women's fête days, as well as the birthdays of all their children. It was she who consulted the astrologers to discover the exact moment when each celebration should begin and end; it was she who gave the orders for the food to be prepared; she who saw to the purchase of the proper gifts; and she who supervised the sending out of each and every invitation, taking enormous care that no lady should feel slighted by the omission of her name from any function she was entitled to attend. On top of all this was the business connected with the school of painting she had founded, and the enormous correspondence she carried on with anyone who sought her advice on the miniatures she loved so much and about which she was such a recognized authority.

Glad to help, Fanny had soon reduced the burden by organizing it properly. There was nothing she could do, though, to lessen the resentment the other ladies felt because Maneka had chosen her to represent her on many an occasion. There were whispered accusations that she brought undue influence to bear on the Rani. To all of this, Her Highness paid no attention at all.

'You will obey my wishes in this, Fanny,' she had commanded gently, smiling one of her increasingly rare smiles. 'It'll cause less dissension in the end, you see. There isn't another lady here who could organize a tea-party, let alone all that I have to do. They aren't trained to do anything like that. If a pedlar arrived with a few baubles, they'd be instantly distracted and nothing would be done! Besides, I don't trust them not to gossip about my affairs and that is something I won't put up with!'

Fanny soon found the school of painting to be the most fascinating part of Maneka's correspondence. The Rani's knowledge of the Hindu myths was unrivalled and she never minded how many questions were asked of her, explaining the details of this painting and that. Over the years, she had acquired a deep insight into the Moghul culture which had first brought the miniature art form to India and she had had no difficulty in marrying that culture to her own. She took a delight in the formalized flowers and animals, the Tree of Life, the arabesques, and the use of the script as a part of the pattern. When these were used to tell the stories of Krishna, or Rama, or to illustrate the Bhagavad Gita, nothing pleased her better.

'Look, Fanny!' she would enthuse. 'Take a look at these flying goddesses. Aren't they beautiful? You see the upper one, dressed only in a *dhoti* and a rope of pearls, with hennaed hands and feet? That attitude is typical of these goddesses all the way from India to China. Doesn't that please you?'

And after a while, Fanny did begin to understand better what it was that she was looking at. However, she much preferred the paintings of small domestic scenes, for, even with the benefit of Maneka's tuition, she was still inclined to confuse one god with another, or any of them with the Lord Buddha, but there was never any mistaking a pert little courtesan making the most of her opportunities as she entertained some great lord or other. With her, Fanny could identify with the greatest of ease and she would wonder why Maneka should laugh at her for saying so.

Then, one day, Maneka had another task for her. When she was summoned to the Rani's rooms, she found Maneka frowning over a letter which she was trying to read at the same time as carrying on a spirited argument with her maid about the heat of her bath.

'Ah, Fanny,' the Rani greeted the other woman, waving the scented paper in front of her, 'the great-aunt of His Highness is leaving Kattyapur to live with her daughter. She lived in the Little Palace up on the hill. Have you been up there? It's beautiful! One can see right across the city even better than one can from His Highness's rooms.'

Fanny managed an interested look, hoping Maneka wouldn't guess how much her reference to Sajjan's view could still hurt her, she would so much have preferred to be the only one to know it well.

'No, I've never seen it,' she said aloud.

'No, I doubt she would have received you, but there's nothing to stop you going there now. His Highness thinks it will be a good place to put the new Political Agent and his wife and it occurred to me you might like to oversee the preparations, as they are British like yourself?'

'Me?' Fanny felt more sulky than ever.

'Yes, you,' the Rani insisted. 'Who else could do it as well as you can?'

Fanny threw back her head. 'How about you?' she retorted.

Maneka's low laugh answered her. 'And have my child born up there? If I start anything I like to finish it. As soon as the baby comes, I won't be allowed out for days!'

Fanny had reason to know the truth of that. The ceremonies at the birth of one of Maneka's babies went on and on for long hour after long hour. Candles were lit to keep the demons and the darkness of the night at bay, and to open a window was unforgivable in case it let in what might be lurking outside, waiting for the slightest opportunity to come in and do harm to either mother or child. It was well known that all spirits are more active in darkness, while humans slept, and so few visitors were allowed in during those dangerous first days; the women kept vigil and the priests were kept busy reciting their prayers, and nobody got any sleep at all, Maneka included.

'Fanny, do it for me?' the Rani begged her.

Unable to refuse, Fanny rose to her feet. 'Yes, Your Highness.'

Truth to tell, all this talk of a British Resident in Kattyapur was depressing to her. She took it as a symbol of her failure to carry out her part of the bargain she had struck with Sajjan when she had first run away with him. Now, although she herself had advised the move, she was resentful that it should be necessary. Worst of all, the British had met Sajjan's request with deep suspicion. She could almost hear them asking themselves what he was up to now. Well, she would have as little to do with the British influx as possible, taking refuge in the *zenana* and pulling the curtains tight around her.

Thus it was that she put off visiting the Little Palace for as long as she could, finding any number of excuses to delay the task, knowing before she started the resistance she would meet from the other ladies, high and low, when it was realized that it was she who was giving the orders. There were times when Fanny imagined that one or two of the ladies actively hated her and she did her best to stay out of their way on the rare occasions when they came to the *zenana*. Devil take the British! How she wished they would stay away and leave her in peace! She could imagine them, even now, strutting about and upsetting Sajjan when they countered any of his plans for the welfare of his people! Nor did she like the idea of these strangers knowing of her own presence there. Only trouble could come from that, she thought.

Yet she didn't like to refuse Maneka. When she looked back over the last few months, she could see that the Rani had been withdrawing from the public part of her life a little more each day. She would still preside at all the major ceremonies that took place in the *zenana*, but her private life had become more austere and she spent more of every day at her prayers.

'As a child,' she had once told Fanny, 'I used to visit the Jain temples in Jaiselmer and I often wished I could be a Jain myself. Their temples are so beautiful!'

Fanny knew nothing of the Jains, but Ila had told her that most of the Rani's dietary restrictions were borrowed from this sect. Only Fanny seemed to think that Maneka was too young to start withdrawing herself from the pleasures of this life to concentrate on the dubious qualities of the next. But then Fanny had always believed in holding on to what she had and living the only life she was certain of to the full.

A few days later, however, saw Fanny making her way to the palace. The men's cries and the sound of the whistle, blasting its warning of her approach, was an everyday experience to her now. Fanny twitched at the curtains impatiently, longing to be done with the whole business.

The Little Palace was the most beautiful building Fanny had ever seen. She was enchanted by the delicate pillars that supported the *chhatris* of the roof, and the walls, tiled in the Moghul style with a multitude of formalized flowers, animals, trees and geometric patterns. Some of the windows were of latticed marble, some glazed with coloured glass in vivid hues of blue, red and green. Everything was delicate and feminine, giving an airy feel to the whole that lent it an appearance of something out of the Arabian Nights. Situated high over the city, it caught whatever breeze was going. If ever anything happened to Sajjan, Fanny vowed to herself, this is where she would live out her last days.

She stood for a long time on the verandah, gazing down at the city below her. She had never been higher than the Fort-Palace before, but from here she could see the roof of the *zenana* itself, painted blue to keep the flies away. The bare rocks of the cliffs shone white in the sun, broken by small scrubby trees in which a myriad of birds chattered and made their homes. Below them from time to time stalked a strutting peacock, raucous as always, preening himself on his elegant beauty, with an occasional vicious peck directed at his drab little mate.

The peacocks were ever-present in the countryside of India, marching and counter-marching with long, stilted steps. Fanny watched them with a sour smile. She had been right to name the game the British played with the Indians the Dance of the Peacocks. It was a territorial game, loaded at the moment in the favour of the Europeans, but she doubted if it would always be like that. India was timeless, and the Indians were a patient people who thought in terms of many lives rather than one. In the end, the Pax Britannica would crumble and India would divide again into its several parts. Was she learning a little of Maneka's wisdom? She hoped so. It was so much more comfortable not to have to feel responsible for every little thing that went on in the world, to know herself to be no more important than a single grain of sand.

Ila was in the main bedroom when she went looking for her, a little resentful that Fanny should expect her to stand between her and the other servants when she would far rather have been at home with Gupta. She wouldn't have come on this expedition if Gupta hadn't persuaded her that Fanny's need was greater than his for the day.

'What will the woman do when she is "out of her house"?' Ila demanded. 'There's nowhere here for her to hide herself.'

'The British don't hide themselves at such times,' Fanny told her. 'They don't think of themselves as being unclean.' She chuckled, seeing Ila's shocked face. 'They even go on cooking for their husbands if they don't have servants to do it for them.'

'How terrible!' Ila shuddered. 'Don't they know anything?'

'Don't you remember how it was with me when I first came here?' Fanny smiled at her.

Ila's eyes rounded with the memory. 'You knew nothing!'

'Exactly,' Fanny nodded. 'Ila, would you like to live here some day?'

The maid laughed. 'His Highness won't want to be coming over here every time he wants to see you! It's different for me. Gupta can live where I live.'

'No, but one day – '

Ila nodded vigorously. 'One day the Yuveraj will give you this palace for your own, somewhere where your children can visit you, and you can grow old in peace. It will be a good place for us to end our days.'

Fanny resolutely turned her mind away from her thoughts of a peaceful old age and back to the task in hand. She knew exactly how it would be: the typical Indian way of doing things, with the workmen walking out of the back door as the Political Agent arrived at the front. She simply couldn't imagine why nothing could be finished on time! It was bad enough that no one seemed to be able to absorb more than one instruction at a time – that she understood very well for, at the hottest times of the year, the most anyone could do was survive from one moment to the next.

'Her Highness is not to be bothered with any of this!' Fanny insisted. '*We* must see to it all ourselves! I wonder if the Yuveraj would help us raise an army of people to deal with everything?'

Ila sniffed, afraid that Gupta might be put in charge of such an army. 'Her Highness will still need to be told,' she maintained stubbornly.

'Yes, and I'll do the telling!' Fanny retorted.

She delayed telling the Rani anything at all, however, until she had reached the point of desperation that the palace would be anywhere near ready for its new occupants.

'Why do you let them get away with it?' Maneka asked her. 'Shout at them a little bit!'

Fanny made a face. 'They still call me the foreign lady. I think they enjoy baiting me.'

Maneka was amused. 'I expect they do. Are you sure you don't want my help?'

'No!' Fanny lifted her chin. 'And don't you dare go behind my back and try to make things easier for me! I must do this by myself!'

'Then go and do it!' Maneka bade her. 'You know nothing will happen unless you oversee it yourself.'

Sajjan knew better than to offer her any advice at all. He had other things on his mind. The British were proving much more difficult to deal with than he had expected and, more often than not, he felt like a puppet of some unknown master in Calcutta who would jerk the strings in a most disconcerting manner, even though there was still no British representative as such in Kattyapur. He was beginning to suspect that the litmus test of his loyalty was going to be how he handled himself when the Paramount Power finally decided to deal with his erstwhile brother-in-law, Hanut. He hoped against hope it wasn't going to mean war! Fanny had advised he should go to Sir Arthur Cunningham, but that gentleman had proved surprisingly elusive recently. Nor was Fanny able to help much.

'Why are you never here when I want you these days?' he demanded crossly of her. 'What's all this about the Little Palace?'

'Her Highness thinks it will be a good place to house the new Political Agent.'

'Oh? What do you think of the place? It's years since I visited it. Can it be made habitable?'

'It's beautiful!' Fanny said softly.

'Then it's yours!'

She turned her face into his neck. 'Yes, but not yet. One day I might like to live there, but at the moment I shouldn't like to be so far away from you.' She gave him a saucy look. 'Unlike Maneka, I plan an active old age! If I had my way, I'd never leave your side, day or night!'

He grinned. 'Nevertheless the Little Palace will always be yours if you should need it. I have been meaning to do something to secure your future if anything should happen to me and now is as good a time as any.'

'The Yuveraj – '

'He belongs to his people, as I do. He may be forced to

do things he doesn't like to keep the peace amongst his people. No, it'll be better if the Palace is known to be yours. Ganesha can inherit from you one day.'

Fanny shook her head. 'Ganesha and I may live there, but the Palace must always belong to the Raja of Kattyapur. I won't accept it otherwise!'

He turned to look at her. 'Wise Fanny! You haven't entirely lost your touch for politics, have you? Do you want to come with me to Hanupur for the celebrations? I'm told the *zenana* there is a hotbed of revolution and potential murder, though I have yet to persuade the British that the female can be just as deadly as the male! I need someone to listen to their conversations and report back to me. Will you do it?'

For once, Fanny felt uncertain. 'Can I be trusted not to disgrace you? I wouldn't have Maneka to rescue me.' She bit her lower lip thoughtfully. 'She says this baby is her last. Does she really mean that, Sajjan?'

'She's an old soul. She wants to start her preparations for the next turn in the wheel of her lives. Don't worry about her, Fanny. She never had what you and I have together. She didn't want it.'

Fanny rolled on to one elbow. 'You love her, don't you?'

Sajjan began to undo Fanny's bodice. 'I shall always love her. She and I have been together for a long, long time, perhaps through many lives. Above all, she is my Rani and she guards my back from the schemes of other women who aren't always what they seem, which is what I want you to do for me at Hanupur. But have a care, my love, it's dangerous work you'll be doing!' He touched her breast with a familiar finger. 'You, Fanny darling, are my wife of affection, the keeper of my heart, and I won't have you risking your life. Listen and report to me every word you hear, but say nothing, not even to the maids you take with you. Is it understood? I can't have anything bad happening to you because you were careless for a single instant! Remember always that I can't do without you! A hundred lives won't be enough to slake my thirst for you! Are you going to come to Hanupur with me?'

'Yes,' Fanny said. Armed with the best advice Maneka could give her, she would go, and in return she would do the little Rani a favour she knew she would be the last to appreciate.

'Maneka's too thin! She has the baby to think of as well as herself. She's hardly eating anything at all!'

Sajjan buried his face in her breasts. 'I'll speak to her about it!'

'Please do,' said Fanny. 'She may be impatient for the next turn of the wheel, but we still need her right here with us!'

Sajjan chuckled reluctantly. 'Oh, not right here, Fanny,' he protested.

Fanny laughed also. 'No, not right here!' she agreed.

An aura of hatred hung over Hanupur like a pall. Fanny renewed her acquaintance with the two ladies who had come out to Sajjan's camp all those years before. They looked like two old women, bent and frightened of their own shadows. Not for the first time, Fanny blessed her good fortune in living in a *zenana* ruled over by Maneka. Here, there was nothing but distrust and fear of Hanut, whose vocation was self-indulgence and his hobby torture.

The women were allowed to watch the evening's entertainment from behind screens, but there was little enjoyment in it. Most of them sat in a sullen silence, their eyes flickering with fright every time there was a movement anywhere near them. Fanny spent her time trying to see where Sajjan was seated and found him eventually, deep in conversation with an Englishman who seemed vaguely familiar to her. Then she remembered that she had last seen him in uniform. Without doubt, it was Mr Walter Gilbert. It would be interesting to know what he was doing here. She turned her attention to the woman sitting on Mr Gilbert's other side and was astonished to find herself looking at a copy of her younger self. *Mary!* Fanny felt quite faint as she recognized her daughter. She tried to decide whether she looked happy, finally coming to the conclusion that Mary was as bored as she herself was of the endlessly whirling *nautch*-girls. She suppressed a smile of amusement at the expression of bland indifference on the young woman's face. She could almost read her thoughts behind that mask, and was sure that they, too, were a mirror-image of her own.

But what could Mary be doing in Hanupur? This was no place for her! Especially not if it came to the battle between the British and the followers of the new Raja that Sajjan expected. He was adamant that the British would never allow his brother-in-law to mount the *gadi*. Whoever was in charge of her should have kept her away! Fanny looked wildly round and saw the whole Cunningham family seated amongst the honoured guests. How smart Lady Cunningham had become! She looked exactly right for the occasion, Fanny noted with approval. That was probably what Mary was doing here – please God, despite his black blood, she was still more interested in Mr Gilbert and wasn't being encouraged to marry the young Arthur Cunningham, whose dissolute ways were already written clearly in his face. Fanny watched his restless eyes going from one *nautch*-girl to the next, a half-smile on his lips.

She shuddered, remembering seeing a similar expression on Lord Bantry's face.

The dancing was second-rate. Fanny was glad Maneka wasn't here to be bored by it. The Rani had a natural eye for such things and was easily put out when she was offered anything less than the best. She saw that Mary, too, was making no attempt to hide her displeasure. She remembered her as she had last seen her, dignified despite the tears that had run down her cheeks, stubbornly refusing to let anyone see how badly she had been hurt and that she cared that her mother was going away and leaving her alone with the monster who was her father. Fanny had never been able to forgive herself for that abandonment. Now, looking at her grown-up daughter, she knew she never would. If only she could talk to her and explain – but that Sajjan would never allow and, most probably, he was right. What was done was done, and there was no going back to do it all over again.

At last it was over. A flutter ran through the women as they watched Hanut get up from his chair and walk over to where they were sitting.

'I thought we were safe tonight!' the woman sitting next to Fanny whispered. 'Why don't the British do something to rid us of him?'

Fanny wondered the same. There had been a great many troops all round the town that afternoon, far more than she would have thought necessary, yet the ceremonies seemed to be going on all the same.

She turned back to the woman. 'There are many strangers in the *zenana* tonight. What are all these women doing here?'

The woman shuddered. 'Hanut has friends visiting. Who are you with?'

'The Raja of Kattyapur.'

The woman spat out the betel-nut she had been chewing. It was typical of the squalor of the place that she made no effort to use one of the spittoons provided, but made a large red patch on the floor that looked to Fanny exactly like a pool of blood.

'The Raja of Kattyapur is a friend of the British. There are those amongst us who say he is doomed to suffer the same fate as the foreign strangers if Hanut has his way.'

'He's a strong man – '

'The strongest of us can die of poison. If you are a woman in Hanupur, it's best to be on the right side of our ruler. Many of his brothers have died already – what's one more?'

Fanny tried to dismiss the nightmare from her mind. 'What woman here could ever reach the Raja of Kattyapur?' she muttered.

The woman shrugged. 'The *nautch*-girls will do anything for money!'

Fanny tried to tell herself that Sajjan wouldn't be interested in anything those tired, dispirited girls could offer him. She had almost succeeded in reassuring herself when the women began to return to the *zenana* in small groups of twos and threes. No one was much interested in what she did with herself and so she went from one group to another to find out what they were gossiping about, looking for anything that would be interesting to Sajjan.

It wasn't long before she found it. All the women were angry and afraid, but none of them more so than the luckless wives of Hanut himself. None of them had any love for him, but most of them had a favoured son they were determined to see mount the *gadi*, thus making all that they had suffered at his father's hands worthwhile. It was one of the Ranis who said, 'Only Kattyapur stands between us and victory!'

486

'Not the British?' another asked sharply.

The Rani pulled her mouth down at the corners. 'They will do as Kattyapur bids them. He is the one who must be destroyed and I am the one to do it!'

Few of the other women believed her. 'How will you do it?' they demanded.

'It's already done!' the Rani claimed. 'The poison was in his cup at dinner!'

Fanny's heart stood still within her. She forgot all about the promises she had made him to stay with the other women until he sent for her. She forgot everything except her own fears. She could taste her fright on her tongue and she felt quite giddy with the despair that gripped her. She must go to him at once and, failing that, she would go to the British and demand their protection for him – if it wasn't already too late!

She didn't know where to find him. Pulling her veil closely over her face, she approached the nearest guard and asked if a message could be given to her lord. The man looked at her as though she were mad, quaking with fear. 'I cannot leave my post, lady!'

'You can tell me where to find him myself, can't you?'

The man shook his head. Then, just as Fanny was turning away, he pointed down the corridor towards another man who was approaching them, the only Englishman Fanny didn't want to see at that moment – young Arthur Cunningham. She stood back into the shadows, hoping he would pass on his way without seeing her. In the opposite direction came another figure she recognized only too well. She knew only bewilderment at the sight of him. What was Edwin Bantry doing here?

'Struck lucky?' Edwin asked young Cunningham.

The young man shook his head. 'Hanut keeps the best of them for himself. Wanted to warn you that your daughter's here, though. Casts a bit of a blight on the proceedings, doesn't it?'

Lord Bantry rubbed his hands together. 'It's time I taught that young lady a lesson! I'll teach her to go behind my back and make a fool of me with the Queen-Empress!'

Cunningham looked more doubtful. 'Her husband is with her.'

'All the better! She's always been far too healthy! My own son may be in his grave, but nothing ever happens to Mary! Well, it will tonight! Come with me and we'll have our sport with her – '

Even Cunningham drew back at that. 'I won't do anything to Mary. My mother's fond of her!'

'She's another one who could do with being taught a lesson! Women! I hate them, every one! They're all above themselves, thinking they're as good as a man, but leave them alone and they come fawning round you, like a bitch on heat! Look at Mary! Couldn't wait to marry that black boy of hers! Well, now she's had a taste of it, she'll probably thank us for giving her a bit more!'

Fanny's blood froze in her veins. Not Mary! For an instant, it seemed she had spent her whole life fighting Edwin Bantry, either on her own behalf or on Mary's. The years fell away from her and she felt as helpless as she had felt when he had taken a whip to Mary to force her to open her door to him. Come what may, and after what both of them had suffered, he was not going to be allowed to add to Mary's miseries once again!

There was one person here who would help, she thought in relief. Hetty Cunningham would be as upset as she was herself. There was no alternative, somehow she would have to find her and warn her that Bantry was in Hanupur, together with her son! Walter Gilbert might also help. From the possessive way he had been looking at Mary, he

488

wouldn't want any harm to come to her. She thought she could trust him for that much at least, though at that dreadful moment she doubted one could ever really trust anyone of the male sex, not when it came to protecting Mary!

She was still hesitating when the trumpets sounded. The military sounds all about her, the trumpeting of elephants, the horses' hooves, and the clipped military commands given in English told their own story. The British had had enough and, having surrounded the town, were moving in closer, waiting their chance to have it out with the new Raja once and for all.

Ashamed that she should have forgotten Mary even for a moment, Fanny bolted down the nearest corridor, leading to the public rooms where she expected to find her daughter. The room was full of flickering shadows from the guttering candles, but Mary was there all right. She was standing with her back to the wall, her father pulling at her crippled arm. Though bigger now, she was recognizably the same person Fanny remembered as if it had been yesterday, a small child trying not to cry as she lay on her bed, broken and crippled at her father's hands.

'Run, Mary!' she shouted to her. 'I'll see about this!'

But the last thing Mary meant to do was run. She reached down under her skirt and brought out the knife her mother had sent her when she had left Delhi. With calm deliberation, she flicked open the blade and rammed it between her father's ribs. She knew nothing but satisfaction as she watched him stagger and fall to the ground, clutching his side.

'You've killed me, Fanny!' Bantry moaned. Cunningham bent over him, trying to staunch the wound. 'I never thought she'd kill me! Fanny! Bitch! Why wouldn't you ever allow me near you?'

Fanny sped across the marble floor, the sound the rings on her toes made making Mary glance her way.

'Run, Mary!' she reiterated. 'Leave this to me!'

She took the knife from her, giving her daughter a push towards the doorway. 'Is he dead?' she asked Cunningham, with all the arrogant calm for which Lady Frances had once been famous.

The young man rose, his face distorted with his hatred for her. 'You won't get away with this, Lady Frances!' he spat at her. 'I was there, don't forget, and I heard his dying words! He said it was *you* who killed him, not Mary! You'll die for this, and there won't be one of us who'll regret it! You haunted him all his days!'

Fanny held the knife out to him on the palm of her hand. 'I shan't deny I killed him,' she said proudly. 'I kept him out of my bed for years with this knife. It was only fitting it should kill him in the end.'

Cunningham took it from her. 'I hope you'll still think so when you swing for him!' he screamed.

Fanny shut her eyes. She hoped so too. But more than that, more than anything else, she hoped Sajjan, if he were still alive, would understand why she had done it!

Chapter Twenty-eight

Fanny had never been anywhere as dirty and unpleasant as the prison in the palace of Hanupur. Her fastidious nature was revolted by the total lack of hygiene. It had been bad enough having to spend hours together in the women's quarters, but nothing had prepared her for this stinking hole, guarded by a couple of cynical soldiers who hated both their own master and anyone who looked likely to succeed him.

For a day and a night, Fanny waited for Sajjan to find her, convinced that no matter what she might have done, he would rescue her and somehow or other make everything all right again. But as the hours went slowly by, she despaired of his coming, deciding he must be dead, and began to wonder what preparations she should be making in order to defend herself from the charges that would be bound to be brought against her.

There were two other occupants of the tiny, stuffy cell: an old woman who was plainly mad, and a younger, pretty female who had earned her living as a dancer before she had fallen foul of Hanut's uncertain temper. At first, Fanny thought she was as recent an arrival as she herself was, but this proved not to be the case; she had lost count of the time, but she knew several months had passed since she had first been thrown in with the madwoman.

'She knew her name when I first saw her,' the young woman told Fanny sullenly. 'Now, I think she wants to forget what she was before she came here.' The *nautch*-dancer easily dismissed the old hag with the matted hair and torn rags. It was her own future that interested her and she immediately sensed that Fanny was important enough to be of some advantage to herself if she curried favour with her.

'What did they put you in here for?' she asked, languidly fanning herself and Fanny with the end of her veil.

'My husband's murder.'

The girl sniffed. 'What has that to do with anyone here?'

'Am I so obviously a foreigner?' Fanny asked.

The *nautch*-girl considered her with care, then she said, 'I can't tell where you're from, but I know you're not from Hanupur from your straight back and your manner. Nobody here lifts their eyes off the ground – certainly not we women! Where are you from?'

'Kattyapur.'

The girl pulled on one of Fanny's bangles. 'Will you take me there with you when you are released? Nobody remembers why I'm here, or even my name. Kattyapur is a good place! Everyone says so! I'd serve you faithfully, dance for you, anything you wish!'

'I doubt the British will allow me to return to Kattyapur,' Fanny answered. 'It was one of the *sahib-log* whom I killed.'

The girl's face fell. 'Who are you?' she demanded.

'My name is Fanny.'

It meant nothing to the girl. 'I will serve you while you're here and perhaps we'll escape together!' she decided. 'If we allow ourselves to be forgotten, we'll end up like that poor soul over there. I'd sooner be dead!'

Fanny could feel only sympathy for that point of view. She was glad to have someone to talk to for, left to herself, her mind went over and over every detail of Bantry's last moments. She had always been afraid there was something of her father in Mary and in that moment she had seen

492

what it was for herself. Mary hadn't hesitated, or shown the slightest remorse, as she had driven the knife home. She had looked as if she had felt she was doing the world a favour! Fanny could only marvel at her daughter's coolness, knowing that she could never have brought herself to do likewise. Even now, she was agonized at the thought of having been the cause of another human being's death. Edwin Bantry had deserved to die a hundred times over, but she could still regret that it had had to be Mary's hand which had dispatched him.

'Are you hungry?' she asked her companion.

'One is always hungry in here. The soldiers eat our food as often as not, and what they don't eat, the rats do!'

Fanny swallowed. 'Rats?'

The girl nodded. A smile glinted between lips which looked bruised. 'The rats are better than other things. They have fur and warm blood. I'm trying to teach one of them to answer to his name.'

Fanny shuddered. She preferred not to think what their other visitors might be. Instead, she went to the door of their prison and began to shout at their gaoler through the door.

'Bring us something decent to eat!' she commanded.

'And who is going to pay?' he asked her, grinning.

'The Raja of Kattyapur!' Whatever she had done, Fanny reasoned, Sajjan wouldn't allow her to go hungry if he were alive and, if he wasn't, it was best she should know it and plan accordingly.

The man opened the door a crack. He looked her up and down, doubting her word. 'You come from Kattyapur?'

She shut her eyes in thanksgiving. If Sajjan were dead, everybody would have known of it by now. 'I'm His Highness's wife of affection!' she announced, already feeling more hopeful.

'Then what are you doing here?' He looked less sure of himself. 'The wife of affection of Kattyapur was lost in the palace. Some say she was killed in the fighting. There were murders galore upstairs, with everyone taking the opportunity of the British coming to settle old scores of their own. How do I know you are who you say you are?'

'Send a message to His Highness telling him where I am.'

He consulted a paper in his hand. 'You were sent here to answer for murder,' he insisted suspiciously.

'An English lord. Send to the Raja of Kattyapur, and to whoever is in charge of the British, and ask them what is to be done with me!'

Her arrogance made him uncertain. He spat accurately on the ground at her feet. 'Foreign lady! Why should I do anything for you?'

Why indeed? Defeated, Fanny settled herself back in the small corner the *nautch*-girl had cleaned for her and leaned her head against the wall, trying to shut her ears to the buzzing of the insects all about her. The heat was intolerable. Straining her ears, she thought she could still hear the sounds of battle going on above them, but then even that stopped and there was no outside noise at all. They could have been alone in the whole universe, the three of them and their gaoler outside the door.

She slept a little. When she awoke her cheeks were wet from her tears and she knew she had been dreaming of Mary putting an end to her father once again.

The door to her cell creaked open. Fanny wiped away her tears on the back of her hands, her mouth curling at the smeared streaks that appeared on her skin. Would she ever feel clean again?

'Lady, you're to come with me!'

Fanny rose to her feet, as graceful as ever. 'Where are we going? Did you send word to the Raja of Kattyapur?'

'It's His Highness the Yuveraj who has sent for you to appear before the British court.'

Hanut, or Hanut's heir, what difference did it make? Fanny's spirits plummeted downwards. Hanut would have enjoyed the sight of her pleading for her life before Sir Arthur Cunningham, for the sheer joy of watching the agony of another human being. She stiffened at the thought, remembering that while Hanut was either dead or the prisoner of the British, Sir Arthur's son was very much amongst the living and was the sworn enemy of both her and Mary.

As she stepped outside her prison, the stench of dead bodies smote her nostrils. Troops swarmed everywhere, forming up into burial parties. At first, she thought they were all British, but then she saw the green coats of Sajjan's army, with their scarlet *puggrees* brilliant in the hot sunshine. She looked back over her shoulder and saw that the *nautch*-girl had taken her opportunity and was following close behind, a filthy handkerchief held over her face.

'What a dreadful sight!' Fanny said in awe. 'How terrible that so many people should have to die in such an evil cause!'

'The British will rule here now,' the guard commented.

Fanny's heart took up a new beat against her ribs. 'Is my lord still here in Hanupur?'

The guard shrugged. He seemed almost friendly, now that he knew she was who she said she was, but she was still doubtful as to how much she could trust him, or anyone else. She felt alone and forlorn.

'You're to be brought before the British for the murder of the Englishman,' he told her with relish. 'I don't know about your lord. All I know is that the dead man was an

495

English aristocrat, known to the Queen-Empress herself! You should have chosen a poor man whom nobody would care about!'

In the distance one of the burial parties moved off, dragging the corpses away behind their horses. Some Hindu priests started reciting their Sanskrit prayers, and the women wailed, huddled together for mutual support. She wondered how much they really cared? No one would mourn the passing of Hanut, certainly not the poor females of his *zenana*, nor anyone else she could think of. She put a hand on the *nautch*-girl's arm, signalling to her that this was the moment for her to make her escape, but the girl stood stubbornly by her, determined to follow Fanny to wherever it was they would take her.

The palace was in a shambles as they passed through the outer corridors towards the main audience hall. British troops were everywhere, intermixed with native representatives from the State of Kattyapur. Nobody gave the two women a glance as they were hurried into the presence of all the leading dignitaries. Fanny saw Sajjan at once, looking as though he had aged ten years in the last two days. Had she done this to him? Inwardly, she wept. At least he was alive! She chastised herself for her lack of faith in him. Nobody but a fool would ever eat or drink unsampled food in this evil place, and Sajjan had never been a fool. She felt his eyes upon her and tried to send him a silent message with her own.

'I am not your judge,' he told her. 'Sir Arthur Cunningham is the one you must look to for mercy.'

'It's you I've hurt,' she answered softly. 'For that I'm sorry. As for the rest, I could do no other. You must see that!'

She longed for some gesture of reassurance, but there

was none forthcoming. He turned his face away, struggling for the impassive dignity he felt was proper to his rank.

'I can't do anything for you, Fanny,' he whispered.

Sir Arthur Cunningham was seated behind a table, a British officer on either side, studiously studying the papers in front of them. A little to one side sat Mary, Walter Gilbert standing behind her, his hand on her shoulder. Mary, too, was ashen-faced and looked about to faint. For a terrible moment, Fanny thought she was going to confess it was her hand that had dispatched her father, and she sent her a quick, warning glance to keep a still tongue in her head. She was limping badly this morning and rubbing her arm as if it hurt her. The sight stiffened Fanny's backbone as nothing else could have done. *Edwin* had done that to her; impossible to tell what injuries were suffered by all the other women he had debased and tortured. It had been only just that he should die for his crimes!

Sir Arthur cleared his throat. 'This is only a preliminary enquiry into the death of Lord Bantry,' he began. He looked directly at Fanny for the first time. 'Do you understand English?' he demanded.

Fanny nodded. Didn't the man recognize her?

Mary jumped to her feet. 'Aren't you going to ask my mother to be seated?' she asked Sir Arthur, in her strange, clipped way. Mr Gilbert pulled her back on to the chair.

'Be quiet, love. Lady Frances is more comfortable as she is.'

Sir Arthur glared at the two of them. 'What is your name, woman?' he roared at Fanny.

'Fanny, sir,' she answered him.

He made a note with enormous care on the paper in front of him. 'We'll take my son's evidence first,' he announced. 'The chaplain can swear him in.'

Mary watched with contempt in her eyes as Mr Cunningham crossed the floor and took the Bible in his hand, stuttering over the oath the chaplain repeated before him. Finally, she spoke:

'Don't listen to him, Uncle Arthur. I told you before, it was I who killed my father. If I hadn't, he would have killed me, or worse. I won't have my mother blamed for this!'

Fanny gave her a furious look, quite as angry as was her outspoken daughter. Why couldn't the silly chit keep quiet?

'Is the English lady necessary to this hearing?' she heard herself asking, a note of desperation in her voice. 'She looks as if she is about to be ill! Take her away to her rooms!'

Mr Cunningham looked increasingly flustered. 'Good idea! She wasn't even there! Mary, you don't know what you're saying! Think of my mother for a change! You owe everything to her – '

'I owe nothing to anybody!' Mary jumped to her feet. 'Can you say it *wasn't* me, Arthur?'

Fanny, seeing Mary was as determined to take the blame as she herself was, went and stood beside her daughter, pulling her veil well back from her face. 'It was I who drove in the knife!' she claimed with immense dignity. 'It was my knife and I'd threatened him with it often enough, as any of his servants will tell you.' She turned and faced the witness. 'Can you honestly say which of us it was who put an end to Lord Bantry's existence?' She didn't dare look in Sajjan's direction. If there was one person in the hall who would guess she was lying, it would be he. He knew her so well! Would he also realize that she had no choice but to do all in her power to save her daughter? Once again, she thought of Mary as she had last seen her, deserted and afraid. No, no, whatever the consequences, this time it was the mother who would have to pay and the daughter go free!

Arthur Cunningham looked from mother to daughter and back again. All he could remember was his mother insisting that he protect Mary at any cost. He thought he would never forget, though, this woman, whom he had always despised, turning on him as if he was something too contemptible to be in the same room with her precious Mary, and he suddenly saw himself, through her eyes, turning into the same kind of sadist as Lord Bantry had always been. India had done this to him, he had excused himself. India and working for a man who would do anything for the lure of gold, and who had dazzled him for a time with his promises of women, money and the friendship of a number of Indian princes who gave him the respect he craved from his own kind, but which was always denied him because his mother had been a superior kind of servant and not the aristocrat she should have been, the kind of person Lady Frances had been before she had thrown it all away, with never a backward glance at the life and ambitions she had left behind her.

'You're very alike!' he gasped out. 'I hadn't realized –'

Fanny raised a brow, smiling that superior smile of hers. 'Alike, Mr Cunningham? Haven't you noticed the difference in our dress? Or my jewellery? How can you say we're alike?'

But they were alike! It could have been Mary taunting him! They were also alike in the way they understood the Indians, even admired them! He clenched his fists, taking in the enormous diamond that decorated Lady Frances's nostril. Didn't the woman have any pride at all? At least Mary was decently dressed!

He pointed to Fanny. 'You killed him! You killed your own husband! Death is too good for you!'

Sir Arthur mopped his face on his handkerchief, a gleam of triumph in his eyes. This was what he had been waiting for. He stared forcefully at his blustering son, wishing he had sired a less spineless individual. God knows, he and Hetty had deserved something better! 'Her husband?' he shot at his son. 'Who do you think this woman to be?'

Mr Cunningham's fury geysered up inside him. 'She's Lady Frances Bantry!'

There was a long, pregnant silence. Sir Arthur mopped his face again. Fanny had the odd feeling he was trying to hide a smile. She turned to face him, some of the fright she was feeling draining away from her.

He leaned forward, his moustaches twitching madly as he addressed Fanny. 'Do you admit to putting an end to Lord Bantry, ma'am?'

Fanny nodded. Her throat was so stiff and sore she couldn't speak.

'Then I don't believe we can bring a case against you. My son says you are Lady Frances Bantry. The Lady Frances Bantry was killed by dacoits in Delhi years ago. An inquest was held and she was declared to be dead. Lord Bantry married again soon after, which he hardly would have done had his legal spouse been alive. I'm not about to make a fool of myself by trying ghosts, ma'am! If Lady Frances is already dead, what would be the point in condemning Lady Frances to die, eh?'

Mary clutched at her husband's hand. 'Mama, you must come to us – ' she began.

But Sir Arthur hadn't finished. 'Sit down, Mrs Gilbert!' he barked at Mary. 'The woman Fanny is wife of affection of the Raja of Kattyapur, isn't that right?' He waited for Fanny to nod her head once again. 'Then it is for him to deal with you, not me! You must wait on him to know your fate.' He stood up, his chair scraping against the marble floor. 'The court is dismissed!' he snapped. 'With so many dead from yesterday, what's the death of one more?' he added. 'Let the dead bury the dead. We have other things to do here. Mary, leave that woman alone and go back to your Aunt Hetty. She won't be happy until she sees you safe and sound for herself!' He cleared his throat noisily. 'As for you,' he went on to Fanny, 'the best I can do for you is to recommend His Highness to treat you mercifully. Lord Bantry wasn't a pleasant man, and it may be you aren't as guilty of his death as you've claimed here before me, though I hope you won't see fit to burden me with the truth of that. Goodbye, Fanny.'

Fanny gave him look for look. 'Goodbye, Sir Arthur,' she said. And she could have sworn that he winked at her. She turned quickly to find Sajjan, but he had already left the hall. Was he still angry? She felt a sudden urge to burst into tears. She was free, yet she had a terrible feeling that, for her, the worst was yet to come.

The thunder and lightning was the first intimation that another dust storm was about to sweep across the burning desert. Fanny watched it from the security of the *zenana* of the palace of Hanupur, wishing she were anywhere but there. The noise the other women were making depressed her. There was a gleeful expectancy that ran through the official mourning which was unpleasant to watch. They were all waiting to hear whose son, or brother, was going to mount the *gadi*, giving them the power they all secretly hoped for. Fanny longed to be home at Kattyapur; with Maneka, who wouldn't have allowed any of this strife for a moment; and with her own children, who would never rule anything and would be all the happier for it.

'Lady, there is someone here to see you.'

Fanny looked up in astonishment. 'To see me? Are you sure?'

'An English lady.'

For a brief moment, Fanny had thought she was to be summoned into Sajjan's presence at last. It was a second or two before she could control her hurried heartbeat and the droop of disappointment that followed with the realization that he still wasn't ready to see her.

'I'll come,' she said.

As soon as she saw Lady Cunningham standing forlornly in the centre of the crumbling courtyard, a pack of screaming women all about her, Fanny remembered what it was that had first made her like the other woman. It must have taken courage to venture here on her own, the more so as Lady Cunningham was essentially a conventional person who couldn't be enjoying anything about her visit to Hanupur.

'Oh, Lady Frances!'

Fanny smiled at her, holding out a hand to her. 'Lady Frances is long dead.'

'Yes. Sir Arthur attended the inquest, you know. We thought he should for Mary's sake – ' Her voice shook as she realized what she was saying.

'I have much to be grateful to you for, haven't I?' Fanny put in quickly. 'Did you never wish me in perdition for what I did to you?'

Lady Cunningham bridled at this accurate reading of past emotions. 'No, no,' she protested, 'I was always ever so fond of Mary! Not that I alone could have done what I wanted for her, but there, you'd seen to it the Queen would take an interest in her, hadn't you? She was kindness itself, even taking the trouble to write to me in her own hand – once she'd satisfied herself I was a suitable person to have charge of her goddaughter!'

'I'm glad of that.' It obviously had meant a great deal to the other woman, Fanny saw with amusement. And she had made good use of the connection, there was no doubt about that.

'So you can see I was well rewarded for taking Mary in,' Lady Cunningham went on, wincing at the renewed wails that went up from the other women. 'How do you stand that cacophony, my dear?'

'Not easily,' Fanny admitted. 'It isn't at all like this in Kattyapur. Our Rani wouldn't allow it for a moment.'

Lady Cunningham's eyes rounded with shock. '*Your* Rani? Do you – do you see much of her?'

'We're friends, yes.' Fanny thought it better to change the subject. 'Tell me about Mary!' she commanded. 'She is married to Walter Gilbert?'

'Oh yes.' Lady Cunningham preened herself happily. 'Mary wouldn't look at anyone else, which was awkward, as you must admit – Well, maybe *you* wouldn't have seen anything to object to in it, but somebody had to think of the child's future, didn't they?'

'I take it that his Parsee grandmother came out of the cupboard. Poor Mr Gilbert! That wouldn't be easily forgiven him.'

Lady Cunningham had forgotten how she had admired Lady Frances for her easy mastery of what would pass, and what would not, in society. Despite her barbaric dress, it seemed she hadn't changed all that much. She didn't even sound disapproving!

'Yes, well, Mary wouldn't make the attempt to ask her father to allow the marriage. I was a bit cut up at the time, seeing only unhappiness all round if she persisted in her choice. But Mary isn't easily beaten, not she! Off she went to England, to visit the Queen, and she came back Mrs Gilbert, married in the Queen's own church, and with her paying for everything, even her dress! Imagine that! Such a kind message she sent me! And the child so happy! Which I never would have believed, for she doesn't take to men easily, if you know what I mean, not after the way her father treated her!'

'Yes, I do see,' Fanny said with feeling. 'Do you like Mr Gilbert?'

'Oh yes!' Lady Cunningham said artlessly. 'If I don't see much of him, it's because there aren't many who understand that he's just as British as the rest of us. One has to be careful not to give offence. You of all people can understand that, can't you? I mean, Mary's position was invidious anyway, without her marrying one of them! Which is what I knew they would say, or at best would be thinking! And so they did! Though much that young lady cares!'

'Indeed, I do understand!' Fanny reassured her. She smiled suddenly. 'Do tell me, Lady Cunningham, how did the dinner party go?'

The other woman crowed with remembered triumph, relieved that she was not to be hauled over the coals for allowing Mary's mésalliance, and glad to be presented with a safer topic of conversation. 'It was a success,' she said with obvious understatement. 'I was ever so grateful to you, Lady Frances!'

'You'd better call me Fanny –'

Lady Cunningham was flattered. Despite the extraordinary way Lady Frances chose to live, she was still the daughter of an Earl. 'And I'm Hetty,' she murmured. She was silent for a moment. 'It's a terrible thing to say, but how glad I am that Lord Bantry won't bother us any more! He did his best to corrupt my own son! And I'll never forgive him for what he did to you and Mary! Never! Sir

Arthur can call it murder all he likes, I call it a blessing for the rest of mankind!'

Fanny shrugged. 'His time had come,' she said casually.

'And it wasn't you who killed him,' Lady Cunningham perceived. 'I'll never believe you did! That's why I'm here now! I wanted you to know there's one person in the world who knows that all you did was take the blame. I don't know that it helps much, but I admire you for it! It could have been very nasty for Mary, whereas I don't suppose anything will happen to you, will it? Why should that Raja of yours care?'

Fanny suppressed a shiver, knowing she would infinitely prefer death at British hands to the prospect of Sajjan's displeasure at the risks she had taken. He might understand, but could he overlook the fact that she had been prepared to put her daughter before all that he wanted to achieve with the British for Kattyapur?

'Don't let Mary dwell on her father's death,' she pleaded with Lady Cunningham. 'It would have happened anyway. If it hadn't been she, it would have been another. Who's to say it wouldn't have been I – who's to say it wasn't? Our actions are like messengers we send to the future and we don't always like where they lead.'

Lady Cunningham threw her a startled look. 'That's just the sort of thing Mary would say!' she marvelled. 'I don't begin to understand one half of what she and Mr Gilbert talk about together. He tells me not to mind her philosophizing. And I don't, as long as she doesn't try to tell me all those indelicate stories the Indians seem so fond of! They don't know any better, poor things, or they wouldn't go around half-naked – ' She broke off, dismayed by what she had said. 'I don't mean – '

'It does strike one rather forcibly at first.' Fanny tried to help her out. 'It took me a long time before I understood how practical these clothes are for the climate here. Also they're much more modest than they seem.'

Lady Cunningham was doubtful about that. She could see quite a lot of Lady Frances's flesh when she could bring herself to look at her and although she had to admit she looked lovely – in an exotic, *pagan* kind of way! – she couldn't see anyone one knew taking up such a fashion!

Fanny saw her visitor to the door of the *zenana*, giving instructions that she was to be taken back to her own quarters.

'It was dear of you to come and see me! I always did like you so much better than anyone else I met in Delhi. You are a good, kind woman, and Mary couldn't have had a better substitute mother. We'll both of us be for ever in your debt! However, I think perhaps you'd better not come again, don't you? Sir Arthur might not like it. Lady Frances would be a different matter, but Fanny, the Raja of Kattyapur's wife of affection, isn't a suitable person for your notice – nor for Mary's either. You might give her a hint to that effect?'

Lady Cunningham was not going to admit she already had, not that she had been sure Mary had listened. Mary went her own way, no matter what anyone said!

'You're still Mary's mother!' Lady Cunningham declared.

'I gave her life. I forefeited any feeling she might have for me long ago – the day Lady Frances died and left her alone with her father.'

Lady Cunningham saw the force of that. 'You're very brave, my dear. And so I shall tell Sir Arthur! Yes, yes, I know Lady Frances must stay dead and buried, but I can see a great deal to admire in Fanny – even if it has to be that I never see you again!'

Fanny stood and watched her go. Behind her two

women were rolling on the floor, trying to tear out each other's hair. The time had come, she decided, to leave. In a sudden whirl of activity she clapped her hands, summoning the maid she had brought with her, and began to tell her what she wanted done. 'And tell that *nautch*-girl from the prison she's to come with us,' she instructed as an afterthought.

'The girl's a thief!' the maid objected.

Fanny was amused. 'Is she? I don't suppose she'll steal anything from me.'

The maid sniffed. 'It's the rest of us who have to put up with her! I'll tell her if she takes another thing from any of us, you'll order her to be whipped – or better still, you could tell her that yourself!'

The storm was closer now. Fanny slept restlessly, knowing even in her sleep that she was nervous of the coming meeting. She was awakened by a crack of thunder directly overhead and gasped, half with fear and half with remembered pain. Silhouetted against the open window stood a man's form. Sajjan!

'What are you doing here?' he asked her. 'Did I send for you?'

She shook her head, a pulse beating in her throat. 'You know you didn't,' she murmured. 'I couldn't stay in the *zenana* a minute longer. This is a terrible place, Sajjan.'

'Terrible indeed.'

She knelt on the pallet she had had made up in the corner of his allotted room. There was no movement from him. He wasn't even looking her way.

'Weren't you pleased by Sir Arthur's decision, Sajjan?'

It was as if he hadn't heard her. 'I hadn't realized how like Mary you are. When you stood beside each other, I could see how Cunningham might not have known which one of you put an end to Bantry.'

Fanny tried to think of something to say. 'Do you mind?' slipped out before she could stop it.

He lifted her on to her feet, his hands holding her beneath her elbows. 'I talked to Mary, Fanny. I had a long talk with her. There's no mistaking the fact that she's your daughter!' His face puckered with pain. 'I only wish she were my daughter also, and not the daughter of some other man! She has the courage of a Rajputana!'

'You can't wish you were her father more than I!' Fanny exclaimed. 'If there had been no Mary, no Edwin Bantry, nothing to run away from, I still would have followed you to the ends of the earth. Will the British force you to punish me for killing my legal husband?'

'Is that how you think of him?'

Fanny shook her head slowly. 'I can't forget he was a man – '

Sajjan hushed her by putting a finger over her lips. 'Your daughter understands better than you do that we must all make our own lives – and our own deaths.'

Fanny blinked. 'Have I spoilt our life together?' she asked him sadly.

'I don't know, Fanny. What I do know is that I can't keep you with me here. You must go home to Kattyapur at once. By the time I return, I'll know better if the British are prepared to let sleeping dogs lie. I cannot put you before my State – as you put Mary!'

Tears filled her eyes and ran down her cheeks. 'Sajjan, wouldn't you have done the same for the Yuveraj?'

'It wouldn't have arisen.'

That much was true. Fanny sighed. 'I had to do it. Please believe that! But I shall never see Mary again, I promise you.' She forced a smile. 'A married lady has no need of anything more from her mother!'

'I think the need was always yours more than hers, and much more than mine! I thought you different from other women, Fanny. I thought you to be the woman of my dreams, my other half, who would share my interests and duties, not go running off, putting her life in jeopardy over her own affairs. If the British had found you guilty of murder, there would have been nothing I could do to save you. I shall never allow myself to be put in such a situation again! Do you hear me?'

The helplessness in his voice touched her as nothing else could. 'Oh, Sajjan, I wouldn't have hurt you for anything in the world, but nor could I abandon Mary a second time! I hate this place, and I hate myself for being the cause of all this trouble!'

Outside the thunder took on a deeper note, the lightning cracking the sky in two, but Fanny was unaware of it. She hid her face in Sajjan's chest, still shaking with the last of her tears. She had thought herself too weary even to sleep, but when his mouth took possession of hers she felt the first stirrings of desire, her usual zest for life flooding back into her limbs. If his need for her was merely physical just now, perhaps she would one day be able to restore what they had had before, before she had placed their life together in jeopardy for the sake of her daughter – something she didn't think he would ever truly be able to understand.

'Don't trust anyone here,' she urged him. 'Everyone is at war with everyone else, hoping to gain power for themselves. Don't trust the British either,' she added. 'They'll make use of you and then blame you if anything goes wrong. One can smell death everywhere in this horrible place! You won't delay your return to Kattyapur, will you?'

'A couple of weeks will see me at home, bringing our new Political Officer with me.'

Fanny made a face. 'More strangers!' she sighed. 'I shall hide myself away and do my best to forget they're there!'

He laughed shortly. 'Whatever role they force on me in the future, I shall always need you to help me with these British!'

She wasn't best pleased by that. She would have been much happier never to have seen another person of her own race again. But she knew better than to push him too far in his present mood. 'You have Maneka to do the honours socially, what need is there for me to entertain them? They'll never forget what happened here – and nor will I!'

'No,' he agreed softly, 'none of us will ever forget, but we can learn to understand, as I am beginning to learn to understand you. As long as I have need of your advice, Fanny, can you deny it to me?'

Her shoulders sagged. 'No.'

'Then that is the penalty I impose on you for Bantry's murder: that you face up to all that the future brings as you faced the past, with all the courage I have learned to expect from my very dear wife of affection!'

Chapter Twenty-nine

The Little Palace was finally beginning to look habitable. Fanny enjoyed wandering through the rooms, admiring their proportions and the new furnishings she had brought in to fill the empty spaces, trying a mix of Indian and European in a manner that was pleasing to her, if to no one else.

Today, the Rani had determined to see for herself that everything was in readiness for the Political Officer and his bride. Fanny had had to do no more than mention she was coming for there to be a sudden spurt of activity on the part of all the workmen. Everything that had been impossible for days was suddenly put into effect, the impossible being possible after all.

Now she was gone again, leaving Fanny to take a last look round by herself, a kindness Fanny much appreciated, much as she had enjoyed playing the hostess to the little Rani.

Earlier the sound of the whistle and men shouting had told her that Maneka's approach was near. Seating herself on one of the new sofas, she had nodded to Ila to have refreshments brought for the heavily pregnant woman. It wasn't very comfortable, she found, and she pulled her feet up under her with a sigh of relief. This was fun, she had decided, for although she had frequently entertained Maneka in her own rooms, carefully keeping away from any of the food she offered her, here she felt more like the hostess of old, in command of both herself and her household.

Maneka had seated herself on a pile of cushions, looking about her with interest. 'Have you thought the Political Officer may have a wife?' she had opened their conversation.

'All the more reason for me to stay away!'

'His Highness hoped you would make her welcome among us. There will be many things which must seem strange to her at first!'

'What an embarrassment I would be to her! The women are worse than the men for pretending that the Indians don't exist, unless they can render some service, of course!'

Maneka had slanted her a glance. 'I can remember someone who thought us a lot of barbarians for slaughtering a horse!'

Fanny laughed. 'Was I unbearable?'

'No, no, a little frightened, I think. It's hard to come to terms with the unknown. Don't be too harsh with the newcomers if they need your help. You may enjoy their presence here more than you think.'

Maneka had made Fanny show her everything, wandering through the rooms and exclaiming over the strange furniture Fanny had had brought from Jaipur. She had checked the water supply, counted the pots and pans in the kitchen, insisting there were far too few family-sized plates in case the Political Officer should be married. When Fanny explained that English people ate off their own individual plates, using their own implements, and not out of a communal container, using pieces of flat bread as spoons, the Rani had shown herself to be fascinated.

'How strange!' she had exclaimed at intervals.

'Not so strange,' Fanny had answered. 'I have all my own things in the *zenana*.'

Maneka had turned sad eyes on her. 'You have no caste, you can't eat with anyone else. I was hoping you would visit here and be with your own people from time to time. You are too much alone!'

The Rani had been a fine one to talk. She very seldom ate at all when anyone else was present. It was as if it were as private a function to her as going to the lavatory. Fanny had been flattered when she had agreed to eat in the same place with her today, more than half expecting her to make some excuse at the last moment. Better still, she had eaten far more than she had at any time recently. No doubt Sajjan had spoken to her about taking the austerities of her new regime too far.

'You're determined I shall be friends with these new people!' she had dared to tease her. 'Will you visit them also?'

'If His Highness permits it.'

'Really?' Fanny had been astonished. 'I shouldn't have thought you'd want to have anything to do with them!'

'Why not?' Maneka had been offended. 'If the only British woman I know is one of my dearest friends, why shouldn't these new people like to be my friends also?'

How to tell her that despite her being the Rani of Kattyapur, they might still treat her little better than a servant? 'Oh, Maneka, don't expect too much – '

'Fanny, the other is only a part of ourselves.'

Feeling snubbed, Fanny had distracted herself by showing the Rani upstairs, where Maneka happily prodded the beds and poked about the bathroom until she was satisfied everything was in apple-pie order, coming up to her exacting standards.

'You've done well,' she had approved at last. 'You see, the workmen did pay attention to you in the end!'

'After you'd threatened them several times over.'

Maneka's face had fallen ludicrously. 'They told you? I

said no one was to tell you, that you wanted to do it all by yourself! Who told you?'

Fanny had chuckled. 'You just did.'

'I did?' The Rani had been about to deny it indignantly. Then she had shrugged her thin shoulders. 'You tricked me! Nevertheless, I don't think you'll have any trouble in the future. Sometimes one must be very firm and insist on having one's own way. If you laugh with them, and say please too much, nothing is done! You must shout and stamp your feet! Then, when everything is finished, you can be more friendly and it won't be forgotten that you mean what you say!'

'I'll remember,' Fanny had said meekly.

The Rani had given her an apologetic look, the ready laughter back in her dark eyes. 'You won't need to remember very often. I gave instructions that your orders are my own. Now, don't tell me I shouldn't have done it! You've been here far too long for them to go on calling you the foreign lady.' An annoyed look had crossed her face. 'I'll not have *anyone* using that excuse any longer! Not even you! You hear me?'

'Yes, Your Highness.'

With Maneka safely installed in her *doolie* and already almost out of sight as she was carried back to the Fort-Palace, Fanny had gone out on to the verandah looking over the city, determined to watch the sunset before she sent for her own palanquin and left the palace behind her for the time being.

It was a beautiful evening, such as is never seen in Europe, with the golden lights of the day transformed into the purple of the night. The birds swooped over the water tanks, taking their last drink of the day. Below her, a peacock spread his tail and his hen paused to admire him before scratching at the dry earth for a last mouthful of food.

There was a slight sound behind her and Fanny turned, astonished to see that the lamps had been lit in the room behind her. How long must she have been standing there, dreaming her time away? It was well past the hour that she had promised to return to the *zenana*. Then she saw there was someone standing in the middle of the room, her head a little on one side as she watched Fanny silhouetted against the last of the sunset.

Fanny took a step into the light, unable to believe her eyes. She would have thought her daughter to be as calm as any statue, if she hadn't seen the whiteness of her knuckles as she grasped her useless left arm with her right hand. What was Mary doing here?

It was Mary who spoke first. 'Mama?' she asked.

Fanny covered her face with her hands. 'What are you doing here?' she demanded. 'I must be dreaming!'

'Oh no,' said Mary. 'I've become a most important person who couldn't possibly be a dream! I'm the wife of the new Political Officer!'

Fanny gasped out loud, though whether with laughter or fright she couldn't have said. And, a second later, they were in each other's arms and were laughing and crying together, completely taken up with their joy at finding each other after all this time.

'Mrs Gilbert,' Fanny said. 'Good God, I may be a grandmother before I can say Jack Robinson!'

'Will you mind?'

'Not if you're happy. I treated you very badly – '

'Nonsense! You did what you could for me, and you kept your promise to me in the end. I wish I felt something for Papa's death, but I can't.'

515

'It was his time!'

Mary looked at her mother with frank enjoyment. 'I'm going to love being with you down here,' she said. 'I'm so glad you found somebody to love and took your chance at happiness. I love him already! Life is splendidly arranged, don't you think, when one finds a man worth the loving?'

Fanny was disconcerted. She blinked. 'You're very — frank,' she said at last. Such things had never been discussed between mother and daughter in her day!

Mary was immediately apologetic. 'Oh dear! Have I shocked you? I should keep a better guard on my tongue, but I'm never able to with people I like. Walter says I shouldn't be allowed out on my own! I must be the worst wife any Political Agent ever had to put up with!'

Fanny recovered herself, though she still found it odd that Mary should know about such things. 'He wouldn't have married you if he thought that!' she said a little uncomfortably.

Mary laughed. 'He had no choice, poor man. He was married to me by Royal Command, no less!'

She almost laughed again as she watched her mother perch herself on the sofa beside her in acute discomfort. Without a word, she sat further back and drew her feet up under her, Indian style, as if it were the most natural thing in the world. Fanny heaved a sigh of relief and did likewise.

'I'm sure Lady Cunningham didn't encourage you to sit like this!' Fanny observed dryly.

'No, she didn't.' Mary's eyes twinkled with suppressed amusement. 'Sir Arthur was more indulgent, however. He's a lovely man, as Eileen would say – '

'Eileen? Is she here?'

'She's with Lady Cunningham. She hasn't been the same since Father McGilligan died. I thought she might like to go home to Ireland, but she has no heart for making such a long journey. That's why I didn't bring her her. I wasn't sure what to expect and, as she won't admit she isn't as strong as she used to be, she gets fussed and extremely cross if she feels out of her depth. She's happy with Lady Cunningham, who is unfailingly kind to her and never rebukes her for chattering on about the saints, as others are wont to do.'

'Was Lady Cunningham kind to *you*?'

Navy eyes met navy. It was like looking in a glass and there was a momentary, shocked recognition of the fact between them.

'Always,' Mary answered gently. 'She didn't understand me very well, but she loved me for your sake. She would never allow anyone to tarnish my memories of you in her presence, not even Papa. She's a very good woman, Mama.'

Fanny nodded, satisfied. That had been her impression also. 'And she's learned to queen it over those cats in Delhi!'

'Yes, she has. She carried off my marriage as if it were the one thing she'd wanted all along – which was far from being the case! You see, Mr Gilbert's grandmother – '

'Is a Parsee.' Then she went on in answer to Mary's look, 'I met him once. I liked him.'

Mary leaned forward in her excitement. 'When you sent me that perfectly splendid miniature. I knew it must have come from you! It started my whole interest in the subject. I gave yours away to the Queen, I do hope you don't mind! It was of a much better quality than any other I had managed to buy for myself.'

'I have no right to mind,' Fanny said simply. 'It was the Rani's idea that you might like it.' Her eyes twinkled with self-mockery. 'As always, I did as I was told! You owe me nothing!'

'I think I do,' said Mary. 'I was afraid in Hanupur. You

were magnificent! You weren't at all shocked by what had happened, were you?'

'That you'd killed him, no. There was a time when I thought I wanted to kill him myself. I was more shocked to find you a grown-up, married woman! I've thought of you as a little girl for so long – '

'I was never a little girl!' Mary objected, amazed by the thought. 'I agree with the Rani! In some ways you'll always be younger than I ever was!'

Fanny felt quite faint. 'The Rani? *You've seen the Rani?*'

'I spent the whole morning with her, while the Raja and Walter were busy about their affairs.'

'She spent the whole afternoon with me and she didn't say *one word* about you!' Fanny raged indignantly. 'How could she? My own daughter!'

'Whom you wouldn't have minded never seeing again!' Mary put in, without resentment.

Fanny, however, was decidedly nettled to know that Maneka had deceived her. 'Who translated for you?' she said crossly.

'Nobody!'

'Maneka doesn't speak a word of English!'

'Her Highness, Mama. You should show more respect! What did you call the Queen-Empress?'

'Ma'am, what else?'

'Her Highness – '

'Someone must have translated for you!' Fanny insisted.

'My – brother, Ganesha, tried to at first, but we soon found we could manage a great deal better on our own. I have your ear for languages and speak most of the local ones quite well. I'd have done better to have inherited your gift for friendship, which I *don't* have – I've benefited from your friends all my life!'

Fanny sensed she was being gracefully manipulated. She

518

cast her daughter a mutinous look. 'Let's hope the Rani is still my friend when I've finished telling her what I think of her for keeping such a secret from me!'

Mary merely chuckled. 'I doubt you'll get any change from that one! She's very fond of you and she certainly won't allow you to quarrel with her! If she was gracious enough to receive me, she didn't do it because of the British Raj, or for me, a stranger, she did it for you, Mama! I rather think she wanted the Raja to know that she was prepared to approve my being here.'

'Why shouldn't she approve of you?' Fanny scowled at her.

But Mary refused to be intimidated. 'Because, whatever excuses we may make, I did murder my own father. Many people would see that as a crime beyond forgiveness, no matter what the circumstances, as you very well know! Tell me more about your Raja. Has he made you as happy as my Mr Gilbert makes me?'

'I love him,' Fanny admitted. 'And I'm more pleased that you married Walter Gilbert than I can say, though I had my reservations at first. I've always been afraid your father might have made you think that all men might be like him. For years after you were conceived, I wouldn't let any man come anywhere near me. You've no idea how respectable I was in London! Sajjan taught me differently – '

'Your Raja?'

Fanny blushed. 'I've no business talking to you like this! I forget you're my daughter – '

'I hope we may be friends, Mama?'

Fanny gave her a surprised glance. 'Even close friends didn't discuss such things in my day!'

'They don't now,' Mary confirmed, laughing. 'Mr Gilbert lets me say anything I like to him, and I thought your

519

Raja might be the same with you. Tonight, Her Highness has promised to present me to him officially in the *zenana*. I talked with him in Hanupur, but we both had other things on our minds then besides getting to know one another. He wasn't liking me very much just then, but I hope he'll find it in his heart to forgive me for putting you in danger. I rather hope he may even come to like me – a little.'

'He isn't – he isn't like the men you know!'

'You think him something more special?' Mary teased her.

'To me he is.'

Mary laughed. 'You're afraid I'll look down my nose at him, is that it? Well, I won't. Mr Gilbert was forced to leave the army because of that sort of thing. If it hadn't been for the Queen – ' She broke off, her voice breaking. 'Mama, I want to meet the man who loves my mother, not the Raja of Kattyapur.'

Fanny turned her face away. 'They're the same person, Mary. You remember me as Lady Frances, friend of Queen Victoria, but Lady Frances died long ago. I'm no more than the wife of affection, the *concubine*, of the ruler of a small and obscure State that doesn't matter much to anyone but him, not even to the British, who want the whole of India in the end! What happened in Hanupur came as a shock to him. I'm not sure what terms I'm on with him at the moment.' She sighed. 'He's very much the Raja of Kattyapur, and I wouldn't have him any other way, though sometimes I wish we could forget all that and just be a man and a woman together!'

Fanny hadn't thought she could explain her feelings to anyone who had not actually been brought up in the *zenana*. She was surprised, therefore, by the gentle expression on Mary's face.

'I'm glad it's like that for you,' her daughter said. She

put her arms around her mother. 'How could you doubt me? I'm proud of you for following your destiny and learning to love someone more than life. I think I'll like your Raja very well!'

And, unbelievably, she seemed to mean it. Fanny felt a closeness and understanding with her that she had seldom felt with anyone else. Then the moment passed and they both began to speak at once, verbally pushing and shoving to make their points to each other like a couple of children. And even when the flood of words finally dried up, they could still smile at one another with mutual approval.

'Would you believe,' said Mary, 'that I am universally known as too shy to open my mouth when people I don't know are present?'

'Are you self-conscious about your arm?' Fanny countered.

Mary gave her a mocking look. 'With some people. Never with my Mr Gilbert. I truly believe he wouldn't have noticed how bad it is if I hadn't pointed it out to him. If he doesn't mind, why should I?'

Fanny nodded briskly. 'I like your Mr Gilbert more and more,' she said.

'Why did nobody tell *me* what was going on?' Fanny demanded.

'None of us needed your permission,' Maneka smiled at her, 'even if she is your daughter!'

Fanny bit her lip thoughtfully. 'You don't think His Highness will come to resent her being here, seeing her every day?'

Maneka shook her head at her sadly, as she might have done to an uncomprehending child. 'He fell in love with you, Fanny, when he first saw you. What man likes to think of his woman lying with another man, even if she was the victim and not a willing partner in the embrace? His Highness would always rather have been the first man in your life.'

'But he was in every way that matters!' Fanny protested.

'You forget, he has been the first man *in fact* with every other woman who's shared his bed. He's closed his eyes to much which his pride doesn't like where you're concerned. Leave it to Mary, my dear. She'll win him over, as merely knowing of her existence could never have done. Your daughter is very like you, as he will be the first to appreciate!'

Fanny hadn't realized the evening was to be such a formal occasion until she saw the Rani had already taken her place, a few of her favourite miniatures close at hand to show Mary some of the work of her school. Fanny pulled her veil across her face, going to her own place and, indeed, so intent was she on her own thoughts that she actually missed Sajjan's entrance, bringing Mary and her husband with him. Instinctively, she rose to her feet and put her hands together in the traditional gesture of *Namaste*.

Her daughter, she saw, was prepared to be equally formal, making an obeisance to Maneka that wouldn't have disgraced a woman who had been born and bred in the *zenana*. It was an action calculated to put the Rani at her ease, as was also her carefully worded greeting in Maneka's own language. She felt suddenly very proud that Mary was her daughter, watching the two women embrace as if they were old friends, both of them intent on the interest they had in common. Mary sat down beside the Rani, her feet drawn up under her, hanging on Maneka's every word.

'You see how like you she is!' Sajjan's voice said in Fanny's ear.

'She has better manners – '

'I'll still take the mother, if she'll let me?' he finished, his eyes alight with some secret emotion she had never seen there before. 'May I present you to your son-in-law,' he added in English. 'The Queen-Empress's own choice as her representative in Kattyapur! Do you remember Mr Gilbert?'

Fanny turned laughing eyes on the man who was standing beside the Raja, who still looked exactly the same as the lieutenant who had visited the *zenana* once before.

'Mr Gilbert!' she exclaimed. 'Exactly the right choice for Mary!'

He bowed over her hand. 'Glad you approve, ma'am! I hope you'll think I'm the best choice for Kattyapur as well?'

For once Fanny was tongue-tied and a little uncertain. 'You've made Mary very happy,' she said at last. 'That's all that concerns me. It's His Highness's approval you must seek for the other. You'll forgive my saying, though, that it was a stroke of good fortune for me that Sir Arthur Cunningham was with you at Hanupur! It could have been even more ugly otherwise!'

'It was a relief to me also!' Mr Gilbert acknowledged. 'No one else could have persuaded Mary to let you take the blame, you know, not even after Sir Arthur had dismissed the case against you. She has a great respect for the truth, has Mary, and very little for the inconvenience it can cause sometimes!'

In other circumstances Fanny might have approved of that. 'What was Sir Arthur doing there?' she asked.

'He had expressed a wish to see your Raja in action before he would allow Mary to accompany me here.' A gleam of humour shone in Mr Gilbert's brown eyes. 'It was a nice touch, wasn't it, to leave you to the mercy of your chosen husband for the death of your rejected one?'

'As long as the truth never comes out in Delhi and Calcutta! *That* would be fatal for Mary.'

'You don't mind the world thinking you a murderess?'

Fanny shook her head. 'I have outlived my usefulness to the British. All I want from life now is to be forgotten by them. As Sir Arthur said, Lady Frances is dead; in Kattyapur, there is only Fanny.'

Sajjan grinned broadly. 'Well said, darling! Here, you are first and foremost my wife of affection, no longer my political adviser!'

The endearment that they only ever used when they were alone made her pulses race. Mr Gilbert might think he knew what it meant, but only she realized it was Sajjan's way of telling her that she had been right when she had advised him to make a new treaty with the British and accept the conditions they imposed on him. It hadn't turned out too badly if they never had to suffer anything worse than have Mr and Mrs Gilbert come among them. For a moment, she forgot there was anyone else there as Sajjan held out a hand to her and, disregarding all she had ever been taught about the protocol of the *zenana*, she flung herself into his arms.

'Oh, Sajjan, thank you, thank you for being kind to Mary!' she whispered.

He hugged her very tightly against him. 'I am pleased with your daughter,' he pronounced. He caressed her cheek with a gentle hand. 'If having her with you makes you happy, then I am happy too. Hanupur, and all that happened there, is a nightmare best forgotten by all of us. To have you both safe in Kattyapur bodes very well for our future, as long as you don't forget that I am the love of your life! I love you, Fanny.'

Her lashes hid her eyes from him. 'I love you too,' she said.

* * *

Fanny waited for Sayed to fetch her that night with increasing impatience. It had been an unforgettable evening. Never had she expected to see Maneka, in mixed company, with her veil thrown back, laughing and talking with the Political Officer and his wife as if she had known them all her life. Even more surprising was to see her and Mary having a heated argument as to why the flower patterns that had been first created for Shah Jahan should now dominate all Indian paintings so completely. Both of them had laughed to scorn Fanny's suggestion that it might be because they made pretty, satisfying shapes that were universally pleasing.

'But, Mama,' Mary had insisted, 'there are other designs which are just as pleasing! No, I believe it has to do with the specific imperial images the Shah Jahan wanted to convey in all his buildings. I think he wanted his people to see his creations as a reflection of paradise.'

The Rani had agreed with this. 'It is written in the Red Fort in Delhi: "If there's a paradise on earth, 'tis here, 'tis here, 'tis here!"'

The Yuveraj had caught Fanny's eye. 'Shall you and I play chess?' he had suggested, and Mr Gilbert had laughed. 'How different things are here from Hanupur,' he had observed.

'Very,' Fanny had agreed with him. 'Will Mary be happy here?'

'As she would be nowhere else. As you are, I hope?'

'I am now,' Fanny had said. 'I have everything to make me so!'

Oh yes, it had been a good evening, with everyone happy and laughing, and now she wanted to be called to Sajjan's bed, and she could hardly wait. When he did come, Sayed seemed ponderously slow to her. 'Why didn't you come before?' she demanded, longing to give him a shove from behind as he waddled up the stairs ahead of her.

'I was asleep, lady, like we all should be at this hour. But do I question the Raja's commands? By Allah, I do not! So I didn't ask him why he couldn't call you to him himself, as he usually does these days. Today, you must be brought to him with full honours and – here we are!'

Fanny had eyes only for Sajjan. She ran lightly across the room to him, her pleasure at seeing him written clearly on her face and in her eyes.

'I thought you were never going to send for me!' she began, and then she grew still. 'I thought – '

'You thought we may have had enough excitement for one day?' he teased her, fingering her bodice with impatient hands.

She laughed with him. 'You're so good to me, Sajjan. I wish I could give you more back in return!' She hesitated, oddly unsure of herself. 'You do like Mary, don't you? You don't still resent that she had a different father, do you?'

His hands found her naked flesh. 'I shall always regret the manner of her making, my love, but I long ago realized that in every way that matters I was the first man with you! Yes, I like your Mary. How could it be otherwise when she is your daughter! If I had any fear of her coming here, it was because I thought she might bear a grudge against you, or treat you as a fallen woman, as she may have been taught to do. I hadn't expected to like her so well, nor that Maneka would take to her so easily. Your daughter has respect – '

'As I never had!' Fanny teased him.

'You had respect in your heart. Your daughter, though, quoted her own scriptures to the Rani: "*Ahimsa*, respect

526

for life, is the highest duty." When I heard that, I knew she would never patronize you, or try to come between us.'

Fanny's eyes opened wide in astonishment. 'But, Sajjan, nobody could ever change the way I feel about you. From the first moment I saw you, you've been the breath in my body, the centre of my whole being! Surely you knew that?'

He jerked his head backwards and to one side in the way all Indians do. 'You were born into a different world. It was always possible that after the romance and fascination of my world wore off you'd want to go back to your own.' He touched her face with gentle fingers. 'I was afraid Mary would remind you of all you had lost and that I might lose you. Are you really mine, my Fanny?'

She kissed his fingers before carrying on her undressing where he had left off, smoothing her clothes away from her without any sign of the impatience she felt showing on her features. When she was totally naked, she turned and looked at him. 'Sajjan, I want you to listen very carefully because I may never have the courage to tell you this again. You gave me life as my parents never could; only fear and hatred. You gave me children to whom I could be a real mother; something poor Mary has never known. You gave me joy where I knew only guilt. When I sat in that prison at Hanupur, convinced they would put me to death, my only regret was that I should have to leave you, or that you might not understand why I had to do what I did, putting your love for me in jeopardy, and that I'd bring you hurt and the contempt of the British. I knew then, better even than I'd known it before, that without you I have no life worth the living. If they had taken me away from you, I shouldn't have wanted to go on living.'

He reached out for her, only to have her side-step his embrace. 'I should have joined you in the next life,' he told

527

her stiffly. 'In every life our love will still call out to us!'

She smoothed the frown from his face. 'What if we only have this life, as I was taught to believe? Let's not miss one minute of it! You promised me one last child, remember?'

He stood completely still, his every muscle poised for action as he strove to control himself sufficiently to take her into his bed before he made love to her. She was the only woman who could have this effect on him with a mere look and a smile. With a gasp, he caught her up against him, kissing her hard before he pulled her after him towards the pile of cushions on the floor.

'*Hare-Ram!*' he exploded. 'God, Fanny, let's go to bed!'